THE DRAGON & THE DAMSEL

CLAIRE DELACROIX

DEBORAH A. COOKE

The Dragon & the Damsel
By Claire Delacroix

MORE BOOKS BY CLAIRE DELACROIX

THE WOLF & THE WITCH

THE HUNTER & THE HEIRESS

THE DRAGON & THE DAMSEL

ONE KNIGHT ENCHANTED

ONE KNIGHT'S RETURN

THE CRUSADER'S BRIDE

THE CRUSADER'S HEART

THE CRUSADER'S KISS

THE CRUSADER'S VOW

THE CRUSADER'S HANDFAST

THE ROGUE

THE SCOUNDREL

THE WARRIOR

THE BEAUTY BRIDE

THE ROSE RED BRIDE

THE SNOW WHITE BRIDE

The Ballad of Rosamunde

THE RENEGADE'S HEART

THE HIGHLANDER'S CURSE

THE FROST MAIDEN'S KISS

THE WARRIOR'S PRIZE

THE MERCENARY'S BRIDE

THE RUNAWAY BRIDE

THE PRINCESS

THE DAMSEL

THE HEIRESS

THE COUNTESS

BLOOD BROTHERS

A MEDIEVAL SCOTTISH ROMANCE SERIES

The three sons of a notorious mercenary should never have met...but now that they are sworn allies, the Scottish Borders will never be the same...

1. **The Wolf & the Witch**
(Maximilian and Alys)

2. **The Hunter & the Heiress**
(Amaury and Elizabeth)

3. **The Dragon & the Damsel**
(Rafael and Ceara)

4. **The Scot & the Sorceress**
(Murdoch and Nyssa)

∾

DEAR READER

The Dragon & the Damsel is the third book in my *Blood Brothers* series of medieval romances, in which the heroes are all sons of a notorious mercenary. This is the story of Rafael, who has ridden with the Compagnie Rouge under Jean le Beau's command, and Ceara, the woman who believes that he is a man of honor despite his history.

Ceara first challenged Rafael in **The Wolf & the Witch** and the battle of wills began between them then. When Rafael returns to Kilderrick at the beginning of his own book, he's determined to have satisfaction from the woman who taunted him. All changes when he realizes that bold Ceara is a maiden, and she needs to know why. When Rafael defends her, Ceara knows there's more to him than his reputation, and eventually, the pair join forces in her brother's quest for vengeance. I love their story of slowly dawning trust, and how they each help to heal each other's scars of the past. I think they are a wonderful if unconventional couple and I hope you enjoy reading their tale as much as I loved writing it. We get a glimpse of the other characters from the series in this book, as well as evidence of the vow sworn by the brothers at Château de Vries in the prologue of **The Wolf & the Witch.**

The Dragon & the Damsel, like **The Wolf & the Witch**, is available in ebook, trade paperback and a hardcover collectors' edition. Next in the series will be Murdoch's book, **The Scot & the Sorceress,** coming spring 2023. Murdoch is a bitter soul who blames Maximilian for his father's demise —when he would take vengeance upon his adversary, he finds Nyssa, the seer, in his path. I'm looking forward to writing this story of redemption, forgiveness and love everlasting, and hope you join me for Murdoch and Nyssa's tale. There are pre-order links for The Scot & the Sorceress on my website.

You can, as always, find additional resources on my website. There is a list of characters in the series, which is updated after each book. I have a Pinterest page for the series—there's a link on the Blood Brothers tab on my website—which is a work-in-progress and will give you a glimpse of my inspiration. There are also a number of blog posts, linked on each book's landing page, about my research for the series.

And of course, you can sign up for my medieval romance newsletter, *Knights & Rogues*, to receive an alert when I have a new release, and to hear my news as well as any special offers or sales. There's also a link on my website under the *Newsletter* tab. You can also follow me at many portals—those links are on the **About Claire page**.

Until next time, I hope you have plenty of good books to read.
    All my best
    Claire

PROLOGUE

Beaupoint, England—May 19, 1376

maury de Vries could not sleep.

The moon was new and the lands around Beaupoint's tower were shadowed in darkness. He surveyed them, using the glass from Elizabeth's father, frustrated by his sense that something was amiss. There had been an uncommon amount of activity on both firth and road of late. Warriors were arriving and departing from Stonehaven and Workington, as if a great force was being mustered, but he knew not where or why. Lord Henry Percy, the Warden of the Middle March on the English side, professed indifference to these tidings, since the warriors did not linger on English soil—they were sailing north. All of Amaury's enquiries to his northern neighbors had gone unanswered, which hinted to him that they knew more than they were prepared to divulge.

On this night, he remained in the solar, watching and listening to the soft rhythm of Elizabeth's breathing as she slept. Amaury's dog, Grise, had readily taken his place in the bed and snored contentedly beside his wife. The large grey dog was protective of Elizabeth, which suited Amaury well. Bête, the largest and fiercest of his dogs, was undoubtedly asleep in the great hall below as had become his custom.

Only sleek little Noisette was awake with Amaury, paws on the sill, ears alert and nose twitching as if she shared his concern.

The tide had come in since sunset and the water in the firth was as smooth as a dark mirror. The opposite shore was black, not a single lantern's light piercing the shadows. Even the stars were obscured by a thin layer of high cloud. The wind was light but steady, blowing from the sea and bringing its scent.

Amaury scanned the view from east to west again, then he saw it.

A company of horses appeared on the road, riding east toward Carlisle. Without the aid of the glass, they would have been simply shadows against the darkness, but Amaury could discern some detail. One dapple destrier was in the lead, flanked by two more warhorses, which galloped slightly behind. Amaury counted at least a dozen horses, perhaps five warriors and numerous squires. They even hauled a wagon, its axles greased so well that it ran stealthily.

And the insignia flying from the first was familiar.

It was the flag of the Compagnie Rouge, the banner carried by Jean le Beau and later Maximilian as the mark of their army of mercenaries. Amaury had seen it on his arrival at Château de Vries in Normandy less than a year before and still the sight gave him a shudder. The reputation of the Compagnie Rouge was brutal and they were known in all lands for their savage efficiency.

But why did they arrive here? Jean le Beau had died and passed the leadership of his company to his eldest son, Maximilian. But Maximilian was wed to Alys Armstrong and resident at Kilderrick, well to the east and north of Beaupoint. Amaury's half-brother had disbanded the Compagnie Rouge and made his life in Scotland, abandoning his former trade.

Amaury lowered the glass as the horses moved past Beaupoint and out of view. It could only be that Rafael, the third of the half-brothers and formerly Maximilian's second-in-command, had reassembled the company and returned to Scotland. Had he been hired by a baron in these lands? Or was the Compagnie Rouge part of this mysterious mustering? Amaury knew the powerful allure that gold held for his half-brothers, particularly Rafael. He imagined that mercenary would do any deed for the right price.

Or could there be another explanation? Amaury recalled that Maximilian had been invited to besiege Château de Vries, the very holding that Maximilian had once considered his birthright. The keep had been seized upon Jean le Beau's death by the brother of his widow, Gaston de Vries and Maximilian's uncle. Maximilian had chosen to leave for Kilderrick rather than wage war against his kin. The invitation had come subsequently from Gaston's son: when Maximilian had declined, Rafael had gone instead. It stood to reason that Rafael had gathered the army of mercenaries again to undertake that quest.

But why did he arrive here and so soon? To be sure, even this group of riding warriors would not come close to carrying the full military power of the Compagnie Rouge. Perhaps Rafael had failed in his quest. Perhaps the mercenaries had declined to follow him in Maximilian's stead.

Perhaps whatever drew other warriors to this region possessed a greater allure.

Amaury did not know Rafael well and he did not wish to. That man had little honor and cared only for his own advantage: he was a true spawn of Jean le Beau. All the same, he was not witless or whimsical. There had to be a good reason for Rafael to undertake such a journey.

Did he intend to oust Maximilian from Kilderrick? That seemed unlikely, as Rafael had despised these northern lands. 'Twould not be a ready victory either, as Maximilian not only had the loyalty of those in his holding but the alliance of the king.

Did Rafael arrive in triumph, having claimed Château de Vries, with the intention of coaxing Maximilian back to his old life? Amaury doubted the keep could have been claimed so speedily and he doubted even more that Maximilian would be tempted. Alys had written to Elizabeth with the tidings that she carried Maximilian's child, and Amaury knew that nothing could tear him from Elizabeth's side now that she, too, had conceived. He and his older brother, Maximilian, had that much in common, at least.

Had Rafael failed and came to beg for some favor from Maximilian's hand? That made an increment of sense, but Amaury doubted the success of such a scheme.

What would Rafael do when thwarted? He might be nigh penniless by this point, and a mercenary without advantage might be as unpredictable as a cornered wolf.

Others should know of these tidings. Someone at the port, be it Whitehaven or Worthington, might alert the King of England or his representatives, for both were on English soil. As English Warden of the Western March, Amaury would notify the English king through his barons. But the border was treacherously close and Rafael's destination might well be Kilderrick. The King of Scotland should be warned, as well.

An army of mercenaries was not a detail to be underestimated, and one beneath Rafael's command might be unpredictable, indeed.

Amaury would not sleep well until he knew his half-brother's intent.

CHAPTER 1

Kilderrick, Scotland—May 22, 1376

*R*afael di Giovanni could fairly taste success. Oh, he knew that his half-brother, Maximilian, formerly known as the *Loup Argent*, insisted he had no desire for Château de Vries, but that could not be the truth. Château de Vries had been Maximilian's goal for as long as Rafael could remember, a dream that his older brother believed to be both his future and his destiny. Maximilian had been furious when cheated of the prize and had ridden to Scotland as a result. Rafael had known from the outset that Maximilian only retreated to plan his strategy and that Château de Vries remained his brother's greatest desire.

Subsequently, Maximilian had declined Philip de Vries' invitation to besiege the keep and make it his own, but that could only have been to avoid sullying his own hands. The place was important to Maximilian, for he had grown up there, and 'twas only reasonable that he did not wish to be the one to damage it, even in conquest. Rafael had undertaken the quest instead, knowing that his brother only delegated the capture of the keep.

As was right and good, Maximilian would claim the reward.

The more he considered the matter—and Rafael had thought of it endlessly since securing the seal of Château de Vries in his purse—the more convinced he became that the entire situation had unfurled according to Maximilian's unspoken plan. It had been Maximilian's expectation that Rafael should succeed, that he should claim the keep and its seal, that he should assemble the Compagnie Rouge again, and that he should return to Kilderrick triumphant with the evidence of his success. Only then would the *Loup Argent* abandon this ridiculous pretence of making a home in a remote Scottish keep and return to the life he knew best.

Maximilian was a strategist, first and foremost, and a man who kept his secrets close. The Compagnie Rouge would ride forth again under Maximilian's lead, striking terror into the hearts of their victims, driving hard bargains with those who opposed their will and gorging themselves on plunder.

Rafael could scarce wait to begin.

Nor could the mercenaries who followed him, a rough and restless group who chafed for the call to war—and with each passing day, their impatience for battle grew. Only four had followed him to Scotland while the rest waited at Château de Vries, defending the prize. Even with five warriors, they were not a small company—four squires rode with them, requiring ten palfreys and five destriers. The women who might have followed the company had been abandoned in Normandy, for Rafael declined to pay for their passage. Women could be found in every port without much trouble, after all, and one was much like another.

Despite that conviction, Rafael found himself haunted by the memory of one woman, a bold wench left behind at Kilderrick. The red-haired temptress who had lived in the forest with Alys was more than a beauty. She had deceived Rafael, left him mired in the mud, stolen his horse, left his favored knife to implicate him in a theft—not to mention blunting the blade in so doing—laughed at his vexation and slit a guard's throat with swift skill he could only respect. Doubtless Rafael's fascination was because she had both challenged and surprised him. Truly, he had never met her like.

Ceara. They called her Ceara. And Rafael vowed silently that he would have his due of her before he left this benighted land again.

To be sure, he doubted she would regret the experience.

He would ensure as much.

After a short delay in Carlisle for the men to sample some local wares, Rafael led the company up the valley to Kilderrick on a pleasant afternoon. No trap had been set for passing travellers, as in the previous autumn. The air was a bit cooler than in France, but the sun shone and the lands were verdant. He could see that there was a brief season of abundance in this land.

Finally, Kilderrick itself loomed before them and Rafael noted that the keep was more imposing than he recalled. Maximilian had been busy—or his masons had been. The walls were higher and broader and the gate more fortified. There was still a camp of masons outside the walls on the far side and the village in the distance was more active than Rafael recalled. Smoke rose from a number of huts, a sign that the number of peasants had increased. Sentries walked the top of Kilderrick's walls and Rafael heard the whistle pass through Maximilian's troops, proof that his arrival had been spotted.

They would be greeted now as champions, feted and celebrated, as they rightly deserved. Rafael urged his destrier to a quicker pace.

"Set camp here," he commanded his men when they cleared the forest, gesturing to the broad slope where Maximilian's company had camped the previous fall. He turned Phantôm with a flourish, anticipating his welcome. The dapple destrier pranced, tossing his dark mane with pride as he cantered toward the gates.

The gates remained closed and the sentries crouched low to watch.

Undoubtedly, he had not been recognized.

"Hail, Maximilian de Vries!" Rafael shouted, raising a hand in greeting. A pair of arrows drove into the ground ahead of him in that very moment. He pulled the horse up short, but Phantôm had already halted. The stallion snorted, stamping with agitation.

Had his brother been ousted?

"Maximilian!" Rafael roared. "Have you no welcome for your own brother?"

"Not one who approaches with an army," Maximilian shouted, his words terse. The gates of Kilderrick opened, revealing a mounted warrior on a destrier behind the portcullis. The iron gate rose and the lone rider passed beneath it, the portcullis dropping behind him with a resonant thud. Maximilian was garbed in his customary black, armored and helmed, his black destrier impatient to run. He held up a gloved hand to stay the archers and rode to meet Rafael alone.

What was amiss? Rafael held his ground and waited, despite his impatience. "Has this land become more perilous in my absence?" he demanded when their horses were a few paces apart.

Maximilian lifted his visor. His gaze was steely and his tone less than welcoming. "All lands are perilous when mercenaries ride through them. You cannot expect me to be glad to see the Compagnie Rouge at my gates, nor to wonder at your intentions."

Rafael shook his head and smiled. "You have become one of those barons we used to despise. Is this what happens to a warrior when he claims a holding in earnest?" He meant it as a jest but Maximilian's expression did not soften.

"Numerous people rely upon my protection at Kilderrick. It would be irresponsible to do less than demand an explanation of you."

Rafael's annoyance stirred, for this distrust was unjustified. They were *brothers*. They had fought back to back in the most vicious battles, relying only upon each other. This was unwarranted. "I come in peace, of course, returned from the quest you yourself granted to me," he said, his tone as cold as Maximilian's.

That man nodded toward the mercenaries making camp. "I bade you gather no army. I granted no permission for these men to enter my lands. I certainly did not summon a company of mercenaries to my very gates."

"And how did you imagine I would seize Château de Vries without force?" Rafael asked with scorn. He gestured to the company behind him, knowing his men watched intently. "'Twas only because of this army that Château de Vries fell and did as much with such speed. I am not such a fool to ride in possession of a prize without escort."

"De Vries fell?" Maximilian's tone was sharp and he urged Tempest forward a step. "So quickly as that? Nay, it cannot be."

"Do you call me a liar, brother mine?" Rafael asked, his voice silky in his anger.

Maximilian frowned. "It cannot be thus. You only departed for

France in December. Given the journey there and back, if you succeeded, you must have done as much within a week."

"Two days," Rafael provided with satisfaction, his contentment growing when he saw that his brother was impressed. "I gathered our company on my journey south and appeared at the gates of Château de Vries at the end of March. Philip met us there, for I had sent word to him of our approach." He smiled in recollection. "Yet Gaston, Lord de Vries, declined to either grant us admission or surrender the keep."

Maximilian smiled a little, the cold expression proving that he was yet the warrior Rafael knew. "You cannot have been surprised." He raised a brow. "Or unprepared."

Rafael laughed. "Hardly that! We loosed a volley of Greek fire upon the walls during the night. No less than a dozen flaming vessels, one after the other in relentless succession. The flames licked the walls and more than one roof burned to ashes. I have never witnessed such a magnificent sight." He could not restrain his enthusiasm or pride. "Never has my aim been so true. Never have my missiles found such perfect tinder. The flames spread within the walls with deadly efficiency. Meanwhile, my men drove a battering ram against the gates."

"The relentless rhythm," Maximilian said with satisfaction. "It would have driven the occupants mad."

Finally, they were in agreement and all would proceed as anticipated.

Rafael grinned. "But Gaston still would not receive us or relent. The second night, we repeated the assault, but it lasted longer and was more vehement. By dawn of the second morning, Gaston called for parlay. He surrendered the seal without hesitation. The prize was secured in less than two days and we did not lose a man. Indeed, they did not strike a single blow."

"The Greek fire did your labor, as befits an attack by the dragon himself."

"Indeed."

Maximilian remained watchful, as if he awaited more. Rafael produced the seal from his purse with a flourish. He saw a predictable glint in Maximilian's gaze.

He tossed the seal to his brother who caught it easily.

"Château de Vries," Maximilian murmured, turning the seal in his hand with what could only be wonder. He flicked a sharp glance at Rafael. "How heavy was the damage to the keep?"

Ah, he was concerned with the state of his prize. Rafael shrugged. "The wooden sheds within the walls are gone, burned to naught. The roof of the solar was also incinerated and some of its contents. The stables are gone, but the horses were saved. Some damage was sustained upon the outer walls, but naught that could not put right in a month. I instructed the châtelain to hire masons and to have the roof rebuilt. By now, it might look as it ever did." He had wanted the keep at its best for Maximilian's triumphant arrival there.

"And my uncle, Gaston?"

"The thief who betrayed you has paid the price," Rafael said with satisfaction. "He lies in the churchyard, unlamented."

Maximilian did not look up but simply turned the seal. "Before or after he surrendered the seal?"

"After he strove to deceive me."

Maximilian looked up at that.

Rafael held his gaze. "The fiend invited me to enter the keep alone, the better that he might surrender the keys to the treasury."

"You cannot have trusted him, not Gaston."

"Of course not! And trust was not deserved, for he had two men hidden to attack me." Rafael nodded. "They preceded him to Hell, then he paid the price for his treachery." He shook his head as if saddened. "'Tis a terrible thing to see a man of privilege grovel for mercy."

Maximilian raised his brows. "A sight I might have enjoyed," he murmured, then granted Rafael another intent look. "What of Philip de Vries, his son, who requested this intervention?"

"He celebrated our victory, then we discussed where best to lay his father to rest. He chose to take Gaston to Château Pouissance, for he knew it would vex his sire to leave de Vries forever."

Their gazes met again, Maximilian's now filled with the respect Rafael knew he deserved. "Well done," he said with an approval that made Rafael's heart glow.

Then he tossed the seal back.

Rafael barely caught it, so great was his surprise.

What was this?

"I thank you for the tidings." Maximilian was surveying the Compagnie Rouge and his tone was crisp. "You may camp here for three nights only. If you have need of wine, ale or meat, I will provide them for a fee, and if any of your men enter the keep, they must entrust all of their weapons to the gatekeeper." He spoke briskly while Rafael stared at him in astonishment. "If you hunt in my forests and take a deer, you will pay me the king's fee for poaching." Rafael sputtered but Maximilian gave him a hard look. "If any of the women in the village or keep are accosted, I will take a reckoning from your own person. Do we understand each other?"

Maximilian would *charge* him?

It had to be a jest.

"Nay," Rafael countered. "In three days, you will depart for Château de Vries with us, taking command of the Compagnie Rouge once more."

But this time, his brother laughed. "I will not leave Kilderrick. I told you as much before, Rafael. This is my home and my future."

"But Château de Vries!" Rafael held out the seal.

"Keep it for your own. Or surrender it to Philip." Maximilian shrugged, sounding indifferent to the fate of the holding he had coveted for as long as Rafael had known him. "I have no interest in armies or foreign territories."

His decision was inexplicable.

"Nay," Rafael protested with heat when Maximilian began to turn his horse. "You *always* desired de Vries. You spoke of it as the sole objective that would justify your days of service to Jean le Beau. You yearned for it beyond all other holdings, insisting all paled in comparison to its wonders."

"I did," Maximilian admitted.

"You came here, to the edge of the world, because you were *denied* de Vries!"

His brother was unshaken. "And in so doing, I learned to find satisfaction with what I possess." He turned to survey Kilderrick with undisguised pride.

Rafael was stunned.

Then he noticed the cloaked figure on the ramparts, unmistakably a woman ripe with child. The wind snatched at her hood and her dark braid blew loose, her gaze as fixed upon Maximilian as his was upon her.

The witch! 'Twas her fault. Maximilian insisted that Alys was no sorceress, but clearly she had cast a spell over him that bound him to her will. This madness had come over his brother since he had taken Alys to wife. *She* wanted Kilderrick above all other properties, for the holding had been her birthright, and she had ensured that Maximilian expended his coin to rebuild the ruin. 'Twas hard to believe that Maximilian could be enthralled by the seductive arts of a woman so scarred as Alys, but here was the proof of it.

Rafael would have argued more, but his brother touched his spurs to his destrier's side as if all were resolved. "Three nights," he reminded Rafael, casting the words over his shoulder.

"Am I not even invited to the board?" Rafael shouted in outrage.

Maximilian glanced back with a smile, reining in his steed. "I forget my manners, to be sure. Of course, you are invited, Rafael." His voice hardened. "Alone and unarmed, you are welcome to dine with us this night, provided you treat the ladies with courtesy."

Unarmed? Treat the ladies with courtesy? Had Kilderrick become a monastery in his absence? What Rafael wanted was a celebration, with great quantities of meat and wine, willing women on every side and a night of pleasure beyond compare. He wanted to eat and drink, dance and rut, until he had his satisfaction and he knew it would take all the night, if not most of the next day.

He had expected no less from his former commander, who had seldom savored such earthly indulgences himself but had always ensured that his men had the chance to partake. Rafael deserved a tribute for his success. Maximilian had always understood the necessity of celebration, though it appeared all that knowledge had been forgotten.

The gate closed behind his brother and Rafael glanced back at the company raising their tents. They had little wine remaining, no ale, no meat, and worse, the women at Kilderrick were not to be touched.

Rafael had promised them the *Loup Argent*'s fulsome gratitude, but there was none to be had.

Worse yet, they were to be gone from these lands in three days. He had paid a hefty sum to transport this company to Maximilian, only to be dismissed—and faced a similar sum to return to the continent. What would he do with Château de Vries? He had no desire to rule a holding himself and he did not trust any of Gaston's lineage to keep a vow. He put the seal in his purse, mightily irked by his brother's reaction.

How could the man who had been the most successful mercenary captain in all of Europe be content with a single keep in a veritable wilderness?

He glanced up at the walls again to find Alys still there, watching him.

Witch. The fault for this was hers.

Rafael turned his horse and could fairly taste the impatience of the mercenaries who followed him. The tents were being raised with speed and there was raucous laughter coming from the camp already. They had expectations, expectations he had to deny.

He only hoped there was sufficient wine in the camp to sate them this night. He would not buy any supplies from the Laird of Kilderrick and his fiendish wife.

'Twas a matter of principle.

"Four bucks," Royce complained. A mercenary who had arrived with Maximilian and remained at Kilderrick, the large bearded warrior always accompanied Ceara when she rode to hunt. She was consistently amazed by how quietly Royce could move, given his formidable size. He also was keenly observant, despite having lost one eye long before. "Two would have been sufficient, but you cannot leave it be, can you, Ceara? When you spot prey, you must always loose your bolt."

"No meat goes to waste," she said, then referred to the cook at Kilderrick. "Denis would not tolerate it."

Royce paused his steed to glance back at the two squires, struggling to bring back the kill. Louis and Nicholas had made a sledge of tree boughs and loaded the deer upon it. Their palfreys pulled the makeshift structure, neither horse particularly pleased with the burden or their uneven progress through the forest. "Four," he muttered beneath his breath and eyed Ceara from beneath his bushy brows. "And we will not even count the hares. You were a fiend this day. What awakened your blood lust?"

Ceara knew she would have taken more if Royce had not stopped her. The sole thing that distracted her from her worries in these days was the hunt and the concentration it required. They were not even back within Kilderrick's walls and her thoughts were already spinning with dire possibilities. "Denis will be glad of the meat," she said simply. "You will see. The company is large these days."

Royce harrumphed and urged his horse alongside her own. The mercenary towered over her, both because of his size and that of his destrier. Ceara preferred her nimble palfrey. They approached the river and Ceara's chest tightened with an increasingly familiar trepidation.

When would Edward pursue her? She had always known that her betrothed would hunt her down. That he had not done as much yet meant only that he did not know where to begin his search. That must have changed. Since Godfroy's death and the return of his followers to the Lord of the Isles, Edward's knowledge of her location would become a certainty. It could only be a matter of time. The tale of her killing of the sentry—a fierce red-haired maiden—would have been repeated and when Edward heard the tale, he would guess the rest.

She had no doubt he would act upon that information—with haste and malice—and the old betrothal would be forced upon her, regardless of her view of the matter. Indeed, she was of no import to this bargain: it was her legacy Edward desired and she knew he would pay any price to secure it.

On the other hand, her brother, if he still lived, should return now that Godfroy was no more. He might have also learned of her location. Which warrior would come for her first? Ceara knew which possibility she preferred.

She had wrestled with the option of leaving Kilderrick, but there was much to be said for being within strong stone walls at night. She was torn between the desire to wait in hope for her brother's return and the urge to flee where Edward would not find her. She had spent the winter improving her knowledge of Norman French, restless to do more.

And hunting. The task was her sole consolation. It was both necessary and active. Ceara had assumed the responsibility for providing meat to Kilderrick's kitchens in Amaury's absence, knowing she needed the wind in her hair and the feel of a swift steed beneath her. She would never have asked but she had been relieved when Maximilian insisted that Royce had to accompany her each time she rode out.

"You are restless this spring and I know it well," Royce said now, surprising her yet again with his perceptiveness. "Do not imagine that the change has gone unnoticed."

"I am not," she protested, though it was untrue.

Royce scoffed. "You jump at every sound. More than once you have cost us a kill. It is not like you to be less than bold, Ceara. Something troubles you."

Ceara bit her tongue.

Royce sighed. "You can hunt until the forest is empty and the river runs with blood, but that will not diminish your concern, whatever it might be."

"What do you recommend?"

"Confide in someone." The big man shrugged. "It need not be me."

"I talk to Nyssa." Ceara referred to her friend and the fourth woman who had shared Morag's hut in the forest before Maximilian's arrival at Kilderrick.

Royce rolled his eyes. "And she will conjure a dream for you. Nay, confide in someone who can see you protected from whatever you fear."

"You still do not believe in Nyssa's charms and forecasts?" She had to tease him a little.

That did not even merit a reply from Royce. "You and I are among those who act. It is our way to resolve any concern rather than let it fester. Make a choice, concoct a plan, and see the threat banished."

"It cannot be so readily done."

"*You* tell me this," he said and shook his head. "The huntress who killed a guard with a single stroke to see Maximilian avenged?" His gaze bored into hers. "You are no weak and docile maiden, Ceara. Do not conduct yourself like one. You are a warrior through and through, just as I am. People of our ilk do not cower in fear and wait for the worst. They face the enemy and eliminate it."

It was the longest lecture she had ever heard from Royce. She was tempted to confide in him, but hesitated, uncertain that a mercenary would understand why she had fled a marriage arranged by her family. Royce might urge her to accept her fate.

Who could she trust to take her side?

Not Maximilian. Not even Alys, now. Nyssa knew more than anyone and advised only patience, a trait Ceara did not possess in abundance.

"But you have battled men," she felt obliged to note. "I only hunt for meat."

"The ill-fated sentry might argue that."

"That was the decision of the moment, not a choice of trade."

Royce waved away the distinction. "Solve your dilemma and soon, or Maximilian might solve it for you."

"How so?"

"Men believe there is only one solution to the restlessness of women." The mercenary fixed her with a look from his remaining eye. "Choose a man yourself before he selects one for you."

Ceara was shocked. "Maximilian will not compel me to wed!"

"He might."

Would he? And who would he choose? Sadly, Ceara could not think of one man at Kilderrick she wished to take to husband.

The most interesting—and untrustworthy—candidate had left.

The boys began to argue behind them in that moment, debating the best way to force the sledge across the river. Royce shook his head and dismounted, striding back toward them, perhaps relieved by the distraction.

As usual, he was decisive. "You cannot use this device to cross the river at any rate," he said, stripping one of the long boughs. He bound the feet of one buck to it, then indicated that Louis seize the other end. "We will carry this one to Denis while you stand guard over the rest," he told Nicholas. "Then we will bring back some assistance."

The boys nodded approval of this scheme as the first buck was hefted high. Nicholas stripped a bough to prepare the second one and Ceara accepted a brace of hares before riding onward. She scarce noticed that Louis, a dark-haired boy with great enthusiasm, strove to do more when she was looking toward them. She noted the way Royce smiled and shook his head, but could not guess what amused him.

There was a matter of greater import ahead. Their small party crossed the river and left the shadow of the forest, then Ceara halted her horse to stare. An encampment had taken root on the empty slope before Kilderrick in their absence, as if conjured from naught at all. There were tents and men and horses, a fire burning and a bustle of activity.

For a heartbeat, she had the curious sense that she was inexplicably returned to the previous fall, when the *Loup Argent* had first arrived in these lands with his army of mercenaries.

But nay. The keep of Kilderrick still rose tall and proud after its reconstruction, the masons still shouted to each other on the far side of the structure as they worked and the recently-rebuilt village bustled beyond them. The sun shone and the promise of summer turned the hills and forest verdant, a marked contrast to that cold and rainy autumn day.

And this company was markedly smaller. Who were they?

Royce strode past her in that moment. He was carrying most of the weight of the deer himself, she did not doubt, and Louis scrambled to match his pace. Royce also halted to stare, prompting Louis to stumble, then grinned.

"For the love of all that is holy," he whispered. "'Tis the Compagnie Rouge!" He hooted and dropped his burden before crossing the shallows of the river with purpose.

Ceara followed Royce, her curiosity roused. If the Compagnie Rouge came to Kilderrick, who had led them here?

She knew who she wished it might be, though it was folly to desire to meet Rafael once more.

"Lambret Bonecutter!" Royce roared and a burly man with a bald head turned to look at him. That man's face creased in a smile and he shouted a reply as he waved a greeting. "You old dog!" Royce strode toward his former comrade with outstretched arms. "And Helmut! How is that hand?" This warrior was missing a hand, but he waved his arm cheerfully as he came to meet Royce. "Bernard!" A man more fastidiously attired than the others, with a trimmed fair beard, bowed to Royce. Royce shook his hand formally, then looked at the fourth warrior. "And who is this?"

"Raynard, as cunning a fox as ever there was," Lambret supplied.

The tall man with auburn hair shook hands with Royce, his expression remaining impassive. His assessing gaze slipped over Ceara and she lifted her chin, hiding how her throat tightened.

It could not be.

The warrior's gaze slipped past her, as if he found naught of interest in her appearance, and Ceara concluded that she was mistaken.

Meanwhile, Royce was lost in conversation with the other three warriors, all of them slapping each other on the back and greeting each other with enthusiasm. Four boys emerged from the camp, undoubtedly drawn by the noise, and it appeared that Royce recognized two of them. Tales were exchanged then amidst boisterous laughter. The men were scarred and tanned, muscled and unshaven, their language in a mix of languages that she found incomprehensible.

Their horses, though, were most fine. Two of the boys returned to tending a veritable herd of horses, most of which had been divested of saddles and trap. The horses were being brushed, their tails swinging and ears flicking as they watched Royce's greeting with obvious curiosity. Ceara had not seen such fine creatures and could not resist the chance to see them more closely. She spotted at least four destriers, magnificent stallions every one of them, and eight—nay, ten!—palfreys, any one of which would fetch a fine price in Carlisle. They all had glossy coats and bright eyes, signs that they were well-fed and well-tended.

Ceara could not resist. She left her horse and the hares with Louis, who already held the reins of Royce's destrier, and went to look more closely at the steeds. She was wearing boots and chausses, as always she did when she hunted, along with a laced jerkin of boiled leather and a light cloak. Her gloves were tucked into her belt alongside her dagger and her hair hung in a long braid down her back. Her crossbow was slung from her saddle and she carried a quiver of bolts. Her choice of garb was so routine that no one at Kilderrick took note of it any longer.

The same could not be said of the arrivals.

"Woo hoo," Lambret said, turning from Royce to survey her with open appreciation. "Do you share your whore, Royce?" Another gave a low whistle. That Raynard simply watched her, his intense gaze making the hair prickle on the back of her neck.

"Are they all so pretty in these lands?" demanded Helmut with a leer. "We are due for a celebration, so bring them all!"

Ceara could not understand all that they said, but their expressions told her all she needed to know of their intentions. They encircled her and she felt her trepidation rise.

The horses would wait.

Her hand dropped to the hilt of her knife. Several men found this amusing and Ceara decided they would feel the weapon's bite first. She nigh jumped for the heavens when a man's hand landed heavily on her shoulder. The gathered men laughed as she drew her blade and spun to face her assailant.

Rafael.

God in Heaven, he was more handsome than she recalled.

Her heart leapt as he stared down at her, the weight of his gloved hand still on her shoulder. The blade trembled a little in her hand, for she had never stood so close to Rafael before. She knew his eyes were blue but to be so close to that piercing sapphire gaze made something flutter deep inside her. He towered over her, though she was not short, and his broad shoulders filled her view entirely. He was gloriously male, his attention locked upon her. Ceara stared up at him and could not summon a word.

Rafael looked as dangerous and disreputable as Ceara recalled, his eyes gleaming with a cursed confidence in his own allure. His smile as he surveyed her was slow and seductive, and she was struck once again by how different he was from others she knew. 'Twas impossible to miss that he came from abroad, from foreign lands and wider vistas, and that the gleam in his eyes was born of experiences beyond her own. His skin tanned to gold, his hair almost black and glossy in the sun. He had several days' growth of dark beard, which only made him look more like an unpredictable ruffian—and more attractive, to her view.

He wore a laced dark leather jerkin with a white chemise beneath it, a combination that made him look virile and hale. The shirt was open at the throat, offering a glimpse of his tanned skin and the tangle of dark hair upon his chest. He wore a necklace that she did not recall but perhaps had never been sufficiently close to notice, the heavy gold chain visible but the pendant hidden beneath his chemise. It was more than his aura of power that intrigued her.

Holding his gaze, the blood hummed in her veins and her skin heated.

Rafael had returned and she was treacherously glad.

She also would do any deed to ensure he never guessed as much, for there was no telling what a man like Rafael would do with that truth.

Ceara stared up at him, knowing that she would give a great deal to find out.

CHAPTER 2

*R*afael's gloved hand slid from Ceara's shoulder to her chin with unwarranted familiarity, yet she could not summon the will to step away. This man held such an allure that he could distract her with a glance—and his touch could compel her to forget her own name. He tipped her face upward so that she met his knowing gaze and she wondered whether he would kiss her.

That would be inappropriate—yet she hoped for it all the same.

"*Ciao, bella*," he murmured so that only she could hear his words. The low murmur combined with his sultry expression heated her to her toes and he watched her, as if keenly aware of her response, his lips curving in a slow smile of satisfaction.

How could such a wicked man be so alluring? It defied belief. She admired men of honor and duty, men of principle and valor—not those driven by their own advantage.

At least she had, until meeting Rafael. Ceara realized that she had challenged him in the past solely to gain his attention—but now she wanted more than a glance or even a touch.

No matter the price.

Then he arched a brow and raised his voice. "Few are as fair as Ceara," he informed his men. He said her name differently than she had ever heard it pronounced before, softer and sweeter, the *r* rolling off his tongue like a caress. She had not realized that he even knew her name but now wanted him only to repeat it again and again.

Perhaps to whisper it against her flesh, while they lay entangled abed.

Her blood heated an increment more at the thought. This was a man who would know how best to seduce a woman. Ceara could not imagine that she would regret a night with Rafael.

He slid his thumb across her chin in a languid caress that made her shiver in a most delicious way. She let him see her reaction and his smile broadened, the warmth in his eyes making her heart race. "I advise you not to trifle with this bold maiden, though," he continued in a low rumble, his gaze unswerving. "She is adept with a knife and unafraid to use it."

The men chuckled but retreated, perhaps because they perceived that Rafael made a claim.

"I thank you for the compliment," Ceara said in careful French, watching his brows rise.

"I thought you did not understand that tongue well," he said, his gaze searching. "Or was that another deception?"

"I have learned more of it since you left Kilderrick."

"Why?" His perusal became more intent, still lazy but more thorough. The sounds of the other men faded and Ceara forgot them all.

There was only Rafael, his hand on her chin, his gaze holding her captive, his presence making her simmer to her very toes.

Ceara rubbed her cheek against his hand, watching him inhale sharply. "I hoped you would return, of course."

Rafael's laugh was hearty. "You wished to speak with me so much that you learned another language?" His men chortled with him, evidence that they still listened. "Am I to be so flattered that I drop to my knees and pledge myself to your service? Or should I compose poetry to win your favors?" His sparkling eyes made the possibility of that most clear.

"I should not recognize poetry if I heard it," she said, her words breathless.

"Of course, you would. Hair like liquid fire," He lifted her braid.

"Cheeks that glow like roses. Eyes that shine with all the shades of the ocean." He lifted a brow. "In a tempest."

Ceara smiled despite herself. Even when he teased her, she was seduced.

Rafael leaned closer, his gaze boring into hers with such intensity that her mouth went dry. "But what I would do with you, *bella*, requires no words." His voice was a low purr, a murmur as smooth as velvet. His fingertip slid down her throat to her shoulder, then hesitated. She felt her nipple grow taut, so certain was she that he would caress her boldly. Then his eyes glinted with mischief and his fingertip eased down her arm, until he captured her hand in his.

He planted a kiss on the back of her hand, then turned it over.

Ceara caught her breath when the warmth of his lips touched her palm. She could feel his desire like a palpable force—no less her own urge to surrender. A more prudent maiden might have retreated to safety, but Ceara suddenly had an idea.

A man like Rafael was precisely the ally she needed against her betrothed. Rafael would not shirk from killing a man, and he would not care for her reasons for asking that the deed be done. Royce or Maximilian might urge her to keep the betrothal vow, but Rafael would not care about a broken promise.

He would have his price, of course, and it would be a predictable one, but her freedom was more important than her chastity. She grew no younger and she would take a chance upon this rogue.

Rafael was the solution she had awaited and this was the moment to act upon opportunity.

Indeed, it felt both daring and right to encourage his interest.

BEFORE CEARA COULD DOUBT the wisdom of her impulse, she placed her hand on the bare skin of Rafael's chest. His eyes widened slightly, in either surprise or admiration, but he did not retreat. Nay, his smile heated with satisfaction in her choice and the challenge in his gaze made her heart skip.

"And now you would taunt me again," he warned softly. "Careful, *bella*, lest you win more than you expect."

"I do not taunt or tease, Rafael," she said, feeling bold indeed. "Not this time." She spread her fingers and flattened her palm against his flesh. She had never touched a man thus, and was aware that Rafael was taut and watchful. He was muscled and hard, warm, and utterly still. She moved her hand slowly lower, letting her fingers slide beneath the open front of his linen chemise. She then leaned closer, inhaling the scent of him. She watched his eyes glitter as she ran her fingers through the curly dark hair on his chest, then her fingertips found his nipple, hidden beneath the cloth. She flicked it and it tightened, just as her own might do if similarly provoked. Rafael caught his breath, a most encouraging hint that she had some power in this exchange.

He wanted her, just as he had before. That was her asset in this exchange.

Ceara touched her lips to his throat and felt his surprise. "I need you to kill a man," she whispered so quietly that no one else would hear.

"Do it yourself, *bella*," he replied just as quietly, his words a vibration beneath her hand and a breath in her hair. "I saw you kill that sentry and 'twas artfully done. You have no need of me."

As gratifying as it was to have her skill acknowledged, Ceara knew this was not true. "But he did not know who I was. I was able to trick him."

Rafael waited in silence, his heart beating beneath her hand.

"This man knows me. I could not surprise him."

"A challenge is good for a warrior. It keeps one's reactions quick," he noted wryly, stepping back.

"He will hunt me."

"And you are a skilled huntress yourself." His voice roughened with impatience. "Get yourself to the keep, *bella*, if you fear an assault—or find another man fool enough to do your will." He nodded to the warriors who followed. "There are candidates aplenty in this vicinity."

Ceara did not retreat. "But you are my choice, not a stranger."

His eyes narrowed as if he suspected her of trickery. "You could ask Royce or Matteo." Both mercenaries had arrived with Maximilian and remained at Kilderrick. "Indeed, Matteo would be my choice. The man is as stealthy as a cat and his aim is true."

"They will confer with Maximilian first." She grimaced, making her view of that clear. "I would rather have you do the deed."

Rafael studied her with gleaming eyes. "Nay," he said with quiet heat.

She could not understand. "But you are a mercenary, a man whose loyalty is bought and sold with regularity. Why not once more?"

He leaned closer, his gaze darkening so that they were nigh as blue as the midnight sky. "Because I do not trust you, *bella*," he murmured. "And my dagger with its blunted blade reminds me why."

He had kept the weapon she had damaged? Ceara was perversely pleased by this, although she knew that he might not have done as much to remember her. It was undoubtedly valuable and that would be the detail of import to him. "I thought you would have a smith repair it."

"I prefer the reminder of my misplaced trust."

She could not stop herself from smiling. He *had* kept it because of her.

"And you are pleased. You must know, Ceara, that you are unlike most women."

"Perhaps that is why you like me," she ventured and he laughed so heartily that she found herself smiling.

"Perhaps," Rafael admitted, not denying the charge. He drew the dagger then and spun it so that it caught the light between them.

It was the same blade. It could have been no other with that elegantly twisted hilt. Sure enough, the tip was bent ever so slightly, the result of Ceara driving the blade into the sheriff's wooden table the previous autumn.

Even his dagger seemed to come from another world, a richer one far beyond the lands Ceara knew. The hilt was shaped like a great braid, beyond the art of any smith she knew. The pommel was the globe crystal she recalled, the one said to have a shard of the true cross within it.

There was something trapped within it, to be sure.

"In any other demesne, I might have been executed, thanks to you casting suspicion upon me." Rafael's voice was a low purr, one that stirred every fiber of Ceara's being. "'Twas Maximilian's knowledge of my nature that cleared the charge and I do not doubt you regretted my escape." He stole a kiss then, moving so quickly that she was startled. The brief caress left her lips burning, and his men laughed when she took two steps back, her hand rising to her mouth in pleasure and agitation.

"I need your help."

Rafael shook his head. "You cannot pay my price."

"Not in coin." Ceara saw his gaze brighten and knew she had named his desire. She touched the top of her chemise, drawing his attention to her cleavage. "But I have other means of compensation."

Rafael froze as if he might be tempted, then shook his head curtly. "A man who does not learn from his mistakes is doomed to repeat them. Not this time, *bella*."

"I give my word!" she said with some indignation.

"And I do not trust it." He shrugged. "There is more to this commission than you confess. I suspect, in fact, that any attempt upon the life of this unnamed man will see me assaulted as a result. Doubtless, you would be glad to have two dead instead of one. Who is this fiend?"

"My betrothed," she confessed. "The match was arranged when I was a child and I do not wish to wed him."

"Then break the betrothal. Or wed another."

"'Tis not that simple…"

"Did you ask him?"

"There is no point. He will refuse my request and insist upon the match."

Rafael was dismissive. "Why must the man die, simply because you do not want him? What was his crime?" He shook his head with resolve. "He is a man, not a hound, *bella*. I will not take his life just because he declines to cede to you."

Ceara had to convince him. She moved closer again, stroking his chest with her fingertips and running them beneath the chain. "What would change your mind?" she whispered, hoping to tempt his curiosity. She hooked the chain with her fingertip and would have lifted its burden into view.

His hand locked over hers, ensuring that whatever hung upon it remained hidden from view. Her hand was flat over his heart, captive between his hand and his chest. His gaze roved over her as if he sought the solution to a riddle. "Naught," he said with a heat that indicated otherwise.

Ceara smiled. "Who tells a falsehood now?"

He snorted but did not reply. Nor did he release her hand.

She felt his heartbeat quicken.

Ceara moved closer, so her breasts were against his chest. "Please, Rafael," she whispered, savoring the sound of his name upon her own tongue. "I pledge I will surrender to you in return." Before he could argue, she stretched up and touched her lips to his, fleetingly. She meant only to offer a taste, but Rafael gave her no chance to retreat.

"And you lie," he murmured against her mouth. "Again." He caught her nape in one hand and lifted her to her toes, slanting his mouth across hers in a decisive and possessive kiss, one far more demanding than her own.

Ceara froze in surprise, struggling against the impulse to tear herself free. She would not win his assistance if she fled. In the span of a heartbeat, pleasure coursed through her from the movement of his mouth against hers, awakening a most pleasurable sensation, and she had no desire to halt their embrace.

Ceara had never been kissed in passion, not like this, but the same was not true of Rafael. He knew his objective and how to achieve it. He drew Ceara into his arms when she did not know what to do. His kiss coaxed her to join him, his arm sliding around her waist, as his men began to jeer and hoot. It was a glorious kiss, one that made Ceara yearn for more. She found herself melting against Rafael, desperate for more of this dizzying pleasure. She arched against him, her hand sliding into the thick curl of his hair, and his growl of approval thrilled her to her toes.

"That one is claimed, to be sure," said one of the men. "Do you not protest her loss, Royce?"

"She would never have been mine," that man said easily. The men laughed together and Rafael broke his kiss, holding Ceara captive as he stared down at her. His fingers worked in her hair, caressing her with a

27

slow persistence that tempted her to moan—or rub herself against him like a wanton.

"Do not mistake me for a man of honor, *bella*," he warned, his low words vibrating in his chest so that she felt them as well as heard them. He smiled down at her, his eyes gleaming sapphire, and the sight weakened her knees. "In my trade, the victor takes whatever he desires and abandons it when he has had his due." Rafael watched her, a hunger in his gaze that thrilled her to her marrow. "You play a dangerous game this day. Be warned that if you touch me again, no man will keep me from my reward."

He released her abruptly and pivoted, leaving her wavering on her feet. Ceara could only stare after him, yearning. She felt stirred and disheveled, awakened and aroused, from just a single kiss.

Rafael did not look back. 'Twas as if he had forgotten her, even after that kiss, which stung her pride. She took a step to follow him but the company of men moved smoothly, barricading her from the camp.

And from Rafael.

Their eyes glinted as they watched her and Ceara strove to gather her wits. She could not fail to note the interest in more than one gaze and heeded Rafael's warning. She tugged the hem of her shirt, tossed her braid over her shoulder and turned back toward her horse as if she kissed men with such ardor all the time. The mercenaries studied her in silence and she knew they would watch her all the way to the gates, just as she knew she did not manage Rafael's insouciance.

He had awakened a desire in her that might prove impossible to deny. Could she keep her wits long enough to see her objective won? Did she dare to embark on a contest of wills that she might not win?

Truly, that kiss proved that Ceara would not regret whatever price she paid to Rafael, whether Edward was dispatched or not.

And that was a perilous realization indeed.

CEARA'S KISS had set his very soul afire.

It had certainly left Rafael craving more.

The warrior maiden was as beautiful as he recalled, even with her fiery hair bound back. It was the flash in her eyes that had beguiled him from the first, for it hinted at an inner fire, one that he now had kindled. A single kiss had proven that she was as fiery as he had hoped and Rafael was not one to ever forgo the prospect of passion.

He had thought to warn her that she tempted him too much with a kiss. He had not expected her to tolerate his embrace, let alone return it, but the truth of it seared him to his marrow. He had expected reticence, even outrage, but she had met him with an answering passion that fed his own desire.

Unpredictable and alluring wench, as irresistible as a siren. Rafael wanted more.

He wanted all she could give.

He wanted both immediately.

He already doubted a single coupling would suffice.

Rafael had to put distance between himself and the temptress, the better to consider Ceara's possible objectives in asking for his aid. He could not think beyond earthy need when his fingers were tangled in the silk of her hair and her lips were swollen from his kiss. When her breath mingled with his own and her breasts rubbed against his chest, her nipples taut.

Rafael pushed a hand through his hair and willed himself to consider her deeds. In the past, Ceara had teased and tempted, but had never allowed so much as a caress.

But now she offered a quest and a reward. Rafael had not even known that she had a betrothed, much less that she wished the man in question to die. Was it even true? Why would she create such a tale? Rafael had no doubt that she manipulated him for her own objectives, and he could only wish that he was not so susceptible to her wiles.

Already he was impatient to see her at the board, like a lovesick swain who could not bear to be parted from the object of his desire, not even for a moment. He was not smitten, though—he was merely ardent. Another kiss might sate him—but there was unlikely to be another in Kilderrick's hall.

Beneath Maximilian's eye, Ceara would not be so audacious. Rafael refused to be disappointed. There was no real prospect of a seduction, after all. He spared a glance at the sky, vexed even so that the evening meal was hours away.

For the moment, he would savor the memory of that kiss and the kindled fire in his blood. He found her kiss persuasive and not just because he had been alone so many nights of late. Nay, there was a sorcery about Ceara, and when she tempted him, he could not readily deny her.

He thought of Alys and her hold over Maximilian and knew no woman would ever hold him so in thrall.

Perhaps the four women were all witches, as the residents of Rowan Fell had once insisted, and they contrived to bind warriors to them.

Rafael snorted. He reminded himself that Ceara had tricked him before.

But still. Had he ever met such a woman? He halted in the shadow of his own tent and turned to watch as Ceara rode toward Kilderrick. The chausses and jerkin left no doubt of her admirable shape and she rode with the ease he remembered. Aye, her bold manner was familiar as well.

A number of rabbits hung from the back of her saddle, evidence of her success at the hunt. He liked that she did not cringe from making the final blow. She would not be a woman to tremble and weep in the midst of war: she would be more likely to insist upon defending his back. That made Rafael smile. He liked her ferocity and resolve.

He was sorry when she vanished through the gate of the keep. Royce trudged behind her, leading his horse and carrying one end of a large stick with a deer bound to it. Louis had the other end of the stick and struggled with the weight of it. They all entered the keep.

Rafael guessed that Amaury had not returned from his pursuit of the abducted maiden, Elizabeth, and that this was Kilderrick's new hunting party.

Royce and Louis reappeared moments later, the squire running down the slope ahead of the warrior's steady steps. That boy was one of the squires who had remained with Maximilian, dark-haired and diligent. Rafael had not missed the boy's adoring stares after Ceara this day, either, though Ceara seemed to be oblivious to the squire's admiration. Denis, the cook, and Yves, the castellan, appeared next, following Royce. As Rafael watched, Yves beckoned to a large dark man whom Rafael recalled as Tynan Smith. Rafael folded his arms across his chest, wondering whether their errand was with him.

But nay. This company crossed the river and vanished into the forest.

In mere moments, they appeared again, this time with Nicholas, another of the four squires who had stayed at Kilderrick. He was the youngest of the boys who had stayed with Maximilian, fair and stocky. The party was now burdened with three more bucks and an additional number of rabbits. Rafael respected the effectiveness of the expedition. Clearly, the game was plentiful at Kilderrick.

Yet Maximilian had forbidden him to hunt.

Rafael called and his new squire, Antonio, appeared.

"Aye, sir?"

"Go to the hall of Kilderrick and ask the laird if he might spare a buck to provision the Compagnie Rouge. Remind him, if you please, that hungry men are less predictable than those whose bellies are full."

Rafael did not doubt that Maximilian would come to the same conclusion, but the reminder could not hurt.

The boy bowed, then pivoted and ran for the gate. He was only ten summers of age and small, but possessed considerable resolve. Antonio never allowed any of the older and larger boys to best him, no matter the cost. He was already a handsome boy, as well, with his dark eyes and curly dark hair, and blessed with a smile that would make him popular with women in a decade or so. Indeed, he might have been a younger version of Rafael himself, save that Antonio had a defender in the warrior he served as Rafael had not. It might make all the difference to his future.

Antonio caught up to the party and spoke to Royce, who glanced back at Rafael's camp then urged the boy ahead of him through the gates.

Rafael thought of Ceara as he ducked into his tent and his blood quickened. He would not step readily into any trap that discredited him before Maximilian. He would have to be patient, but he could ensure that he made the best argument in his own favor with his appearance.

He would bathe in the river and don his best garb before arriving for dinner.

To himself, he could admit that he was curious as to what Ceara might do.

No less, what additional proof she might offer of her willingness to keep the promise that so tempted him.

IN THE FOREST, three men watched the exchange between brothers and conferred quietly in Gaelic. They recognized Maximilian de Vries, Laird of Kilderrick, but had no notion of the new arrival's identity. Of greater import than his name were the mercenaries who accompanied him, for one glance proved that they were accustomed to the business of war. They were a rough and scarred lot, fierce and undoubtedly brutal.

Their camp was rapidly filling the empty slope between the keep and the river.

So many eyes.

So many opposing blades.

The leader of the trio rolled to his back, considering their course, while the others waited for his decision. It was unfortunate that he had not been able to hear the words exchanged by the two horsemen.

"We watch and wait," he said in Gaelic. "Opportunity may come of this."

"At least we know her location," said the second.

The first nodded. "We will have but one chance to surprise them and her. We must choose wisely. We will each take a watch while we await opportunity." They nodded agreement then faded into the shadows of the undergrowth, following his command.

ALYS DUCKED through the portal from the ramparts to find Maximilian awaiting her. She was surprised, though she knew she should not have been. The man could move as quietly as a sunbeam and as swiftly as the wind. He smiled and offered his hand to her, but she noted that the smile did not light his eyes.

"You are displeased," she said as the warmth of his hand closed over hers. She leaned on him a bit as she descended the three steps, feeling that her balance was more precarious these days.

"Nay," he acknowledged. "Not precisely displeased."

"But not precisely pleased," she countered, her tone teasing.

His smile flashed and he raised her hand to his lips, his eyes fairly glowing. "You know me well, my Alys."

Still he was grim so she teased him more. "And you would rather I did not? That is not gallant, sir."

His smile broadened a little more as he tucked her hand into his elbow and led her toward the solar. "It still surprises me when another guesses the thoughts I would hide."

"Even me?"

"Even you, though when you protest, I know it is unjust. If anyone should guess the secrets of my heart, it should be my beloved."

"But you were unloved for a very long time," she noted, understanding this well.

Maximilian looked down at her, his gaze filled with familiar warmth. Alys marveled yet again that she should love this man more with every passing day. He touched her chin with a gentle fingertip. "I thought you slept this afternoon."

"I could scarce miss the sound of an army arriving."

He inclined his head, and she could see that he was still thinking.

"I thought you would be glad to welcome Rafael," she said when he said no more.

"I am glad to know that Rafael is hale. I am less glad that he has brought the Compagnie Rouge to my gates when I am compelled to disappoint him."

"Surely he is the one disappointing you."

"How so?"

"You sent him to Château de Vries, to accept Philip's wager. Why is Rafael here at all?"

"Because he has succeeded."

Alys frowned. "But the season for warfare only began after Easter, and that celebration was late this year. It cannot be more than thirty days, yet he has journeyed from France to Scotland as well."

Maximilian chuckled. "The season for warfare," he echoed and shook his head. They entered the solar and he closed the door, securing it behind them. "Such edicts, my lady, are made by those who would heed all rules. In my former trade, we attacked when we were ready to do so, regardless of the season or date. If one's opponent is not prepared, then victory can be easily won, and I need not remind you of the potency of surprise as a tactic."

Alys' heart sank. "He brought you the seal," she guessed, her words softly uttered.

It was her worst fear. Maximilian had pledged to her that he would remain at Kilderrick forever and that it was his home, but she feared otherwise. She knew—mostly thanks to Rafael—that the possession of Château de Vries had been her husband's sole goal for decades. She would only believe that he could turn aside from lifelong temptation when he did. In this moment, she feared his next words and she knew her grasp tightened on his hand.

"He did." Maximilian kissed her temple. "And I told him that I had no desire for it. Your concern was for naught, my Alys."

Relief weakened her knees, but she strove to hide her reaction. It felt disloyal to have doubted him at all, though she knew how potent a dream could be. The life they shared together filled her with joy though she had not even dared to dream of such happiness in her years of solitude. "I am sorry for my doubts."

Maximilian watched her closely, though, as aware of her secrets as she was of his. "You should have believed me," he chided in an undertone and Alys felt her cheeks heat.

"I feared it was your heart's desire."

"I have my heart's desire," he insisted, urging her toward the bed. He bent to kiss her. "And it is you."

"And I was a cur to doubt you," Alys said. "I am relieved that the temptation has come and gone."

"As am I," Maximilian agreed with a smile. "'Twas easier than I had feared it might be. I, too, wondered how hard that particular holding would be to decline."

"You loved it."

"I did and do, but not as much as I treasure Kilderrick."

"You had no doubt Rafael would triumph."

"None." He unfastened her cloak and set it aside, then shed his own, a welcome sign that he intended to remain with her. "He confessed also that Gaston is dead."

Alys was surprised and could not hide her reaction.

Maximilian nodded. "It seems he strove to deceive Rafael, which is never a wise choice. My brother does not tolerate disloyalty or disappointment." His gaze flicked to the window. "This is why I ponder the situation."

"I do not understand."

"Rafael is unpredictable when thwarted. He came all this way in haste to surrender that seal to me, fully expecting me to sail south with him to possess the prize of de Vries. Instead, I declined its burden, then ordered him to leave within three days, without me."

Alys could take no issue with that decision, though she recognized that Rafael might. "What will he do?"

"I do not know." Maximilian spoke deliberately, clearly considering the possibilities. He went to the window of the solar and looked over the camp that now occupied the slope between the keep and the river. "But I do not have the men to turn aside the Compagnie Rouge should they attack, even with this smaller force." Alys' heart clenched, then her husband pivoted and met her gaze steadily. "I trained the Compagnie Rouge, after all, and they are a fearsome foe."

"But you trained these men, too."

He winced. "They have not the taste for war of the Compagnie Rouge."

"Would the mercenaries not still have some loyalty to you?"

Maximilian shrugged. "If they do, it offers no guarantee to anyone else." He crossed the chamber then, and framed her face in his hands, his gaze suddenly bright. "I taught Rafael to exploit a man's weakness and he knows I have only one." He kissed her with urgency and heat. "Promise me that you will not let yourself be alone, my lady," he whispered when he broke his kiss. Alys shivered at his tone. "Not even for a moment." He pulled back and held her gaze until she nodded agreement.

"I think you should remain with me and within the walls," she said and his eyes began to twinkle.

"As ever, lady mine, our thoughts are as one." He kissed her again, then swung her into his arms and carried her to the pillared bed. Alys found herself laughing with relief when he jumped onto it, still holding her fast against his chest. They tumbled together across the mattress until she was beneath him, his weight braced over her and his face wondrously close to her own. He still wore his armor, the chain mail cool against her hand, but she loved that he was both playful and impatient.

"How fares the babe?" he whispered, curving his hand over her ripening belly.

"As hale as the last time you asked, mere hours ago."

He smiled in truth then. "And the lady?"

"Fine indeed." She reached up and pushed her fingers through the tangle of his blond hair, her heart full to bursting. "I love you, Maximilian," she confessed, her voice husky.

"And I love you, my Alys, which means we must be vigilant."

"Until the Compagnie Rouge is gone?"

"And even after that," he concluded. "Rafael is most adept with a feint."

"Because you trained him well?"

"Of course. There is little point in training anyone badly." Maximilian laughed when she swatted his shoulder, then bent his head to capture her lips in a most satisfying kiss. He would protect her to his dying breath, Alys knew it, but she did not want anyone to die.

She would be vigilant, just as Maximilian advised.

CHAPTER 3

𝒯he mood at Kilderrick was festive as the sun set. The smell of roast venison carried through the entire keep, ensuring that appetites were whetted. There was gossip aplenty about the arrival of Rafael and his men, as well as lively speculation over what that mercenary might do. As much as those in the company knew Rafael had been loyal to Maximilian in the past, his arrival at their gates with even part of the Compagnie Rouge aroused a frisson of uncertainty.

Ceara and Nyssa had moved from Morag's hut in the forest into the keep after the Yule. The tale had been that their assistance was needed —Ceara to hunt and Nyssa to watch over Alys. But the idea had been Maximilian's and now Ceara wondered whether he feared some retaliation for Godfroy's death. The Laird of Kilderrick had not been a mercenary for decades without that labor leaving its mark on his expectations. Had he ordered Rafael's return with a mighty force? It was entirely possible that could be the case and she would not know of it. The laird was as impassive as one of Nyssa's standing stones.

Ceara came to their chamber late, hoping Nyssa would have already gone to Alys. She did not want to answer her friend's inevitable and perceptive questions and was glad to find the chamber empty.

She opened her trunk and smiled at Alys' gift of earlier in the year.

Ceara had never worn the garments given to her, but on this night, she had to dress to tempt Rafael and was glad to have the means.

She was well aware of Dorcha, Nyssa's raven, watching her with bright eyes from his perch in the corner, as if the creature understood all.

How strange that Rafael's kiss seemed to have awakened her to sensation. She ran her hand over her new garb with appreciation for its softness and fine texture. Alys had been generous indeed. Ceara donned the linen chemise and admired how sheer and light it was. It felt smooth against her skin.

Next was the kirtle of deepest green which laced at the sides, the one with gold embroidery on the hems and cuffs. The sleeves laced tightly to her forearms as well. Ceara's heart was skipping in anticipation as she pulled on her stockings and fastened her garters above the knee. Truly, it felt audacious for her thighs to be bare, even beneath her skirts. The chemise brushed against her skin in a most distracting way, making her wonder about the feel of a man's hand there.

Not just any man, though. She flushed as she recalled Rafael's strong grip. It was easy to remember the seductive caress of his fingers in her hair, the weight of his hand as he slid it down her back. The man could stir anyone to a fever.

Did he decline her offer because he was protective of her? Ceara could not imagine as much. A warrior like Rafael had surely despoiled maidens in every territory—and left them hoping for his return. Nay, he simply did not trust her. She had to convince him to take her quest.

'Twould be a bargain, no more and no less. Ceara would not suffer unreasonable expectations, even in herself. When she surrendered to Rafael, it would be no heartfelt mating. There would be pleasure, to be sure, but then Rafael would forget her for the charms of another. She would be next of his conquests, no more and no less, and the loss of her maidenhead would be no asset to her future. If they came to an agreement, she would pay her due, then they would part forever.

"He will never love me," she informed the bird, who nodded wise agreement. "Only a fool would expect as much."

Dorcha cawed assent.

She would find affection with a man later, once she evaded Edward's claim.

All the same, Ceara could not wait to see Rafael again. In his presence, she felt a tingle of excitement that had been absent from her life of late.

Perhaps that would be her lesson from their exchange, a newfound desire to live each moment to its fullest and to dare to be bold in all matters. 'Twould not be a bad legacy, to be sure.

In the trunk was a small pouch Ceara had hidden there, one of her few possessions and the one purported to be of greatest value. After the chemise and kirtle had been removed, she could see it. Ceara brushed her fingertips across it, feeling the shape of the key secured inside it. Though she preferred to have its weight hanging from a cord around her neck, of late she had felt that it was safer here in the chamber. On this night, she closed the trunk, leaving the key in place.

She said a silent prayer for her brother as she secured the trunk's lid.

Ceara had been given a pair of fine leather shoes, but she could not abandon her tall boots. Her belt, wide and richly embroidered with golden thread, was sufficiently sturdy to carry the scabbard with her hunting knife, which she was never without. She had no jewels but no wish for them either. She combed out her hair until it shone in copper waves down her back, then braided a section of it to wrap around her head like a circlet, leaving the rest loose. She bit her bottom lip to make it look fuller and redder, then pivoted to Dorcha and lifted her hands.

"Will I be sufficient?" she asked the bird, which cawed in apparent agreement. Why should her usual confidence abandon her, over a change of garb? She recalled the heat in Rafael's eyes and knew he saw no flaw in her—save that she had tricked him before. "Of course, you are right. I am always sufficient, if not more than that."

Dorcha bobbed his head with vigor.

Ceara blew the bird a kiss then marched to the hall, the weight of her skirts swinging around her legs in a most unfamiliar way. More than one paused to survey her with surprise and appreciation, and she noted the gleam in the eyes of Matteo, who stood guard at the portal to the great hall. The mercenary kissed his fingertips in tribute as she passed, but Ceara ignored his salute.

"I wager you have a scheme," Nyssa murmured as she joined Ceara, her eyes bright with curiosity.

As ever, Nyssa could sense a secret.

"There is to be a celebration," Ceara said. "Why not wear my new kirtle?" She held it out and spun in place, inviting admiration.

Nyssa laughed, obviously knowing there was more to the story.

Before she could comment, the old blind woman, Eudaline, who had come from Château de Vries with Maximilian, plucked at Nyssa's sleeve. "I could not save her," she whispered in French, concern in her words. "Not from *him*."

"Him?" Nyssa asked gently.

"Jean le Beau, that fiend with his unholy appetites!" The old woman shook her head, clearly upset. "We could not save her. We could not. Alas!"

Clearly, the talk of Château de Vries this day had put the older woman in mind of the first arrival of the Compagnie Rouge at those gates. Nyssa bent closer to console the older woman in soft tones and Eudaline's French became unintelligible to Ceara since she spoke in dialect.

There was a stir at the portal and Matteo cried a welcome as Rafael appeared. Ceara watched openly as the two former comrades shook hands and embraced.

Rafael wore a magnificent long-sleeved tunic that fit him closely, wrought of black silk embroidered with blue and edged with gold. His belt was made of gold pieces and slung low over his hips, the scabbard obviously empty. A deep blue cloak was slung over his shoulder and she could see that the lining was silver fur. He wore black hose, fitted more closely than any chausses, and tall black boots. A gold ring flashed on the smallest finger of his right hand. Now she could see what hung upon the gold chain beneath his chemise, for he wore it over his tunic this night. The chain gleamed against the dark cloth as did the large crucifix hung from it. It was a splendid piece, made of gold with swirling details in more gold. A red gem that had to be a ruby was mounted in the middle, an emerald dangling from the ends of each of the cross arms. A large amethyst hung from the base and there were at least three pearls at the top. Ceara had never seen the like of it and knew it came from distant shores. Rafael looked powerful, disreputable and elegant, a guest from another land.

When his gaze landed upon Ceara, he smiled.

She smiled back, heart thumping.

She had noticed earlier that his hair was longer, but it was washed and combed now, falling to his shoulders in glossy ebony waves. He had shaved since their earlier meeting and Ceara could not decide whether he was more alluring bearded or not. He could have been a wealthy townsman or merchant trader on this evening—though, in a way, she preferred the disreputable rogue she had met earlier.

He left his cloak with Matteo and strode toward her, both graceful and predatory. The blue in his garb made his eyes seem a more vivid hue and she could scarce take a breath for awareness of him.

She would die if he left before seducing her thoroughly.

Ceara's heart fluttered when Rafael bent over her hand, brushing his lips to its back. "Perfection," he said, smiling as he surveyed her. He lifted his hand and turned her in place, smiling as he watched her. "You should dress as a lady more often, Ceara."

There. He did it again, saying her name in that luscious way that was both familiar and exotic, setting her heart to skipping with a single word. "Perhaps I should. I confess I had almost forgotten how."

"I doubt you forget much at all," he murmured.

"I expect we have that in common."

He laughed easily. "To your misfortune."

Ceara felt herself flushing at the reminder of how she had tricked him and Rafael winked. Apparently, he was not burdened by resentment. That was encouraging.

"You should be cautious in wearing such a token," she said, gesturing to the crucifix. "God might smite you for blasphemy in wearing his symbol."

Rafael chuckled. "If the divine chooses to so punish those in this realm, the list of those who have earned His wrath is so long that I will be dead by other means before He reaches my name."

"You cannot be certain of that."

"Shall I tempt His fury before your very eyes?" He lifted the crucifix which was as broad as his palm, his eyes dancing with challenge. He kissed it, watching her then glancing toward the roof before he shrugged.

"Perhaps you are lucky."

"Perhaps He knows I do not wear it in His honor, but to recall the one who surrendered it to me."

Ceara was intrigued. "Surrendered by choice or at the point of a sword?"

"Does it matter? I possess it either way." He lifted his palm, his tone mocking. "Behold the sum of my birthright."

Ceara did not think the gem was the sum of his legacy from his father, Jean le Beau, the notorious mercenary, but she did not say more.

Rafael shook his head. "Your disapproval is clear, Ceara, though you do not know all of the tale. I should think that you, of all people, would understand the merit of a story surrendered in increments." To her regret, he dropped her hand abruptly then, putting space between them as Maximilian and Alys appeared at the portal.

The laird's gaze flicked over his guest and Ceara thought Maximilian could specify the precise distance between herself and Rafael. By his grim expression, it was not sufficient.

Had the former comrades disagreed?

Rafael strolled toward Maximilian and Ceara regretted that she had not continued their negotiation while she had the chance. She watched as he bowed low and the pair greeted each other, if less warmly than she might have expected. Even Alys looked wary.

What had the brothers argued about?

If she had thought to have another chance to speak to the new arrival after he greeted his host, Ceara was doomed to disappointment. Yves, the châtelain, clapped his hands in that very moment, ordering them to their places as a squire appeared in the doorway with the soup. There was a flutter of activity and to Ceara's disappointment, Rafael was gestured to a seat at the opposite end of the table from her own customary one. She thought to sit closer, but Yves was at her elbow, urging her to her usual seat.

She felt the weight of the laird's gaze upon her and knew that Yves' intervention had not been an accident.

Ceara bit back her disappointment. It appeared she would have more time to plan for her discussion with Rafael and she would make the most of it.

What precisely should she say to win his support?

And how could she win the opportunity to speak with him?

THE HALL of Kilderrick was remarkably fine, considering that it had not existed the previous October. From his place at the end of the high table, Rafael admired the high ceiling and the painting upon the beams, the broad wooden floor strewn with herbs. Even at this time of year, the air was chilly at night and a blaze roared in the large hearth.

He stifled a shiver. Why would anyone choose to live so far north? The sun barely visited these lands, even at midsummer. He could not bear to imagine what it was like in January: November had been too cold for his taste. Though he did not have a destination for the Compagnie Rouge when they left Kilderrick, Rafael decided they would go south.

The Compagnie Rouge had been preparing their feast of venison and passing the last of their wine around a large blaze when Rafael left his tent for the hall. Maximilian had surrendered one buck to the Compagnie Rouge, at least. The men had been singing with gusto and Rafael knew they would become only louder as the evening progressed. They whistled and teased him about his garb, then wished him success with so many lewd winks that he had only been able to laugh.

Of course, he was required to surrender his dagger at Kilderrick's gate. Maximilian never forgot such details and neither had his gate-keeper. Rafael thought he had hidden his annoyance well.

If the dagger was lost or damaged, he would not be so quiet.

Ceara seemed to have recalled her own charms, for she wore feminine garb that was even more beguiling than her usual chausses. In a way, Rafael was glad to have been seated such a distance from her, for he did not trust himself much more than Maximilian apparently did.

They had known each other so long.

Rafael's place was near the end of the large trestle table along one wall of the room. In the middle was a large carved seat, not unlike a throne, for Maximilian, its back against the wall and opposite the fire. A smaller carved chair was at the laird's left for his lady wife. Two benches then ran alongside the table, one to Maximilian's right and one to Alys' left. Nyssa was seated on Maximilian's right side and Ceara at the opposite end of the table. Next to Alys was Victor with Royce beside him and Rafael at the end of the table. Matteo remained at the portal to the great hall.

Rafael was as far from Ceara as it was possible for him to be, and he doubted the situation was accidental. He stole a glance at her and she smiled at him quite openly. If she was so obvious in her interest, 'twas no wonder Maximilian was aware of it.

He strove to ignore his natural pleasure in her smile, reminding himself of this woman's previous treachery. There had to be more, far more, to this invitation to defend her cause than she had surrendered. If she meant to see him sacrificed in pursuit of her goal, he should have the wits to evade the trap.

'Twas folly even to be curious.

A second long trestle table had benches on either side and a goodly company of villagers and tenants settled there to partake of the meal. Among them were those who had come from de Vries with Maximilian. The old blind woman, Eudaline, was helped to the board by Nathalie, who was clearly no longer a maiden. She rounded with child, though was less ripe than Alys, and was followed by Tynan Smith. It appeared the large quiet blacksmith had wed Nathalie, for they sat together.

Henri came from the stables with his young son, the ostler bowing to Rafael in recognition as the pair took their places. The hall was soon filled with a happy chatter of conversation and the glow of firelight, from the numerous torches set on the walls and the hearth itself. There were no windows in this chamber, for a corridor for the sentries wrapped around it on three sides and there were smaller chambers behind the hearth. The air was redolent of roast venison and Rafael's mouth fairly watered in anticipation of Denis' fare.

He was glad to see his former comrades again and they exchanged a

44

few tales of common acquaintances as the squires bustled about the hall with the soup. He nodded to Louis, Mallory, Nicholas and Reynaud as the boys prepared to serve the meal. All of the boys had grown taller since his departure and he was amused to note how Louis' gaze clung to Ceara. Denis and Marie greeted him politely while Yves was more fulsome in his welcome.

"You must later share the tale of the fall of de Vries," Victor prompted.

"I should be delighted to do so, if the laird so desires." Rafael glanced up as Yves poured him ale.

"I am certain he would invite as much." The older man nodded approval and moved to fill Royce's cup.

"We must hear of every missile," Royce said.

"Every flash of Greek fire," added Victor and Rafael wondered whether his former comrades missed the adventures of the Compagnie Rouge.

"We are reduced to whittling bowls with our knives," Royce said, gesturing to the wooden bowls set before each of them.

"He complains but he likes the labor," Victor added.

"He excels at it," Yves said with pride. "We are well supplied for guests."

"They are most fine," Rafael said, lifting one to admire it. "You made them all?"

Royce grinned. "I did."

"Tell us of the wenches," Victor whispered, his thoughts clearly returning to war.

"The spoils," Royce added. "The gems and gold and fine wine."

"The rich cloth and the studded daggers."

"How much coin did you claim? This tabard is most fine."

"But the gem is not new," Victor said with a smile. "He has worn it before to impress."

Both mercenaries turned to look openly at Ceara and Rafael swallowed his smile.

Yves leaned closer to interrupt. "Excuse me, sir, but Lord Gaston is truly dead? You are certain of that?"

Rafael nodded. "I did the honor myself."

"Excellent," that man said with approval and there was a smattering of applause from those who had followed Maximilian from Château de Vries. "That fiend deserved no less." There was a cheer of agreement. Yves paused before turning away. "I do not suppose you informed Lord Amaury of the tidings on your way to Kilderrick?"

Rafael frowned. "I would not know where to find him."

"At Beaupoint, of course, on the English side of the Solway Firth. If you came to port at Worthington, you would have ridden right past his newfound abode." He smiled. "Perhaps he witnessed your arrival. 'Tis said that he keeps a stern eye upon all activity in his environs."

Rafael doubted that would be for the sake of piracy. Nay, his half-brother had been raised in a fine family with every luxury. Likely he defended the borders for the king, and for little reparation than the honor of a task well done.

"He is Warden of the Western Marches, now, to be sure," Yves continued, as proud of Amaury as if that man had been his own son. "It is a most suitable position for him."

"That knight has found himself a sweet nest," Royce growled when Yves turned away.

Victor gave Rafael a nudge when it was clear that Rafael did not understand. "The woman he followed," he growled. "Lady Elizabeth. She was an heiress as well as a beauty."

That explained Amaury's failure to return to Kilderrick.

"The one who tended his falcon?" Rafael asked.

"Aye, the timid one," Victor agreed.

"'Tis said the meek will inherit the earth," Rafael mused in an undertone. "I always believed 'twould take longer."

Royce guffawed so loudly that Maximilian turned to look, but Rafael merely saluted him with his cup. Victor meanwhile chuckled, repeating Rafael's words so that Royce laughed again.

The boys brought the venison into the hall then and there was applause for Denis' skill. Royce called for Ceara to take credit and she stood, smiling as she accepted the tribute of the company. Rafael appreciated the opportunity to admire her again without attracting his host's ire.

Once the roast and the hunters had been saluted, the other dishes were presented in a dizzying array. There were two soups, dumplings, two different venison stews and a gravy for the roasted meat, eggs prepared five ways, a rabbit tart and a rabbit stew, roast partridge, bread and greens and ale aplenty.

This was no camp fare. There were three different sauces with the venison and four for the hares. Rafael had not eaten so well in a long time and he savored every bite. He laughed with Royce and Victor, then with the encouragement of the company, he stood and recounted the tale of the Compagnie Rouge's attack upon Château de Vries. He particularly enjoyed sharing the details of the Greek fire. At the conclusion, he held up the seal of that estate to thunderous applause.

"All hail the Dragon!" Maximilian cried and Rafael bowed again before taking his seat.

"Why is Rafael called as much?" someone demanded and Rafael gestured to Maximilian, that his host might tell the tale.

"He was given that name by our father, because of his knowledge of Greek fire," Maximilian said. "When Rafael joins the battle, fire rages, reducing all to cinders. The formulation of Greek fire is a secret known to few and mastered by fewer still. Rafael has the honor of being the most skilled with that weapon in all of Christendom."

Rafael bowed at the tribute, which was all true, and there was an awed smattering of applause before he took his seat again.

The hour had to be late, but musicians appeared from the village and struck a tune. Rafael found that promising, but even better was the purpose in Ceara's expression when she left her place and strode directly to him.

She nigh stole his breath away. Rafael had no interest in coy women, and Ceara clearly had a goal. Not only was she dressed in delightfully feminine garb but her hair was loose. He had only seen her fiery tresses unbound once—in the fen—but her hair had been dark from the rain that day. Now, it flowed behind her like a fiery silken curtain, inviting his touch.

She was glorious.

She had bared her breasts to him that day, too, which was not a recollection to bolster his patience. He took a steadying breath and waited, willing himself to remember her treachery.

She was utterly untrustworthy.

But then, so was he.

"Sir," Ceara said when she halted before him, her gaze filled with challenge. There was purpose in her expression and he knew that she meant to pursue their negotiation.

Despite himself, Rafael felt his anticipation rise. Those around him fell silent and he could fairly feel Maximilian's disapproval, but he did not care.

"Will you dance?"

Aye, Rafael most surely would. This was not an invitation he was destined to decline and Maximilian could have no quibble with a dance requested by the lady herself.

CEARA HAD FEARED Rafael would refuse her after their earlier parting. To her relief, though, he swept to his feet and came around the board, claiming her hand with a flourish. The one long table where the villagers had been seated had already been removed, and the benches set around the perimeter of the hall. Maximilian and Alys' chairs remained and the other tables were removed, as well, leaving a fine space for dancing. The musicians nodded to each other and began to play, the villagers clapping along to the familiar tune.

Of course, Rafael was a superb dancer. Ceara was spun through the steps at great speed, his arm securely around her waist. He moved with grace and she was keenly aware of his proximity. He smelled divine, clean and male and warm, and her toes curled within her boots each time he looked down at her.

As much as she could have simply enjoyed the dance, Ceara knew this opportunity would not last forever. Maximilian was glowering at them, and this might be her sole chance to speak her mind.

"I need your help," she said when a spin brought her close to Rafael's chest.

His brows rose. "I have heard that tale already this day," he murmured, then they parted again.

"I mean it, truly," she said when they were toe-to-toe once more. "This is no jest but a matter of dire import."

Rafael danced her around the circle, spinning her effortlessly as they went.

"I believed you once," he noted with a stern look. "And those boots smelled so badly of the fen that they had to be burned."

She was whisked away then, weaving through the circle of men, taking one hand and another, until she was back before Rafael again.

"This is different," she insisted, as he spun her around.

"Aye, 'tis, for this time, I decline to trust you."

"But he must die," she said through her teeth and watched Rafael's brows rise just before the dance parted them again.

"I *loved* those boots."

His words trailed after her and she could not wait to return to his side.

Rafael looked resolute when she faced him again, and bent to whisper in her ear before she could speak. The fan of his breath there made her shiver. "My services are expensive, *bella*," he said softly. "Consider another assistant."

"I want you."

"'Tis not the same matter we discuss," he said with a wink.

Once again, Ceara threaded her way around the circle, smiling as if her thoughts were not consumed with Rafael.

"I offer a day and a night with you when he lies dead," she said softly when she was before him again. "I put myself utterly at your disposal."

He faltered in his steps for a moment, which was most gratifying. "You jest."

Ceara shook her head and he frowned. She knew he had made a choice.

Rafael spun her to a stop as the music ended, then bowed deeply. "I feel sympathy for your betrothed that you despise him so much." He kissed the back of her hand. "Alas, I do not involve myself in such personal disputes."

Ceara parted her lips to protest.

Rafael held her gaze and the glint in his eyes should have warned her. "Unless my price is paid in advance."

She gasped. "But then I should have to trust you to keep your word."

Rafael grinned wolfishly. "Sauce for both goose and gander."

Ceara's resolve faltered. If he did not keep his pledge, then her situation would be even more dire. She might be compelled to wed Edward, and she doubted he would treat her well when he discovered that she was no longer a maiden. He had to die first!

"I cannot pay in advance," she whispered.

"Ha!" Rafael whispered. "But I suspect you have no plan to pay your debt to me at all."

With that, he was gone, leaving her flustered.

How could she do as he asked?

Did she dare to trust him?

Ceara stared after Rafael as he walked directly to Maximilian. Even as Victor spun her into the next dance, she saw Rafael bow before the Laird of Kilderrick. Whatever he said pleased Maximilian, for that man's stern expression eased. In a moment, the laird was nodding and shaking hands with his guest. Ceara wished she could hear their words.

Rafael then headed for the door, pausing to confer with Matteo as he retrieved his cloak. The two warriors embraced again, then without a single glance in her direction, Rafael left the hall.

Nay!

He could not leave so early as this!

But the moments passed and Rafael did not return. The dance finished and Ceara hastened to the door. There was no sign of Rafael. With a single glance at the hall to ensure that no one watched her, she darted out of the hall and went to a window overlooking the slope. She spotted Rafael's dark silhouette as he strode toward the camp of the Compagnie Rouge. He did not glance back once.

Indeed, she thought she could hear him whistling. What made him so merry when she was so vexed?

Curse him! How would she speak to him now?

'Twas clear he had no desire to negotiate further. He had set his price and the sole question was whether Ceara would accept his terms.

Irksome man.

There was naught for it. Ceara would have to pursue Rafael into the camp of the Compagnie Rouge this very night. She would have to trust

THE DRAGON & THE DAMSEL

the rogue and hope for the best. The realization made her heart race, but any deed had to be better than being compelled to wed Edward de Leslie.

She would pay Rafael's prize, in advance.

And she would do as much this very night.

WHAT A BEWITCHING BEAUTY. Rafael refused to regret that he had set the price high, so high that there could be no agreement.

'Twas better this way, though he might still regret a lost opportunity.

He was relieved to have his dagger back in his possession and fingered the hilt as he walked back toward his tent. Again, he was puzzled by the contrasts in Ceara. She danced with the grace of a noblewoman, or an aristocrat's daughter, taught from a young age to attract the eye of every man in her vicinity—yet she had lived in the forest with three other women, in comparative poverty and undefended. She rode like a warrior and hunted with vigor—yet appealed to him like a damsel in distress and did as much so well that he was swayed to take her cause.

Even though he knew 'twould be folly. She had to be deceiving him again, and yet, Rafael would be saddened to leave her at Kilderrick.

He could only hope that she accepted his wager. She was sufficiently bold for any audacity.

The sky was filled with stars and there was a light cool wind—in this moment, he could find no fault with Maximilian's haven. He could not even hear any wolves and guessed that the new laird had driven the predators from his borders. The scent of roast venison both followed Rafael from the hall and greeted him as he approached the camp. Most of his company had retired, a hardy pair finishing the last of the wine as the fire burned down to coals. He was hailed, and exchanged a few words with Helmut and Lambret before retiring to his tent.

Three days and one was gone. Where would he lead the Compagnie Rouge next?

Antonio had prepared for Rafael's return with his usual efficiency.

A trio of oil lanterns burned on the trunks and thick rugs had been unfurled on the ground. Rafael's bed was piled with furs and the boy brought hot water as soon as Rafael stepped into the tent. Too restless to retire, Rafael dismissed the boy for the night and paced.

He would not sleep soon, to be sure, the temptation of Ceara still stirring his blood.

What an irksome day it had been. Instead of a triumphant reception, he had been greeted by a changed Maximilian and a trouble-making Ceara. He heartily disliked that his expectations had been so disappointed.

And he burned for earthy satisfaction, no doubt as Ceara had intended. He felt no triumph that he had named her wiles and evaded them. She was a temptress, to be sure, and one he doubted he would ever forget. 'Twas the consequence of denial, a ploy she used with success.

He should have surrendered to temptation, relying upon his own wits to evade whatever fate she had schemed for him. Surely 'twould have been worth the price.

But she was within Kilderrick's walls and he was not, at least until morning—which seemed very distant in this moment.

He supposed he could walk to Rowan Fell and seek out the smith's daughter who had previously met him merrily, but Rafael possessed no conviction that Isobeal would be as willing as she had been six months before. Also, Maximilian had chastised him for taking his pleasure in the village and insisted he pay the maid for the ride. Earning Maximilian's ire was the least of Rafael's objectives.

Had it been any other man who ruled this holding, he would have demanded a ransom to ensure their speedy departure. He doubted that strategy would succeed with the *Loup Argent*.

Rafael swore under his breath and paced the width of the tent again.

He had a wineskin of *eau-de-vie* and poured the last precious drops of it into a cup. Every detail drove him back to France, including the weight of the seal in his purse, yet he was reluctant to go.

Why?

Ceara.

The truth was both unwelcome and inescapable.

CHAPTER 4

*C*eara. A puzzle, a riddle, a temptation and a distraction. Rafael should have sampled her already and banished her hold over him. He had returned to Scotland with the excuse of offering the seal to Maximilian but in his heart, he knew it was the promise of seeing Ceara again that had brought him north.

Nay, it had been the prospect of *possessing* Ceara. But would one coupling be sufficient? Rafael sipped and he paced, considering the power of the hold she already had over him. And now, this outlandish proposal of hers complicated matters. As she accused, he could accept his payment in advance and abandon her, without killing her betrothed.

It seemed a churlish deed, even in the thinking.

Why did she want him to kill the man at all? It seemed unnecessary. Betrothals were broken all the time. Had Ceara found a more advantageous suitor? If so, why would she not ask the new suitor to dismiss her former one? Rafael doubted she would choose a man with no ability to defend what was his own.

If naught else, her request proved that she was no witch, for a sorceress could have simply cast a spell to kill an unwanted suitor.

What would Ceara deem a compelling match? It was difficult to imagine her as being concerned with wealth and worldly goods. Perhaps she believed in the folly of love, as so many women professed to do. He wondered at her willingness to meet him abed and could not grant that notion any credit. 'Twas clear that attacking this man would end badly for Rafael and she would never pay that debt.

Why was there peril in attacking this man? Had he powerful allies?

Why was the man pledged to Ceara at all? She said they had been betrothed at childhood, but that was a riddle in itself. Children of aristocrats were bound to each other to create strategic alliances, but Ceara apparently had no kin, much less any affluence.

The difficulty was that Rafael's unanswered questions bred a veritable army of additional ones. What if this man she called her betrothed was not pledged to her in truth? What if he was a threat to Ceara for another reason? Who could he be? A brother? A cousin? An enemy of her kin? How had she come to be living in the forest of Kilderrick with the other three women if her hand was of such import? What—or who—had driven her from her home, wherever it might have been?

Why would she not ask Maximilian to aid her in this matter? Rafael had more questions than answers—at least Ceara, if naught else, was distracting him from the greater riddle of Maximilian not desiring Château de Vries.

Or at least insisting that he did not wish it any longer. Rafael removed the seal from his purse and turned it in the light, mystified by his brother's reaction.

Keep it yourself. Never had Rafael heard such an improbable suggestion and never would he have expected it to fall from the lips of Maximilian.

'Twas clear the *Loup Argent,* the man he had known and followed, was no more.

The world, to Rafael's view, was filled with mysteries on this night, and he would not unravel them alone. He finished the *eau-de-vie* with regret and set the cup aside, still bristling with impatience. What he needed was a distraction. Nay, what he needed was a woman, a lusty wench who would not be satisfied with less than a night of pleasure, a woman whose desires were uncomplicated and one whose favors could be dismissed as readily as they could be obtained.

There was, of course, no such woman to be had in his vicinity.

That was yet another reason to despise this land.

He tucked the seal away again, then doused two of the lanterns. The camp was quieter now, only one mercenary singing quietly to himself by the fire. It sounded like Helmut, the most robust of all the men in his appetites. Rafael heard one of his men hail the singer, then his footsteps faded as he made a circuit of the camp. That would be Bernard, who always took first watch.

Rafael set aside his belt and dagger with care. He was unbuttoning his tunic when he heard a footstep outside the tent and he straightened, listening.

Another step closer, and another.

It was neither Helmut nor Bernard, for the tread was too light.

Silently, Rafael unsheathed his dagger and moved to the tent flap, the blade bared. He stood in the shadow, listening as the intruder moved closer. The steps were too stealthy to belong to anyone he might welcome.

The bottom of the tent flap moved and the toe of a boot was revealed.

There was a long pause and the faint sound of breathing from outside the tent.

Then the intruder ducked inside with one smooth step. Rafael pounced upon the fool who dared to enter his domain unbidden. The intruder was tall but slender and wore a heavy cloak. Rafael caught him up in a tight grip, and the stranger fought him until the cold steel of Rafael's knife touched his throat.

His captive froze in the same moment that Rafael realized he held a woman. He remained motionless and she twisted in his grasp to look back at him. Her hood fell back, her red hair tumbling over Rafael's arms, her hazel eyes wide with surprise.

Ceara!

Rafael was shocked. How had Ceara left the keep at this hour without being stopped?

How had she crept into his guarded camp unobserved?

Ceara suddenly smiled, feeding his suspicions anew even as she stirred his blood. Without a moment's pause, she put her finger beneath the blade and pushed it away with a confidence that should have been undeserved.

"I come to pay your price," she murmured, then spun in his embrace and kissed him with unexpected fervor.

Again, she astonished him. Again, she beguiled him with her touch. As much as Rafael knew he should not be seduced, as much as he doubted that she confessed the truth, in this moment, he could not resist any invitation.

Not when the temptress was Ceara. This was their second kiss in mere hours and no less potent than the first. Rafael caught her close with one arm, replacing his dagger in its scabbard before enclosing her in his embrace. He expected her to recoil or squirm free of him, at least to protest, but Ceara made a soft moan instead. The sound nigh drove him wild, and he lifted her to her toes to kiss her with all the passion she deserved.

To his satisfaction, she kissed him back as if she could do naught else. She seemed to have gained new confidence since their earlier kiss, boldly meeting him touch for touch in the night's shadows. 'Twas a wondrous kiss, one that could make him forget everything except the woman in his arms. He scooped her off her feet and carried her to the bed, suspecting her ruse would be revealed too soon for his preference. Aye, she would turn him aside or spurn him, perhaps try to use his own dagger against him. Rafael was prepared to abandon the course if so.

But Ceara wrapped herself around him, a siren whose call he could not deny. Her legs were around his hips, her hands in his hair, her lips parted as she invited him to partake of all she had to offer. She was warm and willing and utterly intoxicating.

Rafael deepened his kiss and Ceara pressed herself against his chest as if she would meld their very bodies together. In so doing, the sweet press of her softness and the scent of her skin took his passion to a fever-pitch. He slid his hand beneath her skirts and rested his palm on her bare thigh, expecting she would demand that he stop.

Instead she caught her breath for a moment, as if her very heart had stopped. She then resumed her kiss, her cheeks flushed and her gaze averted.

What was this?

Rafael lifted his head, watching her as his hand moved ever higher. She appeared to be lost in pleasure, as if he had imagined that momentary reaction.

Had he? A maiden might respond thus in her uncertainty, but his seductress could be no innocent.

'Twas a weakness of his to enjoy the sight of a woman lost in pleasure and the sight of Ceara in rapture was one Rafael knew he would not soon forget. His fingers slipped into the slick heat of her and she gasped aloud. He watched as her flush deepened, that pink blush rising from her breasts to suffuse her cheeks. He caressed her, transfixed to see her eyes sparkle and light with a pleasure he had kindled.

He might have believed all to be well, but her throat worked, as if she was not as at ease with this act as she would have preferred him to believe. Once he had noticed as much, he could not fail to become aware that her fingers dug into his shoulders, as if she did not know what to expect.

Rafael had believed her well-practiced in the arts of love but in this moment, he would have sworn she was a maiden.

A virgin. The very notion sent a chill through him.

Or did Ceara pretend as much to awaken his noble urges?

She should have known by this time how few of them Rafael possessed.

If she would turn him aside, he would look upon her first. He dropped a hand to the lacing at the sides of her kirtle and she smiled, unfastening her belt even as he unlaced the garment. Again, she was willing. In a moment, the kirtle was cast aside, only the pale gossamer of her chemise remained. To his delight, she untied the lace and shed it as well.

She was glorious, all lean strength and pale skin. Her boots rose to her knees, her garters tied just above them, her thighs bare. They were perfect, of course, pale and smooth, yet muscled. He left her boots on, too aroused by her beauty to care about them. Rafael flattened the palm of his hand upon the inside of one knee and slid his hand upward, enticed beyond all reason.

Ceara's eyes darkened, turning from hazel to green. She swallowed and her lips worked though she made no sound. She certainly did not stop him but there was an uncertainty about her response, as if such a caress was new to her.

Was it?

Rafael bent and pressed a hot kiss to the inside of her thigh, feeling her pulse leap. He looked up at her, watching her breasts rise and fall in agitation. Her nipples were taut and rosy, and the scent of her arousal was the sweetest invitation ever.

Still, her discomfiture was clear. "Do you not like this?" he asked in a low murmur.

Her smile seemed forced and her voice tight. "Of course!"

She might not have experienced this particular intimacy. That would not surprise him, for there were men who ignored this seductive pleasure.

Rafael could not resist it. He ran a trail of kisses up Ceara's thigh, her warmth and willingness feeding the fire within him. He slid his hands around her and gripped her hips, liking the smooth strength of her, then kissed her gently in that most intimate of places. She jumped and shuddered to her very toes. When she made a murmur of contentment, Rafael settled to his feast.

The taste of her was sweet and potent, the slick heat proof that she enjoyed his touch. He kissed her again, letting his tongue slide into the softness of her and Ceara trembled as she moaned. He did not cease but teased her with his touch until she shivered and gasped. Her thighs parted and she fell back as if helpless to do otherwise. Her low moan of capitulation was the finest sound Rafael had ever heard and the quiver that awakened within her was as sweet to him as the finest music. Her fingers tangled in his hair, she whispered a curse that made him smile, and Rafael began his amorous assault in truth.

He could only conclude that she had never been worshipped in this way, but Rafael was more than glad to introduce her to this pleasure.

58

He moved slowly to ensure her delight, but her thighs clenched, a hint that he went too far.

Rafael abandoned his quest, moving to lay alongside her. He noted her satisfaction as he replaced his mouth with his fingers and guessed this was more familiar to her. He caressed her gently, easing first one finger inside her tight heat and then another. She moaned and pulled him closer. He kissed her deeply, languorously, his thumb moving across the most tender part of her.

"You taste like sin," she whispered and he chuckled.

"You taste like heaven," he replied, loving how she smiled.

"Nay, it cannot taste thus," she said, eyes sparkling, and he laughed aloud.

He coaxed and coerced, triumphant as she surrendered to sensation and welcomed his caress with more enthusiasm. She arched her back. She writhed in pleasure. She parted her thighs and granted that delicious moan yet again, the heat of her skin rising beneath his hands. Her kiss became more demanding as she, too, used her teeth and her tongue to insist upon more. Rafael felt her tremble, and it was all good. He urged her ever onward, wanting to see her satisfaction complete.

Ceara gasped and became suddenly tight with need, uttering a wordless entreaty. Rafael nigh devoured her mouth, his fingers moving with greater demand and she clutched at him. She was squirming and moaning, inundating him with her seductive scent, desperate for her release.

He gripped her nape, a fistful of hair twined around his fingers, and held her captive to his kiss in the same moment that he drove his thumb against her clitoris. Ceara roared in a most satisfactory way, arching from the bed and rocking as the release shook through her, as fierce in pleasure as she was in all else. She shook with the power of her release then finally collapsed to the bed as she strove to catch her breath.

Then she smiled, pushing her fingers through his hair and rolling her hips. Her hair was a vibrant tangle, her cheeks were flushed crimson and her eyes shone. Her nipples were taut, inviting his touch, and Rafael could not resist the urge to pinch one between his finger and thumb. Ceara chuckled and arched her back, looking so satisfied that he could not wait to join her in pleasure.

"So that is why people rut with such enthusiasm," she whispered, then laughed a little. "The priests have their challenge in convincing anyone to deny themselves such pleasure. I confess I cannot regret the introduction."

Rafael stared at her in shock.

She *was* a maiden!

Ceara had never imagined that such wondrous pleasure existed, much less that a man could conjure such a reaction from her own flesh. Rafael's caress had been a revelation and she wanted only to repeat the deed.

But something was amiss.

She spoke, intending only to complement him, but his dismay was clear.

He rolled away from her, rising smoothly to his feet and putting the width of the tent between them with a trio of steps. When he turned to confront her, his expression was inscrutable. "You knew naught of that," he accused, his words low and hot. "You have never experienced a release before."

She realized then she had erred, though she did not know precisely how.

"It is true," she said, hearing her own hesitation. "I have never felt such delight. You are a most skilled lover, sir."

Rafael swore and shoved his hand through his hair, then turned his back upon her. "You must leave," he said in that same tight tone.

Ceara sat up. "Not so soon as this," she said, trying to sound enticing. If there was to be only one night of intimacy, she would not end it so soon as this. When Rafael did not move, she rose and strolled toward him, reaching to kiss him. "I want more," she whispered and heard him catch his breath. She looked down to see his fists clenched by his sides.

"You are a maiden," he said through gritted teeth, then spun to face her, fury lighting his eyes. "You *lied*."

"Nay," she lied. "It has simply been long…"

Rafael caught her face in her hands and raised her to her toes, kissing her with such passion that she was left breathless. She strove to return his embrace, but was overwhelmed by sensation and when he stepped back, lifting his hands away, she feared her legs would not support her.

"Innocent," he concluded crisply, not missing an increment of her response.

She folded her arms across her chest. "Hardly that."

"But a maiden all the same."

"I…"

"That was not rutting," he said fiercely. "It was but the preamble."

Ceara cursed herself for flushing more deeply. "Of course. That was what I meant, but I have never felt such a sensation…"

Rafael placed a fingertip over her lips to silence her, more serious than she had ever seen him. "No lie, Ceara," he said with soft vigor. "Not in this matter. Are you a maiden?"

She could feel the weight of his will, as if he would conjure the truth from deep within her. She understood that he would stop if she admitted the truth, which meant he would not take her commission, though she could not fathom why that might be. Why was her innocence of such value? Surely he had claimed dozens of virgins. There had been Isobeal in the village—who had not actually been a maiden before Rafael seduced her.

Ceara eyed him, disliking that she might lose all advantage in surrendering the truth. All the same, she found it impossible to deceive Rafael in this moment, after he had given her such satisfaction.

Her mouth opened, then closed again, then she shook her head. "I have never known a man's touch," she admitted. "Until this night."

"And still you have not surrendered your maidenhead." He did not wait for her confirmation, merely stepped back. He pointed silently to the keep, dismissing her with that gesture.

"You do not understand. I need your help and I will pay your price," she insisted. "I vow it."

"But I have no taste for maidens." He picked up her chemise and cast it at her. "Go!"

Ceara was outraged. "Now, you are the one who lies!" she cried. "What difference if I am innocent or not?"

"All the difference in the world," he said with heat, though she could not understand his vehemence. Before she could ask, he placed a fingertip beneath her chin, compelling her to meet his gaze. "Why?" he demanded crisply. "Why do you pay with a gift you can surrender only once?"

She faltered for a moment, then knew only the truth would suffice. "I have naught else you might desire."

He shook his head, discontent. "If you want rid of this man, you could wed another first."

"And my betrothed would only slaughter him to claim what he believes to be his due," she said, her tone bitter.

Rafael's eyes narrowed. "If the loss of your maidenhead will eliminate his affections, there is an entire army of men who would be glad to indulge you."

"He will not care. The match is not about me."

Rafael studied her, his curiosity clear. "What else have you to offer, *bella*, but yourself? Are you an heiress?"

His guess was too close for comfort. "When you kill him, he will be unable to avenge himself. That is the detail of import."

Rafael made a dismissive sound. "You should return to the keep, unless you are willing to surrender all of the truth." It was clear what he believed she would do. He picked up her chemise and cast it toward her.

Ceara let it fall. She folded her arms across her chest, declining to be of assistance. Rafael dressed her as if he dressed unwilling women all the time. Her chemise was pulled over her head and the lace tied. He tugged the kirtle over her head, his gestures brusque and his brow furrowed as he saw it laced as well.

"I will not wed him," she said again. "I will do whatever must be done to ensure that he does not claim me."

Rafael studied her. "Why? Do you prefer another?"

"Nay."

"Is he cruel, disfigured, ancient, unworthy of your affections in some other way?"

She eyed him, knowing her rebellious thoughts showed. "We were but infants when all was arranged."

"And so it is about alliance between families," Rafael concluded. "And what will be lost if this match is denied? What will your betrothed sacrifice if you do not put your hand in his? Is this why you cannot ask Maximilian to support your cause, because he will not?"

"It is complicated."

Rafael laughed lightly but it was not a merry sound. "Aye, it always is." He buckled her belt then stood back, folding his arms across his chest to survey her. "Return to the keep, *bella*. The hour grows late for maidens to be abroad."

She glared at him, blood simmering. "I thought you wanted me," she said with quiet heat.

"I do."

"Then why deny me?"

His lips hardened into a grim line. "I do not take maidens to my bed. Ever."

"You knew Isobeal Smith was not innocent."

"I most surely did, though later she tried to lie."

"Why do you not seduce maidens?"

He shook his head and spoke with impatience, as if the confession was unwillingly made. "Because I have seen what women's lives become when they no longer possess the one asset that could win them a husband's protection. I will not inflict that fate upon any maiden." His gaze was hard. "If a woman has already chosen that path, then aye, I may savor a merry night in her company, but I will not force her onto that path."

"You could wed me."

He laughed but it was a harsh sound. In this moment, he was the merciless warrior with a blade for hire, the man who could be trusted only to ensure his own best interest, and Ceara knew she should have feared him more than she did. "I will never take a bride, even one as beguiling as you." His eyes flashed dangerously and his voice dropped low. "*Go.*"

"Because you are tempted?"

Rafael smiled. "Because you are in the midst of a camp of warriors who do not share my view. Shall I summon them?"

Ceara turned away, tears blurring her vision. Rafael would not be swayed.

She had erred beyond expectation.

She left his tent and did not look back.

INFURIATING MAN.

Ceara had never felt such a muddle of emotion. Rafael had kindled a fury within her, encouraged it until she was certain she would not survive his caress, then cast her into a realm of potent pleasure beyond all expectation. And then, when she was prepared to do whatsoever he asked of her, he guessed the truth and cast her out.

A little late, she recalled horses rutting in the fields and recognized what had not occurred. She had been overwhelmed and had spoken too soon, without thinking. If she had remained silent, she might have experienced the fullness of intimacy this night.

Why did this man prompt her to be such an impetuous fool?

Ceara was uncertain whether to be more annoyed with herself or Rafael. Who would have guessed that he of all men should have at least one principle—and that it should be the sole one that could undermine her plan? Who would have guessed that he would adhere to it, even to the point of denying himself what was willingly offered?

Troublesome, irritating, unpredictable ruffian.

Beguiling, alluring, handsome rogue. Even the memory of his kiss would keep her awake this night.

If not more. How wondrous that had been! And to think it was only part of the measure.

Ceara marched toward Kilderrick in the darkness, knowing her way well enough. There was a glimmer of light beneath the gates ahead, reminding her of the tale she had told the gatekeeper of visiting Nathalie this night. She would have to think of a different tale to allay his suspicions but she would think of something.

For the moment, she wanted to think of Rafael.

Ceara pulled out her dagger and turned it in her hands, debating the merit of returning to Rafael's tent to make her demand at knifepoint. He would only laugh at her or worse, disarm her. She growled in frustration and kicked a stone, marching onward. What other enticement might he accept? She was tempted to surrender the key, but it was not hers to offer to anyone.

It was held in trust for her brother, for his use when he returned.

But what if Niall never returned? Then the legacy would be hers. Without Rafael's aid, she would be wed to Edward then be forced to watch him seize the prize.

It was almost sufficient to make her wish Godfroy had not been killed at all. Matters had been much simpler when there had been no chance of her location being discovered. She shook her head and marched onward.

Then someone grabbed her arm.

Ceara barely managed to emit a sound of surprise before a large hand shoved a cloth into her mouth. She was seized and lifted off her feet, wincing when she felt her dagger slip from her grip. She saw the silhouettes of two other men even as she struggled for freedom with all her might. Her attacker held her arms fast against her side, a second man unfurling a length of rope. She kicked him, but he only grunted before roughly binding her ankles together.

Ceara panicked then, thrashing as hard as she could, but the low chuckle of the man who held her captive sent a chill through her blood. He turned her so she could discern his features even in the darkness and her heart stopped as he smiled.

"Hello, Ceara," Edward said, his voice soft and predatory. She would never forget the features of this dark-haired man, no matter how long they were parted, or his shrewd expression. His eyes were a clear green, as pale and clear as the sea on a sunny day, and they always sent a chill through her. They revealed that he was always calculating his own gain, independent of the price to others. "Well met, bride of mine."

Ceara tried to roar but the cloth silenced her. Between the three of them they had her bound helpless in no time and the largest of them tossed her over his shoulder. Ceara's heart filled with despair when all at Kilderrick remained still. No one raised an alarm.

No one had witnessed her abduction.

No one would even know to pursue them.

She could only look back at the camp of the Compagnie Rouge as the trio carried her into the shadows of the forest. Even Kilderrick would soon be far behind them.

Her worst nightmare had finally befallen her and there was naught Ceara could do.

RAFAEL WOULD NOT SLEEP this night, not with such conflict raging in his soul. He prowled his tent, recalling every word, fairly tasting the memory of Ceara's release. His body yearned for a satisfaction it would not have; his errant heart congratulated him for doing what was right; his mind chided him for wanting more than was his right to claim. He cursed his memories, especially the ones responsible for his convictions, and cast the crucifix onto his trunk only to glare at it.

He smiled just a little, recalling a night when he had informed Maximilian that he could have slaughtered an entire village for another wineskin of *eau-de-vie*. On this night, he could have amended that threat to include an entire army.

Alas, he knew there was no more to be had.

Rafael strode into the night. Lambret had joined Helmut for the last of the wine and the pair dozed together before the embers of the fire.

It seemed his company felt safe beneath Maximilian's tower.

Rafael was not in the mood to tolerate any laxness. He walked the perimeter of the camp himself. He could have taken on an invader alone, armed with only his dagger, in his current mood, and he marched with such vigor that he almost missed the glint of steel on the ground.

He did see it, though it was beyond the perimeter of the camp. Rafael bent and picked it up, recognizing it as Ceara's favored blade. He had seen the hilt of it in her scabbard and Rafael never forgot a weapon. Why would it be loose upon the ground? Why would she have removed it from the scabbard on her way to the keep? Why would she have cast it aside?

She would not have done as much.

Not willingly.

The hair pricked on the back of his neck and he turned slowly in place, peering into the shadows.

There was no sign of Ceara, no sound of any person abroad.

But Rafael felt a fearsome dread.

What if he had cast her into peril by sending her back to the keep?

RAFAEL'S SENSE that all had gone awry only became stronger with each inquiry he made.

He strode immediately to the gates of Kilderrick but the gatekeeper confessed that Ceara had not returned. "She went to the village after the feast, sir, to visit Nathalie Smith. I did not expect her return before morning."

Rafael fairly ran to the abode of the smith and his new wife, pounding on the portal when they did not immediately respond. The couple were startled by his presence, but he was not truly surprised to learn that Ceara was neither there nor expected.

He went through the camp of the Compagnie Rouge, rousing all and sundry, searching each and every tent for a maiden who had vanished into naught. He set his men to searching for signs of intruders, guessing none would be discovered. He went through the ranks of tethered horses and stirred every squire to wakefulness.

Ceara was gone.

She had been taken by the betrothed she feared. Rafael could think of no other reason for her disappearance. A bit late, he wished he at least knew the name of the man in question.

He returned to the place he had found the dagger, taking a lantern in case there was some small sign to be discovered. Dawn was hours away, despite his impatience, but Rafael would be prepared to lend chase at first light.

He should have accompanied Ceara to the keep himself, and he did not need Maximilian to tell him that. It was his fault that she was in peril, which made him the obvious candidate to be her champion. 'Twas an unlikely task for a man of his repute, but Rafael would not abandon Ceara to her fate.

He liked her too well for that.

He would ensure she never learned that truth.

To see this matter set to rights, he would have need of one who spoke the infernal language of this land. Rafael glanced between village and keep, wondering who he might trust to accompany him, then spotted Raynard crouching over the ground. That man moved slowly and steadily toward river and forest, clearly studying some mark on the ground.

He had only joined the Compagnie Rouge this previous winter, but some of the other men knew him as a valiant and trustworthy warrior, quick with a knife. Rafael had taken him on, based on those recommendations. Raynard confessed to being originally of these lands but did not wear their garb. He wore a hauberk that had seen much battle and sturdy boots. He was distinct in the company for carrying an axe as well as a crossbow and sword.

"What do you see?" Rafael asked when he approached that man's side. He held the oil lantern high, illuminating the ground.

"Three men, one with a burden that drives his steps down into the mud," Raynard said, pointing. "They crossed the river here."

"Ceara feared to be seized by her betrothed and forced to keep that vow."

Raynard nodded. "I wager that has been her fate, then. He must have traced her to Kilderrick."

Rafael wondered how that might be, and why that had occurred only now.

Raynard straightened and met Rafael's gaze, his own steady and cool. "What will you do?"

"She asked me to kill him for her. I declined the task but find myself warming to it."

Raynard smiled.

"Ride with me?" Rafael asked and that man nodded once in agreement. "We take two squires, an extra palfrey and ride out as soon as possible."

Raynard bowed his head and Rafael noted that he was already armed. "I await your command."

Rafael called for Antonio as he returned to his tent. He issued commands, then began to don his own armor, unable to quell his smile of anticipation.

Ceara's betrothed might be killed by his blade, after all.

And soon.

CHAPTER 5

$\mathcal{T}$was the worst night of Ceara's life. She glanced toward Edward at intervals and feared it would not hold that status for long. His expression had remained stern and his commands to his fellows were terse. He was rough with her in a way that did not bode well for her future.

Once he secured her legacy, she would die.

But what could she do? Her dagger was lost, her arms were bound to her sides and she was silenced by a filthy rag. Once they had journeyed a distance from Kilderrick and reached three ponies tethered in the forest, she had been compelled to walk while the men rode. One companion, after a quiet consultation that she had not been able to overhear, had ridden on ahead of them, urging his pony to race. Edward and his remaining comrade rode ponies at a slower pace, while Ceara stumbled onward between them.

They never stopped. They never paused. She walked through streams and over rocky outcroppings, through the forest and the fen. Her boots were wet and her feet were sore, but there was no reprieve. She had always thought herself to be strong and stalwart, but that night of forced walking nigh finished her.

She thought the dawn would never come.

There were no sounds of pursuit to her dismay, which meant no one even knew that she was gone. Her own tale to the gatekeeper now worked against her, for no one would seek her at Nathalie's cottage until the morning. No one would even think to look until Rafael revealed that she had visited him, if he confessed as much. He might ride away from Kilderrick or spend the day with his men—her absence might not be discovered until the evening meal.

Who knew what might befall her by then?

Her captors said little to each other, but each kept a hand on the hilt of his blade and looked avidly from left to right. Ceara suspected she was not the sole one to hear naught at all.

She was likely the sole one disheartened by that.

Aye, Edward's expression began to turn triumphant. She imagined he was reviewing the details of her legacy—and what he would do when he claimed it. With her brother gone, there might be even more to claim. Doubtless Edward had an inventory.

The sun rose and they carried on. Any hope that they might pass a village or settlement was only to be disappointed. Ceara became certain that their route had been calculated to ensure that no one caught a glimpse of their small party.

The sun was almost at zenith and Ceara's feet had to be bleeding when they finally crested a rise and halted. A small cluster of buildings nestled in the valley ahead of them and she felt a moment's hope. Then even that was dashed, for she saw that the small village was abandoned. The roofs were not thatched and most cottages were open to the sky. The fields were not tilled, and there were neither gardens nor livestock, no voices raised in greeting or sounds of children calling.

A single tendril of smoke rose from the roof of one cottage, the one set beside a small stone church. There looked to be a garden around that hut and Ceara perceived movement, perhaps of chickens pecking the dirt. A trio of goats grazed the sparse growth.

Edward dismounted and came to her side. "You will behave," he said in soft threat, fixing her with a look so cold that she shivered to her marrow. "Do not imagine that I will shirk from correcting any error on your part. The priest lives alone, having entered a life of contemplation after the villagers died or departed. It would be the work of a moment to silence him forever and ensure that no one ever knows what he witnessed this day." His gaze bored into hers. "Recognize that I will not hesitate to do it."

Ceara dropped her gaze, wondering whether the priest in question would survive the day either way. This must be one of many villages that had been abandoned after the plague ravaged the country and claimed so many lives. She had seen numerous empty homes when she had fled south years before. Though she might have taken refuge in one of them, she felt them to be haunted and had always continued on.

Until she had found a haven at Kilderrick.

"Mungo has ridden ahead to ensure that all is ready for the exchange of our vows," Edward continued and she noticed the pony tethered outside the chapel. "You and I will pledge to each other, as promised by our fathers, before witnesses here. The match will be consummated immediately thereafter, making the MacRuari heiress mine forevermore."

Ceara could not keep herself from glaring at him. 'Twas not the heiress he wished to possess and she knew it well.

Edward smiled, a cold expression that hinted at the wickedness in his heart. "Or you can tell me the location of your legacy here and now, and we can forgo the formalities." He dropped his voice to a whisper. "I promise you that your death will be quick, but I will have my due of you first. That might not be so quick, given your avoidance of our vow."

Ceara was glad to have left the key at Kilderrick, for she knew that she would not manage a single breath after he had taken it from her.

Edward leaned closer. "Where is your legacy hidden?"

She held his gaze with defiance.

He roughly removed her gag and asked again.

"Hidden," she said. "And it shall remain thus."

"Tell me where it is!"

"Safe, so safe that only I can retrieve it. It is safe for Niall."

His eyes flashed and he slapped her hard. "Niall is dead and you know it well!" The blow took Ceara to her knees and left her gasping at the sting.

"Yet all the same, I do not have the legacy," she said through her teeth.

He seized her hair and pulled her to her feet, staring into her eyes. She stared back at him until he smiled. "I believe you, which means my favored plan is the one we will follow. I will keep you alive until you surrender your inheritance. I suspect it will not take overlong." He unbound her arms and she rubbed her hands. "Do not dare to say one word to the priest or give one hint that you are not a willing bride."

"Or I will pay the price?" she asked. "Surely I will pay it either way."

Edward shook his head. "Remember: the priest will pay the price if you err."

"Even before the vows are exchanged?"

His eyes darkened and she knew he would not hesitate to do as he threatened. "Marriage is the one sacrament that does not require a priest. It is better to have witnesses, but Lachlan will suffice if needs be." He gave her a push in the direction of the church, one hard enough to make her stumble. "Onward, and no tricks."

Ceara could not imperil a priest.

The two men led their ponies onward and Edward held her hand, albeit so tightly that Ceara's fingers were numb by the time they reached the chapel. The priest came to greet them, his ready smile and kindly manner adding to Ceara's resolve that no toll would be taken of him. He was not a large man, but one who would be easily overcome and she felt protective of him.

The companion who had to be Mungo appeared. He nodded a greeting and took the reins of the ponies, evidently intending to watch them. He was stocky and fair, the tall man who had carried her away from Kilderrick. He had the same cold gaze as Edward and his other comrade, Lachlan, and Ceara could not decide which of them would be the most terrifying captor.

Edward was charming to the priest, though his companions said little. The priest was encouraged to share the history of the village and the chapel itself, chatting merrily as he led them inside.

He was apologizing for its humble state when Ceara stared upward in wonder. The roof was timbered, which was unusual enough, but the greater surprise was that the interior of the roof was painted a glorious heavenly blue. There were star shapes where the stone was visible, and it was clear that the task of painting the ceiling was only partly done.

The hue of it was a marvel, though, reminding Ceara of the finest of winter nights.

"Have you seen the cathedral in Carlisle?" the priest asked, following her gaze. Ceara shook her head. "I did and it filled my heart with wonder. The labor is a meditation."

"I have never seen a grey star," Lachlan noted and Edward snorted.

"They will be gold," the priest explained. "In the style favored by the French kings, azure and gold. A veritable glimpse of the New Jerusalem, here in our humble sphere." He then cleared his throat. "At least, that will be so when the Almighty provides for that amendment. In the meantime, there is much blue to paint."

Ceara understood that the priest wished them to know that he had no coin. Perhaps he feared Edward's intentions, and rightly so.

"It is beautiful," she said and meant it. The plain stone walls and small dimensions were familiar to her, but the painted ceiling made the chapel feel particularly sacred. There was a small cluster of wildflowers in a vessel on the altar, and Ceara recognized violets as well as yellow cowslip in the bouquet. That such a place of worship and tranquility might be defiled made her throat tighten.

If Edward injured this gentle priest, she would contrive a way to cut out his heart before she died.

Perhaps she would cut off another part of him first.

Edward squeezed her hand with sufficient force to crack her fingers, as if he guessed her mutinous thoughts, but Ceara granted him a brilliant smile. He appeared to be reassured, which meant that he did not understand her at all.

She might yet have the opportunity to use that against him.

They stood before both priest and altar, Ceara on Edward's left, her right hand fast in his. Lachlan was on her left.

What could she do? Lachlan's blade was on the left side of his belt and he kept one hand over the hilt. Edward's was on his right and he did the same. The priest had no weapon. There was a cup on the altar but it was small, made of earthenware and empty. There would be no communion this day, but she would not have expected as much at a wedding, especially one unplanned.

There was not so much as a bench in the chapel, the altar being made of stone and seemingly part of the structure itself. The rafters were just high enough that she could not reach them, and she spotted nothing near the beams. Even a candle would have been welcome, but there was none. She could think of no way to use a cluster of flowers as a weapon, unless she could cast the water from the vessel in an assailant's face.

Never had Ceara been in a place that offered so few opportunities for defending herself. Even the floor was swept fastidiously clean, and she knew she would not be able to gather a handful of dirt to cast into Edward's eyes.

She was doomed to wed this fiend. Despair welled up within her as the priest cleared his throat to begin.

Just then, she heard the ponies nicker.

Edward and Lachlan did not seem to have noticed, but it sounded to Ceara as if the ponies had spied another horse or pony. Whose? The village was abandoned. Had someone pursued them? She scarce dared to hope. She strove to keep her features composed even as she tried to listen to sounds beyond the priest's melodic voice.

Had someone spoken, merely a word or two softly uttered?

Had something heavy fallen to the ground?

What was that repetitive sound, as steady as footfalls but not foot-falls? It scraped sometimes, like steel against stone and Ceara could think of no explanation for it.

It was faint, though, and perhaps not of import.

"I do," Edward said with authority and she realized her fate was nearly sealed.

Suddenly the door to the chapel was kicked open, crashing hard against the wall, and all three of them spun to look. The priest craned his neck to peer over them at the interruption.

Rafael smiled as he strode into the chapel and Ceara thought her heart would never beat again.

Gone was his embroidered tabard and jewelled crucifix. On this day, he looked the dangerous mercenary she knew him to be, armed and prepared for battle. His chain mail hauberk was visible beneath his fitted *jupon*, which was deepest blue but graced with no insignia. A mail aventail covered his throat, having fallen back from his head like a coiff, and his helm was tucked beneath his left arm. His hands were gloved, his arms were covered with mail and plate armor defenses, as were his legs above his boots. A belt embroidered in red and gold was slung around his hips, and she could see the hilt of his dagger as well as her own.

He had found her blade!

His right hand rested on the hilt of his sword. The same full fur-lined cloak was clipped to his shoulder and flared behind him as he entered the chapel's shadows, his ebony hair gleaming. He was magnificent, a visiting champion from a distant and marvelous realm.

The four of them stared at him in silence and—Ceara thought—a measure of awe.

With his free hand, Rafael held up a small gold circle between finger and thumb. "*Bella*," he chided softly, then continued in fluid French. "You forgot your ring."

'Twas the gold ring from his right hand.

He strode closer, filling the chapel to bursting with his powerful presence. Ceara felt her knees weaken, for she had never been so glad to see anyone in her life.

YOU COULD WED ME.

Ceara's impish taunt had echoed in Rafael's thoughts when he realized her captor had taken her to a chapel. He knew she had only suggested as much to vex him, but it gave him an idea. This destination proved that she had been seized by her betrothed and that the man was determined to seal their lives together. Rafael sensed that there was more behind the agreement than Ceara's beauty, but she had to be rescued either way.

'Twas sufficient for him that she did not wish the match.

Feigning that they were already wed was the perfect ruse. She knew his notions about matrimony so would understand immediately that 'twas a feint.

Mercifully, he had arrived in the very nick of time.

Rafael surveyed the rustic chapel, the astonishment in the priest's expression and the glint of malice that briefly lit the gaze of the man beside Ceara. Her betrothed was a warrior to be sure, a man muscled and trim. He was likely of an age with Rafael but a little shorter, though there was a malevolence in his cool gaze that indicated they might be evenly matched in battle. He wore plain chausses and boots, along with a simple tabard and cloak. Though he was dressed as simply as his companion, it was Rafael's impression that he wished to be overlooked. He stood with the pride of a man accustomed to privilege and luxury, despite his garb. His hands were too clean for him to be a peasant, his hair trimmed and his chin cleanly shaven.

Untrustworthy cur. Perhaps a deceitful one, as well. Rafael knew his ilk. He had already stolen a bride and undoubtedly would do worse, given the opportunity. He would have at least one hidden weapon and he would strike to kill.

If anything, Rafael was reassured to be confronted with an opponent who shared his own assumptions about the importance of victory at any cost.

Ceara was unkempt, her kirtle dirty, her hair tangled and her boots mired. But her eyes lit with relief at his appearance and her smile would have induced Rafael to fight any foe.

"I thank you, sir," she said. He noted how she had to pull her right hand hard to escape her betrothed's grasp upon it and wondered whether her fingers were bruised. She walked toward him, giving no sign of any injury—until she lifted her left hand for the ring and he saw that her hand trembled. What had his fierce huntress endured? Rage rose hot within him to see her avenged with all haste. "I am heartened to see you after our disagreement last eve."

"And of what import is a small disagreement to those destined to be together?" he replied gallantly, well aware of how keenly they were watched.

Did her betrothed understand Norman French? What of the priest?

Rafael inclined his head to Ceara as she halted before him, and noticed then the red mark on her cheek. The fiend had struck her? Rafael inhaled sharply, hiding his furious reaction. He guessed that Ceara had noticed, probably in his eyes, for she shook her head minutely.

It took all within him to smile at her, as if naught was amiss. "It is the way of all partners to air their views and debate the merit of each, to better choose their course. There is no cause for another to intervene, when the weapons are words alone." He slid the ring onto her middle finger and was gratified that the fit was perfect. He bent to kiss her cheek, watching her two captors through his lashes. "How many?" he murmured.

"Three," she replied in kind, laying the flat of her hand upon his chest as she touched her lips to his jaw. She was shaking, his valiant warrior maiden, and he understood then the depth of her relief that he had followed.

He would not think of how her day might have proceeded otherwise.

"Two," Rafael corrected softly. He drew back in time to see her eyes widen. Her smile filled with admiration and, as she pivoted before him, he felt her lay claim to her own dagger from his belt. 'Twas neatly done. He caught no glimpse of the weapon, for it vanished into her skirts, but he was glad that it was in her possession again. Since she stood between him and the other three men, likely they did not realize she was armed either.

What a marvel that their thoughts were so readily as one. He could have battled alongside another warrior for a year and not felt such intuitive understanding as he did with Ceara.

"But," the priest sputtered. "You are already wed?"

"My wife was abducted by barbarians," Rafael said, letting outrage fill his tone as he flicked a glance at the betrothed.

"Married?" that man echoed, then frowned as he shook his head. He reached for Ceara's hand. "Claimed by a warrior and used for his pleasure is not the same as holy matrimony. I will yet keep my pledge to you, Ceara, despite your experience."

The lady inhaled sharply as she evaded his touch. "Married," she said crisply. "With vows exchanged before a priest."

"What priest?" he demanded.

"The one I returned to France this past winter," Rafael lied smoothly. "Though there are witnesses aplenty at Kilderrick who will recall the day in question." He held that man's gaze in challenge, wondering why he was so intent upon making Ceara his bride.

This was not a man who followed his heart or even his desire.

"I had no opportunity to explain," Ceara said to the priest. "I was seized and silenced." The would-be groom's eyes narrowed. His companion took a step back, as if to come at Rafael from the other side, then gave a low whistle, one that Rafael was undoubtedly not to notice.

He bit back his smile. No one would reply to his summons.

He was amused that they thought they would surround him. Surely this man did not imagine that Rafael had failed to anticipate such an obvious strategy? He waited, giving them time to realize that no one responded from outside the chapel. The companion took a step forward, but Rafael drew his dagger in a flash and touched the tip to the other man's chest. The man halted, gaze fixed upon the point of the blade, then slowly lifted his hands away from his belt.

"If you intend to hail your companion, alas, he cannot respond," Rafael said with a cool smile, watching alarm light the other man's eyes. "I would ask you to remain until our dispute is resolved. Witnesses are of such import in these delicate matters."

The air simmered with animosity, a sign that matters would soon become most interesting.

The priest was not oblivious to the change of atmosphere. He paled and looked between the three warriors with horror. "I would remind you that this is holy ground," he whispered, but no one acknowledged his words.

"There is no dispute to be resolved," Ceara's captor said. "The lady and I have been betrothed these many years and today, we wed. Whether this ruffian has carnal knowledge of my intended or not is of no import."

"Rafael and I are wed," Ceara insisted.

"And where is the evidence?" demanded her captor. He gestured to Rafael. "We are to take the word of a lawless brigand?"

"I am delighted that my reputation has preceded me," Rafael said smoothly. He pulled a linen chemise from his purse and cast it at the priest, glad that he had taken a moment to prepare for this challenge before his departure. The priest fumbled with the garment then held it up to display a dried blood stain.

"It could belong to anyone!" Ceara's captor roared.

"Yet it is mine," Ceara lied so smoothly that even Rafael almost believed her. "I thank you, Father," she said, lifting the garment from his hands as if too modest to have this proof of the consummation of their match displayed before strangers. She folded it neatly and hooked the garment through her belt, hiding it in the folds of her skirt. Then she stepped back to Rafael's side and dropped her gaze demurely. He could have laughed at the change from her usual manner. "I thank you for keeping the evidence, husband," she murmured.

She was a marvel.

"I could do naught else, *bella*. You are mine, and mine you will remain." He kissed her hand again, noting the gleam in her eyes. They stared at each other, as if so smitten as to be oblivious that they were not alone. In truth, Rafael was taut, expecting an attack.

"But she is my betrothed," his opponent protested. "You had no right..."

"*I* had no right?" Rafael rounded on the other man, ensuring that Ceara was behind him. "You had no right to seize my wife! What manner of barbaric land is this that a woman cannot visit the latrine without an armed guard?" he demanded. "What kind of scoundrel seizes the wife of another to satisfy his own lust?" He raised a gloved hand to the red mark on Ceara's cheek, and let the fury he felt in truth fill his tone. "What blackguard strikes a woman even as he insists he would pledge himself to her and cherish her above all others?"

The priest nodded agreement, his expression turning grim. "You speak aright, my son, but this is all most unexpected." His hands fluttered in his agitation as he looked between the warriors.

"She has been my betrothed since childhood," Ceara's captor growled. "I have the prior claim."

"Yet my *wife* since October," Rafael countered with heat. "We were wed before the *Loup Argent* dispatched me on an errand from which I have just returned." He held the other man's gaze, noting his recognition of Maximilian's former nickname.

"*The Loup Argent?*" the companion whispered.

Concern flickered through the captor's pale eyes, and so it should, to Rafael's thinking.

"And you were escorting a priest to France?" that man said, his doubts clear.

"At the command of my comrade and friend, the *Loup Argent*. Among other tasks." Rafael bowed. "In point of fact, he is my brother."

The captor and his ally exchanged a quick glance.

"But there was no word of this wedding beyond Kilderrick's walls," Ceara's captor argued.

"And who would hear the tidings from a company who speaks another tongue? Who has left Kilderrick with tidings to share?"

"The companions of Godfroy Macdonald," muttered the companion. He dropped his hand to his belt, revealing the hilt of a hidden blade, but was halted by a terse command in Gaelic from his leader.

Rafael eyed them, sensing again that there was an important detail he did not know. "What concern was his demise to you?"

"I have no complaint with his loss," Ceara's captor said smoothly. "Though there are those who will wish for recompense."

Rafael raised a hand, inviting an explanation.

"Godfroy Macdonald was the son of the Lord of the Isles by that man's first wife, Aimil MacRuari," his opponent supplied. "The tale is shared of his death at Kilderrick by the hand of the new laird—"

"A justified punishment for that man's attempt to abduct the laird's bride," Rafael interjected, sparing a glance to the priest. "Are such deeds habitual in this savage land?"

Edward's lips tightened but he ignored the question. "—and also that one of Godfroy's company was killed by a red-haired huntress, quick with a blade." He smiled. "I knew immediately that I had found tidings of my errant betrothed. Her family have always been warriors and gallowglasses."

This last word Rafael did not know but clearly none would explain it to him. "And you would be?" he invited.

"Edward De Leslie," that man confided.

Rafael did not bow, as the other man clearly expected of him, nor did he offer his own name. It was a moment when it would have suited him well to know the details of this match.

Who, precisely, was Ceara? There was a detail of import in this Edward's words, but without a knowledge of local alliances and disputes, Rafael had no notion what it was.

"You must have been watching the keep of late," he said lightly to Edward. "Did you not take note of the feast last night? My wife and I celebrated our happy union again upon my return to these lands." He kissed her fingertips. "'Twas a joyous night indeed." He was aware that Edward inhaled angrily, and knew the moment he awaited had finally arrived.

Rafael did not have to urge Ceara to one side for she already stepped out of harm's way, as if she had anticipated the same result. Edward snatched for her in the same moment that she moved, and his companion snatched for his blade. Rafael drew his sword, tossing his dagger to the other hand, ensuring again that Ceara was behind him. He tripped the captor so that he stumbled to the floor, and nicked the companion's chin with a flick of his sword. That man flinched and retreated, then Edward rose to find the tip of Rafael's sword against his chest.

That man's gaze simmered before he looked away. Rafael welcomed his fury, for it might ensure that he erred.

"You would accost me in a church?" Edward demanded with an innocence that could not be believed.

"I accost villains wherever I have the misfortune to find them."

"As do I." Edward moved suddenly, drawing his own blade as he ducked beneath Rafael's blade. He spun to his feet and lunged toward the altar.

The companion had sprung toward Ceara, his blade drawn, but shouted in pain when Rafael's dagger opened a slit in his forearm. His blood flowed as he spun to attack Rafael savagely, the pair clashing blades as they moved back and forth across the narrow space. Rafael fought fiercely, backing the companion into a corner. The man was like a rabid dog, or a cornered wolf, slashing at Rafael without a solid plan. Ceara made a slight sound as Rafael stabbed at the companion, driving his dagger into the other man's belly. The companion brought the blade of his dagger down at Rafael's fist, where it was deflected by the armor on Rafael's gloves, then pushed past him and fled for the portal.

Rafael was content to let him escape, for he would not go far.

He turned to find Edward holding the priest at knife point, Ceara watching warily. "I will kill him," Edward muttered and Rafael rolled his eyes.

"Vermin," he said with a sad shake of his head. "No warrior of merit kills a priest."

"I warned you," Edward muttered to Ceara. "I will kill him if you do not cede." Her lips set as she put down her blade on the floor and stepped away from it. Edward turned to Rafael. "I will see that you are blamed if I must kill the priest. I will see that you are charged and tried, and that you are found guilty. It will be my pledge against your own, that of the godson of the king against a foreign mercenary."

Godson of the king. There was an intriguing detail.

Ceara was no orphan abandoned in the forest with neither kith nor kin, to be sure.

Rafael set down his sword on the floor with care, giving every indication that he had chosen to comply. He placed down his dagger beside it with care.

He raised his hands and stepped back, inclining his head to the apparent victor.

Triumph lit Edward's eyes and he shoved the priest toward Rafael so that the holy man stumbled. Rafael instinctively caught him. Meanwhile, Edward seized Ceara's hand and hauled her toward the portal, as he whistled for his companions.

Rafael knew that yet again there would be no reply.

He pulled the knife hidden in the back of his belt and threw it at Edward with deadly accuracy. It sank into the flesh of that man's upper arm in a most satisfactory way and blood began to flow. Edward had been holding Ceara captive with that hand and released her abruptly, then spun to pull out the knife. Rafael had already snatched up his dagger and sword from the floor and was in pursuit. Ceara, showing her keen wits, fled to the front of the chapel while she had the opportunity and stood behind the altar with the priest. Her dagger was at the ready to defend him.

Edward took one look then bolted through the door. He had mounted his pony by the time Rafael stepped into the sunlight and was giving the creature his heels even as he tried to staunch the flow of blood. The pony cantered toward the west.

If he thought he had outwitted Rafael, all the better: in truth, Rafael let him escape by design. It would be better for the man to incriminate himself with his own words, and before an authority in these lands, before he met his due.

Raynard stepped out of the shadows alongside the chapel and handed Rafael a crossbow, offering a trio of bolts on his outstretched palm. Rafael calmly loaded a bolt into a crossbow, then fired it after the fleeing Edward. The bolt passed close by Edward's head, and that man cried out. He bent lower over the pony and urged the creature to greater speed.

"The ear," Raynard murmured with admiration. "Always a fearsome quantity of blood."

"Indeed," Rafael replied. "And inevitably a lasting scar. We will know him when we see him next, no matter his disguise."

The other warrior nodded approval, then strode after Edward to try to retrieve the bolt. The two boys picked up their shovels again, digging the graves for the other two warriors a little bit deeper.

Rafael turned to find Ceara beside him, her eyes flashing with a fury he should have anticipated.

Ah yes, he had failed to kill her betrothed.

But he had been right that there was more to the tale. He would have it all before he risked so much as a hair for this temptress again.

CHAPTER 6

$\mathcal{Y}$ou should have let me do it," Ceara said bitterly to Rafael. "I would not have missed." She could not believe his aim was so faulty, given his trade. An opportunity to eliminate Edward forever had been lost!

"I did not wish him to be injured," Rafael said inexplicably. She looked up to find him watching her and knew her astonishment showed "I wished only to hasten his departure."

"Why?" Hot fury filled her. "This is no jest! I would have killed him when I had the chance."

"Yet I would have all of the tale before I execute the godson of a king." Rafael smiled but his eyes were cool, so pale a blue that they reminded her of steel. "A legacy of my experience, *bella*."

"You could take my word."

"I would base my trust upon more than that." His brow lifted. "That is also a legacy of my experience."

"But can you not see that naught has changed? I am as vulnerable as a day ago."

He leaned closer and lowered his voice. "Yet the choice of winning my aid by trusting me with the truth is entirely yours." Their gazes locked in a battle of wills.

Rafael's challenge was clear, but Ceara found herself reluctant to take it. Confiding in a mercenary might only invite him to try to claim her legacy, instead of Edward doing as much.

What should she do?

She realized that the priest had come to stand beside her and bit her tongue, planning her defense to Rafael when they were alone again.

That moment could not arrive too soon, to her thinking.

Edward had vanished into the distance, even the sound of his pony's hooves having faded from earshot. The other mercenary from the Compagnie Rouge strode back toward them, tossing the retrieved bolt and catching it with one hand.

Only then did Ceara realize what had caused the sound she'd heard earlier. Two boys were digging graves in the churchyard, their shovels striking the earth with regularity. She thought she recognized the dark-haired one from the camp of the Compagnie Rouge and assumed both boys had come with Rafael. She certainly recognized the auburn-haired warrior with the assessing gaze, the one returning with the bolt.

She could have believed that she knew him, if his gaze had not been so cold. Her suspicion had to be wrong, more a sign of wishful thinking than aught more.

There were two ponies still tethered behind the chapel, along with Rafael's destrier, a second destrier and three palfreys. The steeds seemed to be untroubled by events, all of them searching for green growth on the ground.

Mungo and Lachlan lay on the ground, both clearly dead and with enough wounds to ensure that they remained as much. As Ceara watched, Raynard approached the fallen warriors and called to the boys. Together, they lifted Mungo and dropped him into a shallow grave, then did the same with Lachlan. The boys began to shovel soil over the two corpses.

Rafael watched with approval, as if he supervised such burials all the time. He removed his glove to rummage in his purse, examining each coin he brought to light. He smiled when he found what he sought. He might have been buying a bun in the market for all his concern.

"They will require funeral masses," he said, offering a trio of silver pennies to the priest as Ceara blinked. "If you might be so inclined?" It was incomprehensible to her that he should care about the immortal souls of the men he had executed, but perhaps he meant only to win the priest's support.

The priest looked between the corpses and the coins, then at the weapons on Rafael's belt. He swallowed even as he stretched out his hand for the coins. His hesitation encouraged Rafael to add another silver penny.

"A donation," that man said with smooth assurance. "To aid in the embellishment of the chapel. With my wife's gratitude."

The priest smiled and bowed, undoubtedly planning to spend the funds on paint or gilt.

"And now, *bella*, we must make haste homeward." Rafael smiled at her with the innocence of an angel and Ceara wished she knew exactly how to eliminate that cocksure smile.

A well-aimed kick might be tactless in the presence of a priest.

Could he not see that naught was resolved at all, thanks to his choices?

"Of course, husband," she said sweetly, thanking the priest again, then Rafael lifted her to the saddle of his destrier. "I can ride alone, my beloved," she protested, though his proximity and his grip upon her waist stirred her in troubling ways. "I am not so injured as that."

"I could not risk your welfare again so soon, *bella*," he said smoothly, then his voice dropped. Though he smiled, 'twas clear he spoke through gritted teeth and for her ears alone. "At least pretend you are biddable. Surely even you can maintain the ruse for a moment."

Their gazes locked for a sizzling moment and then Ceara smiled at him. "As you wish, husband." He led the horse away from the chapel door and she knew from the set of his shoulders that she was not the sole one who was annoyed. The priest retreated to the door of the chapel and waved a cheerful farewell. The other mercenary strode to assist the boys in completing their task.

"You will return the ring," Rafael muttered for Ceara's ears alone.

It was his intention, then, to act as if this interval had never occurred.

"We could be wed," Ceara countered.

"Nay, we cannot be wed." He spoke with impatience. "We will not be wed." He flicked her a dark glance. "I thought you would understand the ruse."

"I did. We could pretend to be wed," she insisted, but he halted and turned to confront her.

"This is no jest, Ceara. You do not know what you ask of me." His gaze flicked over her. "Nay, you do know but you choose not to enlighten me."

"Nay, it is no jest," she replied, her words hot. "If we are not wed and you do not defend me, I shall find myself beneath that fiend and dead soon. And that, sir, is a fate I will defy to my last breath, whether you will aid me or nay."

Before he could argue, much less swing into the saddle behind her, she gave Phantôm her heels and left Rafael standing alone outside the chapel.

Let him explain *that* to the priest.

THE WOMAN LIVED and breathed to challenge him, 'twas clear.

Raynard swung into his saddle immediately. Rafael had only to give a nod and the other man galloped in pursuit. Rafael watched them grimly, telling himself to be content to let Ceara savor her fleeting triumph.

Vexing creature.

"Is all well?" the priest demanded, appearing abruptly at his side.

Rafael granted a broad smile to that man. "You see how tempestuous she is. I can only assure you that her passion is worth enduring. I could never love another as I do my own bride."

"She is fortunate to have you as her champion and defender."

"Aye, although there are moments when she is less appreciative of my merit." Rafael bowed to the other man. "I thank you for the funeral masses and bid you farewell."

The priest, reassured, wished them well as Rafael mounted the palfrey they had brought for Ceara. Antonio knew better than to say much—the squire held Rafael's stirrup then raced to mount his own palfrey. The pair of them rode in leisurely pursuit of Raynard and Ceara, Gervais trailing behind.

The woman made an art of confounding him. It seemed Ceara only drew breath to irk him. Rafael could have regretted how readily she succeeded in that quest.

But this time, Ceara would be the one surprised. Her decision to steal his destrier the previous year had prompted Rafael to teach Phantôm a new trick. He bit back a smile, anticipating her reaction when she learned of it.

He rode in pursuit, not racing after her, wanting to ensure there was distance between the small party and the priest. When they crested the summit of the hill and passed out of sight of the chapel, Rafael gave a three-note whistle. Phantôm halted so quickly that Ceara was nearly thrown from the saddle. She swore, glancing back at Rafael as he rode the palfrey toward her at an easy pace. Raynard also halted his steed, but kept his distance. Ceara slapped the stallion's rump and tried to urge him onward. The destrier stood, hooves planted so solidly against the ground that they might have taken root.

"You!" she said furiously to Rafael.

He dismounted when he was close beside her and cast the palfrey's reins toward Antonio. "Me," he agreed readily. "I was compelled to teach him a new feat after he was stolen by an unscrupulous scoundrel."

"I am not unscrupulous." She flushed a little. "At least not entirely so."

"I choose to believe otherwise."

She clicked to the destrier and touched her heels to his side, but Phantôm dropped his head to graze and remained in place. "Will he ever move again?"

"Only when I grant him the command to do as much, and that will not happen until you pay my price."

Ceara met his gaze warily. "I offered to do as much already but you spurned me."

"My price for releasing you is different." Rafael smiled as her eyes filled with suspicion. "Tell me who you are in truth."

"I do not know what you mean. I am Ceara, no more and no less."

She was flustered, though, her color high as she strove to keep her secrets.

Rafael sighed. "That is not even half the truth," he chided softly. "Your betrothed is the king's godson, by his own admission."

"He might not be."

"Does he lie?"

"Nay," contributed Raynard who had ridden closer.

Ceara glared at the other man, to no discernible effect. The warrior remained impassive and watchful.

"It is never wise to foil the godsons of kings without knowing the fullness of what is at stake," Rafael continued. "You will surrender the truth to me, all of it, immediately."

Her chin lifted in defiance. "And if I do not?"

"I will leave you here and return to Kilderrick alone with the horses. I will also reclaim my ring, one way or the other." He glanced down at the hilt of his dagger and she caught her breath.

"You would not," she insisted, her left hand closing into a fist.

He would not, but she did not need to know that. Rafael was prepared to be feared and distrusted by this particular maiden, in the hope that would diminish his temptation.

He lifted a brow. "I recall that you abandoned me in perilous circumstance once. It might be a fitting vengeance to do the same to you." He glanced over his shoulder. "Doubtless the priest would be kind to you."

Ceara inhaled furiously.

"I feel compelled to remind you, *bella*, that I am most decidedly *not* a man of honor," Rafael said.

She lifted her chin, her eyes flashing with a magnificence that stole his breath away. "You are not so fearsome as you would have others believe."

The statement sent alarm through Rafael but he regarded her grimly, hiding his thoughts. "There is the word of a foolish maiden. Any faith you have in me, *bella*, is utterly misplaced."

She looked as if she might argue but Raynard chuckled darkly. She looked between the two warriors with newfound concern, a sight Rafael welcomed.

"Do we have a bargain?" he asked.

"How do I know you will keep your part of the wager?"

"You do not, but it seems you have little choice than to trust me." He smiled wolfishly, purely to annoy her and her eyes flashed at his success.

Her lips tightened as she eyed the other warrior, then she met Rafael's gaze steadily. "I will tell you as we ride to Kilderrick."

"Know if you fall short of expectations, I will have no compunction in abandoning you somewhere just as inconvenient as this place. Perhaps even more so, for there will be no ponies to be stolen within proximity."

"You are the most irritating person I have ever known."

"I assure you that you share that honor," he said, and swung into the saddle behind her. He locked his arm around her waist and pulled her tightly against him, not trusting her in the least. Sadly, the feel of her curves pressed against him awakened urges he would have preferred to forget. He reminded himself that the ride to Kilderrick would not take that long. He would surrender her to Maximilian's protection, then ride out with the Compagnie Rouge immediately.

With any luck, he would think of a destination by then.

"You desire more from me than a tale," Ceara taunted, rubbing her buttocks against him. His body responded with predictable enthusiasm and she looked up at him with dancing eyes. "I will have my original wager yet."

Rafael halfway feared she was right in that.

He did not imagine that she truly wanted to be wedded to him. He was no champion, much less a faithful husband who would see her sheltered and with child. He certainly had no desire to wed any woman himself, yet even though Ceara knew as much, she insisted upon the merit of a match.

She wished only to use him for her own purposes, and Rafael would not be seduced.

He kept his expression forbidding. "You possess an optimism entirely undeserved," he said and felt a cur when the light died in her eyes. He touched his heels to his destrier's sides, leading the way to Kilderrick as the others followed behind.

~

CEARA HAD NOT CONFIDED in anyone for so long that she could not immediately decide where to begin. She was keenly aware of the mercenary who accompanied Rafael, for that man watched her so avidly that she could not forget his presence. He also undoubtedly listened and she was not entirely at ease with him hearing her tale.

She had to share it with Rafael, though. He was right that 'twas only fair. He had pursued her and defended her, and she would not see him pay a fearsome price for his intervention—that his choices showed a chivalry he insisted he did not possess only made her more grateful for his intervention.

He tightened his grip upon her, making her both aware of his hard strength behind her and the distance they had already journeyed.

She recognized the move as a command to begin.

"Once," she said, "there was a warrior known as Somerled, who was victorious in battle and claimed rulership of Argyll, Kintyre and Lorne. He married the daughter of the King of Mann and added that territory to his domain as well as the Islands. He was known to be a leader of men and a fair judge, and he had five sons and a daughter. Of those six children, two sons survived to establish dynasties of their own: from Dugald descended the Lords of Argyll and clan MacDoughall, and from Ranald descended the Lords of the Isles, clan Donald, clan MacRuari and clan MacAlister. The blood of Somerled runs in the veins of all these families."

Ceara realized that Rafael's companion had moved closer. That man's destrier, a fine bay with white socks, rode alongside Phantôm but behind Ceara. Not for the first time, she cursed the limitations of not riding astride, for she could not see that man at all. She could see the two squires, but that was less satisfactory.

"I have heard tell of the Lord of the Isles," Rafael said. "He was the father of Godfroy, the lost betrothed of Lady Alys, was he not?"

Ceara nodded. "Aye. Eòin Macdonald holds that title now, and he is wed to the King of Scotland's daughter."

"And will the death of his son pass without repercussions?"

"He had abducted Alys and tried to kill Maximilian," Ceara reminded him.

Rafael nodded but said no more.

"Our family is clan MacRuari. Our lands are to the north and west, the heart of it called Garmaron. Ardnamurchan and the islands of Uist as well as Benbecula were our traditional holdings, though later Moidart and Kintail were added, as well. We are warriors all and our menfolk often labored abroad as mercenaries. Aherne MacRuari was my own forebear. He was the third child and youngest son of Ruari MacRuari. Ruari was the MacRuari chieftain and had a daughter by his first wife, name of Aimil. He had a son by another woman who was not his wedded wife. That was his eldest son, Raghnall. And then, he had a second son, Aherne."

"By a wife or a mistress?"

Ceara shrugged. "It depends who recounts the tale. It is said that when Ruari was without wife or mistress, he encountered a mermaid and that she bore him a son."

"A mermaid?" Rafael's skepticism was more than clear.

Ceara twisted around to fix him with a look. "It is the tale."

He smiled, the sight making her heart leap. "Aye, I can believe that there is a siren in your lineage, one whose descendants might beguile and deceive unwitting men."

"Yet killing the godson of the king would not see me hunted until I was dead?"

Ceara faced forward, hating even the sound of that prospect. She knew Rafael could defend himself and did not truly fear that Edward would be able to injure him.

But his point was well taken.

"She was not deceptive," Ceara said hotly. "They loved each other in truth."

"Which does not explain your betrothal to this Edward," he noted.

Ceara continued her tale. "Ruari's courtship of the mermaid was ardent, and he could often be found on the rocky shore, talking to her as she combed her hair. Then one day, Ruari disappeared and could not be found. He was believed to have drowned, perhaps in pursuit of the enticing mermaid, yet his household were astonished when he returned after a year and a day. There was sorrow in his eyes and 'twas clear to all that his heart was heavy. He told tales of the mermaid's palace and her treasure, of her love and her beauty. He confessed that his beloved mermaid had died in the birthing of their son. Overwhelmed with grief, he had left the infant with her kin."

"Did he not regret that choice?"

"If so, there was little he could do about it. He knew he would never find the mermaid's hidden realm on his own. Ruari's son was lost to him, unless his wife's kind chose to return him to land. He had recurring dreams then, dreams of his lost son returning to become the tanist and proving himself worthy beyond all others."

"The tanist?" Rafael echoed.

Ceara frowned, uncertain how to explain the term.

"His official heir," Raynard explained. "The tanist is the named heir of the chieftain. He may be the chieftain's oldest son, but he may not be. Birth order is of no import. He is the most worthy leader after the chieftain, and should be a man experienced in the arts of war and diplomacy. He should be trusted by his kin and respected by both his allies and enemies. It is similar to your assumption of the leadership of the Compagnie Rouge—that was less about your kinship with the *Loup Argent* than your experience and skills."

Ceara glanced back to see Rafael nod. "A man other than the eldest son may be named heir, if he is better suited to the task."

"Aye," Ceara said in unison with Raynard.

"Yet I will wager that Ruari's other son believed himself to be the better candidate."

"Of course," Ceara agreed. "Ruari's eldest son, Raghnall, tried to gain his father's support, but Ruari had never been close to this son. Raghnall had a fearsome temper that could drive him to rash decisions, while his father was more temperate. They often argued bitterly. Ruari's hopes were entirely fixed upon his lost son and he returned to the spot where he had met the mermaid each and every night, watching and yearning."

"That can only have made the other son bitter," Rafael speculated.

"Aye, and perhaps the daughter, as well. Slowly, despair claimed Ruari's heart. More than seventeen years after he had lost his mermaid and returned home, Ruari took to his bed, slowly fading from this world."

Ceara blinked back her tears. This part of the tale always upset her.

"His son, Aherne, arrived on his own eighteenth birthday, come of age and seeking his father, but he was too late. Ruari had died a mere day before and the siblings declined to acknowledge him."

"A tragedy," Rafael murmured. "Who became chieftain?"

"Raghnall claimed the chieftainship, but the clan was divided. Aherne left the MacRuari lands, persuading a large number of local men to follow him as gallowglass mercenaries."

"Gallowglass?" Rafael echoed.

"Mercenaries like myself," Raynard contributed. "Warriors from Scotland who battle in Ireland. We share a language but have no family loyalties in those lands."

"Ah, mercenaries who can be trusted to have no conflicts." Rafael nodded approval of this.

"Indeed," Raynard agreed. "The Gaelic is *gallóglaigh*, foreign warriors."

"And so, this Aherne undermined the fighting power of his rival, by leading warriors to other battles," Rafael concluded. "'Tis a clever tactic."

"To buttress his claim, Raghnall allied with Eòin Macdonald, Lord of the Isles, by betrothing his sister, Aimil, to Eòin."

"I will guess it was a powerful alliance."

"Aye. Raghnall was a decisive leader. His fury in battle ensured that he saw much success. He seized Kintail with such vigor that the king was compelled to cede it to him, taking it from William, the Earl of Ross, who bitterly resented the loss. Raghnall was the earl's vassal, but they seldom agreed, and finally, when they were both summoned to Perth to the king's parliament, William seized the opportunity. He and his men ambushed and killed Raghnall with several of his men at Elcho Priory in 1346."

"The king cannot have approved of that choice."

"He did not, but he was more concerned with ensuring stability in the west. He granted Raghnall's territories to Eòin, declaring that they belonged to the Lord of the Isles as the inheritance of Aimil, his wife."

"And Aherne?"

"There is a tale that he returned to the MacRuari family stronghold in 1347 while Aimil and Eòin were in residence, seeking the chieftainship. One tale insists that he was rebuffed, then departed his homeland in disappointment. There is yet another tale that he arrived and was ushered into the presence of those two, then never seen again."

"Yet if he is your forebear, he had progeny."

"A son and myself," Ceara agreed. "My mother had disagreed with Aherne's choice, thinking he took too great a risk, but she had remained in Ireland at his insistence with my brother. She would have accompanied her husband, but she was ripe with child and he insisted she remain in safety. By the time of my birth, she had lost all hope of seeing her beloved again. When my brother had seen eighteen summers and was as valiant a warrior as could be, she took us both to the Earl of Ross. She entreated that man to support my brother's claim of the chieftainship, which had been vacant since Raghnall's demise, and also to see our family legacy reclaimed from the Lord of the Isles. The earl, chafing at the favor shown to the Lord of the Isles, was glad to comply."

"What favor was he shown, bella?"

"In 1350, Eòin forged a new alliance with the king, and in so doing, he divorced Aimil without cause to wed the daughter of the king's official heir. He put Aimil aside, disinherited the three sons they had together, and wed Margaret, and the king writ a decree assigning Aimil's inheritance to Eòin and his children by Margaret." She held up a hand. "They have eight children and the MacRuari legacy is claimed by the Macdonalds, unless my brother can change matters."

"What of this Edward?"

"When my mother took me to the court of the Earl of Ross, they agreed that I should be betrothed to his only son, also named William. My mother and I remained in William's household for protection, which was where I learned to ride and hunt."

"With your betrothed?"

"Nay, William was never robust." Ceara frowned, recalling the sweet but sickly boy. She had become fond of him, though she would never have been glad to call him husband. "He died in 1357, the same year

96

THE DRAGON & THE DAMSEL

that King David was released from English captivity. We had high hopes of my brother's success then. My mother and I left Ross for my grandfather's holdings to await my brother's triumphant return."

"I will guess that did not transpire," Rafael said, his tone wry.

"Nay, the king taxed the nobility heavily to pay for his ransom and unrest spread through the land. In 1366, the Earl of Ross led a rebellion against the king, thereby inciting royal fury. The rebellion was crushed, but William had lost the king's favor. Perhaps he was uncertain of that, but when he strove to entail his earldom to his half-brother, Hugh de Rarichies, the king forbade this choice. Instead, the king insisted that William's daughter wed a knight he favored highly, one Walter de Leslie, and that the earldom of Ross pass to Walter through her."

"Why did the king favor him so mightily?"

"Walter de Leslie was a crusader and knight, and thus earned the king's admiration. King David also betrothed Walter's bastard son to me to secure the alliance between our families."

"And better to secure the earl's conquest of the MacRuari lands," Raynard said softly.

Ceara ignored his comment, though she knew Rafael took note. "I never liked or trusted Edward or Walter: when my mother died that winter, I fled south alone."

"You had no defender," Rafael said softly, and Ceara nodded.

"When King David died in 1371, William tried to contest Walter's claim, but the new king, Robert II, upheld the previous king's decision. Robert also became Edward's godfather in David's stead, declaring that he would ensure the interests of Walter de Leslie were defended." Ceara nodded. "By then, I had come to live in Kilderrick's forest."

Rafael's tone became crisp. "But that was several years ago. It is inexplicable that he should suddenly pursue you now."

"He did not know where to find me, not until there were tales of Godfroy's demise."

"But, Ceara, you no longer have a legacy." Rafael was impatient. "Your brother is gone, the lands have been claimed by others and you cannot become chieftain. Why does this Edward seek you with such vigor?"

"He and his father have a scheme to blend the families, to ensure that the lands of our clan are assumed by the earldom." Ceara knew the reason sounded feeble, but she would not hasten to share all of her secrets.

Rafael made a dismissive gesture to their surroundings. "These lands are empty, *bella*, devoid of value to any who do not already hold them in affection. There are no crops, no gold, no markets, no items for trade. Of what import who holds this hill or that valley? This is a wasteland of rocks, to be sure."

Ceara pretended to consider this. In truth, she had to decide whether to confide more. Acknowledging the existence of her legacy, though, was not the same as surrendering it.

"I suppose then," she continued with apparent reluctance. "They must desire the treasure."

She felt Rafael's surprise, then his lips were against her ear, his voice as low and soft as silken velvet. "Treasure? What treasure?" There was an urgency in his tone that she should have anticipated, yet it disappointed her all the same.

She should be glad. Her confession had been a success. She had his undivided attention, just as she had hoped.

The heart of a mercenary was bought in gold, to be sure.

Her sole value to any man was her legacy and that was more disappointing than Ceara could have expected. Would she ever be desired for herself alone?

Treasure?

Rafael had his doubts of this tale. The revelation was too timely. Ceara had deceived him before, after all, and she had made it clear that she still wanted his aid. When he looked at these stony hills and barren fields, he could not imagine that there were riches to be claimed within any distance.

Was it true or had she simply discerned the most reliable way to win his agreement?

He had a weakness for gold and riches, to be sure.

For the moment, he would feign belief, the better to discern Ceara's ruse—whatever it might be.

"The mermaid's treasure, of course," she agreed, granting him a smile that was entirely untrustworthy. "Did I omit that detail?"

"You did," he acknowledged. "And surely not by accident."

"*Dìomhair na maighdeann-mhara*," Raynard said softly, his eyes alight. Rafael gave him a look. "The mermaid's secret. 'Tis an old tale in these parts and the hidden hoard grows with every telling."

Ceara flushed, a hint that there was truth in these words. Perhaps the treasure was no more than a single cup or a trio of Viking coins. It might be worth the trouble of collecting it. "The treasure is unclaimed, for its location was hidden and hidden well. It was the legacy of the mermaid to her son, Aherne, and the rightful legacy of his descendants."

"Including you."

She nodded. "It is said that when Ruari returned from the home of his beloved, he brought a trove of treasure, gifts from her kind in the hope that wealth might ease his sorrow. It did not, of course, and he hid it away, unable to bear to look upon it."

"Did the Lord of the Isles not claim possession of this prize upon his marriage to Aimil? I thought he had wed her to claim her family holdings."

Ceara smiled at him. "You listen well."

Rafael smiled back at her. "It can be a most helpful habit."

She did not seem to know what to make of that, and he savored the fleeting sight of her uncertainty. Had she created the tale as she recounted it? Or had she modified it in part? Rafael would recall every detail she had surrendered and listen for any deviation.

"Aimil never knew of the treasure's location. Ruari would never have told her, nor would Aherne."

"Particularly if she and her husband ensured his silence," Rafael noted. "But all the same, perhaps another has claimed it."

Ceara shook her head. "It is there yet, safe."

In her confident claim, Rafael smelled a trap. Somehow Ceara would ensure that he undertook the challenge of accessing the hoard and she later claimed it. Perhaps the siege would cost his life. Perhaps he would be captured. He was wary, to be sure.

"And you will undoubtedly tell me not only that you know its location, but that it has lain undisturbed all these years and that only you can lead anyone to it." Rafael could not hide his skepticism.

Even Raynard snorted in disbelief.

"Not only me," she said. "My brother could tell you of its site." There was a softening in her tone, and Rafael was touched by her affection for her sibling.

Undoubtedly that was her scheme. "The one who has not returned?"

She nodded. "I hope he has not breathed his last. There are many relying upon him."

"Who is to say that he has not claimed the treasure and left these lands forever?"

Ceara's eyes flashed. "He has not. He would not!" She lifted her chin, her expression turning stubborn. "He is a man of honor. I know it well."

Rafael sighed mightily. "Even men of honor are tempted by fortunes awaiting claim."

She shook her head. "Not Niall. Never Niall."

Rafael looked toward Raynard whose expression remained impassive. "You will need better bait for your lure, Ceara."

She turned to face him, her tone imploring. "But you must believe me! If the hoard had been found, there would have been a tale." That was not entirely implausible. "And there has been none, not a whisper to be heard. Eòin Macdonald would not have been able to keep himself from gloating over it, or displaying it. Walter de Leslie would have done the same. Both men would have granted gifts from it to the king and his allies. It would be *known*."

Rafael found his gaze rising to Raynard again. That man shrugged, evidently finding the argument persuasive. "'Tis a sparsely populated land, yet tales travel with ease," he said in his rolling accent. "I agree. 'Twould have been known."

"But you have been abroad. You might not have heard."

"I hear much more than you guess. I have kept contact with former comrades at intervals and there are many of us who once fought together now fighting abroad." He nodded grimly. "'Tis a treasure of much repute. If it had been unearthed again, I would have heard."

Rafael looked down in time to see Ceara's triumphant smile. "Of course, there is one additional detail that might have ensured its security."

Rafael lifted a brow, inviting the confession she obviously wished to make.

"It might have been the missing key." She held his gaze with resolve, fairly challenging him to guess its location.

A tide of desire rose hot within him, demanding that he seduce her until she was breathless, overwhelming her with his touch and compelling her to share her secrets in exchange for satisfaction. Had she not been a maiden, Rafael would not have hesitated, but he could not allow his bold huntress to dismiss his sole principle.

Her dawning trust in him was spellbinding, to be sure, but 'twas also perilous—and he knew that Ceara alone would suffer any results. He had to discourage her faith in him, even to frighten her, but with words alone.

This treasure and its key would provide the perfect means to do as much—though he would feel a cur, it must be done.

For Ceara's own sake.

CHAPTER 7

I see no key," Rafael noted, watching Ceara's eyes sparkle. "I have kept it safe."

"And where is the lock?"

"I cannot simply confess every detail to a known mercenary seeking his own reward," she chided as if he were no more dangerous than a hungry hound. "You might seize the key and abandon me while you claimed the prize." She shook her head. "Nay, you must take me with you and defend me until the hoard is in our possession."

He laughed. "I should take an army to a destination unknown on speculation alone? I think not, *bella*."

"Then I will hire the Compagnie Rouge to escort me to the treasury. They can defend me when I make my claim."

Rafael watched her, considering. She was resolute, to be sure, and that made him wonder whether the treasure existed in truth. "You will not like our price," he growled.

"Name it." She was undeterred and he knew he should have anticipated as much.

"A third of the hoard, plus expenses."

Ceara gasped, her expression one of such dismay that Rafael wanted to laugh aloud. "A *third*?"

Rafael shrugged. "Plus expenses."

"Plus?" Fury began to simmer in her eyes, and he knew he should be glad that her opinion of him changed so quickly.

"Of course. My men must eat and drink, as must their horses and their squires. Their transport must be paid if there are to be voyages on ships, and their keep at inns must be covered, if indeed there are inns to be found in this land." He sighed. "Clean water, of course, can also become an expenditure, depending on the locale, and, be warned, *bella*, that if they are obliged to fight, the price only increases."

She stared at him. "And a *third* in addition to that." A fire raged in her eyes. "That is a healthy fee. Do you even know the extent of these riches?"

"Nay and that is the concern. Were you to supply me with an accurate inventory, we might negotiate a lower increment, should the hoard be of sufficient size."

"I cannot do that. No one has seen it in decades."

"And those who have seen it are dead," Raynard contributed. He shrugged. "Unless one counts the *mermaids*." He grinned as he said this last word and Rafael chuckled.

Ceara glared at each of them in turn.

"And it may have been plundered," Rafael said, his tone reasonable. "The journey may be futile. How will you pay our fee then?"

"It is not gone," Ceara said with heat. "It cannot be. The treasure was secured in a secret location by Ruari's command, where it remains hidden to this day. The mermaids defend it."

"A fable told to children," Rafael replied with a yawn.

"The truth! When you take me to it, you will see."

In fact, Rafael was more curious than he suspected was wise. Ceara's quest would give the Compagnie Rouge a destination. If there was a treasure, a measure of it would be a welcome addition to his funds. If there was not a treasure, they would still depart from Kilderrick in a timely fashion.

They had no other offers for their skills.

And then there was the company of the fair Ceara to be considered. As much as he would have denied it, he was not content to abandon her while Edward de Leslie was yet in the vicinity. Doubtless that man still lusted for her hand—or her family treasure. Doubtless that was the compelling lure.

He cleared his throat. "Should we undertake this venture, I will keep a tally of expenses that you might subsequently reimburse me, whether there is a treasure or not, in addition to the third."

"That share is outrageous." Ceara pivoted to look at Raynard, who smiled.

"I expected him to demand half," that man informed her. "That is the customary fee of the Compagnie Rouge."

"Outrageous," she whispered with heat.

"Unless there is to be a battle," Rafael noted.

"Of course," Raynard agreed easily. "Another ten per cent for opposition and twenty for war."

"That is scandalous, immoral and predatory," Ceara complained.

"Of course," Rafael agreed readily. "Recall that we are *mercenaries*."

"Although many in the Compagnie Rouge would pay to ride to war, purely for the pleasure of the endeavor." Raynard smiled when Ceara sputtered. "Perhaps Rafael is convinced that this is a considerable collection."

"I cannot agree to a third," Ceara said with heat.

"'Twill be forty per cent by the morrow," Rafael said smoothly and Ceara turned upon him with fury. He was tempted anew to kiss her and put that passion to good use. "Our price invariably increases with any delay in the negotiations."

Then something dawned in her expression and he had time to dread her next words. "If you were my husband in truth, you could claim half," she noted. She held up the hand with his ring upon it, her expression filled with familiar challenge.

Rafael laughed. "If I were your husband in truth, I could claim it all and you could not make a word of protest in any court of law. You would be mine, along with all your dowry and legacy."

His laughter halted at the truth in his own words.

Their gazes met and locked for a potent moment.

Was marriage such a high price to pay for a fortune?

After all, they did not have to remain wed forever.

This was the opportunity he had awaited.

~

CEARA'S WARINESS dawned as Rafael began to smile. He looked dangerous and unpredictable again, a combination that made her dread his intentions. Her treacherous heart skipped with awareness of his allure and she knew that if he touched her, her wits would be addled indeed. They drew close to Kilderrick and it seemed suddenly there was insufficient time to plan.

"You would not wed me, seize the treasure, then cast me aside," she said, but she heard the uncertainty in her own tone.

He smiled, his gaze dark. "Why not? Your own king would not take your side, given his own choices in the past."

"But I am a maiden and you have no interest in maidens."

"You speak aright in that." He bent low, his voice a soft murmur in her ear. "And best of all, a match that is unconsummated can be dissolved with ease." He snapped his fingers.

Nay, nay, she would not be used by him to line his purse, then cast aside! "Nay, you would not do this," she insisted, wondering even as she spoke who she sought to convince. "That is why you refused to wed me. You would not be so dishonorable. You would not *cheat* me."

Rafael considered her, that smile curving his lips as he arched a brow. He could not have appeared to be more wicked, if he had tried. "Have you forgotten my trade, *bella?*" he asked softly. "Have you forgotten our price?"

"Nay, and neither have I failed to note your nature. Though you would try to hide any honor in your character, you did not have to pursue me. You did not have to ride to my aid."

"Perhaps I only amused myself, *bella.*"

"Nay. I do not believe it. You are a man of principle."

Raynard snorted heartily, as if trying to disguise a laugh. Rafael chuckled darkly. "For a maiden with her wits about her, she is readily deceived," he said to his companion.

"Aye," that man agreed. "But then, she does believe in mermaids."

The two warriors laughed together and Ceara's cheeks burned that their merriment was at her expense. It could not be so. Rafael was not a villain in truth. She would not believe it. He was not of Edward's ilk. He had protected her.

But what if that had been merely a ruse to disarm her?

~

Ah, his huntress was uncertain and discontent. As much as Rafael yearned to reassure her, he knew this situation was best.

They were crossing the stream at the base of Kilderrick's valley, and Rafael heard the stamp of horses and low murmur of men's voices. He slowed Phantôm as the camp of the Compagnie Rouge came into view through the trees. Rafael spotted a familiar figure outside his tent. Maximilian was armed and upon his black destrier, the breeze lifting his cloak and the sunlight glinting in his blond hair.

He could only assume that Ceara's absence had been discovered and that he had been blamed. Rafael exchanged a glance with Raynard, then rode into the cluster of trees that grew beside the stream before pausing again.

Maximilian looked markedly grim.

The laird's presence was not the sole surprise, though. Maximilian was not alone. Another man was mounted on a destrier with elaborate caparisons, the lion rampant of Scotland emblazoned on all his garb. There was no doubt of his identity, given the pennant bearers and attendants crowded around the king, and the size of the striped silk tent pitched at the highest point, opposite the gates of the keep.

Why had the King of Scotland arrived at Kilderrick?

It seemed too much of a coincidence, given the tale Ceara had just recounted and the enemy they had routed. Rafael had a hundred guesses, but doubted Edward could have located his godfather so quickly.

The king's presence, though, would dictate Rafael's own choices. Thanks to Ceara, he knew that monarch was allied with the Lord of the Isles by marriage. That meant leading the Compagnie Rouge to the east, north or west would attract a scrutiny Rafael did not welcome. They would ride south first, as if leaving the area, retracing their path from Carlisle. They would need passage by ship to retrieve a mermaid's treasure, and he could only hope that such passage might be found from England's western shores. There was a challenge to solve later.

For the moment, his half-brother Amaury held the keep of Beaupoint on the English side of the Solway Firth. That would serve as their initial destination. Amaury might be compelled to assist Rafael, if only to rid his holding of the Compagnie Rouge.

First, Rafael had to ensure their escape from Kilderrick, even with the king's watchful eyes upon them. So long as Ceara's full identity was unknown, it might be done.

Rafael's thoughts flew. Maximilian might insist that Rafael wed Ceara, given how that man had become as conservative as any baron. She would produce the chemise, his own feint, and use it against him, if he declined.

But Rafael would not decline. He would claim this fiery maiden as his wife, thereby ensuring her protection—though the timing of his choice would convince her that he desired only the treasure. Theirs would be a match of convenience and would remain unconsummated, the better that they could part once he had retrieved this fabled hoard. If it truly existed, the gamble would pay well. Ceara would have sufficient wealth to choose the spouse she desired, he would have riches untold for his own, and in the shorter term, the Compagnie Rouge would have a destination.

'Twould be perfect.

First, they must leave Kilderrick behind.

CEARA WAS DISMAYED to see the king's banner and his company of men newly arrived at Kilderrick. Had Edward sent word to his godfather to ensure that her betrothal pledge was kept?

What would Rafael do?

He pulled the horse back slightly to survey the company on the slope, his eyes darting over the company. She had no doubt he estimated their numbers and power exactly. Then she thought he chuckled softly. His eyes gleamed with an intensity that made her dread his intentions.

But there was no opportunity for her to make another appeal.

Rafael turned to Raynard and said something quickly in a language she did not comprehend. It sounded like an order. That warrior replied, nodded grimly, then rode away with haste, clearly intent on fulfilling some task. He rode into the forest, following the path of the river, as if he would enter the camp of the Compagnie Rouge from the side furthest from Kilderrick's keep.

As if he would keep out of view of Maximilian and the king.

At Rafael's gesture, the boys followed Raynard, leaving her alone with this unpredictable mercenary.

"Where is he going?" she asked.

"You need not know," Rafael said sternly. "Do not challenge my claims in this exchange."

"What claims?"

He touched his lips to her ear, the fan of his breath making her shiver. "Here is the wager we will make: we will wed this day, purportedly at Maximilian's dictate, then you will lead me to this treasure. Upon recovering it, we shall divide the spoils, half to me, plus sufficient to cover the expenses of my men."

Half? "What madness is this?"

He shook a finger at her, continuing in that smooth undertone that she should not have found so persuasive. "And then you will be safely delivered to whatever town or keep you prefer."

Delivered? Ceara propped her hands upon her hips, more than prepared to argue these terms. "And what of you, *husband?*"

Rafael smiled wickedly. "You will never see me again."

She found herself gasping again. "But you said we would wed. That is not a marriage! I will not be bound to you before God then abandoned at your choice."

"It could be worse," he said. "You could be bound to me and *never* abandoned." There was a glitter in his eyes that made Ceara wonder whether it truly would be worse to spend her life with this man, seeking adventure each day.

Then celebrating their union abed each and every night. The very prospect made her flush. "You wish only to alarm me with such threats," she said, for lack of a better reply.

His gaze hardened and she wondered why her accusation should so offend him.

"Our marriage will not be one in truth, but no one will know as much until our wager is completed. Then and only then, we shall reveal that the match was never consummated and alas, our ways must part." He smiled and she braced herself for his next words. "You can spurn me when the moment comes, if you prefer. I will not be offended."

"Nay, you will be gone."

His smile broadened.

"Think, Ceara. You will be affluent and able to choose whatever man you desire—if indeed you desire one at all."

His solution was neat, to be sure, but Ceara instinctively disliked it. She knew she should be glad of having Rafael sworn to her cause for any increment of time, but this proposal irked her. "But Edward…"

"Will not lay a hand upon you," Rafael interjected with ferocity. "While our paths are joined, I will defend you with my life." He bent and locked his gaze with hers. "Upon that, you have my most solemn pledge."

Ceara believed him and not just because of the gleam of resolve in his eyes.

Indeed, his vow made her heart flutter.

She eyed him. "But half?"

He laughed, reckless and dangerous and utterly enticing. "Half, *bella*. And the agreement will only be finalized when I hold the key."

"The price was a third but moments ago."

His brows rose. "It will be two-thirds if you delay longer."

Ceara exhaled in annoyance and he chuckled before his gaze rose to the two knights. His eyes narrowed and his amusement faded. "Why do you think the king is here?"

Rafael shrugged and she knew he had already considered that question. "It seems overquick for Edward to have found his godfather. There may be other danger afoot." He met her gaze, his own incisive. "Will he recognize you?"

Ceara considered the question, then shook her head. "I have never seen him. Even Eòin last saw me as a child. 'Twas the last king, David, I met with William, the earl of Ross."

"Both dead, a matter of much convenience. What of your family?"

She frowned. "I am said to resemble my mother, but she never met Robert."

Rafael nodded approval, then his voice dropped low. "Then we shall proceed. Do not mention your kith and kin or even your surname. You are simply Ceara, no more and no less."

"Will they accept that for the vows?"

"They will be compelled to, since your origins are a mystery." His smile was wicked and curiously reassuring. "Let the king divine who you are when it is too late to intervene."

"The sooner we depart the better," she said with some trepidation.

Rafael did not reply. He turned Phantôm and let the destrier charge noisily through the trees. The beast moved with a confidence his master shared, and Ceara thought Rafael must look like a conquering hero when Maximilian and the king turned to look. Phantôm pranced when he emerged from the shadow of the trees, shaking his head proudly then stepping high as he cantered toward laird and king.

Rafael's gaze was fixed upon the men and Ceara's heart soared to be with him. She slid her arm around his waist then, and felt the tension in him. He gave every appearance of bold indifference, but she knew he was braced for a surprise—and in a way, that was yet more reassuring. If there was to be a battle, she trusted him to see her defended. She dropped her hand to the hilt of her dagger and heard his minute sound of approval.

"Diplomacy, *bella*," he growled. "Tact goes further in winning the day."

"Especially when one is prepared for more than words." She surveyed him. "You are enjoying this."

He smiled then, flicking a glance down at her, and she could have stared into his twinkling eyes forever. "As should you, *bella*," he murmured. "'Tis peril that quickens the blood and makes one most aware of being alive."

Ceara found the argument compelling and strove to savor the moment.

Rafael halted his destrier before Maximilian with a flourish. The beast tossed his head before stamping a foot and exhaling in a snort.

Maximilian's destrier nickered and Ceara felt the weight of the king's stare.

She remained silent, finding the task easy for once in her life.

"And so you are returned, brother, having retrieved the errant maiden," Maximilian said, coolly surveying Ceara. She held his gaze unchastised, for it had not been her decision to be abducted. She might have corrected him, but Rafael's grip tightened on her waist in warning and she bit her tongue.

Diplomacy was a skill she had never learned.

"And you, brother, entertain a most noble guest." Rafael spoke with uncommon charm, his manner sufficient to win the favor of any man. He bowed to the king, who acknowledged him with a slight nod. "I apologize, your majesty, that our camp has occupied so much of the space beyond the walls of Kilderrick, and hope that you have not been troubled by our presence. I had no notion that my brother expected such an exalted guest."

Neither laird nor king replied, and Ceara concluded that Maximilian had not known of the king's intent. Why *had* the king come?

She recalled the reputed splendor of the mermaid's treasure and fixed her gaze upon the ground beside Phantôm's hooves. The king continued to study her and her pulse raced, even as she let her hair disguise her features from view. Beneath her cloak, she gripped the hilt of her knife.

Rafael waved a hand toward the camp of the Compagnie Rouge and continued. "I have given orders already that we should move closer to the river, ceding the higher ground to your majesty and your men. It will be done with all haste. Please accept my most humble apologies for any inconvenience. I know my brother is always honored to receive you and wishes for your utmost comfort at Kilderrick." He bowed toward the king and Ceara ducked her head yet lower.

"I thank you for this courtesy," the king said, even as there was a shout. They all turned to watch as the largest tent of the Compagnie Rouge was struck. Ceara assumed it was where the men gathered at meals, for it was a large canopy, patched in many places. When it fell to the ground, Ceara could see squires leading horses down the hill to the river and other tents being taken down. The entire camp had erupted in activity with remarkable haste. She spotted Raynard pointing and directing the efforts and knew this had been his assigned task. That great tent was raised again, closer to the river and also closest to Kilderrick. She could not help but notice that much activity was obscured by it in that location.

What was Rafael's scheme?

"You will not distract me from the matter at hand with your courtesy," Maximilian said wryly to Rafael.

"It surely is not my intent to do as much, brother." There was a thread of steel in Rafael's tone.

"We have spent much of the day seeking this maiden, only to learn that she fled to your tent last evening before you both vanished from Kilderrick." Maximilian's tone was hard. "This after I warned you that the women of Kilderrick must be untouched while your men make camp here."

"I apologize for your concern this day, brother. I felt haste was of import in pursuing my reluctant bride." Rafael's grip tightened on Ceara's waist. "I return with tidings of success, though, for I have finally convinced her to accept my humble self." His smile was so dazzling that Ceara blinked.

Maximilian surely did as well. "You mean to wed?"

Ceara could only watch as Rafael lifted her left hand and kissed his ring upon her finger. "Aye, brother, we have already pledged each to the other. In this triumph, I am the most fortunate of men."

"*That* ring," Maximilian murmured with apparent surprise.

"*That* ring," Rafael echoed, his eyes narrowing. "For it is appropriate beyond all others."

The two brothers eyed each other for a tense moment and Ceara wondered whether the king and his councillors were as uncertain of the import of this particular ring as she was.

Then Rafael smiled down at Ceara. "Indeed, I must confess that the pursuit of this lady's affection was the main reason for my speedy return to these shores."

"If you have come to such an amicable agreement, then you cannot take offense at my insistence that you exchange your vows again before me," Maximilian said.

Ceara had the impression that the two brothers sparred with words, each more aware of the other's nature and intention than she could ever be. There was a tension between them, as if each deliberately provoked the other. She hoped neither succeeded, even as she wondered what was at root.

Then she wondered whether it was a ruse for the benefit of the king. Doubtless he did not welcome any suggestion that Maximilian, as his ally, still had connections with a company of mercenaries.

Rafael inclined his head politely. "Only if the king will also attend the ceremony. There is no blessing so potent as the goodwill of powerful men, in my view, and I would be honored to have his majesty stand witness to our pledges."

"We will assemble at the chapel within the hour," Maximilian said, as if he did not trust Rafael to do as much.

"Must we ride all the way to Rowan Fell?" Rafael asked then grinned down at Ceara. "I find myself eager for the marital bed after a long journey already this day."

Ceara flushed and the king shook his head in disapproval of such base desires so openly declared.

"Nay," Maximilian said. "There is a newer and smaller chapel within the walls of the keep. You have not seen it, but it surely will suffice."

"It surely will," Rafael agreed with a smile.

He rode then to the gates and into the bailey beyond, dismounting as all those gathered there watched and whispered. "The key, *bella*," he murmured just as he was lowering her to the ground. He fixed her with a quelling look, one that others might mistake for adoration. In truth, the vehement blue of his eyes made her heart thunder. "Fetch the key immediately."

Of course. The treasure was his true desire.

She could not afford to forget that this was all a feint, for the benefit of claiming the treasure. It was a feint that would save her from Edward as well, and Ceara knew she should be grateful for it for that alone—yet she found herself wishing there might be more.

Even the recollection of Rafael's seductive caress of the night made her quiver deep inside.

Could she provoke him to grant more, before their alliance ended?

Did she dare?

She raised her chin and smiled, as if unaffected by the grip of his hands upon her waist.

"I must wash and braid my hair again," she said for the benefit of others. "Forgive me, sir, for the delay, but I would look my best for our exchange of vows." She lifted her hands and looked down at her kirtle in apparent dismay, then stretched up to kiss Rafael's cheek. She was surprised when he caught her close, as if he could not bear to be parted from her for a moment.

He spoke with resolve, his lips against her ear. "Know that if you betray me in this, *bella*, I will deliver you to Edward de Leslie myself."

And there was the truth of it. She had been warned of the consequences and informed of the sum of her value. Ceara forced a smile, as if Rafael had whispered an endearment and strode to her chamber like a merry bride.

She reminded herself that she had won her goal. Rafael would protect her, at least until the treasure was in his possession. He would take her to the mermaid's secret and surely he would overcome any obstacle to claim it.

Then he would cast her aside.

It felt like less of a victory than Ceara had hoped. Even half of the reported wealth of the treasure was insufficient reward.

Nay, she wanted more, much more, from Rafael di Giovanni. She wanted him to look at her as if she were the prize. She sensed that when he granted himself to a cause, his loyalty was unswerving and she wanted that devotion for herself. She wanted to journey to those distant lands, to see the marvels of the world, to fight at his back and savor all the pleasure that could be found on this earth.

He was her means of denying Edward's claim. He might be the way to find Niall again.

Ceara was placing the key on its lace around her neck when she wondered if she could win her desire in the time allotted to their union. 'Twas true that Rafael could abandon her, as he threatened, regardless of the law. But if their match was consummated, 'twould be harder to annul the marriage. She gripped the key, determined to tempt

Rafael to possess this maiden, hoping that would be sufficient to prompt his loyalty.

If naught else, the notion gave Ceara a plan.

ALYS MIGHT NEVER SLUMBER AGAIN. The previous afternoon, she had awakened to the news that Rafael had arrived at Kilderrick with the Compagnie Rouge to offer the seal of Château de Vries to Maximilian. She suspected she would always feel that had been a closer matter than she would have liked, less because Maximilian was unreliable than because she loved him and Kilderrick so very much. Having lost all once, Alys would prefer to keep all she had won.

Then on this day, she scarce opened her eyes when Hilda, her maid, confessed that Ceara was missing. By the time Alys was dressed that morn, there was word that Rafael had vanished as well. That could be no good portent, to Alys' thinking, and she searched with the others in the hope of finding Ceara hale—or at least untouched.

Ceara's favored palfrey was still in the stables, and Royce knew naught of Ceara riding to hunt again. Ceara had not been in the village, despite the gatekeeper's conviction that she had visited Nathalie, and Maximilian had searched the tents of the Compagnie Rouge to no avail. Both Ceara and Rafael were absent, which did not bode well for her former companion to Alys' thinking.

Despite her concern, Alys had been convinced by Maximilian to retire to the solar that afternoon. She had slept deeply but briefly, only to awaken to find the King of Scotland himself setting camp outside the walls.

"Ceara has returned with Rafael," Hilda confessed, her excitement evident as she aided with the laces on Alys' widest kirtle. "And they mean to wed this very day!"

"Who decided as much?" Alys demanded, fearing that her friend was being compelled to wed the ruffian against her will.

"Rafael declared that Ceara had accepted him, it is said, before my lord Maximilian could insist upon it. 'Tis said he was warned twice to leave the women of Kilderrick untouched. Ach, my lady, you will need another kirtle soon. This one is just barely decent."

Alys looked down at the sides where her chemise was visible between the laces. "I will wear the short cloak this day," she decided and the maid nodded approval even as she turned to the trunk. Hilda, fortunately, could work even as she chattered, for she was much enamored of gossip and speculation. Indeed, Alys relied upon her for tidings of all those beneath Maximilian's hand.

"It is whispered Ceara herself seems most satisfied with the arrangement, my lady."

Alys wondered at that. Had Rafael taken Ceara by force? Alys would not have expected that crime from her husband's half-brother, but it was difficult to be certain. Ceara certainly had taunted him in the past, and had the better of him more than once. There had been an awareness between them, to be sure, and both possessed fiery tempers.

Perhaps they were well-matched.

"She kissed him of her own will in the bailey and fairly ran to prepare for the exchange of their vows," Hilda continued. "Do you think, my lady, that the course of love runs true? Perhaps they vexed each other previously to disguise their admiration."

"Perhaps," Alys ceded. "I should like to speak to her to be certain."

"Not so hasty, my lady. Your garters are yet unfastened and you must look your best when the king visits his lairdship. You will be on Laird Maximilian's left hand, after all."

Alys frowned, knowing that Hilda could make a feast of a crumb when she felt inclined. It might take hours for her attire to be deemed acceptable by her maid. Sadly, she was no longer sufficiently nimble to evade Hilda.

She would gather tidings instead. "Do you know why the king has arrived?"

"Has he need of a reason? Perhaps he wished to see how fine Kilderrick grows. Perhaps he desires it for himself!" Hilda smiled at that, though the notion sent a chill through Alys. "Perhaps he comes to confer with his lairdship or invite his assistance." She stood up, beaming as she surveyed Alys. "But he is here for the wedding feast, by virtue of his arrival this day."

Alys wondered at the timeliness of it all.

"And we are blessed indeed that Ceara and Royce hunted with such success yesterday," her maid continued. "There will be fare fit for a king this night! I hear Denis is hard at labor in the kitchens already."

"I must speak with Ceara, with all haste."

"I would add a finer trim to your kirtle, my lady. 'Twill take only a moment…"

"Immediately, Hilda. The kirtle is fine as it is."

The maid pouted a little. "Yves awaits you, my lady, outside the solar, to confirm the preparations, and he is nigh as impatient as you." The king's arrival would have Maximilian's châtelain in a fluster for he was much concerned with propriety, but Alys knew Yves' questions could not be evaded.

Yves was indeed waiting for her, and his queries began immediately —he would confirm the meal, the king's accommodation, the preparedness of the hall and the abundance of supplies, the seating at dinner and the arrangements for the chapel. He shared the concerns of Denis in ensuring that the fare suited the royal palate.

Alys tried to move down the corridor to the chamber shared by Nyssa and Ceara even as she allayed his concerns. Yves was not the sole obstacle, for the narrow passage was already congested as all within the keep approached the chapel. Servants, villagers and villeins crowded together, all chattering with excitement and moving toward the small family chapel at the other end of the keep. The king's men mingled in the crowd, identifiable by their gleaming armor and colorful tunics, and she could hear Maximilian's deep tones somewhere in proximity. The entire assembly moved slowly but steadily until the corridor filled and they were compelled to halt. The mood was merry and someone began to sing, the familiar tune taken up by the others gathered for the ceremony.

In the distance, Alys saw Ceara appear from her chamber—which was nearer the chapel—her hair brushed to a red gleam. Alys shouted, but her call was lost in the din.

"How lovely she looks," Hilda said, sighing at the romance of it all. "There is naught so fine as a wedding, is there, my lady?"

Rafael awaited Ceara at the portal before the chapel, that jewelled cross gleaming on his tabard and his expression filled with satisfaction. He might have been claiming a king's hoard. His appearance was striking, given his dark good looks and his dark tabard with gem upon it.

Alys saw him smile as Ceara approached him, then he kissed Ceara's hand.

Did Ceara wed him willingly? Alys moved forward, excusing herself as she tried to make progress.

The chapel itself was a small space, intended for the family of Kilderrick alone, and the king would have filled it to overflowing with his closest retinue. The wedding vows would be exchanged before the doors where more could witness them. Alys watched Rafael draw Ceara closer to his side and wished she could see her friend's expression. She spotted Nyssa, halfway between herself and the chapel, obviously trying to reach Ceara, as well.

Maximilian appeared then at the summit of the stairs with the king by his side. The king continued toward the chapel at Maximilian's gesture, while he waited for Alys. The crowd parted to make way for the king, who halted alongside Rafael. In the moving throng of well-wishers, Maximilian was like a rock that all flowed around—and his very presence commanded the company to make way for Alys. She was glad to feel the strength of her husband's hand close over her own.

"Is she happy?" she asked in a whisper.

"That is of no import," Maximilian replied quietly. "She has been claimed and he will not defy me again on Kilderrick's soil." He flicked her a look as cold as steel. "It is done."

"But her happiness must be assured!"

"She accepted him willingly, by all appearances." Maximilian drew her closer to his side as they approached the couple and the chapel. His voice dropped to a low murmur. "Fret not, Alys, I believe they are well-suited, though it may not be affection that draws them together."

"What then?"

"Desire?" He shrugged with an indifference Alys did not share. "It can only be this way, Alys. You must see as much. She has lost her maidenhead and he must wed her. This is no battlefield or realm where the laird's edict can be defied. I will not tolerate as much."

"Not even by your half-brother."

Maximilian's lips tightened. "Especially by him."

Alys sighed, knowing he was right but hoping Ceara would be happy with her match. They reached the doors of the chapel and the priest nodded a greeting. Then Ceara turned and smiled, her eyes lighting with a pleasure that even Alys could not deny.

Relief flooded through Alys at this sign that Ceara desired the match. Though Alys doubted it could be a happy one, it was her friend's choice and her husband's dictate, and so it would be. If Ceara ever came to her for aid, Alys would welcome her. That and a proper wedding was the best she could offer her friend.

Alys hoped it would be enough.

As the priest raised his hands to welcome all, Alys said a prayer for Ceara's future.

CHAPTER 8

*C*eara had never been one to dream of her nuptials or her future husband. Given that her betrothed had first been William, a feeble young man of no allure at all, and later Edward, a sly man with no regard for her, this was no surprise. Ceara had dreamed instead of a life of her own choosing, one in which she was unfettered by betrothals and obligations. That destiny might be available to her after she was widowed, perhaps. After being sworn to Edward, she had even imagined how she might ensure that she was widowed sooner rather than later. Her mother had spoken often of her love for her husband and Ceara's father, as well as of her hope that Ceara should also know a great love. For years, Ceara had assumed that to be impossible.

And yet she stood, her hands clasped in Rafael's strong grip, and found herself tempted to believe. Rafael had saved her from Edward. He had lied for her and he had killed for her. Despite his insistence, she could not believe he felt naught for her at all—much less that her instinctive trust of him was misplaced. What would it be like to win his heart in truth? She already guessed that nights in his bed would be wondrous, but how much better would any mating be if their hearts were allied? As she made her vows to honor and obey this man she barely knew, Ceara felt her heart fill with hope for a marriage based upon love.

With Rafael.

To her thinking, she had until they claimed the treasure to seduce him fully, both to consummate their match and capture his heart. She did not doubt the challenge would be considerable but the glint in his eyes as he smiled down at her only fueled her hope.

Ceara had given Rafael a glimpse of the key on the lace around her neck when they met at the chapel doors, proof that she kept her pledge, and he had nodded approval. She liked how they could be in agreement so readily or even anticipate each other's actions. She admired that he felt no need to insist that she be feminine and demure—indeed, he seemed to admire that she hunted and rode with confidence. He had brought her back her dagger, so was not offended that she knew how to use it.

There was promise in this match, a promise that Rafael himself might not yet see, but Ceara would convince him of it. She was already certain that she would never meet another man like him. What if she could seduce him? What if their match could not be annulled? What if their lives were bound together for all eternity?

The very notion made her dizzy.

It was not that far to the sanctuary of the treasure—it might take them a week with the Compagnie Rouge riding with them, or it could be reached more quickly if they departed alone.

What precisely was his plan? Ceara did not doubt that Rafael had one.

Undoubtedly, he had several more to address surprises and eventualities. She liked that she could rely upon him to anticipate challenges—and prepare for them.

In the meantime, what would he expect of her? Would he be fool enough to expect her to be a biddable wife and to forget her own opinions, to agree with him always?

"You smile," he whispered when their vows were made and he kissed her cheeks in turn. "What jest have you planned at my expense?"

"None!" She smiled as his brows lifted. "I hope only that you do not expect obedience in truth, dear husband. To be biddable is not my greatest skill, much less my inclination."

"You cannot think that to be a revelation to me." He took her hand and turned her as the priest swept open the chapel doors. That man led them to the altar, the king following, then Alys and Maximilian behind. As they walked together, Rafael cast her a sidelong glance and spoke in a low murmur. "But who knows what will change?"

"I will not."

"Nay? But there may truly be a miracle performed in this chapel on this day. One can never discount the possibility of divine intervention." His eyes were sparkling and Ceara fought her urge to laugh at his playful manner.

"You cannot wish me to submit to your will in all matters."

"Never," he replied, his tone silky and guided her to kneel before the altar. His eyes glinted when he leaned toward her. "I like naught better than a rousing contest of wills, as you undoubtedly suspect."

"I wager we will have more than one." Ceara said and his smile flashed.

"I think there is no uncertainty in that, *bella*." He eyed her, the admiration in his gaze heating her to her toes, and Ceara could not find a single objection to that scheme. "I should be disappointed if you became docile."

"Why?"

He leaned close, his breath against her ear. "Because there is no triumph in claiming what is readily surrendered," he said, his voice so dark that she shivered with delight. "A conquest over adversity is always sweeter."

Ceara bowed her own head as her face flushed.

Then Rafael continued, his voice so soft that only she would hear his murmured words. "Not that there will be a conquest in this case."

She blinked, fighting to ensure that her dismay did not show. The fact was that she enjoyed Rafael's company and his bold assumptions. His scheme, to retrieve the treasure and leave her wealthy in a place of her choice, was the best and fairest offer she had ever received from a man. Though 'twas possible he told a tale concocted to ensure her compliance, Ceara did not believe that to be the case. He really did intend to follow that plan, then return to his former life, granting her the ability to live as she chose.

The key brushed against her breasts, cool and heavy, and Ceara reminded herself how much had changed in a mere day.

She dared to hope that it could change markedly more by the time the mermaid's secret was claimed.

~

RAFAEL WAS impatient with the formalities, but he understood that it would be folly to vex Maximilian.

Yet.

He smiled as he made his vows, he nodded and he accepted the blessing of the mass. He shook hands and welcomed the felicitations of laird and lady, king and companions, of villagers and villeins and servants. He noted that Nyssa, the blond woman who had lived in the forest with Alys and Ceara, seemed discontent. He did not fail to observe that Ceara avoided her former companions. When Alys might have spoken to Ceara after the service, Rafael stole a kiss, one that left his new lady flushed and silent, her eyes sparkling with wonder.

He escorted her to the hall, making a triumphant procession of it. The king was seated at Maximilian's right with Alys at the laird's left, while Ceara and Rafael were seated in the middle of the other long table, facing the other trio. They were surrounded by well-wishers as they crossed the floor of the hall to their places, and he guessed that Ceara was popular at Kilderrick. A toast was called immediately and cups raised.

In mere hours they would be gone, and though Rafael itched to hasten away from Kilderrick, he dared give no hint of his intentions. The king was seated opposite Ceara and seemed most intent upon studying her, a bad sign to Rafael's thinking. She might have been a riddle he was determined to solve.

Darkness could not fall soon enough.

He would not give one hint of his impatience to be gone.

~

THAT RING.

Maximilian sat at the board beside Alys, wondering at Rafael's choice. He knew his brother well enough to recognize that it was not a coincidence that Ceara now wore the ring that was the sole token Rafael possessed from his mother. They had jested over the years that Rafael would only surrender that ring when he was dead or when his finger was sliced from his hand. It was not overly valuable in itself, being a mere circle of gold, but it represented much to Rafael.

Even Maximilian did not know the fullness of that tale, but he knew there was one.

And why Ceara?

Who was the maiden who had been Alys' companion in the forest? What had been her life before she came alone to Kilderrick and found shelter in the forest? Maximilian did not know and he was uncertain Alys knew more—but he could not ask her outright with the king by his side. That man was staring at Ceara as if he would draw a tale from her by force of will.

Was a secret identity the reason Rafael had wed her? Maximilian was well aware of his brother's views of marriage and they did not include Rafael ever pledging himself to a single woman.

There was something of great import that Maximilian did not know, and it was far more than a passing detail.

"I must say that I am relieved," the king said heartily after the health of the new couple had been toasted. He drained his cup and Maximilian nodded to Yves, who already hastened to refill it.

"Indeed, my lord?" Maximilian said, uncertain what could have soothed the royal spirits.

"When I heard the Compagnie Rouge arrived in Scotland, I feared their intention, and when I heard they made for Kilderrick, I confess I imagined the worst."

"My loyalty, your majesty, is beyond question."

The king did not reply to that, but only chuckled. "To think that an entire army would set sail from France, simply so their commander could claim a bride." He toasted them again and drained the cup once more. "Theirs must be a love worthy of a bard's tale."

"There was an attraction between them from the first," Alys said with authority, prompting the king to glance her way. She smiled.

"When my husband first came to Kilderrick last fall, Rafael and Ceara were often together."

"But he left her behind all the same."

"I never imagined my half-brother would wed," Maximilian said.

The king laughed. "But the heart will not be denied. Excellent!" He quaffed another cup of ale, then complimented Maximilian upon it.

"There is a skilled brewster in Rowan Fell. We were fortunate this day that she had a new batch of ale available."

"Fortunate indeed. This is most fine." Again, the king sipped with enthusiasm. "Tell me," he said then, his tone becoming somber. "Who is the bride? Has she kin in these parts?"

Maximilian gave Alys a nudge beneath the table. The change of the king's tone warned him that this was a matter of concern. "She has been a companion of my lady wife these many years."

"But who is her family? From whence does she hail?"

"We do not know, your majesty," Alys said politely. "There were four of us who took shelter together in the forests."

The king wagged a finger at her. "And one was Elizabeth d'Acron of Beaupoint, an heiress in her own right. I have not forgotten that detail."

"But we knew her only as Elizabeth," Alys said.

"How can this be? You must have spoken of your various histories!"

Alys shook her head. "We had an agreement never to do as much. I assumed that the others were as content to keep their secrets as I was."

"But you must have wondered," the king persisted.

"There are women aplenty who find themselves assailed by men when they would rather not be," Alys said quietly. "The tale is sufficiently common that one need not share it."

The king was not content with this. "You must know something of the bride, beyond her uncommon beauty."

Why was the king so determined to know more of Ceara? Maximilian did not trust this curiosity a whit.

"She has a skill with horses," Alys said. "And is a fine huntress. Beyond that, I know only her friendship."

"Horses," the king mused and sipped of his ale, watching Ceara with narrowed eyes. "And a huntress."

"Is either of import, my lord?"

"Likely not," the king replied with a smile. "But if she is local to Kilderrick, both are uncommon. There are so many more ponies in these parts and few women have been taught to ride to hunt."

"Perhaps she came from the south," Alys said with a shrug. "Or even the east."

"Perhaps," the king mused, then turned a cool smile upon Maximilian. "If I did not know better, I might guess she was a nobleman's daughter, though I do not know of one missing." The king considered this then continued easily. "As mentioned, I find myself relieved that this army comes only for a wedding."

"And they will depart within two days," Maximilian felt obliged to note.

"Do they?" The king nodded. "That is most satisfactory. One can never be too accepting of a military force of uncertain loyalties within one's own realm." He turned then to meet Maximilian's gaze, his own steady and cool. "I find you a welcome ally, Maximilian de Vries, but should I find myself compelled to choose between established and newfound alliances, you may be sure that history will rule the day."

"I understand, my lord," Maximilian said, holding the king's gaze as he took note of the warning. He felt Alys' agitation and claimed her hand, raising his cup as he hailed the company. "A toast to the good health and long life of the happy couple," he cried, and the call was taken up by the company.

There was something about horses that had stirred the king's recollection.

Maximilian wondered whether Rafael knew what it was.

"He stares at me," Ceara murmured and Rafael smiled as if she spoke of the meal.

"Perhaps he has not seen such a beautiful bride in a long while."

"I make no jest," she said with some agitation. "'Twill all go awry."

Rafael caught her chin in one hand and leaned close. The company hooted as he claimed a long and sultry kiss, then he withdrew only an increment. "Not unless you give cause," he whispered to her, his words hot.

Her lips parted then closed again, her flush hinting that he had aroused her with that kiss. She swallowed and obviously strove to appear calm, but Rafael was not fooled.

She was fearful, his bold huntress, and if any other guessed as much, they would wonder why.

"We must leave," she whispered, her gaze flicking to the other table.

"We will when our departure raises no suspicion, *bella*," he confessed, then kissed her soundly again. He kissed her until her lips softened against his, until her arms stole around his neck, ignoring how the company cheered and stamped. He kissed her until he felt the resolve grow within her and her determination rise, until she kissed him back and he knew that familiar fire would be in her eyes. By then, his own heart was thundering and he caressed her cheek as he broke their kiss. "Trust me," he instructed soundlessly, the words barely moving his lips.

She smiled, flushed and nodded meekly, appearing to be so biddable that even Rafael was nearly fooled.

He caught Maximilian's gaze and saw a warning in his brother's eyes. What had the king said to him? Rafael itched with impatience to be gone.

The king certainly could not have found fault with the feast. There had been endless courses and even now, the last of them, tarts with apples and custard, was being removed. A goodly quantity of ale had been imbibed, and candles had been lit when darkness fell.

Soon.

The musicians from the village appeared to a rousing greeting and the tables were cleared so they could be folded away. Rafael escorted Ceara to one side of the room, calculating how few dances were required before they left the hall without looking like they fled.

Matteo appeared beside Rafael, and Rafael guessed that his former comrade had tidings to share. "No sign," he murmured to Ceara, who cast him a smile and pretended to be enthralled by the musicians.

He had no doubt she listened.

"Ale was sent to the Compagnie Rouge," Matteo informed Rafael.

His choice of Norman French meant that others might listen, as well. "And a number of dishes from the kitchen that they might also celebrate the day."

"That is most generous of our host."

The other warrior lowered his voice and changed to Venetian. "I suspect he wants rid of you, and would give you no cause for complaint."

Rafael smiled into his cup of ale, keeping his voice low. "We will be gone soon enough."

"How soon?"

Rafael only held Matteo's gaze.

The other man's eyes lit. "Take me with you," he whispered with urgency. "This is no life for me. I should never have lingered."

Rafael nodded once. "Make haste," he counselled. "Bring your steed and the lady's possessions as well."

"They will guess."

"Nay. Use the excuse that you have sold your horse to me for my wife, as I have always admired it." Rafael smiled. "You could say that you wish to collect the coin before I change my offer. As all know, I am cursed unreliable."

Matteo chuckled. "Not you!"

Ceara cast Rafael a glance that proved she did not understand.

The other man's expression lit. "I could linger to hear the tidings from my former comrades."

Rafael nodded. "Take word that my lady desires a bath this night. It must appear that we intend to remain the full time Maximilian has allotted to us, or even longer in defiance."

Matteo nodded and straightened, clapping along with the music as he watched the dance. Rafael felt the weight of Maximilian's gaze and feigned surprise when he found his half-brother watching him. He raised his cup in salute, gestured to the hall and kissed the fingertips of his other hand in gratitude. The laird smiled reluctantly, then nodded before turning to the king. That man's gaze lingered on Ceara but Rafael disguised his unease.

They had to depart. He dared not delay much longer.

"What is happening?" Ceara asked in a murmur, leaning toward him as if she would claim a kiss when Matteo stepped away.

"We dance but once," Rafael murmured, offering his hand to her rather than answering. "Then retire." He let his gaze sweep over her. "I find myself most ardent this night."

"Even for a maiden, sir. I am surprised." She nodded with uncharacteristic meekness and took his hand. "As you wish, husband."

Rafael sensed that she mocked him in this, but there was no mischief in her gaze. What scheme did his biddable bride possess? He would truss her and toss her over the saddle himself if she tried to impede their swift and secretive departure. He would defend her to his last breath—and every warrior of his acquaintance, even those who knew him by reputation alone, would recognize that she was his weakness by that very fact alone.

Truly, Rafael had begun to suspect that this magnificent woman with her fiery nature and fierce resolve, with her determination to challenge him and her ability to entice him, might be his ideal partner —if he had ever intended to be with any woman for more than a night or two. The very notion was troubling, which meant he had to keep it well hidden.

Ceara was sufficiently clever that she might guess the truth.

Better she believed that he wed her for the treasure and was as ruthless a scoundrel as he was reputed to be—not a man in peril of losing his heart, the heart no one believed he possessed.

And that was a secret Rafael would take with him to his grave.

RAFAEL'S TENT was almost empty in marked contrast to the previous night. For a moment, Ceara thought she had entered the wrong tent. Most of the chests were gone and the carpets had vanished. The bed had disappeared and there was only a single lantern, hanging from the wood that supported the canvas. It was muddy underfoot and chilly.

This undermined her scheme of seduction. She had planned to greet him nude, adorned with only the key on its chain, in the hope that base desire would lead to the consummation she desired. But in this muck? She was reluctant to drop her cloak to the ground.

Even as Ceara stared about herself, Rafael's squire opened the last remaining trunk and unpacked items from it with efficient gestures. He set out a plain tunic, along with a dark cloak and sturdy boots. Rafael's hauberk was laid out for him, arranged on the open lid, and the padded aketon he wore beneath the hauberk. This mystified Ceara. The squire spoke to her, but in a language she could not decipher—was it the same one Rafael had used earlier with Raynard and Matteo?—and she could not say whether he meant to reassure her or warn her. In the next moment, the boy bowed and left the tent.

Why did Rafael need his armor?

Was he going to abandon her so soon as this?

What about the mermaid's secret? She had been sure he desired the treasure.

Rafael laughed with his comrades at close proximity, accepting their congratulations, but Ceara hesitated to embark upon her plan of seduction. She unfastened the cloak she had flung over her shoulders before leaving Kilderrick and shivered at the chill in the air.

To undress might be folly.

But she had to persuade Rafael to meet her abed. It was the sole way to ensure that the law would be on her side if he chose to leave her.

She was untying the laces on her kirtle when he appeared suddenly, ducking into the tent and halting to stare. "What is this you do?" he asked tersely.

He carried a small bag and his manner was impatient. The boy followed him, rapidly unlacing the back of his tunic even where Rafael stood.

"It is our nuptial night," she said with care, troubled that she had to remind him as much.

He shook his head, but that scarce reassured her. The crucifix disappeared and Rafael shrugged into his aketon and hauberk, tugging the plain tabard over top. She had never imagined a man could change his garb so quickly. Indeed, he might have forgotten her presence.

The boy held Rafael's plain tall black boots as Rafael fastened his belt. He flung the cloak over his shoulder and was once again the unpredictable warrior whose presence stirred her very soul.

He surveyed her, smiling a little at her obvious confusion. "We will not linger here this night," he whispered, then indicated the back of his tent. She followed him and his touch revealed a place where the cloth overlapped. He pulled it back and she was startled to see that the camp behind his tent was gone. The boy packed away Rafael's more elaborate garb and departed with the final trunk. Ceara saw the silhouettes of two horses and heard their trap.

"We ride," Rafael whispered when she met his gaze, barely mouthing the words.

Ceara was both relieved and disappointed.

"Do you not wish to leave the king, with his curiosity, behind?"

"Of course, but it is our wedding night."

"Ours is no conventional match, *bella*."

The squire returned with another man, both of them working together to strike the tent. Even as the cloth wavered over her head, Ceara hesitated to step into the night.

"Immediately, *bella*," Rafael added with a measure of heat and she understood that he interpreted her hesitation as resistance.

"But my palfrey is in Kilderrick's stables."

"She is your steed no longer. You ride with me."

"But..."

"I could not secure her without arousing suspicion. If possible, she will be restored to you later."

Ceara was pleased that he had even considered the matter. "I must have my chausses."

He smiled and presented the small bag he carried. "Now," he mouthed and she opened the drawstring with haste. Her belongings were inside it, her few clothes bundled together with haste by someone else.

Who?

Ceara tugged out her chausses and kicked off one boot. Rafael waved to the men who left the tent. He then untied one lace of her kirtle while she finished unknotting the first. In moments, her kirtle was packed away along with the fine belt, and she was dressed as was her custom, in her chausses, boiled jerkin and boots, her cloak thrown over her shoulders and her knife in her belt.

At a murmur from Rafael, the boy returned and took the bundle of her garments with a bow. The others reappeared and continued to strike the tent.

Rafael touched a finger to his lips and she nodded understanding. She ducked out the back of the tent with her hand held fast in Rafael's strong grip. Phantôm was saddled and waiting. She quickly braided her hair as Rafael spoke quietly with a cloaked man. They watched the last tent fall with obvious approval, then Rafael gestured. The other man mounted his steed and she recognized first Matteo's destrier, then that warrior himself when his hood fell back.

Meanwhile Rafael pivoted to grip her around the waist and lift her to the saddle. The sole tent remaining was the large one that blocked the view of the others. Rafael's tent was bundled up with remarkable speed. The horses had vanished as well as the squires and most of the men, only mud left in the shadow of the great tent. Rafael's squire was the last one, hurriedly packing the last of Rafael's possessions.

"I trust I seized all of import," Matteo said softly to Ceara, nodding at her attire.

"Aye," she acknowledged with a grateful smile. "Thank you."

To her surprise, he flicked back his cloak and revealed that he had her bow as well. Rafael swung into the saddle behind her in that moment and Ceara asked Matteo to keep the weapon for her. She had her dagger, which would be sufficient. Rafael's arm locked around her waist again, his heat and strength reassuring her. He would defend her again as he had this day and she knew it, no matter how he insisted upon reminding her of his chosen trade.

He waited until his squire climbed into his palfrey's saddle then clicked his tongue. The three horses moved toward the river, Matteo beside Rafael and the squire fast behind. They moved soundlessly into the shadows and the other two horses dropped behind as Rafael rode south along the stream's banks.

Ceara's heart was skipping but she was glad to leave Kilderrick and the king behind. Her sole regret was that she had not had the opportunity to talk to Nyssa, but that woman would understand.

And in truth, they embarked on an adventure, in pursuit of her family legacy. There was no better partner to undertake this quest with her than Rafael, a notion which made her smile. Though he was a warrior and a mercenary, a rogue with a small army for hire, she trusted him, not just to keep their wager but to see her protected.

Was that folly? Ceara could not be certain but she already suspected that she would never regret whatever passed between herself and this man. He was like no other she had met and she was thrilled to ride with him.

Aye, he spoke aright. Peril made her feel more alive and Ceara could never regret that.

THE COMPANY RODE south in darkness and comparative silence. The moon was waxing to its first quarter but the skies were overcast and the wind was wild. They kept close to the river, the horses guided into the water at intervals to disguise their scent. Tree branches tossed overhead and Rafael caught glimpses of the dark turmoil of the clouds overhead.

"Will you make camp before it rains?" Ceara asked quietly when Kilderrick was miles behind them.

Truly, Rafael was astonished that she had remained silent for so long. "Nay."

"The storm will be a violent one," she continued. "We will be soaked to the skin."

"And yet we will be alive. That must be of some merit."

She twisted to look at him, her gaze searching. "Do you think the king guessed?"

"Not while we were there, but I would be beyond his reach when he discovers the truth."

She nodded and turned around again. Her agitation in the hall was banished with distance and she was once again the huntress he so admired. "You ride for Carlisle," she said finally, which was sufficiently close to the truth for Rafael to agree. "Where is the rest of the Compagnie Rouge?"

"They await us ahead."

"At the clearing, where the river bends to the east," she guessed with an accuracy Rafael found unsettling. She must have sensed his surprise, for he heard the dismissive sound she uttered. "'Tis the only place large enough for such a company to gather," she chided, as if his surprise was due to an assumption that she was witless. In truth, he preferred to hold his secrets close and 'twas troubling to have a comparative stranger spy them so readily. "You forget that I have ridden to Carlisle many times these past years."

"And done so without detection," he agreed. "But I did not doubt your skill."

"What then?" She glanced over her shoulder when he did not immediately reply.

He smiled. "I am not accustomed to having my secrets discerned."

She laughed a little. "Then you should disguise them better. The location of your men cannot be much of a secret, given that there is only the one place sufficiently large for them to gather. And they cannot have ridden far without your leadership." She shook her head. "Any soul who knew these lands would have guessed their location.

That was a chilling assertion, for no doubt those who served the king were familiar with the area. Rafael recalled that Ceara was no stranger to keeping secrets herself and found it curious that they shared this trait. She had been reluctant to share the tale of the mermaid's treasure and still he wondered what details she had not surrendered.

More importantly, in this moment, he realized the import of her experience. It was the routine of the Compagnie Rouge to hire guides when they entered unfamiliar territories, often young boys who knew the main roads and the hidden ones. He had been uneasy that he knew these lands so poorly, no asset when a king's men might be in pursuit. But Ceara was the resource they needed this night.

"You know these lands well," he said and she nodded immediately.

"I have ridden to Carlisle at least twice per year this past decade, often more."

Rafael, in contrast, had undertaken that journey only a few times, most times with the Compagnie Rouge and thus on larger roads. He had endeavored to follow Ceara to Carlisle once—when she had stolen the very horse he rode this night—but had never even glimpsed her before his return to Kilderrick.

She knew the smaller paths, to be sure.

"Chart our course," Rafael invited and she started.

"Me?"

"Who else? I know only the large roads, but we will not evade detection upon them."

"Though our passage will be faster." She considered the question for a moment. "It is a question of speed or stealth."

"As is so often the situation."

"If you would ride to Carlisle, it would be best…"

"Nay," he said, interrupting her. "We would ride around Carlisle and enter England without detection. Secrecy is the greater concern on this night."

The bend in the river became clear ahead of them. There was no sign of the Compagnie Rouge, but Rafael had no doubt they awaited him there. "And where do you go in England?" Ceara asked.

"Must you know?"

She fixed him with a look that was surprisingly stern. "I trusted you in leaving Kilderrick. You must trust me in sharing our destination, that I might ensure we reach it more quickly even in stealth."

Rafael chose to take the risk. It was admittedly small. "Beaupoint." Beyond that, he was uncertain as there were several ports, but they would decide once there.

Perhaps Amaury would have counsel for him.

"Elizabeth's home, held now by Amaury." Her glance was quick and thoughtful. "Will he aid you?"

"Who can say?" There was the nut of the matter. There was little affection between himself and that half-brother, but it was too late to regret any choices of the past. He needed little from Amaury beyond information and haven for a night.

Though Rafael knew even that might be too much to ask.

"He might arrest you or summon the king," she said, echoing Rafael's own concerns. "I did not think there was much fondness between you."

"But there is blood and a vow of which I will readily remind him."
At her obvious doubt, Rafael dropped his voice. "I do not intend to
linger. He will grant my desire willingly to see us gone from his
borders."

"And if he would arrest you instead?"

Rafael smiled. "I wish him luck."

Ceara studied him for a moment, then nodded. "I do not know
Beaupoint's location, though."

"Yves said the keep overlooks the firth. He thought Amaury must
have seen our arrival."

"Then it cannot be difficult to find."

It was Rafael's turn to nod.

"I would turn east from here instead of riding south," she said with
conviction. "For then we would be hidden by the forest. There is a trail
that leads ultimately to Bewcastle."

"I remember hearing tell of it last year."

"Of greater import is that it passes no towns or farms. We will be
able to reach the border without detection."

"But the Scottish king summoned Maximilian to Bewcastle last fall.
Is it not a busy keep?"

"It is a large keep but not a well-tended one. It falls to the king's
hand, for there is no current lord there. It is a shelter, no more and no
less, and likely used by others than the king. While he is at Kilderrick, it
undoubtedly lies empty save for the creatures of the forest." She cast
him one of those wicked smiles. "Even I have taken shelter there, when
it suited me."

Rafael nodded, indebted to her knowledge of the terrain. "And
then?"

"At the southern end of the forest, we will be close to the border.
The land is cleared on either side of the old Roman wall that marks the
old border."

"And the current border?"

"It is in dispute and moves often, depending upon the dictate of
either king. We should cross the wall and ride south a goodly distance
before turning west." She looked up at the sky. "You should know that

the lands around Bewcastle are frequented by reivers. It is known as the Bewcastle Waste."

Rafael felt his protective urge rise. "But you have ridden through it alone?"

Ceara cast him a quick smile. "Not of late. It has been years since I came this way. It may be perilous."

"We are mercenaries, *bella*."

"Aye, but I did not wish for you to be surprised." She looked up. "The moon is just past new and there are sufficient clouds that we should be unnoticed. How quick is your party?"

"Not as quick as a rider alone, to be sure."

"We should make the wall by daybreak."

"And Beaupoint?"

She cast him a confident smile. "You will be able to dine with your half-brother three nights hence, no matter how circuitous our path."

Rafael chuckled. "Assuming he invites me to his board at all."

"That, sir, is your challenge, not mine." He saw her sit taller before him and scarce heard her murmured words. "You must be in the habit of hiring guides in a new locale."

"Aye," he agreed warily.

"Do you pay them?"

Rafael felt his eyes narrow. "Of course."

"Then I will take a tale as my compensation." She held up her left hand and he noted the challenge in her manner even before she spoke. "Tell me the import of this ring."

CHAPTER 9

$\mathcal{I}$t has none," Rafael protested, but Ceara only scoffed. "Then why did Maximilian so comment upon it? He was surprised that you bestowed it upon me. The ring has significance and you will not convince me otherwise."

Rafael shrugged, striving to dismiss her interest in this particular tale. "Perhaps he was surprised that I surrendered it, for I own only the one ring. There. You have your tale and owe me three days guidance."

"Nay," Ceara insisted with a confidence that surprised him. "It cannot be that valuable in itself. It has an emotional import, like the crucifix that you wear to recall the person who surrendered it to you."

Rafael's heart chilled at her perceptiveness.

She twisted around to face him. "Who *did* surrender it to you?"

He could only make a jest to deter her. "You wish that tale as well? Your guidance becomes expensive, *bella*. Perhaps I should leave you here and take my chances with the southern road."

"I simply learn from your example. The longer the negotiation, the more the price increases."

"But only if your services are indispensable."

"You need me."

"We shall see." His voice dropped to a low growl and he felt her shiver in response. "Do not push overmuch, *bella*." In truth, the feel of her against him undermined his noble intentions and made him think of making camp, taking his pleasure, and accepting the consequences.

But not until they were out of harm's way. He had not come this far to lose all to mere lust.

"Yet you are claiming the lion's share of my legacy." Ceara glanced back at him. For a moment, he thought her unaware of his turmoil, but then she ground her hips against his lap, a knowing gleam in her eyes. If she tried to seduce him, he knew he would be lost. "Be warned, sir. I will know the importance of both pieces before our ways part."

"Or?"

"Or we might not part at all, sir." She ran her hand down his thigh, setting his very blood afire with her caress. "I will not forget that you owe me a tale, and I never leave a debt uncollected. You might surrender the tale simply to be rid of me."

He might.

They reached the perimeter of the clearing and Rafael spotted his men hidden in the shadows. "You have not gotten us to Beaupoint yet, let alone all of us hale and uninjured."

"Nor have we claimed the mermaid's reputed treasure. It seems we both have debts outstanding, each to the other."

She was so confident and beautiful that Rafael could not entirely stifle his smile. "You dare much, bella, in tempting the dragon," he warned and she laughed.

"Aye, I do. What is the merit of waking another day if one does not live each hour fully?"

Rafael had no reply to that, which clearly pleased his companion.

She tapped his shoulder with a fingertip. "You will tell me both tales and willingly, the first when we reach Beaupoint. The second you can save for after the treasure is retrieved."

"You have no shortage of conviction in our success."

"With your boldness and skill, and my knowledge, I cannot doubt it." She surveyed the waiting company in the shadows. "Summon your men. 'Twill not be my fault if they are left behind. Speed and silence are both of import this night."

With that, she snatched the reins from his own hands and spoke to Phantôm. The beast listened to her, as if she had trained it and not

Rafael, but Rafael did not interfere. If naught else, he trusted her understanding of horses. He could always command the destrier to halt and the creature would follow his bidding over hers.

Rafael gripped Ceara's hips and let her guide the steed across the river, then beckoned to the Compagnie Rouge with an imperious gesture. They moved immediately out of the shadows. He felt rather than heard them close in behind Phantôm and was impressed yet again by how stealthily the vast company could move.

The sky was churning with dark clouds, reminding him of his first arrival at Kilderrick. At least there would be no witch's trap this time. The wind gusted and a tree cracked in the distance, then the first cold drops of rain came pelting down upon them. Ceara did not acknowledge it, so intent was she upon guiding the horse. Rafael saw the shadowed trail only in the last moment before they plunged into the shadows of the forest. It was dark all around them, but Ceara clicked her tongue and the destrier trotted onward. The company followed behind them, the wheels of the carts creaking.

She had to be as tired as he but she gave no sign of faltering. Perhaps it was because she led them now and felt the responsibility to succeed. Having surrendered the lead, Rafael felt the full weight of his exhaustion. He had dined with Maximilian, pursued Ceara and her captor, returned to Kilderrick, taken a bride and departed that keep in darkness. He ached from so many hours in the saddle and only as Kilderrick and the king fell into the distance behind them, would he let the tension ease from his shoulders.

Had their departure been unobserved? He had been in his trade too long to have many doubts.

Rafael closed his eyes to listen as the forest closed around them. He knew that doing as much made him more keenly aware of his other senses. It certainly made the press of Ceara's curved buttocks against his thighs much more difficult to ignore, much less the satisfactory feel of her hips beneath his hands. He was tempted to grip her more tightly and draw her close, but he told himself that he would not distract her from her task.

Closing his eyes also sharpened his hearing and he willed himself to pay attention to the sounds around them instead of imagining what he might do with Ceara—or how he might persuade her to give that cry of pleasure again.

Rafael was not surprised when he heard the faint sound of pursuit. One horse. One rider. A messenger, a spy or an assassin? A reiver riding alone? Or a villain in the service of another?

Only time would reveal the truth.

THE HAIR on the back of Ceara's neck prickled. If she had ridden alone, she would have concluded that danger stalked her path. Since she was so keenly aware of Rafael behind her, it was possible that peril was much closer. His hands rested on her hips, his grip firm but not tight, and she could feel his warm strength against her back. The power of his thighs pressed against hers and 'twas impossible to forget his presence, much less to keep herself from recalling the surety of his caress.

More seductive than his proximity, though, was his trust. She was pleased that he let her guide his company and she would not fail him. The path was wreathed in shadows, the forest uncommonly quiet. There should have been more creatures afoot on a night lit by this silvery crescent of a moon, but Ceara felt that the very forest was watchful. The Compagnie Rouge was quiet and she could not complain about their passage.

Bewcastle Waste, though, felt haunted to her.

They rode for hours beneath the chilly onslaught of rain, and the horses had trudged through so much mud that they were mired to the knees. The wagons became stuck only once, to Ceara's surprise, but the men had not even spoken as they freed them from the mud. Their progress was a given and each man knew his task. Despite the twisted path Ceara had led, the company had moved steadily onward.

They passed several clearings that had been burned since last she had ridden this way. The fires were long cold, but the trees were yet charred and black. The rumors Ceara had heard at Kilderrick clearly were truth. The reivers had moved eastward after Kilderrick had become too much of an obstacle to their movements across the border.

They had chosen well, to her view, for there was no one to defy them in these lands.

Rafael took the reins at the first of these places, leading the destrier in a broad circle around the damaged ground. She wondered how much he could see in the moonlight, but 'twas evidently sufficient. She felt the sharp prick of his attentiveness and knew naught would surprise him this night.

They rode on, ever to the south and east, taking a convoluted path that they might not be readily followed. Once or twice, Ceara thought she heard something behind them, but it must have been an echo of the forest. Instead of hastening onward, Rafael urged her to slow their pace several times and she knew he listened.

At least the rain had stopped in the middle of the night, though she was still cold and wet. Rafael had wrapped his fur-lined cloak around them both, his arms locked around her waist, and the heat that rose between them did more than warm her flesh. She was tingling with his proximity, impatient to feel his hands upon her skin again. The softness of the fur against her chin made her recall other sensations, the weight of Rafael's hands upon her, the sure caress of his fingers in that most intimate locale.

Whenever they halted, she would pursue her scheme of temptation, meeting him adorned only with the key. He might insist that he had no inclination to sample maidens, but Ceara knew she could persuade him to forget his sole principle.

Truly, it was doubtful she would remain a maiden for long. She could scarce wait for Rafael's seduction. It could only be more wondrous than his kiss.

'Twas almost dawn when the company approached the lip of the forest. Ceara could see light ahead, piercing the shadows of the forest. The trees had been thinning for a while and the path growing steadily wider. When she looked up, there were larger gaps in the canopy and she could see the lightening of the sky overhead. They had made good time and covered a considerable distance, despite the many twists and turns she had chosen. She was impressed that the men had neither faltered nor complained, though she could not be the sole one who was tired beyond all.

"England lies just ahead," Ceara said. "We could cross the border immediately." She frowned when he did not reply. His breathing was slow and steady behind her, as if he slept, and had been thus for the entire ride. She twisted around to face him and his eyes flew open, their vivid blue startling her.

He nodded once, then captured the reins, drawing his destrier to an abrupt halt. The beast exhaled mightily and stamped a foot, but did not protest beyond that. Rafael was out of the saddle immediately, and Ceara smiled when he closed his hands around her waist and lifted her from the saddle.

"Show me," he commanded. His eyes were a vivid blue and his lips were drawn to a taut line. She seized his hand and drew him toward the edge of the forest, assuming he wished to see the territory ahead. Brambles snatched at them as they made their way through the last of the undergrowth and wet branches trailed against their garments. There was mud aplenty underfoot and a stream ran audibly nearby.

She halted in the last of the shadows, her heart leaping with triumph. They had emerged precisely where Ceara had planned to lead them. She was aware that every gaze was fixed upon Rafael, each member of the company awaiting his command in silence behind them.

"You know this place, *bella*?" he asked, sounding less pleased than she.

"Aye. It was my destination."

Flat pasture stretched before them for a long interval, the shadow of a forest on English soil appearing as a blurry haze in the distance. The open fields were divided by the old stone Roman wall that ran across their path, intact as far as Ceara could see to left and right. Clouds covered the sky and mist rose from the fields. The sky was growing steadily brighter to the east and had a pink tinge. There was not a living soul in view, save a hawk that circled lazily overhead.

"The Roman wall," she said to Rafael when there was only silence. When he did not reply to that, she gestured with impatience. "England lies ahead, just as you desired. We could be in that distant forest as the sun breaks free of the horizon."

He only frowned.

Her triumphant mood was clearly not shared.

143

Rafael took another step forward and fairly glared at the open space between forest and wall. What was his concern? There was no one to witness their passage and Ceara was impatient to leave Scotland—and Edward—behind. He scowled at the sky, then peered to the left and right before glancing down her. He did not look pleased. "How do we cross the wall?"

"It is not that tall…"

"Tall enough for a company with horses and wagons." He was curt, his eyes narrowed, his manner brusque.

He must not have noticed the two structures built into the wall. Ceara pointed to the right. "There is an old fort there, though a house has been built within its walls…"

"Nay," Rafael said flatly.

Ceara eyed him in confusion.

He spoke crisply. "Where there is an abode, there are eyes to see. We must cross another way."

She pointed left. "There is a ruined tower there, a milecastle. The wall is broken and a track passes through it. I have used it before."

Rafael peered into the distance, considering the structure and its distance. Still, he looked to be discontent. "How many times?"

"Only once. Usually, I take a more direct route to Carlisle, further to the west." She braced her hands on her hips. She was annoyed, not that he asked so many questions but at her sense that he did not trust her judgement. "Speed is of the greatest import when one would sell horses taken from reivers." If her tone was tart, he gave no sign that he noticed.

"How far?"

"Too far. In daylight, we could not pass Brampton unobserved and there is nowhere to hide and await darkness."

"Where else?"

"How many passages do you need?" Ceara asked with impatience. "Surely one would suffice?"

He granted her a steely glance. Something troubled him and she understood that he would not tell her of it.

"Those are the only breaches I know," she admitted. "To the west, the wall is more broken, but it will be impossible to avoid Lanercost

Priory. The Augustinian priors do not hold themselves in seclusion from the world."

"They do not," he mused. "On the contrary, it is their goal to mingle in society and provoke change."

"To ride north and circumvent it means our route last night was meaningless."

"And to the east?"

"I have never ridden so far as to find its end. Eventually there are more towns in that direction, and a road runs alongside the wall on its southern side."

Rafael nodded once, then pivoted to speak to his men, giving commands in that language she did not understand. Ceara stared after him, wondering why his manner had changed. The men began to dismount, clearly finding naught unusual in Rafael's manner. Some tended the horses, while others arranged the wagons and began to erect tents. They worked steadily and quietly, and she saw that the camp would be smaller than the one erected at Kilderrick.

"I can hunt..." she offered but Rafael shook his head before she could finish her words.

"There will be no fire, thus there will be no smoke," he said tersely and she guessed that the company was in the habit of traveling thus. "We have cheese and bread yet."

"But England..."

"Will wait until we can attain it in stealth. This day, we will sleep. We move at darkness."

Ceara was aware of the purposeful activity that surrounded her yet was at a loss herself. "What shall I do?"

"Naught. Be quiet and still, and do not leave this spot." He might have turned away, but paused and glanced back. He studied her as if realizing that last to be unlikely and to her relief, his expression thawed. "You must be tired."

"No more than you must be." Though she did not wish to appear as a burden, to her dismay, Ceara could not entirely stifle a yawn.

Rafael smiled, the sight making her heart thunder. "You are unaccustomed to our ways, *bella*," he said softly. His fingertip brushed her cheek and she fairly melted at his touch. "Aye, you did well," he murmured, evidently having noticed her response and Ceara did not care when his eyes glowed with such approval.

The weight of Rafael's hand fell upon her shoulder and he drew her against his chest, his arms closing around her. Ceara was only too content to step into his embrace, for his caress bode well for her planned seduction. She was encouraged that he was not indifferent to her and could only believe in the success of her plan.

Then he spoke, as if he had read her thoughts. "Do not look so satisfied, *bella*. I have not ceded to your scheme."

"What scheme?" she asked and he chuckled.

"I merely ensure there are no doubts of your role," he murmured against her temple, then his gloved hand was beneath her chin. His gaze bored into hers. "You might not been mine to savor, but neither will another in my company sample your charms."

His mouth closed over hers with possessive ease before she could speak, his kiss stirring her soul even more readily than before. How had she never guessed that such pleasure could be conjured with a touch? Ceara closed her eyes and surrendered to Rafael's embrace. She kissed him back, feeling the beat of his heart against her own, savoring the feel of his hand in her hair. His kiss was leisurely and thorough and she found herself wishing it might continue forever.

Ceara was breathless when Rafael broke the kiss, and the satisfaction simmering in his gaze warmed her to her toes. If his kiss was a feint to foster the belief that she was his woman in truth, Ceara did not care.

This very day, she would become his woman in truth.

"Tend Phantôm for me," he suggested gently and kissed her temple. "Then retire to my tent."

"Will you join me there?"

"Temptress," he teased, his gaze considering. "I will, with a surprise."

Ceara nodded agreement, her anticipation rising as he turned away. She saw that his squire was busily unloading his belongings. Rafael beckoned to Matteo and Raynard. The trio conferred but Ceara could not understand their words.

She led Phantôm to the central area where the horses were being tended. She was aware that the other three men watched her: there was the burly one, who Royce had called Lambret Bonecutter, the one missing a hand who Royce had called Helmut, and the more elegantly attired one who might have been a knight. He was handsome but surveyed her with an openness she distrusted. She gave him her most chilling glance and set to work.

The boys were becoming familiar, too. Rafael's squire had much to do, with his master's baggage to unpack and three bay palfreys to tend in addition to his own. Raynard's destrier was tended by another dark-haired squire, along with two palfreys. Lambret and Helmut tended their own destriers. A palfrey they evidently shared was tethered nearby. The mercenary knight had a stocky squire and two palfreys in addition to his own destrier. Despite his lofty appearance, he tended the destrier himself. The horses, to Ceara's satisfaction, were all healthy and well-fed, their coats glossy and their eyes bright. She was relieved to see the baskets of horse bread and oats brought from the wagons by the squires. Fresh water was carried from the stream for the beasts as well, and their tails swung as they were tended. Indeed, the destriers were as proud and vain as the men who rode them, their necks arched and their feet stamping.

Ceara brushed down Phantôm, taking reassurance from the familiar task. He was a sleek and beautiful creature, as well, well-bred and well-tended, and she liked the work. At Kilderrick, there was usually a squire or two eager to tend her palfrey after the hunt, though sometimes she managed to insist upon doing the work herself. Before Maximilian's arrival, she had only ridden the horses they stole and sold, and she had savored her long solitary rides to Carlisle. It had been a long time since she had taken care of a fine destrier.

The labor made her recall the home of her foster family, the smell of a clean barn in winter, the reassuring sounds of horses in the early morning. She thought of wild rides across the meadows and along the shore, days of wind and sunshine and fine horses. In a way, she missed that place and those days, of retiring with the slight ache of a solid day's labor, of the satisfaction to be found in simple pleasures.

The horses were surrounded by wagons and tents, confined in a central place, and other boys took away the saddles and packs. 'Twas clear there was a plan, such a well-established routine that no conversation was needed. The horses' tails swung and their ears flicked, both signs that they were accustomed to this rhythm. Once the horses were tended and eating contentedly, the men began to erect the tents. There would only be three raised on this day, Ceara saw, one of which was Rafael's. The contents of the wagons quickly disappeared within their shadows. The boys began to gather and cut branches of trees, adorned with new leaves, placing them around the camp to disguise its presence.

Who did Rafael expect to see them? Or was this a habitual choice?

Matteo returned to the cluster of horses and took up a brush to tend his own destrier, his movements impatient. It was only then that Ceara looked again for Rafael and she barely caught a glimpse of him. He was striding around the camp, instructing the boys in the placement of the boughs. He laughed at a comment from one of them and ruffled the boy's hair, then his gaze rose to Ceara. That smile lingered on his lips as he stared at her, and her chest tightened. He said something to his own squire, who came directly to Ceara as Rafael watched.

The boy spoke to her, then bowed and gestured toward Rafael's tent. It seemed he would usher her toward it and Ceara smiled, knowing he had been instructed to do as much by Rafael. She followed the boy, aware that Rafael watched her, and glanced up just before ducking into the tent. He had turned away abruptly to answer a question and she felt bereft at the lack of his attention.

That would change soon enough.

Then she stepped into the tent and saw that all was as it had been when first she had visited. Had that truly been less than two days before? Carpets were laid upon the ground and the sunlight shone through the tent overhead, casting a dappled pattern upon the rugs. There was a bed in the midst of it all, a bed piled with fur pelts. The boy had unpacked her garments and laid them out on one of Rafael's trunks, apparently uncertain of her wishes. There was a fine bone comb set alongside, a bowl of clear water from the stream, a piece of soap and a thick cloth. He explained and retreated, indicating that he would stand guard outside the tent to ensure her privacy.

Ceara removed her boots and set them by the tent flap, then unbraided her hair and undressed. Though the water was not hot, she had become unaccustomed to that particular luxury. It felt good to clean herself from head to toe, to scrub the dust from her skin and coax her fingers and toes to warm again. She found herself yawning as she combed out her hair to a lustrous sheen. The sounds of the camp were dimming now, and she guessed that more of the men were retiring to rest.

Soon, Rafael would come to her.

She stretched out nude upon the fur pelts, her hair cast across them, and felt wicked indeed. The chain was warm against her skin, the weight of the key between her breasts, and she fingered it, wondering how Rafael would touch her first. Would she have to touch him to begin the seduction? She closed her eyes, imagining how she might begin, recalling his kisses and caresses.

She found herself sinking into the softness of the furs, then sighing contentment at the comfort of Rafael's bed. Ceara intended to close her eyes for only a moment, but exhaustion betrayed her and she slept.

RAFAEL OVERSAW every detail of the camp, refusing to delegate any item. He told himself that he wanted to see whether their pursuer revealed himself, but in truth, he wanted to delay the moment he was alone with Ceara. He knew what he should do; he knew what he had resolved to do, but a night with her fairly in his lap had awakened his desire so that he was uncertain he would be able to deny it. If it had been his custom to make the noble choice, it might have been easier to do so, but he was accustomed to taking what he desired—particularly when it was offered freely—and this was all new.

Trust Ceara to discover new challenges for him.

When he finally could find no more tasks, he dismissed Antonio, sending the boy to sleep with the other squires. Bernard had taken the first watch and waved as he passed, strolling around the perimeter of the camp. Raynard was tending his boots with the impatience of a man unprepared to sleep as yet. Rafael crouched down beside him.

"We were followed," he said and the other man's gaze flicked to him and away.

"Aye?"

"One horse, one rider." Rafael recalled the sound. "A palfrey, I think."

Raynard abandoned his task, his eyes glinting. He spoke as softly as Rafael. "How far behind?"

"A hundred paces, sometimes more, sometimes less." He pointed in the direction he had last heard the sound of pursuit. "All the way from Kilderrick."

"No coincidence then."

Rafael shook his head. "I would know his intent and leave him behind before we ride out."

Raynard nodded and rose to his feet with purpose. He cast his cloak over his shoulder and drew his blade, then left the camp. Rafael watched until the other man vanished into the undergrowth, then headed for his own tent. He opened the flap and everything tightened within him at Ceara's proximity. He closed his eyes and prayed for fortitude, knowing he had little.

He had stepped inside before he realized she was sound asleep.

She was also nude, save for the key he desired. Rafael's blood quickened as he stood for long moments and simply stared. He might have imagined Ceara in his bed, as perfect as a woman could be, but he knew he did not.

He shed his boots and crossed the tent silently, gazing down at her while she was unaware of his presence. Her hair was loose, a tangle of fire beneath her shoulders and cast across the fur pelts. Her skin was fair, her breasts as pale as ivory. That made her nipples look even more ruddy, their taut peaks doubtless a result of the chill in the air and not his presence. He only managed to resist the urge to touch her. Her lashes splayed against her skin, a darker russet hue than he might have expected, and her lips were parted, so rosy and plump that they invited his kiss.

Si bella. She was magnificent. He easily recalled her response to his touch, her willingness and her warmth, and he took a step closer, wanting. If she had been awake, if her eyes had been flashing and the words falling from her lips with haste, he would not have been able to resist her allure.

As it was, he would be a cur to awaken her. She had guided them to this haven, never complaining of their circumstance. She was unlike any woman he had ever known, a warrior to her marrow. Indeed, he thought she had savored the challenge, but that was of no import. He owed her a boon.

He wanted to give her more than that.

Rafael stood and watched Ceara for long moments, enticed beyond belief, striving to recall his own resolve. He would never seize a maidenhead or even accept one freely offered. He would never be the reason a woman lost the chance for a respectable marriage, even if she did not believe she desired one. Ceara would one day encounter the man who would defend her for all his days and nights. That would never be him.

Rafael had that responsibility only for a short while, and it included protecting her from himself.

The key tempted him, but he feared that the slightest touch would awaken her—and doom his good intentions.

He eyed the key and wondered. Could he retrieve the treasure without her by his side? Raynard had recognized the tale and might know the place of which she spoke. With the key in hand, Rafael could leave Ceara safely behind, perhaps at Beaupoint, then return with her share of the treasure once it was claimed. He would not cheat her of her due, for they had an agreement, but he would not put her in peril either. He could trust Amaury to ensure her defense—that man was noble to a fault.

Indeed, she would be safer with Amaury and Elizabeth than with Rafael.

For an ideal solution, it was utterly irksome. He wanted to be with Ceara when the treasure was reclaimed. He wanted to see her eyes flash with triumph when she was proven right. He wanted to argue with her over their respective shares. Just the prospect tempted his smile. She would surrender naught readily, to be sure, and he suspected they would negotiate his fee anew.

She would be better at Beaupoint, if he could contrive the way to leave her behind.

Rafael shed his armor and washed, then chose a clean chemise himself. He returned to look at her once again, unable to resist her allure, cursing himself that his only principle should prove so inconvenient.

With a sigh of regret that he was not the rogue he was reputed to be, Rafael pulled the pelts over Ceara, along with a dry cloak. She nestled more deeply into them with a sigh of contentment that made him ache for a kiss. Instead, he then wrapped himself in his heaviest cloak and lay down on the carpet to sleep. He was close enough to hear the soft noises she made in sleep, to smell her scent, to wonder at her dreams.

What did she desire, his bold huntress? Rafael assumed that all women wished for marriage and children, a comfortable home, but Ceara was different from others he had known. He glanced at her, uncertain what her goal might be.

But such considerations were futile. His future would never be bound to hers. He should take some rest while he could. Rafael had time to wonder whether he would be able to sleep with temptation in such close proximity before his eyes closed and he knew no more.

CHAPTER 10

*T*he Compagnie Rouge were camped outside the city of Venice, in the hills that overlooked that fabled city. Tensions between the Holy Roman Emperor and the papacy meant profit for Jean le Beau and he had divided his forces to raid on behalf of both sides. Maximilian had led a force that rode north to the wealthy towns of Lombardy. Rafael rode as Jean's second in the Veneto, a promotion unexpected.

Rafael was twenty summers of age, having been with the Compagnie Rouge for five years. He had learned much and seen more, but never had a sight been so welcome to him as the vista before him. 'Twas late summer and the abundance of the harvest could be seen in every field. The vines were heavy with grapes and the fields were filled with peasants hard at work. There was abundance and affluence in these lands, making them ideal for plunder.

But Rafael's chest was tight. This was the first time since joining the Compagnie Rouge that he had been close to the city where he had been born and abandoned, the city where he had made his greatest friend.

By the end of the day's ride, Venice glittered even in the distance like the prize she was, the Adriatic shining beyond the city itself. Rafael stood at their last outpost, yearning for something he knew he would never possess. Who had his mother been? Had he no other relations? His background was a mystery. The older he became, the more he wanted the truth. There was a gap in his own history, a hole in his life. He wanted a family, a sense of belonging, a surety of his place in the world.

But Rafael knew he would never have any of that. He was an orphan who had grown into a man destined to wander for all of his days. He was not alone in that destiny, but it chafed at him. He had found a welcome of a sort in this pillaging army, but what might he have become, in different circumstance?

Rafael felt rather than heard Matteo come to stand beside him, and was not surprised by that warrior's presence. They had been friends for as long as Rafael could remember. His every childhood memory included Matteo, for Matteo's mother had raised Rafael. He owed them his very survival, a debt he would never repay. They had been his only family, but he was keenly aware that he had not been blood.

"Will you go?" Rafael asked softly when Matteo did not speak. In that moment, he envied his old friend just a little, even though Fate had led them to a similar destination. Matteo's mother might yet live—and better, they both knew where to find her if she did.

On the one hand, Rafael understood the temptation. This close to Venice, Matteo might have the opportunity to see his mother again. Though it would be defiance to leave the camp, there might be little risk. Jean le Beau might be inclined to tolerance. On the cusp of battle, he would need every warrior who could lift a sword, regardless of any disobedience.

On the other hand, Jean might be in a vengeful mood by morning. He might dismiss Matteo from the company for such a departure, or worse, might see him punished.

And Matteo's mother might have died in their absence.. There had been no means to send her the news of their fate. She might have concluded that her son was dead.

Matteo could lose all in seeking her.

Rafael saw Matteo's nod from the periphery of his vision and was not surprised.

"I must. You know it."

"Aye."

Rafael anticipated the other man's question but was snared between loyalty for the past and ambition for the future. Recently promoted, Rafael was aware that his new stature was precarious. Jean le Beau might punish him more harshly than Matteo—or more leniently. The man loved naught more than *unpredictability yoked to violence, the better to keep all in his company fearful.*

"I would ride there this very night, before the battle on the morrow," Matteo said with quiet urgency. "You know she would be glad to see you."

"If she lives." Rafael could not evade the truth.

"If she lives," Matteo agreed, then heaved a sigh. His impatience to be gone was palpable.

"You will provoke his ire," Rafael warned. "You might lose all."

"He needs us too much to cast us aside before the city is taken," Matteo scoffed. "We are not without our skills, Rafael." There was a measure of bravado in his tone and Rafael hoped his friend was right. He knew by his silence that Matteo would take any risk to go.

In his place, Rafael would have done the same.

He turned to his friend, searching his expression even in the shadows. "You could ask him." The notion gained in appeal as soon as it was uttered. Permission might be readily gained on this night before battle—and if Matteo was refused, he could go anyway, in defiance.

Matteo laughed shortly. "There is no compassion in his soul. He would refuse me. He might ensure that I could not go, simply because he could."

"He might not refuse me." The words were uttered on impulse but had a resonance. Rafael saw hope flare in Matteo's dark gaze. He knew then that his friend did not want to ride out alone.

He could scarce blame him. They had pulled each other from trouble too many times to recall. To undertake any venture in solitude was unthinkable and perilous.

"Ask, but be quick. He already savors the wine." Matteo's expression turned grim. "I will go either way."

"I know." Rafael's decision was also made. He would go to Venice with Matteo this night, with or without Jean le Beau's permission. He would ask Matteo's mother what she remembered of his own mother. She had denied him before, but their reappearance might encourage her to relent.

That did not mean, though, that he would not strive to defend them both from their commander's wrath.

$\sim$

Rafael's resolve must have shown, for Jean le Beau took one look at him and dismissed all others from his company.

They eyed each other in silence. The old mercenary was still trim and handsome, his hair silver at his temples and his face both tanned and lined. There was a youthful vigor about him and his appetites for all pleasures were legendary, though he had to have seen fifty summers. He had seen much more, of course, and had done such foul deeds in his own interest that he was feared the length and breadth of Christendom. Just the mention of his name or the sight of his banner could prompt a surrender, perhaps in the hope of mercy. Rafael had learned in his years of service with the Compagnie Rouge that Jean le Beau possessed no mercy.

To be alone in his presence and have his undivided attention was not for the faint of heart. Rafael held his ground and the older man's stare.

"Speak," the older man commanded finally, his expression shrewd as he sipped his wine.

The quiet of the chamber and the watchfulness of his commander prompted Rafael to boldness. "Why have I advanced quickly through the ranks, more quickly than others of my skill?"

His question prompted a cool smile. "You might be fortunate."

"I have not been thus far in my life."

Jean le Beau chuckled. "Maximilian noted your aptitude. You have him to thank for your progression." He fell silent but Rafael did not speak, hoping the older man would continue. "I admire a man with enthusiasm and you have shown a considerable measure of it in learning the secrets of Greek fire." Jean le Beau nodded. "I also like to ensure that those of great use to me are satisfied with their lot." His voice dropped dangerously low and the air prickled between them. "Is that why you come to me this night? Are you discontent?"

"I would visit the city this night, with your permission."

"Or even without it, I suspect." When Rafael would have protested, the old mercenary waved him to silence. "Do you return to your former trade with your companion? They say once a thief, always a thief."

"Nay."

"Ah, then do you hunt some expert in your weapon of choice? Or do you seek provisions for your secret mixture?"

"Always both, sir."

Jean le Beau rose to his feet, sauntering closer. His posture was casual but

Rafael knew better than to be at ease. The man was a viper, always prepared to attack. "But I suspect you seek another treasure in this city," he whispered, eyes glinting. He reached out suddenly and seized Rafael's right hand, turning it so the golden ring on Rafael's smallest finger caught the light. He peered at it and smiled, his cold gaze rising to Rafael's once more. "I recognized it immediately," he whispered, relinquished his grip, then pivoted to return to his chair.

This time, it was Rafael who filled the silence for he could do naught else. "Are you my father?"

Jean le Beau surveyed him in the act of filling his cup again. He smiled, so clearly enjoying that he had the upper hand in a discussion that Rafael knew his suspicion was correct. "I suppose you have noticed your own resemblance to Maximilian."

"Others commented upon it, sir."

Jean le Beau nodded and drained his cup in one long swallow. "Francesca," he said with satisfaction, the name making Rafael's heart leap in his chest. The name echoed in his thoughts as he savored its sound. He had not even known that much of his mother. He waited, hungry for more, hating that only this man could give it to him. "The ring was the only thing she never surrendered to me."

Rafael found his hand closing into a fist, the better to ensure that he did not lose the ring, his sole keepsake.

"You have her fire," Jean le Beau continued, his tone idle. "I guessed when you were brought to me that day. 'Twas the reason you did not pay so dearly for that theft." He chuckled, nodding toward the dagger in Rafael's belt. "My men knew when I let you keep the prize. There is only one trait that makes a man worthy of such compassion in my camp." The mercenary smiled. "A man so favored is family and thus beyond the reprisal of all, save myself."

Rafael resisted the urge to touch the pommel of the dagger. Indeed, the leniency of Jean le Beau in that instance had awakened Rafael's immediate suspicion that there was more at work than he knew. He had been caught in the act of stealing a dagger from one of the men of the Compagnie Rouge. Not only had he been unpunished, but Rafael had been granted the dagger in question. It made no sense, not until the whispers began in the camp that the mercenary leader had recognized another of his bastards.

Jean le Beau drank his wine, his eyes gleaming as he watched Rafael. "You have my height and eyes, of course, but the same dark hair as she. Lustrous and gleaming." He smacked his lips. "Francesca. Aye, there is a memory." He lounged on his seat, as watchful as a cat. "I suppose you would like a sweet tale of her from me." His gaze turned to granite and his jaw set. "I expected better of you, given your lineage."

Rafael waited in silence.

The older man frowned. "But perhaps I should indulge you, the better that the desire to know does not consume you. You are possessed of an unholy curiosity, after all."

"Curiosity has allowed me to improve the Greek fire, sir. A man without inquisitiveness would have failed in my chosen quest."

"Aye, and there is the difference. Francesca had fire but no fury. She had no taste for battle and warfare, no desire even to defend herself. She simply awaited her due. She did not seek it out. She lacked true passion, your mother, and that was why I tired of her. You should count yourself blessed that you inherited mine." Jean le Beau smiled into his cup. "I like that comparison. You have both the fire and the hunger of a dragon. Let that be your moniker from this day forth. To the Dragon." He saluted Rafael with his wine and drank deeply.

Rafael did not respond lest Jean le Beau stop speaking of his mother. He simply stood in silence—and hoped for more.

"You are dissatisfied, I see." The older man made a dismissive gesture. "She was a beauty, of course. I desire only the best. She had a flash in her eyes that would beguile the most indifferent man, and I was not indifferent, to be sure. She would have denied me, but any argument was futile. I always claim all I desire. I take what is not freely given. She learned that lesson well." He nodded, holding Rafael's gaze. "It was hard and fast, each and every time, neither the best nor the worst that ever I had. Is that what you wanted to know?

Rafael shook his head.

"I took her," Jean le Beau rose to his feet and continued, his voice like steel. "I seized her and claimed her maidenhead within the hour. And then I kept her." He smiled at the memory. "She tried to escape me once, fleeing from the camp in the night, but naturally she was caught. After that, I kept her bound." He considered Rafael with glittering eyes. "Do you desire a token of her? Is that what you await? I have none to give." He smiled. "I gave her all I wished to grant and you were the result." He chuckled to himself and filled his cup once more with wine. "And so you have had your tale. Leave me."

Rafael wanted to steal something from the older man, even if it was his satisfaction in this moment. "I came for permission to leave the camp this night."

Jean le Beau smirked before he sipped. "To visit your beloved mother?" He clicked his tongue, chiding Rafael. "Such tender feelings are a liability in our trade."

Rafael wondered whether Jean even knew Francesca's fate. "I would assess the strengths and weaknesses of the city before we raze it to the ground. I would know where best to strike to bring the townsmen to their knees and open their treasuries."

Jean le Beau laughed with delight at this fabrication. "Your father's son, to be sure." He tilted his head to study Rafael, his eyes narrowing. "But perhaps you show your lineage in another way. Your mother was not inclined to be trustworthy."

"I believe you are relying upon the Greek fire to ensure a quick triumph."

Jean le Beau nodded warily.

"I leave it in your care while I undertake this journey." Rafael bowed as his father's eyes lit with satisfaction. The other men could use the weapon without Rafael's guidance: the Compagnie Rouge simply had no ability to make more without Rafael. "I would have Matteo accompany me that we might assess the possibilities more thoroughly."

"Two thieves returned to the grounds they hunted for years." There was a sneer in the older man's voice, but Rafael was not ashamed that they had survived.

"No one else in the company knows the city so well. We will be efficient on this night."

Once again, their gazes held in silent challenge, the older man seeking some weakness in the younger. Rafael did not even dare to blink, and he strove to hide his hatred of his leader and father. He feared he would fail the longer the exchange lasted.

Finally, Jean le Beau waved a hand, dismissing both Rafael and the errand. "Go. Know that I will set the torch to your tent at dawn if you are not returned."

. . .

RAFAEL AWAKENED SUDDENLY, his eyes flying open. The dream had been so vivid that for a moment he feared that Jean le Beau yet lived, then his gaze darted around his tent and relief flooded through him. This tent was larger than his first in the Compagnie Rouge and more splendidly furnished.

The old viper was no more.

Aye, he had seen him dead at Château de Vries.

Rafael exhaled and closed his eyes for a moment, willing his heart to slow its erratic pace. The light had changed, the sunlight having turned to the gold of late afternoon. He could hear the low murmur of his men and the nicker of the horses, the soft snoring of some soul within earshot. The shadows were deeper and colder outside the tent, a reminder that he was in Scotland. The chill rising from the earth was an unmistakable sign.

Never mind the red-haired beauty slumbering in his bed, her very ease evidence of her trust.

That trust was undeserved. She knew his reputation and had to have guessed at his past deeds. No angels rode with Jean le Beau, after all.

Ceara had not moved much in her sleep, shifting only to one side slightly. Her breathing was still deep and even, and there was a flush on her cheeks as if she had warmed. He had the urge to awaken her with a kiss, or even a caress, but knew that would only lead him astray. He was drawn to her, not simply because of her beauty. It was her audacity that snared his attention, her confidence that prompted his smile.

His father spoke the truth in that: sentimentality was a liability in his trade. To love anyone or anything was to be vulnerable to another and Rafael would not make that error. If he surrendered to temptation in this matter, Ceara would be the one to pay the price.

Rafael rose and dressed with quick gestures, watching Ceara all the while. He donned his chausses, then tugged on his boots. He took his aketon, hauberk and a dark tabard, as well as his belt. The dagger he considered for a moment, memory bright in his thoughts.

The golden ring glinted on Ceara's finger, the sight making his throat tighten. The dream was a reminder of the price his mother had paid for Jean le Beau's seduction, a fortification to his own resolve to never repeat his father's deeds.

On impulse, Rafael gently claimed his ring from her finger, replacing it on his own hand where it belonged. Ceara had no need of it any longer, after all. The sooner their ways parted, the better for both of them.

He left the tent to find Raynard awaiting him, a young boy sleeping by his feet.

"Louis!" he said with surprise and the boy stirred.

This had been the last revelation he had expected. Why would one of Maximilian's squires follow them?

CEARA AWAKENED with the sense that she had missed a detail of import. She sat up, shivering that she was still nude beneath the cloak and disappointed that she was alone. Rafael's fur-lined cloak was on the carpet in the midst of the tent. He had come then. She got up and touched it, her fingers sinking into the softness of the fur, and thought she could still detect the heat of his body.

'Twas then she realized that her left hand was bare. The tug of the ring's removal must have been what awakened her. Who would have the audacity to steal Rafael's ring? Ceara dressed in haste, fearing the worst and knowing its absence would not pass unremarked.

When she burst out of the tent, still braiding her hair, she found Rafael standing close by. His arms were folded across his chest as he listened to the words of the boy before him. He was dressed and armed, obviously prepared to ride, his squire still darting around him.

The ring gleamed upon Rafael's left hand and she breathed a sigh of relief, glad that it was safe. Why had he retrieved it? There could be no encouraging reason, to be sure.

Then she realized the boy was Louis.

She gasped and Rafael flicked a glance her way, his gaze sliding over her in assessment before he turned back to the boy again. Once again, he was cool and distant, and the fact that he had retrieved his ring had to be of import. "Louis brings tidings from Kilderrick."

She went to his side, refusing to be rebuffed.

Louis bowed to her and she greeted him, but the boy was quick to continue his discussion with Rafael. "As I said, sir, at the wedding feast, the king asked of Ceara's name and origin. Lady Alys confessed that she did not know, and when pressed by the king, admitted that Ceara knew much of horses. 'Twas clear the king found import in this detail and I feared you would know why."

Perhaps he repeated the message, for Rafael did not appear to share Ceara's dismay.

"He has guessed!" she whispered. "He must realize that I am the one who fled the court of the Earl of Ross."

Rafael's features could have been carved of stone as he glowered at Louis. "And who granted you permission to pursue us?"

The boy flushed crimson and he lowered his gaze. "No one, sir."

"And you thought it a good choice to ride alone through the Bewcastle Waste?"

"I ensured I was close behind your party, sir."

Rafael was stern. "You should have been within it, or safely at Kilderrick."

"I had to tell her, sir. I had to warn Ceara." He then fixed Ceara with an appealing glance. To be sure, she was uncertain what she had done to earn the boy's devotion.

"You should not have taken such a risk," she chided him. "You could have been injured."

The boy's flush deepened and his expression turned stubborn. "I had no choice," he muttered.

"And you are certain that you were not pursued?" Rafael asked him.

The squire shook his head. "But you may be. That was why I had to come."

Raynard appeared in that moment, leading a palfrey from the middle of the camp. Ceara knew this was a horse from Maximilian's stables. The palfrey was playful, biting at Raynard's hair and swishing its tail, a sign that it had rested and been fed. Ceara smiled herself, enjoying the sight of Raynard's rare smile. He looked younger and less stern in so doing, while Rafael seemed in this moment to be both older and colder.

If Raynard had not laughed at her tale of the mermaid, she would have been certain that her suspicions of his identity were correct. But her brother could never mock a tale of their family, not for any price.

Louis clearly believed Rafael to be vexed with him. "If you surrender the palfrey to me, sir, I will ride back to Kilderrick. You need not be concerned with me."

Rafael shook his head. "I need not be concerned that a squire from my brother's household takes an uncommon risk? You err in understanding my responsibilities, to be sure."

"But..."

"You ride with us," he commanded. "'Twill be safer for you in this land of reivers to ride with the company."

"But where do you go, sir?"

"Beaupoint. Amaury will have to find a way to return you to Kilderrick safely."

Though Louis might have disguised his relief, Ceara noticed it. She suspected his reaction was as heartfelt as her own.

And she liked that Rafael protected this impulsive and loyal squire, as well.

Rafael smiled slightly, apparently unsurprised by her response. "If the king has divined the truth, we must depart with haste." She nodded and he turned to speak urgently to his men. "We ride with all speed. There is no time to delay. Across the wall, then west, upon the road. We can only hope that few are abroad at night to witness our passage." He pointed to the tents, which already were being struck. If anything, the company dissembled the camp even more quickly than the night before.

Ceara guessed from Rafael's manner that they would not halt until they reached Beaupoint itself, no matter how long the ride.

CEARA WAS THINKING, a sure sign of trouble brewing. Rafael could not miss the signs. She glanced at him repeatedly, obviously holding back her words, but her manner was agitated. She had a notion, he was certain, or perhaps a question. Either way, she intended to spring upon him in privacy, perhaps in the hope of gaining a confession he would not have made otherwise, and he was almost tempted to let her ride alone to avoid that situation.

But he did not trust her that much—and she still had the key.

Undoubtedly, she would ask again about the ring, or his mother, or some other secret from his past. Rafael braced himself for her queries even as the company packed the camp. He was not a man inclined to confide in others and she would learn as much by the time their ways parted.

The company gathered in the last shadows at the lip of the forest to watch the sun sink below the top of the tree canopy. The shadows stretched long and the air turned cooler. There was not even a circling hawk to see when they rode out swiftly and silently.

Ceara was fixed upon their goal for the moment, directing him to the milecastle and the path that wound through it. As she had confided earlier, the wall was broken and a path ran through the midst of what had once been a tower. The track was evident but not well worn, and he was reassured that it must be seldom used. If the reivers were active in this region, then people may have moved.

Once on the other side, they turned to the west, readily finding the road Ceara had mentioned. The moon was yet waxing although on this night, they saw it rise, glowing golden. It turned silver by the time it rode high in the sky, still not a full quarter but brighter than the night before.

The area was surprisingly quiet, and Rafael welcomed that. There did not seem to be many residents in the vicinity, another hint of the reivers' activities. They rode past several small villages and lonely farms, but no one challenged them. Rafael was certain they could not be readily identified. Their horses were swift and the wagons rolled quietly on the better road; his men were all garbed in dark garments and cloaks without insignia.

The town of Brampton was larger, as Ceara had indicated, and they rode around that town in terse silence, keeping to the southern roads around its perimeter.

It was when the town had faded from view behind them that Ceara first spoke. "We will reach Carlisle before the dawn at this pace."

Rafael nodded approval, feigning indifference to the softness of her voice and her proximity.

"Why did you retrieve your ring?" she asked finally.

"Because you no longer have need of it." When she did not reply, he found himself continuing. "And wearing it only encourages you to have ideas that are incorrect."

"How do you know what ideas I have?"

He nigh rolled his eyes. "I can guess."

She bristled. "You have many assumptions about women and what they will do."

"There tends to be a certain predictability about the matter."

"But already I have proven that I am less predictable."

"'Tis true, but in the end, you will not be."

"What does that mean?" She twisted around to look at him, though he doubted she could see much of his expression in the shadows. "That you expect me to lose my heart to you, just as *all* the other women do?" Her tone was scornful.

Rafael chuckled. "Not all surrender their affections to me. Some grant only their favors."

She shook her head, not deigning to reply.

"But all women have the same ultimate desire," he continued, wondering even as he uttered the words whether they were true of Ceara. "A husband, a home, children." He yawned mightily. "There is no woman who would choose my life, at least not for long."

"You might be surprised," she replied immediately.

"Aye? And what is your desire?"

This time, she was the one to chuckle. "I appreciate that old jest, that what a woman desires most is her own way."

"Ah, you wish a man who is biddable."

"Not that! Never that."

He found himself smiling at her vehemence. "What then?"

"I would have a man who loved me as I am, not one who wished me to change to please him. I like to ride to hunt. I like to wear my chausses and ride astride. I will never be the woman to sit by the fire and tend to my needlework. I would ride out with my man and work alongside him at whatever task we might undertake."

"No quiet cottage in the forest for you then?"

She laughed. "I would have a hall, wrought of stone, with high walls and a company of servants."

"Ah, you would wed a nobleman."

"I care not for his lineage. The merit in wedding a man of wealth would be that I might have horses." Her tone turned wistful. "In that case, I would breed them and trade them, though I might find it difficult then to sell them." She shrugged. "But what is of greatest import is that the man I take to husband has affection for me, regardless of his wealth or lack of it."

Rafael ensured that he sounded weary. "You speak of love then, as the minstrels do. Surely that is a predictable objective from a woman?"

Ceara straightened and spoke with characteristic ferocity. "My mother told me often of the love she shared with my father, and how both passion and affection brought joy to her life. She wished for me to know the same joy."

"Yet you were betrothed to the son of the earl."

Ceara sighed. "Women have fewer choices and you know it well. After my father disappeared, my mother was reliant upon the earl's goodwill."

"And did you love his son?" Rafael found himself cursed curious.

"William?" She laughed lightly. "Nay, not William. He was never robust, but a quiet boy who often remained in the hall. His father taught me to ride and hunt, and called me the son he never had." Her voice was warm with the memory of it. "His daughter was groomed for a marriage of alliance. She understood the books of the holding, how to dress and dance, how to flatter a man. Euphemia knew her destiny and was uncommonly serene."

Rafael bit back a smile that the two women should be so different. "Yet you learned to dance, as well."

"Aye, they were kind to me." She shook her head. "But William died too soon."

"How so?"

"We never wed. His death did not make me a widow."

"Why were you not wed to him sooner?" Rafael knew that some noblemen saw their children wed at twelve summers of age.

"My mother insisted that the nuptials wait. Each year, she appealed to the earl, arguing that my brother might return, urging him to wait. He indulged her and, in the end, his kindness betrayed us all." She was quiet for a long moment then and when she continued, her voice was husky. "I miss her." Her words were husky and he had the uncommon urge to console her.

"What of Edward?" he asked, changing the subject. "Why do you dislike him?"

"He is a man who sees only his own advantage. He will never care for another, least of all me. Indeed, I think his interest is solely the mermaid's secret." Her voice became wistful. "It must be a glorious thing to be desired for one's own self, not for a dowry or an alliance or the good of one's kin."

Rafael could only believe she was right in that.

"Is there such a place in Scotland you would choose for you and your lover of such merit?"

She wrinkled her nose. "I have no particular desire to remain in the land where I was born. I would rather travel and marvel at the world's wonders."

Her ploy was so obvious that Rafael laughed. "You will not tempt me to take you with me, *bella*. No woman rides with the Compagnie Rouge for long."

"And whose choice is that?" she asked, her manner hinting that she expected no reply. "But what of your plan for the future? Are you like all men, in wanting only to have satisfaction abed at regular intervals and a son to bear your name?"

Rafael shook his head. "I will never wed in truth, so I will have no son."

She looked up again. "None at all?"

"I know what it is to be an orphan and a bastard," he said with resolve, holding her gaze. "No child deserves either fate."

"An orphan?"

"Aye."

She frowned and fell silent, considering that. "But what of you?" she asked finally, her hand falling to his arm. "Do you not deserve a better fate than a life at war alone?"

"I am not alone with a company of men following my command," he said, his tone matter-of-fact. "And war is all that I have come to know. I should not know how to live in peace."

"Even in times of peace, a man with a holding must see it defended. What if you claimed a holding of your own?"

"I should not know how to administer it."

She laughed. "Then you must wed well." She twisted around, her eyes dancing so merrily that he could not halt his answering smile. "Perhaps one raised in an earl's household, where the daughter of the house was expected to understand the books."

Rafael shook his head. "That will not be my fate."

"Whyever not?" she asked in challenge. "I thought the seal of Château de Vries was already in your grasp."

Rafael felt his lips thin. "Only a nobleman can claim the seal of such a holding and my origins are humble."

"How humble?" she asked. "I thought you were Maximilian's brother and he is not humbly born."

"Jean le Beau got me upon a serving maid who had the misfortune to attract his eye."

With that, Ceara frowned. "What else do you know of your mother?" she asked softly.

"Little enough. Her name was Francesca." He was surprised to hear himself confessing the few details he knew. "She died in the delivery of me."

"An orphan," she mused. She twisted to look at him and he was surprised that there was compassion in her gaze. "I cannot imagine what it would be like to have never known my mother." To his astonishment, Ceara's sympathy was for him. He stared as she placed a hand upon his chest, certain that no one had ever cared for his loss. "I am sorry that you were cheated of knowing your mother, Rafael."

He found his throat tight and he frowned at the distance. "It is of no import," he said gruffly. "And was many years ago."

Ceara laughed beneath her breath. "Yet with this detail, I understand so much. 'Tis why you defend others, like Louis and myself, since you were not defended," she said softly, turning to look up at him with a smile. "A protective mercenary."

His heart twisted but Rafael hid his reaction. "You make much of little, *bella*," he said, his tone stern but she shook her head.

"I see that you follow the vows of a knight, to defend those weaker than himself. I do not see so much difference in your choices and that makes you a noble warrior to me." She looked up at him, her eyes bright with challenge even as his heart thumped. "You do not deceive me, sir."

And that was precisely what Rafael feared.

CHAPTER 11

$\mathcal{J}$ was late afternoon when they approached their destination and the horses were cantering with less enthusiasm than before. Ceara knew she would not be the only one glad to abandon the saddle. They had halted only to let the horses drink, pressing on to their destination, but she had not uttered a sound of complaint. She would ride as long as any of the men, though Louis was clearly exhausted.

Finally, Beaupoint's tall tower pointed to the heavens like a sentinel before them. They had asked in a village to the east and been directed by a suspicious miller. That man had stood in the road, hands on his hips, watching them proceed as if he would verify that the keep was their true destination. Rafael guided his company around the village clustered outside the walls of the fortification sworn to Amaury's hand.

"Alas, the lord of this holding has already taken a bride," Rafael murmured in that low voice, the one that made Ceara tingle to her toes. "Otherwise, you might have found your rich husband and raised your horses here."

She glanced back at him to find his eyes sparkling. She smiled that he teased her and chose to respond in kind. They had ridden in silence since his unwilling confession and she suspected she had irked him in provoking it. "I have no regrets in that, for I doubt Amaury would be sufficiently ardent to suit me," she said boldly, laughing when Rafael was visibly startled. "And I suspect I might not suit him either."

"Whyever not?"

Ceara shrugged. "He has chosen to wed Elizabeth and there could be no woman more different from me." Truth be told, Elizabeth reminded her of Euphemia, a woman consumed with duty and obligation. She had never thought Euphemia took much amusement, by her own choice, and now that she was wed to Edward's father, that would not change.

"But he has fared well by the look of it," Rafael mused, apparently unable to disguise that he was impressed by Beaupoint. He directed his men to set camp near the forest to the southwest of the tower.

He dismounted and lifted Ceara to the ground, his hands remaining locked around her waist as he looked down at her. Her heart skipped that she had his attention.

"Dare I trust you to stay in the camp?" he asked quietly, arousing her suspicions.

"Where are you going?"

He spared a glance to the tower. "I must bargain with Amaury." He did not look as if he expected the exchange to proceed well. "'Twill not be suitable for you to witness our discussion."

Ceara felt her eyes widen. "You will not injure him!"

"I may threaten him," he admitted, his eyes dark. Once again, he was a dangerous rogue, one whose presence thrilled her to her marrow. The corner of his mouth lifted in a knowing smile. "I would not have you witness the result."

"I want to go with you."

"And yet you will not. I leave you in Matteo's care, but I will have your pledge to avoid vexing him." He spared a glance to his comrade and she saw his eyes twinkle. "If you test his patience, you may find yourself without his protection."

Ceara was aware then of how many men were in Rafael's company. "You will return?"

"I give you my most solemn pledge, *bella*." He held her gaze as he kissed the back of her hand. Ceara's mouth went dry and she thought of the night ahead, another opportunity to seduce him. It seemed that Rafael's thoughts followed the same path, for his gaze simmered. He turned her hand and kissed her palm, then closed her fingers over the imprint of his salute.

It was not enough. Ceara impulsively stretched to her toes and kissed his mouth, trying to show that she was more than willing to surrender her all. She had only herself to offer and she feared it would not be enough when Rafael stiffened in surprise.

Then he swept her off her feet and bestowed one of those passionate kisses upon her, one that left her convinced that her very soul would erupt in flames, one that left her dizzy and clinging to him as if he was the sole fixture in her world. The man was changeable, indeed, so suddenly ardent that she could scarce recall her own name.

When Rafael set her on her feet, his eyes were blazing and his jaw was taut. Ceara found herself unsteady on her feet. She kissed her own finger as the air simmered between them, then touched her fingertip to his mouth. "Hasten your return, sir," she whispered and his wicked smile flashed.

He nipped her finger with his teeth, then shouted to Matteo. Ceara watched, daring to hope Rafael had changed his thinking.

That warrior appeared beside Ceara and they spoke quickly in that tongue she did not comprehend, before Rafael swung into his saddle. He turned the horse with a flourish and rode toward the distant keep with confidence and purpose.

She and Matteo stood together, watching him, but Rafael did not look back. Just the sight of him made her heart thunder.

"Will he return safely?" She had to ask.

The warrior shrugged. "I doubt he will be very welcome, but he rides alone to ensure that the lord does not see a threat."

"But Rafael has no one to defend him."

Matteo laughed shortly. "You have never seen him fight, have you? The leader of the Compagnie Rouge needs no one at his back." He turned away then, calling to the boys and pointing.

"What is that language you speak with him?" Ceara asked, trailing behind him.

"Venetian."

"Why? Was Rafael raised there?"

Matteo shrugged. "The tale is not mine to share." His eyes twinkled with unexpected humor. "We are not a company inclined to sharing secrets." He pointed to the tent being erected, and she recognized it as Rafael's own. "He will expect you to remain there."

"Out of sight, like a prisoner?"

"Out of view, that others may not be tempted."

Ceara nodded understanding, but doubted any of these men would risk Rafael's ire. "But I would be of assistance. What can I do?"

Matteo eyed her, his doubts clear.

"I cannot be idle," Ceara protested.

He nodded once. "The horses all need to be brushed down and watered."

Ceara followed him, sparing one last glance after Rafael. He drew near the gates and she saw that another horse emerged from the keep, an armed warrior in the saddle. Was it Amaury? She could not be certain, given the distance, but the gleam of the knight's armor gave her pause.

Something was amiss, though she could not name it.

AMAURY WAS NOT TRULY SURPRISED that the Compagnie Rouge arrived at his holding. In a way, he was glad of it, for he had questions. It stood to reason that Rafael had led the men to Scotland because he had tidings to share with Maximilian about Château de Vries. Even though Gaston de Vries was not his father in truth, Amaury knew that man well enough to want all the details explained. Amaury allowed no one to ride out with him when a lone rider approached the gates, for he had little doubt of that warrior's identity. The rider had donned a helm, his armor glinting in the late afternoon sun.

The magnificent dapple destrier left no doubt that it was Rafael.

Amaury's half-brother did not shirk from any deed, no matter how perilous it might be. Though another man might have admired the audacity of his sole approach to Beaupoint, Amaury knew the choice was not a reckless one. Nay, there had to be archers with their bows bent, lurking in his own forests, prepared to strike a blow at some signal from Rafael.

To be fair, his own walls bristled with archers charged with the same instruction, and they had the better vantage.

He heard the gates close behind him as he rode out to greet the arrival, his entire being tense with the uncertainty. What would Rafael do? Why had he come?

To Amaury's surprise, Rafael lifted his visor when he halted his destrier just steps away. "Hail, brother," he said, that familiar trace of mockery in his tone.

"Well met," Amaury replied crisply.

"I bring tidings of Château de Vries in the hope that they will be of interest."

"It is unassailable?"

Rafael laughed, his smile flashing. "It is fallen." He patted his purse beneath Amaury's astonishment. "I have the seal and would have delivered it to Maximilian, but he declined it."

Amaury blinked. He lifted his own visor. "He declined de Vries?"

"I see you share my surprise. He bade me do with it what I would." Rafael shook his head, apparently unable to conceive of any deed he might do with such a holding.

Pillage and theft were his skills, perhaps even rape, but this brother was a mercenary through and through. At least their father had one son to follow in his steps.

"Perhaps the king will pay you for it, so he can bestow it upon a loyal follower."

Rafael wagged a finger at him. "There is a notion and I thank you for it. Maximilian suggested that I might take the lordship myself." He raised his brows at the absurdity of the idea and Amaury smiled.

At least the man knew his own strengths.

He inclined his head. "I thank you for these tidings. And now, you return to France?"

Rafael fixed him with a look. "I have not shared all as yet."

"There is more? You were not gone six months and the season for warfare has only just begun..."

"Gaston led the defense of de Vries," Rafael said, interrupting him flatly. "And when he lost, he strove to deceive me."

"I wager you were not fooled, for you yet live and breathe."

Again, Rafael smiled, looking more like a wolf than Amaury recalled. "I remembered his inclination to trickery, and deceived him instead." He sobered, surveying Amaury. "He is dead by my own hand." There was a challenge in his tone that confused Amaury.

"You suspect that I will not believe you?"

"You were raised as his son. I thought you might challenge me."

Amaury scoffed. "I am more likely to thank you."

They grinned at each other for a moment, until Amaury realized how odd it was to find himself in agreement with Rafael. "And what of Philip?"

Rafael shrugged. "He kept his pledge and surrendered the holding as promised."

This time, only Amaury laughed. "He is his father's son in truth. I would never turn my back upon him."

"Indeed." Rafael did not appear to be surprised.

"Be warned that he shares Gaston's patience in waiting to avenge a perceived slight."

Rafael nodded and Amaury feared his warning had not been sufficiently clear.

"If you left him with the keys to Château de Vries, I hope you are prepared to fight him for its possession upon your return."

Rafael smiled. "I am, in point of fact. I thought he might not be entirely trustworthy. 'Twas his eager grasp of the keys that revealed him, and his obvious desire for the seal."

"Indeed?"

"Indeed. He argued with me about bringing it to Maximilian. He suggested the risk to the seal was too great." Rafael raised his brows. "As if I could not safeguard an item that fits in the palm of my hand."

"But if you had left it, he could have claimed the keep outright."

"Indeed."

This time, the smile shared by the brothers was warmer.

"And now I have a favor to ask of you, as Lord de Beaupoint," Rafael said softly.

Amaury felt as if he had been warned. "Do you?"

"I would be invited to your board this evening, along with my new wife."

Amaury was shocked. "You have wed?"

"In name only, though Maximilian believes the situation to be otherwise and the lady makes some effort to change our bargain." This appeared to amuse Rafael. "You know my bride, for Ceara was one of your own wife's companions at Kilderrick."

"Ceara wed you and willingly?"

Rafael chuckled. "To be sure, she had little choice, or none that was better. I depart at first light with the Compagnie Rouge and would see her safety assured, as she will not be in my company."

"You wish to leave her here."

"I wish to entrust her to your care, without her awareness of my intention."

"That is trickery!"

"And in a way, it is earned. She has tricked me before. More importantly, she will not be safe when I leave these shores, and while I wish many things for this particular woman, I wish most of all that she be defended. Given the perils of our destination, that cannot be with me."

Where was Rafael going? Amaury knew he should not care, so long as the small army of men would be leaving.

"As a result, I ask you to invite us to partake of your hospitality this evening," Rafael said, speaking so crisply that Amaury knew he had planned every detail. "We will arrive, she will dismount in the bailey and I will depart immediately. Her horse will be seized by your men and your gates will be secured, so that she can only watch as we leave these shores." His brows rose. "She will, undoubtedly, be vexed."

This was a marvel, that Ceara could have a fondness for Rafael. Or was it simply the surprise that would annoy her? Amaury knew little of the fiery woman who had been his wife's companion. A bit too late, he wished Elizabeth was at his side, to whisper what she knew into his ear.

What was truly afoot? He could not imagine that Rafael, of all men, was protective of Ceara—much less that Ceara, an accomplished hunter, could not defend herself, wherever Rafael was going.

He did not reply and when Rafael spoke, his words had an under-current of steel. "Do we have an agreement, brother?"

The question had to be asked. The need to abandon a lover would explain Rafael's request. "Have you despoiled her?"

Rafael spoke through gritted teeth. "Not yet, but one more night of temptation will see that matter resolved. She must remain within Beaupoint's walls until I am gone."

Amaury was intrigued. "For you have no desire for a bride."

"Not I." Rafael frowned and averted his gaze, his voice softening. "And she will fare better with a husband with an honest trade. Our match must be annulled, for her own welfare, and that means Ceara must remain innocent."

Well. Against every expectation, Rafael had surrendered his heart. This was a marvel, and the realization changed all for Amaury. Still, he was not unaccustomed to trickery himself, and strove to verify the details. "If I do as you ask, then you will leave, and I will not see you again?"

Rafael smiled and spoke smoothly. "I could not guarantee that. We are both young and hale, brother mine." He raised his brows. "Who knows what will transpire in time? But I will leave your holding now, along with my men." He offered his hand. "Have we a wager?"

Amaury urged his destrier forward and clasped Rafael's hand, looking into his brother's eyes. "We dine at sunset."

Rafael inclined his head. "We will be there. I thank you, Amaury." He smiled, and this time there was no mockery in his expression. Then he lowered his visor and urged his destrier to walk backward, no small feat but one that meant he could continue to watch both Amaury and the archers on the walls.

"What of the lady's situation after the morning?" Amaury called.

Rafael raised a hand. "I have been informed that what a lady desires most is her own choice. Perhaps that is a fitting gift from me. Let her choose her destination. We must seek passage on a ship. Would you recommend Worthington or Whitehaven?"

"Either might suffice. It will depend upon your destination and which ships are at port."

Rafael nodded. "We will depart at first light. I give you my pledge."

He bowed again, turned the horse with enviable skill and galloped back toward the camp.

Dinner and a guest. Elizabeth would be most interested in these tidings. Amaury hoped she could console Ceara.

The gates opened behind him and he turned his destrier more slowly, thinking of all Rafael had told him. He knew he should mourn the man he had been always told was his father, but he could not. The simple truth was that a world without Gaston de Vries was a much brighter place than one compelled to endure that man's influence.

Amaury could not imagine a situation better deserving of a feast.

ONCE THE HORSES WERE TENDED, Ceara saw that Rafael's tent had been raised, though he was still at Beaupoint. She offered to assist the small yet determined boy who labored as his squire, making herself understood with hand signals. He protested but eventually relented and Ceara soon realized why.

She could not believe how much baggage Rafael possessed. She had not taken stock of it earlier. He had to be more vain than a queen, for there were trunks beyond counting, and each one of them heavier than the last. She could not falter in her task, though, for she had invited it—and Rafael's squire worked so diligently that she would not be outdone by a mere boy. It seemed that each item in his tent had its place and the boy fussed, ensuring that all was precisely as it should be.

She wondered whether he would be beaten if an item was set awry, but could not believe Rafael capable of such cruelty.

Then she wondered why she held such a conviction of his good character, given his trade and his obvious satisfaction with it.

To be sure, the man could addle her wits with a mere kiss—though there was little to be underestimated in his caress. To couple with him had to be a marvel beyond belief—and she, unlike many maidens of her acquaintance, was blessed with a healthy curiosity about such matters.

Who better to teach her than Rafael, her husband?

She wondered when he would return.

She wondered what Rafael would say to Amaury. She wondered

how Elizabeth fared, halfway wishing she had been invited to accompany Rafael.

In truth, the wondering wearied her more than the labor. Once all was arranged to the boy's satisfaction, she could only gaze toward the bed with yearning.

The boy vanished and she was sorely tempted to nap.

He reappeared suddenly and silently with a large leather sack of some kind, which she helped to position atop the layered carpets. The leather was boiled and waxed, which was most curious, and she only understood its purpose once the boy began to dump pails of hot water into it.

"A bath!" she declared in French and the boy smiled, then nodded.

He embarked on a long explanation in that infernal language she could not comprehend, then fell silent, obviously realizing she did not understand. He frowned and took a breath. His French was even more careful than her own. "Last night, my lord ordered a bath for you, but we left Kilderrick."

Ceara nodded agreement.

He smiled in relief, then gestured proudly. "Tonight, you have the bath."

Ceara frowned. "But will others come?" She made her fingers walk, as if they entered the tent, then pretended to be surprised at her bath.

The boy looked shocked by the possibility. He shook his head vigorously and pointed to her barren left hand, evidently not noting that the ring was gone. "*Sposa.* Only Rafael. *Si?*" He was so fierce that she could readily imagine him defending the opening to the tent with his life.

"*Si.*" Ceara agreed. "Ceara," she said, pointing to herself, then gestured to him.

He beamed. "Antonio," he admitted with pride and they each bowed.

They smiled at each other, both pleased by the exchange, then worked together to fill the bath with the remaining water. Antonio opened Rafael's trunks with obvious familiarity at their contents, and presented a comb, a rough cloth and a ball of soap to Ceara with a polite bow. The comb she recalled from their camp the night before. The soap smelled faintly floral, and far superior to soaps she had known, even at Kilderrick. It was also a hint that she was not the first woman to bathe in Rafael's tent, but Ceara refused to take umbrage.

She would be the last.

Then Antonio bowed and ducked out of the tent. Ceara could see his silhouette as he stood guard outside the opening. The water filled the tent with steam and she found herself smiling in anticipation of her bath. She undressed and found the water too hot as yet. She cleaned her boots and folded her chausses, then shook out her kirtle and a clean chemise. She eyed the silhouette of the boy outside, then surveyed the trunks on all sides.

What did this man carry with him? He had come all the way from France with these possessions, so they must be of some value.

Watchful of the boy's presence and the possibility that she could be discovered, Ceara silently opened the first trunk. The plate armor Rafael had worn when he had ridden in pursuit of her was carefully packed inside it. There were also greaves that he had not worn and a chain mail hood, as well as heavily studded gloves and a helmet. There was a dark padded aketon in the bottom of the trunk and several sheathed knives that had been rolled in cloth.

The next trunk was a veritable artillery. There were knives, swords and daggers, as well as a fine crossbow and a fearsome mace. All were packed with care and polished to a gleam.

The third trunk apparently contained the treasury for the Compagnie Rouge. It was half-full of coins of mixed origin, some gold but mostly silver. Ceara scooped up a handful and let them run through her fingers, then realized that the boy might hear her. She looked over her shoulder but he had not moved. While it was more coin than she had ever seen in her life, it seemed to Ceara that there was not as much as would have been ideal. To pay passage or keep for a company of this size would whittle the contents of this trunk with speed, she would wager.

No wonder Rafael was interested in her family treasure.

The fourth trunk contained garments, all of the same ilk as the ones she had seen Rafael wear. There were four more fine linen chemises, another pair of dark chausses but made of brocade, a heavy woolen cloak without a fur lining, two more embroidered tabards and a short cloak with a hem embroidered in gold. There was a pair of leather shoes in this trunk as well.

Two trunks for his garb, one for weapons and one for coin. What was in the others?

Ceara opened the next, a shallow box as long as a sword but only as deep as a handspan. It was filled with similar items wrapped in cloth, though she could not identify them. She frowned and removed one, unfurling the cloth to find a dark sphere inside it. She bent to examine it more closely but someone cleared his throat in close proximity.

She gasped and spun, almost dropping the sphere but clutching it to her chest in the last moment.

Rafael. Of course. He stood just inside the opening, watching her, his expression inscrutable. The silhouette of the boy was gone, so he had dismissed him silently.

Ceara felt as if she had been caught at some forbidden deed, but she had only been looking. Surely he expected her to be curious?

"What is it?" she asked, lifting the sphere.

Rafael strode toward her, lifting it from her grasp and examining it as if she might have damaged it. Then he wrapped it carefully in the cloth and replaced it in the box, nestling it into place. He closed the lid, securing it. "Your bath cools," he noted, a challenge in his tone.

"Are they all the same?" she asked, thinking of the rows of similar bundles. He nodded. "What are they?"

"What do you think they are?" He removed his cloak and stretched as if entirely at ease.

She was not fooled. He was watching her too intently.

The vessels mattered.

They might even be one of his secrets.

Ceara wished she could examine one again. If this was a riddle, she wished to solve it. "I do not know. That one is crockery, like a fine cup, but has such a small opening. I cannot imagine how you might fill it." She frowned. "I am not sure why." She bit her lip. "And it has a sheen."

He settled into the only chair in the tent, one that unfolded, and watched her. "You might guess by its location."

"In a trunk in a tent?"

His eyes gleamed. "In *my* tent."

181

The tent of a mercenary. Ceara eyed the trunk of armor and the one of weapons. "Is it a weapon?"

Rafael laughed. "It is *the* weapon."

Ceara did not understand. "You throw poorly fashioned cups at your enemies?"

He laughed again, then leaned forward, bracing his elbows on his knees. "Did you not know that you entered the den of the dragon?"

"The dragon," she echoed. "Do people other than Maximilian truly call you that?"

He nodded.

"It cannot be because of your appetite for maidens," she said pertly. "I know you do not have one."

His smile heated, his gaze flicking over her. Ceara realized she wore only her chemise.

Rafael removed his boots, so at ease that they might have shared a chamber for a decade. Ceara watched him with fascination and anticipation. "Jean le Beau gave me that moniker because of the Greek fire. Only I in the Compagnie Rouge know its secret and it is a formidable weapon, to be sure."

Greek fire. Ceara had heard of that weapon but had believed it to be a fable. Fire that burned on water? How could that be? "What has Greek fire to do with dragons?"

"It has been compared to their fire by no less than Jean de Joinville." His jerkin was cast on the bed and his chemise untucked.

She caught her breath, thrilled that he intended to disrobe, but strove to hide her reaction lest he halt. "Should I know who he is?"

"He accompanied the French king on crusade to Palestine and wrote of the weapon when he saw it used by the Saracens. He spoke first of a missile, then greater detail." Rafael cleared his throat and quoted a passage. *"'The tail of fire that railed behind it was as big as a great spear, and it made such a noise as it came, that it sounded like the thunder of heaven. It looked like a dragon flying through the air. Such a bright light did it cast that one could see all over the camp as though it were day, by reason of the great mass of fire and the brilliance of the light it shed.'"* He nodded once. "That was over a century ago. I still feel the same marvel each time I let it loose."

Ceara looked at the box of odd cups. "Those vessels?"

"Those vessels are one means of delivering the Greek fire. I prefer their size. They must be filled with a mixture wrought from these other ingredients." He gestured to the smaller trunks and boxes. "They must be in precise balance and prepared with every attention to detail. The opening is then plugged with the cloth, the remainder of the cloth wrapped around the orb, then lit with a flame before being hurled at the target."

"That was how you took Château de Vries?"

"Among other places." He came to her then, his gaze simmering, and began to unlace his chausses. "If you do not intend to enjoy that bath, *bella*, then I will."

Ceara's heart jumped but she refused to show her shyness. He disliked maidens. She had to be more at ease in such intimate moments that he might forget her innocence. She cast him a smile, then pulled her chemise over her head and cast it aside.

Rafael froze, his gaze darkening with welcome heat. She braided her hair and wound the braid over her head, securing it with a tie. She felt like a wanton displaying herself to him, but it was thrilling to have him study her with such intensity.

She wore only the key to the treasury, trapped on its lace, when she approached him. "And how is Amaury?"

"Hale enough." His voice sounded tight with strain and Ceara chose to tease him.

She noted that his fists were clenched by his sides when she stopped directly before him. She took a breath, then reached to continue untying the lace of his chausses as if she did as much all the time. She could feel the heat of his skin through the cloth and the ferocity of his gaze. Her mouth went dry at her own audacity. "And Elizabeth?"

"I did not have the good fortune to see the lady."

His manhood strained the fabric and she gave him a little caress through the garment, hearing how he caught his breath. She flicked a glance to his burning gaze, then slid her hands beneath his chausses, slowly easing them downward. He smiled with familiar hunger, his expression reminding her of a wolf. "Did you gain what you desired of him?"

"I believe so." His voice was a low murmur.

"Will we linger here?"

He shook his head, his expression inscrutable. "Nay. But you and I are invited to dine in the hall this night."

"Then you must bathe quickly," she said, her tone mischievous.

Rafael hesitated only a moment, then he murmured something beneath his breath that Ceara did not understand. She could not care when he kicked off his chausses, then discarded his chemise. He was all lean strength, his skin tanned to gold and his body powerful. Ceara hardly had a chance to look before he swept her into his arms. "We must make haste, *bella*, lest we miss the meal," he growled, his smile as wicked as ever it had been.

"Aye," she agreed. "I am most hungry, sir." She reached up to touch her lips to his, expecting to be rebuffed. He caught his breath, then he swore with a savagery that astonished her.

A mere heartbeat after that, Rafael captured her mouth beneath his own in a possessive kiss that made her heart race. Aye, she thought he might devour her and she could imagine no better fate. The Dragon would despoil her and she could not wait.

Her scheme was destined to succeed!

Ceara wrapped herself around Rafael as he carried her to the bath, wanting only to feel his skin against hers. She fully expected him to lower her into the water, but instead, he stepped into the tub himself, then sank down slowly. She gasped to find herself sitting in his lap, his arousal hard against her buttocks, the key snared between her breasts and his chest.

He framed her face in his hands and kissed her, his mouth open and his tongue demanding, as if he could not resist her. Ceara reached for him, letting her hands slide down his chest in the water, but Rafael halted her. He turned her so that she was sitting on his thigh, and placed her hands on the sides of the tub. She could feel his erection against her hip and he nuzzled her neck from behind. He cupped her breasts in his hands and held them above the warm water, the cool air making her nipples draw into taut peaks. He kissed her ear, her throat, her neck, his lips and his teeth setting her very flesh afire.

Ceara sighed contentment and leaned back against him, moaning when he rolled her nipples between the finger and thumb of each hand. He pinched them and teased them, tormenting them with pleasure so that she rocked her hips against him with need. His breath fanned against her neck as he chuckled, then one hand slid into the water. She felt him spread his fingers wide as his hand eased lower, then his fingertips slid into the slick heat between her thighs. Ceara arched back and he turned her slightly, cradling her in his lap as he claimed her mouth again.

Rafael teased her clitoris just as he had her nipples, coaxing it to a hard bud, then his finger slid inside her so that she gasped. He chuckled darkly and swallowed the minute sound, then slid a second finger inside her, working them back and forth so that Ceara thought she might expire from pleasure. That was naught compared to the sensation when his thumb began to torment her clitoris again, his kiss driving her ever higher, his touch making her wild with desire.

She felt the storm rise within her, then he pinched that tender pearl and cast her free, swallowing her cries of satisfaction as she shuddered in ecstasy. When she clung to his shoulders, gasping in the wake of her release, he washed her gently then lifted her from the tub, wrapping her in one of the thick cloths. She reached for him, but he stayed her with a gesture. His gaze locked upon her, his blue eyes burning like flaming sapphires, as he closed a hand around himself.

Ceara understood. He would not claim her maidenhead this night, but his desire could not be ignored. She would not surrender the war, but could cede this battle. She rose to her feet and dropped the cloth, letting him look upon her. His nostrils flared and his lips drew to a line, his gaze snapping with desire. His entire body was taut as he caressed himself, his gaze unswerving, and Ceara took the only step between them. She reached up to kiss him, then as his mouth closed possessively over hers, she slid one hand down his chest and wrapped her fingers around his strength. She gave him only one caress and the release came upon him, compulsive and powerful, making him rock upon his feet as his seed sprayed forth.

He caught his breath and dropped his forehead to her shoulder, his body slick with perspiration. "We will be late to the board," he said gruffly.

"I believe 'twas worth it," Ceara said and he raised his simmering gaze to hers.

"Never doubt it, *bella*," he murmured, then kissed her thoroughly once again. There was something in his tone, something that sounded like a warning or a farewell to Ceara, but as soon as his mouth closed over hers, she could not care about anything other than Rafael's kiss.

CHAPTER 12

*W*hether she was a temptress, a seductress, a siren or a witch, Ceara was impossible for Rafael to resist. He had not been able to keep from succumbing to temptation. Just one moment of her silken skin against his own, or one more chance to watch her gain her pleasure, one last taste of her kisses had been irresistible. He felt his fascination growing and knew their ways could not part quickly enough.

Even this time, the sight of Ceara's release made him yearn to bury himself within her and be satisfied. He suspected, though, that once would not suffice. Better to hasten to Beaupoint and see her protected while he had some chance of treating her with the honor she deserved.

A man of honor would never put a lady's chastity in such peril, but Rafael would not follow his father's lead.

He had spoken to Raynard who believed he could guide Rafael to the location of the treasure. He had arranged for Ceara's safety in his absence, perhaps for all time.

All he needed was the key to ensure the success of his quest.

Rafale shaved after their bath, his thoughts churning even as Ceara hummed a merry tune. His tent was filled with the scent of her and the heat of her, his thoughts filled with all they had not yet done. His awareness of her only increased his urgency to leave her. Already, he found a beguiling ease in her company. 'Twas clear he could readily come to rely upon her companionship, her conversation and her challenges.

It must be this night, and it would be this night that they each followed their own path.

But the key.

Time was of the essence and perhaps he could distract her long enough to obtain the prize. Rafael dressed quickly in his finest, donning also the jeweled crucifix over the black tunic. He set out the fur-lined cloak, noting that Antonio had already polished his boots to a gleam.

Ceara had but one choice of garment, the kirtle she had worn at Kilderrick. She wore it with her tall boots and sturdy belt, her hunting knife at the ready, as ever it was. She braided her hair but had neither wimple nor circlet as befit a married woman. She was radiant and he had no quibbles with her garb, but he had to claim that key.

Worse, he had to claim it without arousing her suspicions. Sadly, she was not witless.

Truly, that was much of her appeal.

Rafael circled her, as if discontent. "I would have you more finely attired," he said finally with a heartfelt sigh.

She surveyed her own garb and smiled, untroubled. "I have naught else. I will suffice as ever I do."

He fought a smile at her confident claim. "Then I must augment. They will only believe you to be my bride if you are richly attired."

"You could give me the ring again," she said, but he ignored her, turning to his trunks.

"Indulge me?"

She folded her arms across her chest, smiled and nodded. "I suspect it does not matter. You will do as you will do, and we *will* be late to the board."

"Do you protest the reason for our delay?"

Ceara laughed. "Not a whit."

Rafael grinned, then threw open trunks in succession. He chose a finer leather belt to replace the one she wore and left her knife aside when he changed it. She tried to protest but he silenced her with a fingertip.

"They will take it from you at the gate at any rate," he chided softly. "Better to leave it here in safety."

Ceara ceded with a frown but she ceded. "What of yours?"

"You are right," he said, and removed his own dagger from the scabbard on his belt.

That pleased her.

Rafael rummaged in the small hoard he had gathered over the years. There was a simple circlet and he had a length of undyed silk, both seized in a long-ago assault upon a keep and nigh forgotten at the bottom of his trunk. He wound the cloth around the circlet expertly, then draped it around Ceara's throat once the circlet was set into her hair.

"How many woman have you dressed in finery?" she asked wryly.

"More than you would wish to know," he said, hoping to evade her questions.

"Nary a maiden in their number?"

"Not a one."

None of those women, though, had been as splendid as Ceara. The fiery red hue of her braids fairly glowed against the cloth and he nodded with satisfaction. He opened her chemise a little further with a fingertip, tracing the curve of her breast until she caught her breath. Her eyes flashed and she flushed a little, but the change favored her.

He stole a kiss intended to melt her knees and her resistance, and when she swayed against him, he knew that she was not the sole one affected. He placed his shorter cloak over her shoulders, though it was not lined with fur, and walked around her again.

"Will I suffice, sir?"

"You always suffice, *bella*, but on this night, we must appear to be as equals to my brother and his lady wife."

"But we are not their equals." Her smile turned impish. "Unless you claim Château de Vries as your holding."

Rafael was dismissive of the notion. "We may appear as their equals in wealth if not stature. Much is determined by appearances, after all."

She nodded understanding and waited his decision.

There was naught for it.

He would have to surrender one of his prizes. He knew the sole one that would do. If he could not return, if he chose not to return, if there was no treasure or he was robbed of it, Ceara would have a goodly measure of wealth as a result of this gift.

Rafael rummaged in the treasury, hearing Ceara catch her breath when he drew out the long string of pearls. And well she should, for they were magnificent. Each was as big as his thumbnail and they were matched in hue. Of all his prizes, they were not just among the finest but had no taint of blood upon them—they had been surrendered willingly to the Compagnie Rouge. They had been a inducement for him to lead the army by another route and Rafael had been so awed by the pearls that he had done as much.

He draped the necklace around Ceara's neck, liking how the pearls gleamed against her skin, how the string fell almost to her knees. She raised a hand to the gems in wonder, but Rafael was busily arranging them. He was also striving to ignore the lace that held the key, hoping Ceara would think he had forgotten it. He looped the string around her throat twice more, then pulled two loops more closely around her neck. The final loop he held up to her waist, looking around the tent as if seeking what he already knew he would use.

"Hold this," he instructed, then retrieved a gold pin from the treasury. It was a small cross with arms of even length, like the one used by the crusading orders, set with garnets. He pinned the pearls to her belt, then stepped back to survey her.

"Much better," he declared and she smiled, as radiant as any queen. He grimaced, feigning dismay, for the moment had come to seize the prize. He could only hope for success. "But this." He touched the hide cord that held the key and grimaced as if disgusted by the contrast of it against the pearls.

Ceara looked down at it and he watched her fight against her suspicions. "I could leave it here with my knife," she said finally, just as he had hoped she would. Relief flooded through him.

"A most excellent notion," he said warmly. "I will secure both here in my small treasury and Antonio will guard the tent. I cannot imagine that we will be detained long at the board of Beaupoint." He winked at her as he made space for her treasures atop the coins. "Amaury cannot wait to witness my departure, after all."

Ceara smiled even as she set the key into the treasury. He felt her doubt but ignored it. She took a breath as he secured the lid, then he adjusted the drape of his cloak upon her shoulders. "Magnificent," he murmured, brushing his lips against hers before leading her to the flap. "Perhaps you might undertake a small assignment for me," he said, wanting only to distract her.

"Of course."

"If you might learn the closest port from your former companion, that would be most helpful."

"Will you not ask Amaury as much?"

"I will, but he might be disinclined to honesty. We will be able to compare their replies, for I doubt Elizabeth would try to deceive you."

Ceara smiled, clearly pleased by her task. "I will do my best." Rafael led her from the tent, watching her eyes light when she realized that another palfrey had been saddled for her. "I am to ride by myself?"

"'Tis only fitting."

He lifted her to the saddle, admiring her confident seat on the horse, even side-saddle. He could have stared at her all the night long, filling his mind with her beauty, but again, he dared not arouse any suspicions of his intentions. He kissed her hand. "You are splendid, *bella*," he murmured and meant every word of it.

"You do not look so poorly yourself," she replied with the mischievous smile he adored.

He would miss her, to be sure, but she would be protected at Beaupoint and that was no small detail to guarantee.

Even though Rafael felt like a wretch for what he would do.

'TWAS A PERFECT SPRING EVENING, the sun just sinking toward the horizon, the sky clear and the wind crisp from the sea. Ceara saw the stars emerging overhead and smelled the tide changing in the firth. It felt good to be riding again, to see the satisfaction in Rafael's expression when he surveyed her, to feel such confidence that this night they would be together in truth.

Even Beaupoint, rising tall and forbidding before them, offered the prospect of adventure. She had never journeyed this far from home, never eaten in a hall finer than Kilderrick. She would be glad to see Elizabeth again, though they two had never had much in common. Better for Elizabeth to be secured within stone walls, like a princess in a tower, while Ceara roamed with Rafael in search of new conquests.

She would be glad of a bountiful meal, to be certain.

Matteo followed behind them at a slight distance, and Ceara knew his hand was on the hilt of his blade. There was a fanfare when they approached the gates and Rafael smiled at the sound. The gates were opened and she could see the torches burning within the bailey.

Rafael gestured and she rode ahead of him, seeing that Amaury and Elizabeth stood on the far side of the bailey to welcome them. Ceara was scarcely aware that Rafael was not immediately behind her, so occupied was she with the unfamiliar sights of the keep. Beaupoint was larger than any fortress she had visited before. The walls were so thick that the guards had a chamber on either side of the passageway. Ceara felt the chill of the stone walls that towered over her and shivered in a sudden premonition of dread. There were two metal portcullis gates to bar the entry after the wooden gates and she was beneath the second when she heard a sound behind and above her.

She glanced back to see that Rafael was yet outside the walls, watching her solemnly.

He raised a hand and she knew.

The cur meant to leave her behind!

Ceara tried to turn her horse but the bridle was seized by a knight immediately beside her. He obviously had been granted this task, as had his fellow who snatched the reins from her hands. Between the two of them, the horse was restrained. Ceara leaped from the creature's back but another knight caught her around the waist. Though she fought him with all her might, she knew her fate when the portcullis slammed into the ground.

"Rafael!" she roared in outrage. She wrenched free of the knight's grasp and flung herself at the portcullis, giving it a hearty shake. It did not even tremble.

Rafael watched, impassive, then blew her a kiss. *"Ciao, bella,"* he said softly, his deep voice echoing in the stone passageway and she knew he had planned all of this.

"You filthy lying wretch!" Ceara cried. "Scoundrel! Blackguard!" She shook the portcullis with every insult, but Rafael did not glance back. It was worse to be ignored than to have been tricked in the first place. "You will not abandon me so readily as this! We are yet wed, sir, for better or for worse—until death us do part."

But it was only Matteo who turned to look at her. Rafael did not glance back, his back straight as he rode out of her life.

And she knew then that their vows were as ashes. Without the match having been consummated, it could be as readily dissolved as if it had never been.

He had done precisely as he had pledged he would do—but she had been sufficiently witless to expect otherwise.

"Fiend!" she shouted but she might have been calling to the wind.

"He meant the best," Amaury said quietly from behind her but Ceara turned on him with fury.

"Do not be a fool," she snapped. "He intends to steal my family treasure and claim it for his own."

Amaury and Elizabeth exchanged a glance.

"He said naught of treasure," Amaury said.

"Of course, he did not! He argued his case that you might agree with him and be of aid in his scheme."

Oh, she could have merrily wrung Rafael's neck.

The worse was that he rode into peril by leaving her behind and these gates ensured she could do naught about it.

Ceara propped her hands on her hips and glared at Amaury, who retreated a step. "The cur lied to me, and I was fool enough to be readily deceived." She spat on the ground then, more furious with herself than with Rafael, then glared at Amaury. "And *you* aided in his scheme. I thought you were supposed to be keen of wit, no less immune to his charm."

"Nay, he does not abandon you, Ceara," Amaury insisted. "He loves you."

"Nay," she protested by rote, but Amaury shook his head, his confidence complete.

Ceara's fury faded like night before the dawn. She knew her astonishment showed as clearly as her skepticism had. "He does not," she murmured, but realized as the words crossed her lips how much she wanted to believe. "He cannot. He would insist otherwise."

Amaury smiled. "He surrenders much to see you defended."

Elizabeth touched the string of pearls with an admiring fingertip. "He wants to protect you," she said. "Whether he knows the inclination of his heart or nay."

"It cannot be," Ceara whispered, looking after Rafael's fading figure.

"He believes you deserve better than he could give," Amaury supplied.

"And a man who has failed to recognize his own merit finds that notion familiar," Elizabeth said warmly. She slid her hand through Amaury's elbow and gazed up at him, adoration in her expression. The pair exchanged a look of such heat that Ceara felt the glow of their love and she frowned as she averted her gaze.

Rafael had almost reached the camp of the Compagnie Rouge.

"When does he leave?" she asked, knowing she had need of a plan.

"With the dawn. He intends to find passage, presumably to France."

Ceara shook her head. "He will not sail for France until he has gone north to fetch the treasure." She leaned her forehead against the portcullis. "And without my aid, he will die in the attempt."

"You under-estimate his resolve," Amaury said gently, but Ceara did not.

Elizabeth took Ceara's arm and led her from the gates. "Come and eat. The meal is prepared and it will do us all good…"

"I have no appetite." Ceara said with impatience, wondering if it was possible to bribe the gatekeeper without Amaury's knowledge. She did not even have her dagger.

Oh, Rafael had deceived her well. She might have been impressed with his skill if she had not been so vexed—and so fearful for him.

"But we can confer more privately at the board," Elizabeth said, an unfamiliar resolve in her tone. She gave Ceara's arm a tug. "Come," she continued, dropping her voice to a whisper. "And pretend to have surrendered this battle for the moment. We will talk later, in privacy."

"Are there spies in your hall?"

"When people speak of treasure, there are always spies."

"I fear for him, Elizabeth," Ceara confided softly and the other woman studied her. "If you do not let me return to him before they ride out, Rafael will seek that treasure and he will die."

Elizabeth's smile dawned slowly and her eyes lit. "Why do I have the notion that he is not the sole one whose heart is engaged?"

And Ceara could only flush at the truth in that.

Raynard had disappeared.

Rafael could not explain it.

He sought the warrior upon his return to the camp from Beaupoint but could find no sign of him. Raynard's horses were gone, as well as his squire, Gervais. There was no sign of his baggage or his tent.

Rafael could make no sense of it. No one had seen the warrior leave and he had told no one of any intent to do so. He had not been seen since they had made camp.

While 'twas true that the individual men were not permanently beholden to the Compagnie Rouge, few left without a word of explanation. Rafael would have expected the same of Raynard, and it irked him to be mistaken.

It irked him yet more that he now had no means to locate the treasure.

Rafael sat in his tent, pondering his own choices. Without Raynard or Ceara, his chances of locating the mermaid's cache were small indeed. Though others might have heard of it, he could spend weeks wandering—and worse, he would not know the locale when he passed through it. Even if he found a guide, his search might not be welcomed, given that he was a stranger to these parts. Rafael recognized a quest with little chance of successful completion—and one that could indeed end poorly for him.

He paced his tent, then packed what few items Antonio had set out. He could lead his men back to Kilderrick, but there was little point in that. They could ride south in the morning and seek passage back to France. That would solve many of his woes, though the notion had little appeal.

His regret in leaving Ceara would diminish with time and distance, though on this night, the loss of her company weighed upon his heart. He disliked that matters were unresolved with Edward and feared for her future.

He also disliked that they had parted badly.

He was becoming soft, to be sure!

Rafael resolved that he would return to Château de Vries and negotiate with Philip for the seal. Once that was resolved, the Compagnie Rouge would ride forth again, seeking opportunity once more.

'Twas his life. There was no reason for the scheme to lack appeal, though it did.

Rafael wondered what Ceara would do when Amaury permitted her to leave Beaupoint. Would she return to Kilderrick? Would she seek her family treasure alone? Would Edward find her and seize her again? That prospect troubled Rafael though it should not be his concern. He had saved her once from that villain and delivered her to Amaury's protection. He had done more than a man of his ilk could be expected to do.

Perhaps he should seek out Edward de Leslie and ensure that threat was eliminated.

Perhaps Ceara had been right about the missed opportunity in eliminating that man.

He recalled her teasing comment about protective mercenaries and frowned. No matter what she said, he knew that riding with the Compagnie Rouge was no life for her. Better that she be left at Beaupoint than in some village far away from all she knew—pregnant, despoiled and abandoned.

Better she was yet a maiden and among friends, so she could make her own choices. Was that not what she said she desired?

Rafael would not consider what he desired.

He locked the trunk that contained his treasury, discontent, doused the last lantern that burned in his tent, and then he heard the nicker of a horse. 'Twas Phantôm, the sound the stallion made when encountering someone familiar to him. But Antonio had to be asleep. The boy was exhausted and when he slept hard, naught roused him before dawn.

Rafael felt his eyes narrow as he heard a footfall that could only be that of a destrier. He moved near the tent flap and listened, straining his ears against the quiet of the night. It was dark and still. He could hear men sleeping and the tails of horses swishing. The fire crackled no longer, doubtless having burned down to coals, and there was no murmur of conversation.

There was another step of that destrier, another nicker.

And the whisper of a familiar woman's voice.

Ceara was stealing Phantôm.

Again!

RAFAEL CAST OPEN the tent flap and stepped outside, enraged. His destrier was a dozen steps away, Ceara standing beside the stallion. Behind her was the palfrey she had ridden to Beaupoint. She was dressed to travel, wearing a heavy cloak he did not recognize. She smiled at him with such audacity that his blood boiled—then he saw the silhouette of Amaury on his own destrier in the shadows behind Ceara.

He had ensured her safety and she cast it away.

"I thought I might have to awaken you with a kiss," she whispered, those eyes dancing. "'Tis a shame you heard my return and cheated me of that pleasure."

This was no jest.

Rafael marched toward her and seized the destrier's reins. He fixed her with a glare. "I left you safely within Beaupoint's walls, *bella*."

"And I declined to stay there."

"Have you no care for your own welfare?" he demanded, nigh prepared to give her a shake.

"I ride in pursuit of my family treasure."

"Have you forgotten your betrothed, Edward? Where else will he seek you but in the lands of your kin?" He flung out his hands. "What merit are the wits you have been granted if you decline to use them?"

She was utterly untroubled by his outburst, though it vexed Rafael to have lost his temper. He heard his men stirring behind him and knew his fury had awakened them. He glared at the maiden responsible, folding his arms across his chest lest he shake her in truth.

"You are only vexed because you intended to seek the treasure without me," she said with annoying confidence. "I had to come during the night to intervene before you departed."

She spoke as if her choice was utterly reasonable, when there was naught reasonable about her decision at all. "I will not take you into such peril under any circumstances." He nodded to Amaury. "Take her back to Beaupoint. Lock her in the dungeon, if you must. *She will not ride with me.*"

"You do mean to seek the treasure, then," she asked, utterly undeterred. He had erred greatly in letting this woman trust him!

"What I intend or do not intend is of no import to you. Our paths have parted. Our match will be annulled. We have a wager and I will keep to its terms."

Ceara shook her head. "But much has changed. Amaury tells me that the galloglass warriors are mustering and there can be only one reason why that is so."

Rafael waited, for he could not guess the import of this. He knew by Ceara's jubilant expression that she believed she knew the truth and he doubted she could remain silent for long.

"My brother returns!" she cried when Rafael did not speak, flinging out her hands. "My brother returns to claim his rightful due as chieftain." Her excitement could not be ignored. "The gallowglass warriors rally to his aid. Our lands will be retrieved from the Lord of the Isles, the chieftainship will be claimed from Raghnall, and my brother will possess his rightful legacy."

Rafael pushed a hand through his hair. "And you know this how?"

"There can be no other explanation. 'Tis obvious."

"I can think of a thousand explanations," he replied drily.

"Because you do not know these lands. This victory has been fore-told and the time is ripe…"

"Why?"

She eyed him. "Because Godfroy Macdonald is dead, of course."

Rafael's gaze slid to Amaury, who remained silent and impassive. "Why is that of import?"

"Aimil, the heiress of Garmaron, had three sons by Eòin Macdonald, all of whom were denied their legacy when he put her aside to wed the king's daughter. The eldest died and the second son, Raghnall, was granted the chieftainship of clan MacRuari." Ceara was dismissive of this. "It is an empty title, though, for he has no lands and no men. His father, Eòin, seized all the lands save one keep, the Eilean Tioram."

"Eòin Macdonald," Rafael echoed.

"Also known as John of Islay, Lord of the Isles."

"I have heard this name before."

"Of course. He was Godfroy's father." She gave him an impatient look, as if he was slow of wit, which Rafael did not appreciate. "With his youngest brother dead, Raghnall is without allies. He is at his weakest point, which means the time has come for my brother to return. He will have dispatched word to the galloglass warriors, who rally to his banner even as we speak." She nodded with confidence. "He will need the mermaid's treasure to secure his triumph. I intend to retrieve it for him."

Rafael shook his head. "I intend to ensure that you do no such thing."

Ceara glanced over her shoulder at Amaury, her pride in Rafael's response obvious. "I told you he was protective of me."

Amaury did not reply, his expression remaining grim. Rafael wondered what else Ceara had told him.

"I am no defender of damsels," Rafael began to argue, but Ceara reached out and boldly touched the ring on his finger even as she held his gaze. He had no notion what she might say, but he was sufficiently intrigued to fall silent.

"I wager Francesca was a beauty to claim Jean le Beau's attention."

Rafael could only shrug at this change of subject. He watched her warily, unable to predict what she would say next—or why.

"Did he give her this ring?"

"The sole thing he gave her was an unwanted babe in her belly," Rafael said bitterly before he could stop himself.

Ceara nodded. "It was her ring, though, was it not?" Her guess was uncannily accurate. "Was it from her parents? Or did she have a betrothed before Jean le Beau despoiled her?"

Rafael met her gaze steadily. "What if she did? The ring is of no import!"

"The ring is of great import, and your every denial only convinces me of that." Ceara leaned closer. "Maximilian was startled that you surrendered it, after all."

"Maximilian is overly sentimental."

Ceara shook her head with conviction. "I will guess that matters did not proceed well for Francesca once she found herself with child, thanks to Jean le Beau's assault upon her."

"You do not know as much," Rafael protested, hearing the echo of his father's triumphant claims in his memory again. He would dream of that conversation all his life, he was certain.

"You would not be so determined to leave maidenheads intact otherwise," Ceara argued. "Nay, he took her, indifferent to the consequences, concerned only with his own desire. What happened to her afterward? Matteo said you speak Venetian to each other. Did you grow up in Venice. Why? Was that her home? Perhaps she returned to a home there or Jean le Beau cast her aside there. But she could not have been welcomed by her kin or her betrothed if you were abandoned after she died in childbirth."

It took all within Rafael to keep from silent as she unraveled his past with fearsome accuracy.

Ceara continued, her fingertips landing upon the ring again. "You said she was a maid. Her family must have denied her because she was despoiled. Perhaps her son was also cast out, a mere infant but a shame to his family, a bastard born to a woman who died. Perhaps this ring, a possession of his mother that was not linked to her family, was given to the child. It might have been on a cord around his neck, a small souvenir of his heritage, a token any orphan might treasure. It hints at a history and a family, perhaps a family he always yearned to have. It hints that he was once loved." She looked up at him, her gaze filled with invitation. "You could have all of that, Rafael," she whispered and he could not believe how he was tempted. "You could keep Château de Vries. You could uphold our marriage. I would proudly bear you sons, even without that ring upon my finger, and I would love you with all my heart and soul."

She had no notion how her words fed a yearning deep within his heart, but Rafael knew that such dreams did not come true. He would only injure her or lead her into danger.

"You promise much to win my agreement, *bella*. What if I took all you offer and abandoned you afterward?"

She smiled, that mischievous expression making his heart squeeze. "You would not," she said with such unwarranted confidence that his temper flared anew.

"You do not know what you suggest," he replied with heat. "You do not know what you invite into your days and nights, and you trust where such faith is undeserved. *I am my father's son.*"

Ceara shook her head. "Nay. You are obviously your mother's son. Your father showed no hesitation in despoiling maidens, after all."

Rafael could not argue with that truth.

"I think you have made the best choices possible in a life blessed with few good options, and now, you have the opportunity for better choices. That is a gift and one you should welcome."

"Ours is no real marriage and 'twill not be one," he insisted, his tone harsh. "You would spin a tale that suits you but not me. I am no lord and no nobleman. I am a warrior and a mercenary, and I will die as I have lived. Do not be so fool as to expect otherwise."

Ceara nodded, clearly unconvinced.

"I will *not* take you north," he said with force.

"You will go alone?"

"My choice is not your concern."

"But the key is a feint," she said and smiled.

Rafael eyed her, inviting an explanation with a glance.

Ceara shrugged. "I do not know what it opens, but it will serve no purpose in claiming the mermaid's treasury. You might as well cast it into the sea."

Rafael glared down at her. "Why would the key be a ruse? Why would you possess a key that has no purpose?"

"To have a plausible tale to tell. My mother advised as much." She smiled with infuriating surety. "The key kept Edward from killing me and prevented you from abandoning me, so perhaps its usefulness is over."

"I do not care," Rafael said. "I ride south at dawn."

"Not to find the treasure?"

He shook his head.

Ceara's lips set with a resolve he knew would not be readily shaken. "I am not going to abandon the treasure, simply because you have no desire to seek it out."

"That is not what I said."

"You said you ride south," she said, her voice rising. "That can only be because you do not wish to claim the treasure. You have the key, after all, and until a moment past, you believed it was of import."

He glowered at her. "I do not know where to seek this treasure."

Her brows rose. "Oh! You should have thought of that before surrendering me to Amaury's protection."

"I did think of that," he said through gritted teeth. "I intended to have Raynard guide me there, but he has vanished."

"Perhaps he seeks it himself."

"He does not have the key."

Ceara raised a brow. "Perhaps he knows it is of no use."

Rafael sighed. "Enough! Dismount. Take the palfrey and go wherever you will, but wait until the morning."

"You should come with me to claim the treasure." She surveyed him, as pleased with herself as he had ever seen her. "After all, I am the true key."

"You? How can that be?"

Ceara laughed. "'Tis the treasure of a *mermaid*, Rafael. I am the key because I can swim."

Rafael could think of no reply to that. He looked at Amaury, who shrugged, then back at Ceara. "'Tis an uncommon skill, *bella*." Rafael would expect the ability to swim to be particularly rare in Scotland, where both air and water were cold beyond belief.

"Aye." She smiled with pride. "But I swim with all the agility of a fish." She wagged a finger at him. "You will need my skills to seize the prize."

"The treasure is hidden underwater," he guessed, intrigued. If that was the case, it might yet be intact.

"Not precisely. It lies in a cavern that can only be reached by swimming underwater. I remember its location well and I can give you a list of the treasure, if you please."

"I thought no one had seen it in decades."

Ceara smiled. "No one but me and my brother. We found it when we were children."

But the brother had not returned, Rafael recalled, wherever he had gone. If that man was dead, Ceara was the sole person who knew the treasure's location.

But Rafael would not be swayed by her tale. He considered that Ceara had need of him for some reason, and recalled his original conviction that she would ensure he met some dire end.

She extended her hand. "I will need my crossbow."

"Safe within the walls of Beaupoint, you had no need of it."

"And you do not require two such weapons, given the extent of your arsenal."

"You should return to Kilderrick," he argued. "And wait until dawn, at least. The roads will be safer." She opened her mouth to argue, but Rafael raised a hand. "Enough, *bella*. You have had your say and my choice is made."

Amaury urged his horse forward at that.

"But something *is* afoot," he warned softly. "There are warriors aplenty riding and sailing for the north, as if a great army musters in Scotland. It is possible that Ceara speaks aright."

"I am right," she interjected but Amaury continued.

"I can learn no tidings of it. One advantage, though, is that you could sail north and attract less attention than would customarily be the case, particularly if the Compagnie Rouge remains here. I would ask you to do as much and bring me whatever tidings you can. If Ceara is right and alliances will be challenged, I would know of it as soon as possible." He smiled slightly. "I would compensate you."

Ceara regarded him, her anticipation of his agreement so obvious that Rafael could only shake his head. He was not so readily manipulated as that.

"I see that you two have contrived a plan," he said and Amaury nodded.

"'Twill be simplest to evade curiosity if there are just the two of you. You might ride in disguise, as mercenaries in seek of employ, with palfreys."

Ceara's eyes were bright with challenge and anticipation. "We ride alone, just you and I, no steeds, and we split the treasure equally when we claim it."

"Equally?" Rafael pretended to be outraged, but he wanted to see her reaction.

"You do not bring an army, thus your former rate cannot stand," she said with heat. "And you are being compensated by Amaury." She was so sure of herself that Rafael was almost reluctant to disappoint her. But she spun a tale that had no basis in fact. She assumed all would proceed her way because she wished it to be so.

But if there was to be war, then Rafael was the one who understood what would transpire.

He leaned close to her, watching her lips curve in a broader smile. "You are a witless fool, *bella*, if you think I will consider this situation for one moment. I ride south with the Compagnie Rouge and if you are too foolish to remain in safety, your demise will be by your own choice."

He saw her eyes light with outrage, then he pivoted to return to his tent. The entire company was watching and listening, his men standing in the shadows, their expressions forbidding. Bernard nodded once toward him before Ceara, predictably, seized the back of his belt.

CHAPTER 13

*Y*ou cannot deny me," Ceara said, aware that Rafael had done precisely that.

She knew he could not abandon her here when her brother's legacy was to be reclaimed. She would not allow it! He liked to let others believe that he was motivated solely by his own advantage, but Ceara knew better. She had to play her part in her brother's triumph and that meant Rafael had to accompany her.

Amaury had decreed as much. If Rafael refused, Amaury would take her forcibly back to Beaupoint. She would never be a maiden locked safely in a tower.

More importantly, she knew the secret that lurked in Rafael's heart and in this moment, she would use it against him.

Rafael turned a simmering glance upon her. "I just have." He pointed to the keep. "Go. Return to Kilderrick in daylight and with an escort. I will surrender your crossbow to Amaury, to be returned to you when he sees fit."

"You cannot treat me like a child!"

"On the contrary, I treat you like the fool you insist upon being."

"You are cursed stubborn, sir. We could ride together and ensure that justice prevails. We could find passage at Whitehaven…"

And that was sufficient. She saw his eyes flash as he strode back toward her, fury in every line of his being. "Have you ever been on a ship with men of war, *bella*? Have you any notion of the peril that would confront you there?"

She straightened with defiance. "You were the one who told me that peril made one feel alive."

"Aye, when one is well defended. Consider that any ship will be filled to capacity, if so many wish to journey north. Horses will be shoulder to shoulder in the hold, and men will be pressed against each other above. All is open to the sky, so if it rains, all will be wet. There will be no fire, no heat, no hot food. There will be vermin and there will be...dirt."

She shook her head, knowing the smell of manure well enough. "I do not fear *dirt*."

"You should fear men."

"I could disguise myself as a boy. I could be your squire. No one would know."

Rafael shook his head. "How many days sail to this Eilean Tioram?" he asked Amaury.

That knight shrugged. "If the wind is with you, it could be less than a week. If not, it could readily be two."

"A fortnight," Rafael said to Ceara, biting off his words. "How will you relieve yourself for a single day, let alone a fortnight, without anyone noticing that you cannot piss over the side of the boat? Your secret will not last a day, and then matters will become interesting indeed. Warriors on ships are bored, for there is little for them to do. There is one amusement that can be pursued anywhere, *bella*." He held up a finger. "One. And I have yet to meet a man who did not favor it. You will be fondled. You might be cornered."

"You will defend me," she insisted. "You have done as much before."

"I am a single man," he said with heat. "I will be outnumbered at least ten times over, perhaps twenty. I will have to sleep and I may well be attacked. I may be killed, or worse, and then your fate will be sealed. You will never arrive intact at your destination."

Her eyes narrowed. "What could be worse than being killed?"

"They might injure me or bind me, then compel me to watch." She was startled but he continued, his words hard. "You know little of the savagery of men, *bella*, but I have seen it all and more." He poked a heavy finger into her shoulder, punctuating each word with a jab. "Listen to me and listen well. I will not take you north and I forbid any man who follows me to do as much in my stead."

She looked beyond him to the Compagnie Rouge, who looked as resolute as Rafael.

"You could take the Compagnie Rouge with us," she suggested.

"To what purpose? We do not even know that the mermaid's treasure exists or can be found. It is a futile venture. We sail south to opportunity." He held her gaze. "Farewell, *bella*."

He turned to walk away from her again and her heart nigh broke that he would deny her. She would never see him again, which meant she had naught to lose. Amaury touched her elbow, but Ceara spun away from his touch, calling after Rafael.

If naught else, he would know the truth.

"You are wrong," she said, not caring that her tone was harsh. "I know all too much about the savagery of men."

Rafael looked back.

"When we finally came from Ireland, seeking news of my father, my mother disappeared. She returned a week later, her body as broken as her spirit. She taught me how to tend her wounds, though I was only a child myself."

He halted watching, wary.

Once she had begun to speak, Ceara found that her words poured forth in a torrent. "She delivered a babe eight months later, a second brother for me, a small babe that came too soon and in the chill of winter. I heard the whispering of the midwife. I heard the accusations made against the character of a woman who bore a child long after she had been widowed. 'Twas years before she told me that the babe had been got upon her against her will when she sought tidings of my father from his family." She took a shaking breath. "I will never forget the love in her expression when she held that child, in those few hours that he drew breath. She told me that his conception was not his fault and that he, too, was a beloved child."

Ceara saw Rafael swallow, but he did not turn away.

"They came in pursuit of her, though she did not betray the existence of my brother and I. They wanted to ensure there could be no challenge from Aherne's children. Whoever attacked her must have realized that she had delivered of at least one child. My mother feared some reprisal from the moment of her return: when she bade us to seek the mermaid's protection one night, my brother and I knew where to hide." She shook her head. "I wish we had not left her," she confessed, her words husky.

Rafael did not so much as blink.

"The next day, we found her in the wreckage of what had been our home. I will never forget my terror when I saw the smoke rising from our cottage, when we raced to seek her in that morning's mist. She had been beaten and abused again. My brother vowed then that he would fight for justice and vengeance, that he would return the honor of my father's nature to the holdings of our kin."

Rafael had not moved, but stood as a man transfixed.

Ceara took a step toward him. "You could argue that I saw only the result of such savagery, that I did not taste it myself, but you would be wrong in that, as well. My mother sought the protection of the Earl of Ross, but I fled Delny after my mother's death. You have met Edward de Leslie. Surely you can believe he had no compunction in insisting that I should surrender to him what would ultimately be his. He assaulted me one day when I was alone and I struck him, earning his ire and necessitating my flight. I will never forget how helpless I felt when he held me down, how desperate I was to escape, how much I feared that I would not be able to repel him."

She walked toward Rafael, holding his gaze in challenge. "I know my father fought for justice and his rightful legacy. I saw my mother fight for the future of her children. I fought for my own survival. You fought for coin, perhaps for honor, perhaps for satisfaction, but you are more than you have been, Rafael di Giovanni. You can be more than your father's son. I invite you to journey north with me, to take my brother's cause and ensure that righteousness is returned to my family lands. I invite you to take the cause of good, though there might be no compensation beyond your satisfaction in a task well done, to defend those who have been denied justice in the past." She placed her hand upon the ring on his finger. "I invite you to be Francesca's son, her pride and her joy."

There was silence for a long moment, a veritable eternity as Ceara stared back at Rafael, wondering what he was thinking. When he pivoted, she thought he would deny her request and was crushed—but then, he spoke to the Compagnie Rouge.

"I have no right to lead you all into this terrain, to pledge your blades to a cause that may offer neither reward nor even satisfaction. But I will sail north with this warrior maiden if only to see how this tale will end. The choice of whether to follow and fight or remain and wait is yours to make. Are you with me?"

Matteo raised his hand. "I am," he said, stepping forward, then there was a roar of agreement from the Compagnie Rouge as the others shouted their agreement.

Ceara could not believe that they had agreed, and she almost laughed in her relief.

Then Rafael spun to face her, his eyes glinting. "You will have need of your crossbow, *bella*," he murmured. "No one rides with this company unarmed." She could not care for his objections any longer. She flung herself at him, loving how he caught her against his chest and lifted her high. "Remind me never to vex you," he said softly, humor in his tone, and she could only laugh.

"You take delight in vexing me at every moment," she retorted and he smiled.

"Not every moment, *bella*," he fairly growled, his gaze sweeping over her with a heat that left her blushing. "My fierce beauty," he whispered, then his mouth closed over hers with that possessive ease, his kiss driving every sane notion from her thoughts.

Ceara did not care what he planned or how the future might be resolved. He would go with her. He had been won to her side, and she could only wish to celebrate that.

She kissed him back, her satisfaction with the situation utterly undisguised.

~

AMAURY HAD SPOKEN ARIGHT. The Irish Sea was thick with ships, all sailing in the same direction. The result Rafael should have anticipated was that there were no ships available of sufficient size to transport the Compagnie Rouge.

They waited two endless days for one to return to harbor, as anticipated, and procured their passage with such haste that Rafael knew he had paid too much.

The truth was that he found it both thrilling and troubling to have Ceara think well of him. It unsettled him to have her assume that he would make the honorable choice, that he could be relied upon, that he was, in fact, an honorable man. He had been assumed to be a rogue and a blackguard for so long that he was shaken by her conviction.

She had to be wrong, yet he was reluctant to prove as much to her.

He wanted her to be right.

But what then? How could Rafael continue his trade as a man of honor? Unlike Ceara, he was not persuaded that the line between knight and mercenary was so very slender. There was the matter of lineage, to be sure. A knight was an aristocrat, the son of a nobleman trained in the use of arms, like Amaury. Rafael was the son of a mercenary and a serving woman. 'Twas not the same. His choices had always been defined by his blood, regardless of what a bold and beguiling maiden with her heart in her eyes believed.

He convinced himself that it was merely a convenience to let her believe what she would of him. Their ways would part shortly, and he hoped to have the satisfaction of knowing that she could choose her own future after he was gone.

He was less certain that he wished to continue his future as he had lived his past.

Ceara's trust also meant that she touched him without regard for consequences. He could have frightened her. Perhaps he should have done as much. But he enjoyed both their easy camaraderie and the hum of awareness in his blood. There was much to be said for temptation denied, at least in the short term.

He dreaded the intimacy of the ship, but in the end, his fears were groundless. Their passage was rough as the wind had changed, and it took them eight uneasy days to reach their destination. Ceara was seasick beyond all expectation and even he, who seldom was uneasy on the water, had a few restless nights.

There was no privacy to be had, though he had not expected otherwise. Ceara spoke to the crew, under Rafael's stern eye, and shared all the tidings she learned. The sailors estimated enormous—and improbable—numbers of warriors who had gathered and forecast war shortly. Indeed, they speculated that the Compagnie Rouge might arrive too late, which was not a notion greeted with enthusiasm.

There would have been outrage if Helmut and Bernard both had not been so seasick that they could scarce move.

On the eighth day, the skies cleared and the sea was smoother. The wind was crisp from the west, driving them onward with welcome speed. The wilderness went on and on, seemingly forever, with a disconcerting lack of towers, steeples and even pennants. It seemed to Rafael that no matter how far they journeyed, the lands were as empty and similar as the days before. Islands and inlets abounded, birds soared above them in quantity, and the sea crashed on an infinite number of shores. Sea and sky were silver and blue, cold hues that joined with the wind to chill him to his very marrow. He came to see a wild beauty in it, one echoed in the merry dance of Ceara's eyes, but he doubted he would ever be warm again.

No wonder Ceara had learned to hunt. This desolate land was home to every manner of creature, save man.

"Tell me a story," Ceara invited as they leaned on the rails together.

"I know no tale fit for a maiden's ears," Rafael responded and Matteo, standing on Ceara's other side, chuckled.

"You should tell us a tale," Matteo invited Ceara.

She looked startled, but Rafael smiled. "Tell us about your grandfather and his mermaid lover," he suggested.

"I told you of them and you laughed," she said, eyes flashing.

"But in this locale, the tale seems more plausible. Tell us again."

She gripped the rail, rocking on her feet as she decided where to begin. Rafael watched her, noting that she had lost a little weight on their journey and that she was paler than she had been. The fire still burned in her eyes, though, and he had no doubt that her passion for justice had only grown stronger.

"My mother used to tell us the tale, but now I wonder how she could have known it. Perhaps she knew only the barest details and embellished them, as those who entertain with tales are wont to do." Ceara's smile was wistful. "She was a gifted storyteller, to be sure. She knew so many tales and her recounting of them was so wondrous that she could make us forget a storm outside, wolves howling in our proximity or the emptiness of our bellies."

Again, Rafael felt a pang that he had not known his mother, but this time, he also was glad that Ceara possessed such potent memories of her own.

"The tale was that my grandfather, Ruari MacRuari, chieftain and warrior, a man of affluence and social position, was saddened by the loss of his wife and his mistress. He was alone, his daughter and son tended by nurses, his holding at peace, his neighbors in agreement with him. He was said to love music and could never resist the sound of a tune. Musicians and minstrels were always welcome in his hall, but there came a winter when none traveled in the vicinity of his keep. Eilean Tioram is a stronghold that becomes an island when the tide is in, save for a single path to the shore. It has a high stone wall encircling it. He took to walking that wall at night in his loneliness and that was when he heard the mermaid sing."

"'Twas said her voice was splendid, richer than the finest wine and as rare as gold. Her song awakened a desire within Ruari, a yearning to see the woman who sang so beautifully, a need to be closer to the song to hear it better. That night, he listened to her from the walls, scarcely aware that the moon was full. He could not discern her, but knew the direction from which her song carried. On the next night, he left the keep to seek her out. Each night that he left the keep, he neither heard her song nor located her. He feared she had abandoned him, that he would never hear her wondrous voice again, and he mourned that he had lost a treasure before claiming it for his own.

"Finally, when the moon was full, Ruari heard her song again. Belatedly, he realized that he had heard her last on the night of the full moon. He fairly stumbled over his own feet in his haste to reach her side. He followed the sound of the song and finally spied her, sitting on a rock near the shore some distance away from his keep. He listened and he watched, noting how she combed her long golden hair, how her tail glistened in the moonlight, how her breasts fairly glowed in that silvery light. His heart was captive, to be sure. He was utterly spellbound by her song and her beauty, but he feared to startle her by revealing himself. At dawn, she dove back into the sea and he returned home alone.

"For the next month, he sought tales of her during the day. There were a few recounted of her beauty and her song, and yet more of her cruelty to men. 'Twas said that she enchanted those who listened to her, that she beguiled them and then deserted them. 'Twas said that as soon as a man could not survive without the sound of her song, she dove into the sea and vanished. That man would be haunted by her for the rest of his life: he would hear her song at intervals, often on the night of the full moon, but at a distance. He would be driven to seek her out, to row out toward her voice or to dive into the sea. Once he had surrendered to the urge to reach her at any cost, he would never be seen again. Eventually the mermaid would appear in another location. 'Twas said that she had been betrayed by a man she loved with all her heart and that she had vowed to avenge herself upon his kind forever.

"But Ruari understood that what a woman desired most was to be loved for what she was, not for what she could become. He did not wish to change the mermaid, but only to adore her. He left a fine ivory comb on the rock she favored before the moon rose full the next month, and stood in the shadows on the shore, waiting for her to appear. He saw her rise out of the water and knew the moment she discovered his gift. He heard her laugh with delight and she called him by his own name, thanking him for the comb. And then she sang with glorious vigor, ensnaring his heart so that he was oblivious to all but her song.

"On the next full moon, Ruari brought her a brass mirror, a circle of metal polished to a high gleam. The moonlight shone upon it when she discovered the gift and her laugh reminded him of a hundred silver bells ringing in unison. Once again, she called him by his name. Once again, she thanked him for his tribute, and once again, she sang so beautifully that he nigh wept at the sound.

"On the next full moon, Ruari left her a strand of pearls. Again, she was pleased and he watched her adorn herself, admire herself in the mirror, then comb her hair. He smiled that she was so delighted, but this time, she asked a question when she called out his name and her thanks. 'What would you have of me, Ruari MacRuari?' she asked, her voice nigh as spellbinding as her song. 'That you would sing forever,' he replied, for it was truth. At that, she dove into the sea and he feared her lost, but she appeared suddenly before him in the shallows. The moonlight shone in her hair and her eyes were wide and dark, her face more lovely than any woman he had ever seen before. 'Is that all, Ruari MacRuari?' she whispered and he stared at her in wonder and longing. 'I would love you,' he confessed. 'You would change me,' she charged but he shook his head, shaken by the very notion, and saw something soften within her. 'I love you, precisely as you are,' he added and her lips parted in wonder.

"She rose from the sea and kissed him, and he closed his eyes at the salt sweetness of her embrace, knowing he would recall this moment for all his days and nights. 'Twas then he realized that she watched him, marveling, before she abruptly dove into the sea. This time, she did not reappear. She did not return on the next full moon or the next one and Ruari despaired of ever seeing her again. He knew that others whispered that he had been enchanted, and he was determined not to fulfil their expectations. He would not waste away, but he would love his mermaid for all time.

"In those times, the MacRuari lands included three islands, North and South Uist and Benbecula, as well as Skye. Ruari was diligent in governing his lands and at regular intervals, he set sail for the islands to hear the concerns of his tenants and hold courts. One day, he and his men sailed across the minch toward the islands but a storm blew up suddenly and the ship was tossed in the rough seas until it capsized. Neither Ruari nor his men could swim, and though he clutched a wooden oar in the hope that he might float to shore, he knew his hopes were meager. He watched his men vanish beneath the waves, never to rise again. He had said his prayers when he saw a glimmer of gold beneath the water."

"She came for him," Rafael said, winning Ceara's smile.

"He thought he dreamed the glimmer, but his mermaid appeared, his pearls yet around her neck. Their gazes clung and he sensed her uncertainty. 'Do you still love me, Ruari MacRuari?' she asked softly and even though the wind and the waves whipped around them, he heard every word resonate in his heart. 'Aye,' he said. 'I could never cease to love you, even though we were apart. I will love you forever, mermaid mine.' She swam closer and put her hands upon his shoulders, wonder in her glorious eyes. He thought the storm had ceased and there was only his mermaid, so close to his embrace. He fairly held his breath as she leaned closer, then closed his eyes as she kissed him sweetly. His heart soared and he knew he could die a happy man having tasted her kiss one last time. A great wave crashed over them then, driving Ruari down into the depths, but to his astonishment, he did not drown. Nay, his mermaid kissed him again and smiled at him, then took him by the hand and led him ever deeper into the sea."

"Then he drowned," Matteo said when Ceara fell silent.

She laughed at him. "Nay! Then he was gone for a year and a day. When he returned to his stronghold, his heart was broken. His mermaid had died in the delivery of my father, Aherne. Her kin visited him nightly for another year and a day, bringing a gift to him and leaving it upon the rock where his mermaid had sung so sweetly. Ruari knew it was a legacy for their son and he secured it for Aherne's return. He lived the rest of his life, awaiting that moment, until he lost hope and despaired."

"And that was when his son Aherne came," Rafael recalled.

"Too late," Ceara whispered, her throat working. She frowned and Rafael had the urge to console her. "But Ruari had known a great love and he never regretted a moment of it," she continued in her usual steady tones. "He won his mermaid's heart and destroyed her bitterness by adoring her as she was. He knew better than to endeavor to change a beloved to suit himself, and that is the lesson of their tale." She looked up at Rafael then, her gaze clear with conviction. "My mother undoubtedly concocted the tale, for the moral was one she held dear. Love can change all, but when one loves, one does not demand a change in one's beloved."

Rafael frowned and stared out at the approaching shore. Her

conviction was well and good, at least in a tale, but he knew he could not give her happiness.

And that meant his love for Ceara must remain undeclared, for the sake of her own happiness. She would find another man and she would be happy without Rafael. He had to believe it to be true, for he knew she could not be content with him, not with time.

He did not have to be glad of it.

AT KILDERRICK, on the night the moon waxed full, the wind rattled the shutters, the trees swayed by the river and Nyssa dreamed. She dreamed of a wolf that devoured the moon, then hungered for the sun. She dreamed of a wolf that would never be sated, a wolf that destroyed all that came within its reach—a wolf that sought more when all around it was a wasteland.

She awakened to the howl of a wolf in the distance and shivered despite the warmth of the chamber. Dorcha huddled on his perch, sound asleep, another shadow in the darkness. The keep was quiet, though she heard the sentries on the parapet and smelled the fires from the huts in the nearby village. She missed Ceara, for her former companion was so pragmatic that troubling dreams were readily dismissed.

On this night, Nyssa had no one to ease her fears.

She rose in silence and darkness to open the shutter and look out at the night. Clouds raced across the sky, seemingly torn free of some mooring, their edges ragged and dark. The moon was coldly silver and she found no reassurance in its light.

There was a flicker in the forest as the wolf howled again, a spark of fire against the shadows. Her heart leapt and she stared intently at the spot, wondering whether she had imagined it. Did someone stalk those who resided at Kilderrick? What did the moon symbolize that the wolf was determined to destroy? Where was the wasteland?

And who was the wolf?

The sole conviction Nyssa possessed was that she would soon know that truth.

MINGARY WAS the destination of all the warriors and Rafael saw as the land became closer that the hills behind the keep were crowded with tents. In time, he could perceive the numerous ponies and many men, most armed with swords and axes. He was astounded by their numbers. Fires burned, sending trails of smoke into the sky, and there was a bustle of activity that was familiar to him.

There was not truly a harbor, simply a natural inlet. At low tide, they led the horses ashore through shallow water, carrying their belongings. Even the wagon was conveyed to safety with a minimum of effort. There were few horses and fewer destriers, which meant their arrival did not go unnoticed. Even without speaking Gaelic, Rafael was aware of the murmur of anticipation among the other warriors when his company reached the shore. Several applauded them with enthusiasm. Rafael was considering where his men might make their camp when someone shouted his name.

He blinked, for he recognized that voice.

He turned in amazement, even as he heard Ceara gasp, then found Raynard striding toward him, hand outstretched. "I feared you would not come," that warrior said, shaking Rafael's hand with enthusiasm. "The Compagnie Rouge arrives!" he shouted to his fellows and a cheer was roused in truth.

"You left no word of your destination."

Raynard grinned. "I thought my sister might tell you."

Rafael looked between Raynard and Ceara as she began to laugh. "I wondered," she said, giving the other warrior a hearty poke in the shoulder. "But when you laughed at the mermaid's tale, I knew it could not be you."

"And in all this time, you have forgotten how I loved to tease you," Raynard said, catching her close when she cast herself at him with joy. He grinned at her joyous greeting and Rafael was startled.

When Raynard's expression softened and he stood beside Ceara, the family resemblance between them could not be denied. Her hair was long and red, while his was short and auburn, but there was a family resemblance in their eyes and their smiles. Rafael felt a fool that he had not seen it sooner, much less guessed the warrior's identity.

"I will assume that your name is not truly Raynard," Rafael said.

The other man chuckled as he offered his hand. "I am Niall MacRuari, but I believe you have guessed as much already."

"And this is why you left in secret."

"I wished to hire the Compagnie Rouge but did not believe I could afford the fee," Raynard said with a smile. He ruffled Ceara's hair with affection and she beamed at him. "I confess that I hoped my sister might be persuasive."

"Where have you been all these years?" she demanded.

Niall shrugged. "Fighting. Learning the arts of war. I was in Ireland for many years with the gallowglass warriors, then journeyed to France with some of them. All the time, I was meeting other Scots who fought abroad and seeking support for the battle I hoped to wage one day. Fortunately, most men like naught better than a fight close to home, one in which they can provide justice for one of their own. I knew I could gather an army when the time was right. I waited for the moment with growing impatience."

He cast a glance over the camp. "As soon as I heard that Godfroy Macdonald was dead, I knew the time had come." He cast an adoring glance at Ceara, who evidently could not disguise her delight. "And when I later heard that in the assault upon Kilderrick that resulted in Godfroy's death, a red-haired maiden had killed a man with her own dagger, I suspected I might find my fierce little sister alive and well."

"That is why you joined the Compagnie Rouge," Ceara concluded with satisfaction.

He nodded. "I had fought years ago for the Compagnie Rouge and recalled Maximilian de Vries well. I had heard the tale of him being denied Château de Vries and riding for Scotland, of course, and soon discovered that he was the one who had killed Godfroy at Kilderrick. I guessed that the new leader of the Compagnie Rouge would ultimately report to him there. I did not initially realize that you were brothers," he said to Rafael. "But that would only have made me more confident of my choice. I apologize that I left without word at Beaupoint. I knew the time came to make our move upon Eilean Tioram and could linger no longer." He shrugged and glanced over the gathered men. "While it is true that many lust for this battle and came with enthusiasm to partake of it, I feared that any delay would see the forces diminish."

"Patience is not generally in the nature of all fighting men," Rafael acknowledged.

"Not enough of them, to be sure," Niall agreed. "And now that you are arrived, we shall attack. The moon is waning, and we can move at night." He smiled at Rafael. "I am uncommonly glad to have the Dragon upon our side."

Rafael smiled, knowing that it was the Greek fire that the other man welcomed most of all. "How far is your target?"

"Farther by path than as the crow flies, and the road is uneven. One long night will see us there. We will have a day to parlay, then can attack at nightfall."

"Surely there will be no agreement at this point?" Ceara demanded.

"I doubt as much, but still there must be a parlay." Raynard smiled at Ceara. "My sister would be disappointed if I did not conduct myself with perfect honor." He pointed skyward, gesturing to the clouds that gathered. "'Twill rain this night and with vigor. I suggest you make camp while you can, perhaps on that slope. The drainage will be good there. I will have some stew and provisions sent to you."

Rafael nodded and directed his men, leaving Ceara to embrace her brother again before following him.

And so, they would fight after all. Truth be told, he was glad of it.

"YOU LOVE HIM," Niall said to Ceara with such conviction that she could only nod agreement.

She grimaced. "He does not believe we have a future together."

"And what of the moment?" her brother asked with impatience.

She drew back to look at him.

"I believe he loves you as well," Niall said. "Indeed, that is what guides his choices."

Ceara nodded, hoping it was true. "That is what Amaury said."

"You have a chance," her brother urged her. "Perhaps your last. Do not surrender it willingly."

She smiled at him and gave him a hug. "Thank you, Niall."

"Thank you, Ceara. Recognize that only you could have convinced the Dragon to lead the Compagnie Rouge here without payment.

"He will claim the lion's share of the mermaid's treasure."

Niall laughed. "Will he?" He did not wait for a reply but kissed her temple. "Your match has my blessing. Make it so." His voice dropped to a whisper. "Be bold, sister mine."

He should have remembered that Ceara needed no encouragement to do as much.

CHAPTER 14

*R*afael sat and stared at the fire long after Ceara had retreated to his tent, watching the moon rise and battling his rampant urge to claim what was legally his own. He told himself to remember the greater good and was unconvinced.

'Twas Matteo who finally dared to sit beside him, doubtless because Matteo knew his dark moods better than any other.

"A man might conclude you did not want her," that warrior said lightly.

Rafael snorted. "Only a fool would imagine as much."

"Yet you are wed. She is yours to take."

'Twas true enough. "But then she would not be mine to put aside."

Matteo snorted at this. "Few men would feel the constraint." He gestured to the camp. "Particularly those of our trade. We come. We take. We vanish with the dawn."

Rafael was thinking of one man's conquest and departure. It was inevitable that he would confide in someone. Matteo had been his closest friend his entire life. Even if they did not share a father, they shared a history. "She is unlike any other I have known."

"Because of her beauty?"

Rafael shook his head. "'Tis her nature. She is bold, reckless even, willing to risk even herself for her beliefs and loyalties. I admire that."

"You are said to be the same. Perhaps you have that in common."

"Perhaps that is why I feel compelled to defend her."

Matteo smiled. "Even from yourself?"

Rafael smiled in return, though his expression was bittersweet. "Especially from me. I understand her, and that means I have the power to destroy her. I will not do as much." His voice hardened. "I will not become my father."

Matteo nodded and they watched the moon rise higher together. Dark clouds were mustering in the west with impressive speed. "'Twill rain soon," the other man finally said.

Rafael could only nod agreement.

He thought of Ceara in his tent and doubted he would be able to deny temptation this night if he retired there. He recalled the coy expression she had cast his way, how she had watched him since their arrival on these shores, how she had smiled at him. He thought of the tale of her mermaid and knew the details had not been a coincidence.

Indeed, he wondered which storyteller had embellished the tale.

She appreciated that he admired her as she was. Rafael knew that was woefully insufficient.

Matteo stood up then and stretched. "I have seen how you look at her. I have seen you put your own best interest aside for her. You are two of a kind and your union would be jubilant."

Rafael met the other man's steady gaze. "It could not endure."

"And what of it?" Matteo asked. "'Tis rare to have even a chance at such joy in a union. Take it, even if you know it may not even survive the dawn. You and I both have seen how abruptly a man might reach the end of his days. Take the chance. Seize it and celebrate it! There is no cause to live with regrets."

"She might conceive," Rafael said. "I will not…"

"By her telling, her mother bore her after her father vanished," Matteo said with impatience. "I do not regret my upbringing, to be sure. I had my mother. I had you. Not all tales of fatherless children end badly." His gaze was hot when he met Rafael's gaze. "Perhaps not even yours," he added, a challenge in his tone.

With one last steady look, Matteo pivoted and strode away. Rafael considered his friend's words as the clouds began to gather overhead.

He thought always of repercussions and results, of the future and not the present.

What if he abandoned the past, and changed his future? What if he dared to believe? He knew he would regret Ceara's absence when their ways inevitably parted.

What if he never knew her touch?

Aye, he would regret that until his dying day, to be sure.

Rafael swore softly and swept to his feet. He marched to his tent, knowing that a single protest from Ceara would cool his ardor. He was snared between what he believed he should do and what he wished to do beyond all else, and it was not like him to be indecisive.

Then he opened the flap of his tent. As Ceara turned to face him, time seemed to halt. There were only they two in all the world, only this moment and this place where all hung in the balance. Two lanterns burned in the tent, filling it with their golden glow, turning her hair to a river of flame. Her eyes shone with anticipation when her gaze met his. Her smile was filled with the invitation of every siren who had ever tempted a man to sample her charms. He saw the mermaid in her then, spellbinding and enthralling. She was wearing the cloak he had surrendered to her and when he closed the flap of the tent, she turned to face him fully. Her hand rose to the clasp and she unfastened it, letting the garment drop to the ground.

She was nude, save for the pearls he had draped around her neck at Beaupoint. Rafael stood thunderstruck by her beauty and her implicit invitation. He was humbled by her trust and stared as his mouth went dry.

"You must be certain," he managed to say.

"I am utterly, completely, and unreservedly convinced," she said, then walked closer. Her hips swayed, her skin gleamed in the light of the lanterns, and Rafael inhaled of the scent of her when she halted before him. She arched a brow. "Unless you would decline?" she whispered, her voice sultry and Rafael could only surrender.

He speared his fingers into her hair, lifted her to her toes and claimed her with a satisfying kiss. There was this night and he would ensure that they both savored it.

~

CEARA HAD BEEN afraid Rafael would refuse her. The longer she waited, the more convinced she became. She had bathed but agitation made her warm again. She paced and she sat. She extinguished one of the three lamps. She considered the merit of retiring before he arrived, but knew she would not sleep. The camp grew quieter and the chill of the night rose from the ground through the rugs.

She feared he would not come to his tent at all.

Then she heard his step. The opening was swept open without preamble and he stood there, his gaze burning as he surveyed her. His expression was stony, his thoughts inscrutable, even when she dropped the cloak. She could not tell whether he was tempted by all she had to offer or not, and her doubted redoubled.

Her palms were damp when she approached him but she saw his sharp intake of breath. His eyes darkened to burning sapphire and his lips tightened, giving her new hope.

And his demanding kiss made her heart soar. It left no doubt of his desire, or of her ability to tempt him. She locked her arms around his neck, surrendering completely to his embrace in her relief. Rafael deepened his kiss, but Ceara welcomed all he had to give. His touch was more urgent and more demanding, as if he was filled with an impatience similar to her own. Ceara welcomed the tempest he awakened, digging her nails into his shoulders, mimicking all he did and noting what he liked.

"*Bella*," he whispered when he tore his mouth from hers and his voice was wondrously husky. His eyes blazed blue as he surveyed her. He raised his hand to cup her breast with a reverence that made her pulse flutter, then he bent to kiss her nipple. Ceara caught her breath when he grazed the taut tip with his teeth and he chuckled as he gathered her closer. He lifted his head, his smile filled with lazy satisfaction when the nipple beaded to a point. He watched her as he teased it with finger and thumb, and she did not hide her arousal from him. Even that made her feel audacious but she did not care.

"I desire you," she said and the light in his eyes flared. She knew 'twould be perilous to admit more than that. "Show me what it is for

man and woman to meet abed. Show me while we still have the opportunity." She retreated a step, claiming his hand, and tugged him toward
the bed. Rafael followed, smiling as he surveyed her. She sat on the side
of the bed then laid back, tossing her hair so it spilled across the linens.
He stood and watched her, taut once again, as he set aside his knives
with care. He did not seem to even blink, so fixed was his attention.

Ceara thought she should give him something to look upon. She
lifted her own hands to her breasts and teased the nipples just as he had
done. The peaks were already tight, but she pinched them and rubbed
them, teasing them to be even tighter and redder. Rafael removed his
belt slowly, so slowly that Ceara could scarce endure it. She smiled at
him then dared to lift her knees and part her thighs, displaying herself
to him.

His smile flashed and he cast aside his tunic. His hauberk followed,
then the padded aketon he wore beneath. He came to her in his
chemise and chausses, bending to kiss the inside of her knee as he had
once before. His gaze was wicked as he met her own and Ceara knew
what he would do. Then she felt the nip of his teeth, the smooth caress
of his tongue, and his warm breath as he trailed kisses up her thigh. His
touch felt both dangerous and seductive, utterly irresistible, especially
when his mouth closed over her and he kissed that most intimate place.

Ceara sighed as she capitulated to his expertise. He gripped her
buttocks and lifted her, feasting upon her. His caress made heat
thunder through her, making her heart race and her very blood boil.
She felt that tide arise within her, just as it had before, but she did not
fight its power. She opened herself to it, wanting only more and more,
and Rafael did not disappoint. He conjured her passion in steady increments, then retreated, leaving her frustrated for a heartbeat before he
launched his amorous assault again. She realized that each foray
increased her desire more so that she was nigh incoherent by the
fourth time. He might have retreated again, but she clutched his shoulders and moaned with need. She felt his chuckle as well as heard it,
then his tongue did some sorcery that cast her over an abyss into a vale
of pleasure that went on and on and on.

It was only when she finally caught her breath that she realized she
had shouted in her release. Rafael grinned at the patter of applause

carried from the other tents, evidence that she had been overheard. Several men hooted and encouragement was shouted in several languages. It was probably better that Ceara did not understand it all. Even as it was, she flushed crimson before she laughed aloud.

Then she reached for Rafael, unfastening the tie on his linen chemise. She pulled its hem from his chausses with impatience and cast it over his head. He was glorious, tanned and powerful, as watchful as ever. Her hand rose to the crucifix, but he lifted its chain over his head, kissed it, then set it aside with the same care he showed with his weapons.

She wondered whether he would ever confide that tale in her.

She wondered whether there would be the chance.

But in this moment, there was much to share. His hair was tousled and unruly, and the glint in his eyes was as dangerous as ever. She ran her hands over his chest and shoulders, loving the strength and power of his body, finding a beauty in it that she could only admire. He shed his boots beneath her roving caress, then his chausses and she continued to touch him, exploring his body as he had caressed hers. When he turned to face her, she felt her eyes widen at the sight of his arousal, but she reached out to caress him all the same.

She watched his eyes close and his head tip back in rapture as she cradled his strength in her hands, then he caught his breath sharply when she stroked him. She felt a wondrous sense of power when he gritted his teeth, for he was so obviously snared in the same maelstrom of desire that had captivated her. Beneath her fingers, he grew larger and harder, his entire body became taut and his hands gripped into fists. She was awed by his restraint, and also yearned to shatter it.

She bent and kissed him, as intimately as he had kissed her.

He jerked and swore, stepping away, his eyes blazing as he whispered her name. There was reverence in that, too, an awe that she welcomed, and Ceara could only smile at him.

"I love you," she whispered, knowing the confession was past due.

"Nay," Rafael said with heat, taking a step back, and she knew she had erred. "Nay!" He spun away from her, seizing her cloak and tossing it toward her. He fell upon his clothes, dressing with uncommon haste, dragging on his boots. His chemise was yet open when he halted at the portal, his cloak hanging from his hand. "Nay, Ceara," he whispered with heat, his eyes snapping. "Not that. Never that."

"But we…"

"Nay." He was resolute. "You recall me to what I know is right." He raised his fist and kissed the ring as he held her gaze, his eyes blazing. "I will be *her* son," he said with fervor and Ceara could not summon a word to argue with him.

He spun then and swept into the night, just as thunder cracked in the distance. Heavy raindrops fell upon the tent and the wind made the canvas flap. The storm erupted and Ceara knew that Rafael would not be back. She cast herself across the bed, wishing she had held her tongue, knowing that she had impulsively spoken the truth of her heart.

She had ruined all with just three words.

But in her heart, she could not regret that she had confessed the truth to him.

∽

SHE LOVED HIM.

Rafael flung himself into the tent Matteo shared with several others, his mood foul. He kicked off his boots and wrapped his cloak around himself, aware of his friend's inquisitive gaze. The rain fell in torrents and the air turned cold.

Matteo braced himself on his elbow to consider Rafael. "I will guess that all did not proceed as hoped," he said in Venetian. Helmut groaned in his sleep and began to snore loudly, denied his slumber on the sea journey. The squires breathed deeply and evenly, proof that they were unaware of the murmured conversation between friends in the darkness.

Rafael scoffed. "She said it."

Matteo chuckled, obviously aware of his meaning. "And you did not respond in kind?"

"Of course not. That way lies folly of the worst kind."

"Aye, blissful union is a situation to be avoided at all costs."

"You jest."

"You would mock me if our places were reversed."

Rafael sighed at the truth of that. "'Tis of no import," he said, his tone cross. "I did not have to reply in kind."

"Because you fled." Matteo nodded with satisfaction that his conclusion had been proven aright. "Love is always of great import to women."

"To what end?" Rafael asked, his frustration raging.

"You could wed in truth," Matteo said, his words faltering as he undoubtedly recognized the issue.

"Men like us do not wed," Rafael said. "There is an abundance of uncertainty in our lives, too much for wives, never mind children."

"You could abandon your trade."

"And do what? I have no skills beyond the battlefield." Rafael continued when Matteo would have protested, his own frustration evident in his words. "We fight and we pillage and we celebrate, then we move on and repeat our actions. Even you noted that we vanish with the dawn. We do the same over and over until we die. We do not live to venerable old ages and we do not die quietly. We are slaughtered, perhaps even by our fellows, perhaps even by a comrade seeking a trinket we have claimed, perhaps in a drunken dispute. And what would happen to a woman then? She would be shared or killed or both, and you know it well."

"But she loves you."

The very words twisted Rafael's heart. "Nay. She loves a notion of me that owes much to tales and less to truth." He sighed. "Women do not love us, Matteo. Most fear us. Some respect us. Still fewer find us useful in settling their own disputes. But love." He shook his head. "Love is for men of honorable repute."

"What of Maximilian? Does his happy situation not prove you wrong?"

"Maximilian was always blessed by Fortune," Rafael argued softly. And Maximilian was of noble blood on his mother's side. That changed all, though it would have been churlish for Rafael to note as much to Matteo. "It is not wise to expect such uncommon luck, much less to rely upon it."

"Antonio calls her your *sposa*."

"Aye," Rafael acknowledged, a lump in his throat. "But he, too, is fond of fanciful tales."

"You mean to leave her at Kilderrick when all is done." Matteo did not add the question of whether they would survive the pending battle. It was an accepted truth that any man who entered a battle might not leave the field unscathed and they never discussed that possibility. It was their habit to assume survival.

Rafael nodded. "Or Beaupoint. 'Twill be her choice."

"I think she will choose to be with you."

He shook his head with resolve. "And she will be disappointed, just as she will be yet untouched." He met his old companion's gaze in the shadows and found unexpected sympathy there. "It must be thus."

Matteo nodded sadly. "I am sorry, my friend," he said softly.

"As am I, Matteo. As am I. But truth is not changed so readily as that."

THE NEXT DAY, Ceara had a glimpse of Rafael's life. She had no doubt that he avoided her, but she followed and watched. There were conferences between men and discussions of strategies. Scouts returned from spying upon their destination, and shared what they had learned. She saw maps drawn in the wet earth and men beneath commanders. All of them were grim and the low grey clouds seemed to echo their mood.

She helped when she could, remaining within the area claimed by the Compagnie Rouge. She fed horses and tended the fire and in the afternoon, she helped to pack up the camp. They rode out at sunset and she did not ride with Rafael. He led the Compagnie Rouge on Phantôm and she was in the midst of the company. The wagon was guarded between the men, just as she was surrounded by them, and she felt her trepidation rise with every step. Niall was confident, but this was no jest. Many of the men would not return from this battle.

They progressed slowly over the rough road and its circuitous path. The sun was rising when they crested the last hill and the valley of the MacRuari stronghold appeared before them. In the distance was Eilean Tioram, perched on the lip of the sound just as she recalled. The square tower of the keep rose from a circle of land little bigger than the base of the keep, the roof of wood. There was a stone wall around the keep, securing a strip of rock from the water that encircled the small island. The tide was in but she saw the shimmer of it receding. The occupants of the keep had to realize their vulnerability for as the attackers rode into the valley and fanned out, archers shot arrows from the keep.

Not only was there a considerable force that had journeyed with them, but it was evident that many had also gathered within the keep. Even at a distance, the sentries could be seen on the ramparts and Ceara knew that the walls fairly bristled with archers.

The pending battle seemed suddenly very real—as did its result. Men would die, this night and on the morrow, men who were hale at this very moment. The realization sent a chill through her.

What if Rafael was one of the unfortunate? 'Twas impossible to watch him, so vital and hale, jesting with his men as he rode onward, and consider that he might not draw breath within a day or two. Even the possibility made her feel bereft and cold.

"Mark the distance," Niall cried. "We set camp around the highest perimeter. Only the Dragon will enter their range and not until sunset."

Ceara's heart rose to her throat, but Rafael did not falter.

Her father had vanished in this place, never to be seen again, and in this moment, that seemed a potent portent of doom.

RAFAEL WAS KEENLY aware of Ceara, even as he fulfilled his duties. Her confession haunted him but he would not be seduced. 'Twas when he began to make his preparations of the Greek fire that she ventured closer to him.

She sat, watching him mix the combination of powders. She had offered to help but he had declined. All who offered to help had been declined and he wondered whether she knew as much, or whether she was insulted. He could not read her expression and he had to concentrate on his labor. The components were all different in appearance and he set them out. He had a small scale and he weighed each component before mixing them together in a large bowl.

Ceara sat in a silence he found remarkable, simply watching.

"The combination must be exact?" she guessed finally, her words tentative. He felt a cur that he had so frightened her.

"Aye. Precision is key."

"What are the powders?" she asked and he shook his head.

"No sorcerer shares his secrets, *bella*. They are the key to his trade."

"But this is not magic." She drew closer and he could not regret as much.

"It might as well be. It is not a formula widely shared, and as a mystery, it gains a repute as sorcery. The response to Greek fire is both fear and wonder." He opened the trunk with the vessels she had called misshapen cups, which Antonio had set out for him, and chose one. He had a small funnel and poured the mingled powders into the vessel, adding a twisted length of cloth when he was partly finished. He added more powder, then wrapped the end of the cloth around the vessel before returning it to the trunk. He nestled it securely into a hollow that kept it in place, then began to fill the next one.

"You must be bored, *bella*," he said much later.

"I like watching you."

He gave her a hard look, but she simply smiled. The sight made him frown and return his attention to his task.

"What will happen tonight?" she asked after a long interval.

"We will attack. Beyond that, no one knows."

"You can guess."

He shrugged. "They will retaliate. There will be fire and bloodshed, but naught compared to the battle that will erupt at first light."

"How can you be sure of the timing?"

"*Bella*," he chided softly, then indicated the keep. "The tide comes in."

She turned to look and he stole a glimpse of her. The silvery sheen of water was rising around the walls of the keep, making it an island. More importantly, she was the bold warrior again, her gaze assessing as she studied the place, her stance confident.

"Doubtless, they think themselves secure for the night, protected by the water. In truth, they are trapped. There is only a narrow route by which they can leave the fortress and no man will cross it and live.

They have given no consideration to my contribution, likely because they have no knowledge that I am here. By morning, when the tide recedes, they will stream from the keep like rats." He nodded as he put another filled vessel in the trunk. "And they will slaughter as many as they can, in retaliation for what they have endured during the night. The battle will be savage." His gaze rose to hers again, his manner deadly serious. "You will remain with the horses and the squires, well away from the battle."

"I will remain with you."

"Nay, *bella*. I forbid it." He glared at her and was surprised when she relented.

"You cannot stop me from using my crossbow," she said with heat.

"I would not even try," he said, his tone reasonable. "A word of advice, though, *bella*. Do not be eager to spend your bolts. These battles always endure much longer than one would expect." He watched her swallow. "There always comes a moment when those who yet have ammunition control the result."

Ceara paled at that, but 'twas only the truth.

Rafael packed another missile, praying that she would survive unscathed. His heart ached at even the possibility of her demise, then she surprised him once again. She moved closer, still watching him work, and dropped her voice low.

"Tell me a secret," she invited and he thought she meant the formula.

He shook his head. "Surely the point of a secret is that one does not tell it to another."

"Surely at this moment there is little left to lose." She sat up, leaning forward so that she could hold his gaze, her own expression deadly serious. "Either or both of us may die in this battle."

He wished she had not realized fully how dire their situation was.

Rafael nodded, for his conclusions were not that different.

"This may be our last chance to surrender a tale."

"I scarce think that of import."

"You will not tell me a secret?"

He shook his head.

"Then I will tell you one."

He glanced up, expecting her to confess a tale of her own history. But of course, his huntress smiled, looking so unpredictable and audacious that his heart squeezed, and he guessed the truth a moment before she spoke.

"You are kind, Rafael di Giovanni."

Rafael laughed at that. "You err, *bella*."

She shook her head. "Nay, you are kind. You are loyal and you are noble. You would hide your good traits, I will guess because they have been seen as weaknesses in the past, but you are a good man."

"You see what you wish to see, no more and no less."

"You have defended me, for no reward at all save that it was the right choice. You have not lied to me or deceived me. You have tried to aid me and I do not think it was solely for your share of the treasure."

"Then I have deceived you with greater success than you know," he said, dread rising within him that she should see the truth of his heart so readily.

Ceara shook her head. "You are your mother's son," she insisted with vigor. "And I wish I might have known her." She lifted her chin to meet his gaze. "She would have been proud of you, Rafael," she whispered and he could not speak, so tight was his throat.

Then he took a breath. "You are wrong, *bella*. I have stolen and I have pillaged. I have made my way as a mercenary for more than fifteen years and I have excelled at the trade."

"You have done what you had to do to survive," she said with conviction.

Rafael worked in silence, aware that she was as captivating as a mermaid sent to hold him in thrall.

"I will tell you another secret," she said finally.

"Surely you have laid all of mine bare."

She laughed a little. "One of my own."

"Ah. The situation must be most dire."

Her smile faded, against his expectation. "I killed three men."

Rafael was startled.

"Not at the same time," she continued. "'Twas one after the other. The worst of it is that I still feel no remorse." She frowned, considering that. "I would do as much again without hesitation."

"Should I fear for my own survival?"

"Nay." Her voice hardened as did her expression. "They did not share your conviction that maidens should be left untouched."

Anger flared within Rafael, a protective need surging to the fore.

"Not me," Ceara said. "After Edward's attempt to claim me, I always encouraged men to believe that I was a maiden no more. I saw that many men favor maidens, though I cannot imagine why that should be."

"Nor I," Rafael agreed gruffly and she smiled at him.

"It only makes sense, to my view, that any endeavor is more enjoyable when there is a measure of expertise."

Rafael had time to nod before she continued.

"Do you remember the fen where I led you?"

"Where I was snared in the mire and in the end had to sacrifice my favored boots?" He deliberately kept his tone light. "Where you stole my destrier and my dagger? Aye, *bella*, I am unlikely to forget that place." He set aside another completed missile, recalling the vision that had prompted him to take those dangerous steps into peril. Ceara had unbound her hair before him and shed her chemise. She had bared her breasts, displaying herself to him, and so perfectly beguiling was the view that he had walked directly into the fen and become trapped there. Had the others in the company not sought him out, he would have slowly sunk and drowned.

He glanced up to find her watching him closely. "I thought then that you had played that trick before."

She nodded, looking down at the ground. "Jeannie used to tell tales of us."

"The sheriff's wife in Rowan Fell." Rafael recalled now how Ceara despised the woman.

"She told others that we were whores, not witches, free for the taking of any man so bold to make his claim. Whenever there was a celebration in the village and ale was readily imbibed, they would come. Often they fumbled, too drunk to be a threat, but once in a while, there was a man with resolve."

"And so you devised a plan." He was grim, knowing that she would have prepared for the defense of all of them, that she would have seen that task to be her responsibility. He was not surprised that she had been effective at it.

"We were maidens, not whores," she said with heat. "But they did not care. They would have taken what they desired, disinterested in the consequences." She sighed. "Elizabeth always hid when we heard them coming, as fearful as a rabbit." She shook her head with annoyance. "I thought the sound of her heart would draw them directly to her."

"She already knew what men would do, given the opportunity," Rafael guessed.

Ceara considered that. "I wager now that she did, though then I simply thought her a coward."

He smiled at that.

"No one wanted Alys, with her scarred face. She would raise a hand, as if to hex her attacker, and invariably the man would flee."

"That left you and Nyssa."

Ceara nodded. "I pretended I had been sampled thoroughly before. I could fight if a man was undeterred. Nyssa is so lovely, though. When Dorcha could not defend her and she did not run fast enough, I offered myself instead."

"Dorcha?"

"Her raven."

Rafael nodded understanding when she raised her hands like claws about to tear.

"Most would follow a willing woman rather than fight a reluctant one. I led two to the fen, a year apart, and left them there to die."

"Did they?"

"Of course." She almost smiled. "A responsible hunter always checks the traps, ensuring that a doomed animal does not suffer overmuch." Her voice hardened. "I checked."

"How much did they suffer?"

"Enough," she said with satisfaction.

Rafael could imagine how merciless Ceara would be against any man fool enough to threaten her friend. "And the third?"

"He ended up in the fen, but he was dead before he reached it." She took a bite of bread and frowned. "He caught Nyssa. I heard Dorcha screaming and found him atop her. He had struck her hard and she no longer fought him. The sight infuriated me so, that he would take what was not his to claim, filled me with rage. I took my knife. I crept up behind him and seized his hair, then slit his throat like the vermin he was. I dragged him to the fen and cast him into it."

Rafael stared at her in astonishment, even as she shuddered.

"I cannot believe even now that I managed the feat." She met his gaze. "He was tall."

"Rage can bring great resolve," Rafael said, believing her.

She nodded. "He had not completed the deed. I was so glad that I had come in time."

"And this is why you despise the sheriff's wife." It made perfect sense to Rafael. "And why you took vengeance upon her, trapping that pig within their cottage."

"Her home is the only thing of import to her. I struck where the greatest wound would be made."

"And since then?"

Ceara smiled. "Since then, I have found myself in the laird's favor, by dint of his bride, and Jeannie dares not speak a word against any of us."

"The men were not missed?"

She shrugged. "I cannot find it in my heart to care."

"Nor I," Rafael said softly. "Nor I."

They remained thus, Rafael working on his missiles and Ceara watching in silence, for the longest time. Rafael found himself speaking with no prior intention of doing so. "You were right about the ring," he said quietly. "But I will tell you of the crucifix and you may think less of me for knowing that tale."

"I doubt as much," she said with familiar ferocity, but Rafael knew better.

This tale was secret for it did not show him in good light. It seemed only fitting to share it after she had made her own confession.

And truly, he might never have another opportunity to tell of it.

CHAPTER 15

*C*eara could see the crucifix in her mind's eye, the splendid gem of Rafael's that had shone against the dark wool of his tunic. She would never forget it, for it was the finest gem she had ever seen in all her days.

"Matteo and I had been five years with the Compagnie Rouge when we approached Venice again." He drew his dagger and spun it so that it caught the light. "But I should begin the tale earlier. I grew up with Matteo. His mother was sickly and we lived together in a small room in the poorest neighborhood of the city. They called her *puttana* and spat upon her, but his mother was no whore. She had been a maid and a son of the household had forced himself upon her. When she became pregnant, she was cast out. She had taken me in and she raised us as well as she could. There was little food and less coin. We became thieves at a young age, stealing whatever we could, to ensure our survival."

"Were you ever caught?"

"Seldom, though we were often suspected. We devised a strategy, that one would hunt, as we called it, and the other would create a distraction. We always watched for each other, and it worked well enough. We moved through the city as a matter of routine, never hunting in the same vicinity two days in a row, or even within a fortnight. As we grew older, we undertook disguises. We stole hats and capes. Once we had a brightly colored tabard that one of us would wear then abandon once the prize was seized. We would retrieve it later and use the feint again."

"You enjoyed it."

Rafael shrugged. "There can be satisfaction in thwarting those who show you only disdain. It troubled Matteo to hear the insults cast at his mother, a sweet and kindly lady, and she, too, became more inclined to remain at home." He nodded. "We were about fifteen when I erred." He held up the dagger. "This was a temptation I could not resist. The Compagnie Rouge were in the city, but we knew only that the streets were crowded with wealthy mercenaries. Gems gleamed on their fingers and gold in their teeth. Weapons shone on their belts and they cast coins at tavernkeepers as if they had a boundless supply. I thought this one dagger would not be missed but I was wrong. I was seized and when Matteo strove to distract my captor, he was caught as well. They understood our ruse only too well and we were taken to their commander, Jean le Beau, at their camp beyond the city walls. My victim was a man of fearsome size who roared for justice, but I was only aware of Jean le Beau. He was uncommonly handsome, but there was a cruelty about him. His eyes were brilliant blue but hard, as if he savored the darkest side of his chosen trade. And he studied me all the while that my victim decried my crime. I could not avert my gaze. I felt that he saw all the secrets of my soul. And when he smiled, I feared what he might say."

"What did he say?"

"He plucked the dagger from the grip of my victim and offered it to me. Then he gave me a choice. I could join his company and keep the dagger, training in the ranks of his men. Or, he could slit me from gullet to groin and leave me to die on that very spot. Whatever I chose, my companion would share my fate."

"What an evil wretch," Ceara whispered.

"No doubt, but still I was surprised to be granted a choice. My victim was astounded and studied me intently, as if he had missed some pertinent detail. When I chose to live, the men always kept their distance from me, treating me with an inexplicable courtesy. I was a thief. I had tried to steal from one of their own, but I had an exalted place in their company. It made no sense to me." He pursed his lips. "Until I met Maximilian."

"You saw the similarity between you?"

Rafael shook his head. "Matteo did. And then the puzzle became increasingly clear, each hint adding credence to the conclusion that Jean le Beau had known me as his son on sight. And so it was that five years after the day we joined the Compagnie Rouge, we approached Venice again. Matteo wished to seek out his mother, for she would have known only that we had disappeared. Departure from the camp was forbidden and severely punished, but Matteo was determined to go. So, I went to Jean le Beau to request permission."

"And?"

"He gave it to me, because I was his son—and because he was reliant upon the Greek fire that only I had fully learned how to make. He also told me her name."

"Francesca." Ceara uttered his mother's name softly then they sat in silence, a silence that he could only see as an honor to his mother.

"Was Matteo's mother alive?" she asked finally.

"Aye. Barely. She was so frail, but so very glad to see him one last time. I asked her about my mother, as I had a thousand times when we were younger, but in facing death, she relented. Perhaps it was because I knew my mother's name. She confessed to me the name of the family who had betrayed my mother."

"Did you know of them?" Ceara prompted when he fell silent.

"Aye! They were one of the richest families in the city. She did not make much sense at that point, but I assumed that this family had been the ones to cast her out. I assumed she had been in their service, a maid assaulted by Jean le Beau when the Compagnie Rouge was in Venice who then lost her post. I could not believe that anyone would cast a woman into the streets because she had been raped and I was furious. Matteo and I went to their palazzo to learn the truth."

"Palazzo?"

"They had such wealth that they lived in a palace, *bella*. It was in the early hours of the morning that we arrived, and I was outraged. The dagger was persuasive in gaining me admission, as doubtless was my fury." He shook his head. "We were barbarians. We kicked down doors and punched guards. We struck terror into the heart of every man who would have denied us entry, and we worked our way steadily to the very heart of the palace. There we found the head of the family, a man some twenty years older than myself. He was startled and displeased by our appearance, but when he saw the ring, he sputtered to silence. I knew then that he knew not only my mother but had realized who I was. His fear revealed his knowledge."

"Did he tell you more?"

"He was almost incoherent in his fear. He said a whore could not be suffered within a decent household. He said it might have been different if she had lived, but I knew he lied. He asked me what they were to do with her bastard? I struck him for that, though he was soft and weak, a man of privilege not of war. When he fell, his nose bleeding copiously, I took the crucifix from him forcibly. I made him kiss it for his devotion to God's goodness and I remember still how he trembled in fear. He thought I would be his reckoning and he was right, but I did not take it then."

"You gave him time to dread your vengeance."

Rafael smiled. Perhaps she did understand him, at least partly. "We left, destruction in our wake, and I paused to look over the palazzo. I particularly wished to observe the design and hue of its roof."

"Greek fire," Ceara whispered.

"'Twas the most curious thing, *bella*, but of all the buildings in Venice, that palazzo was the sole one that burned to the ground in the assault of the Compagnie Rouge the next day. Other buildings had some damage, but not so much as a single stone of that palazzo was unscathed."

"What of the man?"

He shrugged as if he did not care.

She smiled up at him. "It seems we have a certain ferocity in common."

Rafael's gaze flicked over her, his expression inscrutable. "It seems we do, *bella*." Then rose to his feet with purpose. She could hear activity in the camp and hurried to join him.

"You will remain out of sight and out of range," he instructed her. "You will not invite attack and you will not defy me in this."

Ceara could only smile at his stern manner. "My protective mercenary."

"Not yours, *bella*," he said, then turned to leave. His tone turned fierce in a way that made her yearn to reassure him. "Never yours."

Before she could protest, Rafael was striding away, calling to his men.

AT DISTANT BEAUPOINT, Lord Amaury d'Evroi escorted a messenger in the small chamber beside the great hall. The rider wore no insignia but whatever he said to Amaury gained that man's complete attention. The pair were alone in the chamber and Elizabeth's curiosity was piqued. She had details to attend in the kitchens and the hall, but had addressed all of her responsibilities by the time the messenger emerged with Amaury. The younger man bowed to Amaury, who looked thoughtful, then bowed to Elizabeth as he departed the hall. His palfrey had been kept waiting in the bailey and she heard the hoof beats of the horse departing.

Amaury was turning some item in his hands, his brow furrowed.

"What word did he bring?"

"Unexpected tidings. Do you recall a cousin of yours, name of Henry d'Acron?"

Elizabeth frowned. "I have a vague recollection. I could ask Uncle James, for he recalls all such details."

"Later, perhaps. The day is fine and he enjoys the discussion with the masons about the foundation so much that it would be unkind to trouble him."

Elizabeth's uncle had surrendered the seal of Beaupoint and its responsibilities to Amaury, her chosen spouse, in favor of a retreat from the secular world. He was seeing a monastic foundation built on the southeast corner of Beaupoint's lands, and the masons had arrived, as arranged, just a week before. There was much activity in those fields as the dimensions of each building was decided, and her uncle's plans were discussed with the masons who would do the construction.

Amaury smiled and showed her what was in his hand. "This is the detail of greater import."

"A seal. For what holding?"

"For the Barony of Gisroy."

Elizabeth frowned. "Where is that?"

"To the east of Carlisle, along the border. Bewcastle is within its bounds, but the barony has been untended these many years. I have had discussions aplenty with the Baron of Clyffton about the unruliness of the border lands and the reivers."

Elizabeth folded her arms about herself and shivered, for she had a particular dread of reivers given her experience of them.

Amaury put his arm around her shoulders and drew her close. "You know they are ousted from our lands."

"Aye, I do."

"And they are less commonly found in Liddesdale, thanks to Maximilian's efforts in ensuring the peace. There have been tidings that they moved east, into the undefended territories of Gisroy. Your cousin held this seal and was the last Baron of Gisroy, but he took little interest in the holding. His greater properties were further south, where he spent his time. The Baron of Clyffton corresponded with him, and of late, asked him to be more vigilant or at least visit his barony."

"It seems a reasonable request for the sake of those who tithe to him."

Amaury nodded. "When he had no reply, the Baron of Clyffton rode south to speak to his old comrade. Instead, he discovered that Henry had died at Christmas, with neither child nor wife. Your uncle is his heir, so the Baron of Clyffton sent the seal here to Beaupoint."

"But Uncle James has no desire for a holding. He surrendered this one to you."

Amaury tossed the seal and caught it again. "And I would have Gisroy defended. The man who takes responsibility for it must be unafraid to fight for justice or to mete out their due to villains."

"Do you have a candidate in mind?"

Amaury smiled and turned his wrist, displaying the healed scar there. "We swore as brothers to defend each other's interests," he said quietly. "I have not forgotten, nor will Maximilian have done as much."

Elizabeth gasped in surprise. "You would appoint Rafael."

Amaury nodded.

"But I thought you did not like him."

"I have distrusted him in the past, 'tis true, for we are very different. But when last he was here, I understood him better." Amaury met her gaze. "I know what it is to have naught to offer the lady who has captured one's heart. Perhaps Ceara is all he needs for us to be better united."

"But would he take such a responsibility? He has never lingered in one place for long."

"I cannot say. I would like him to have the opportunity, though, for he has the fortitude for the challenge."

"Can you nominate him?"

Amaury shook his head. "I cannot appoint him alone. The lands of Gisroy extend into Scotland as well as in disputed lands. Both kings must approve the choice. I will need Maximilian's aid to argue Rafael's suitability, and we may fail all the same, for his lineage is not noble." He fixed her with a look. "Even a poor barony is a rich prize."

"You will not fail," Elizabeth said with a conviction that made her husband smile. He drew her closer and kissed her temple.

"Do you feel sufficiently hale to ride to Kilderrick? I would confer with Maximilian with all haste. Such an enterprise will not be accomplished swiftly."

Elizabeth smiled up at him. "I would not miss this discussion for any price," she said, then cupped her ripening belly. "I have felt much more robust of late."

"You can ride?"

"I will ride, but if I tire, I may ride with you, sir."

"And I can have no argument with that." Amaury smiled, the love in his gaze warming her so thoroughly that Elizabeth could only feel gratitude that she had won such a man as her spouse. She stretched up and kissed him, loving how his arms closed protectively around her.

This man had claimed her heart in truth, and with each day—and each choice he made—he secured his possession of it all the more.

As soon as darkness fell, the drums began.

Ceara was fascinated. The man had made preparations all the day long under Niall's instruction, and her brother had frequently conferred with Rafael. 'Twas clear both had besieged strongholds before and relied upon each other's experience for a triumph here. She remained with the camp and the horses, well out of range of the archers at the keep, and suspected that they watched as avidly as she.

Brush and wood had been gathered from far and wide and laid in a large arc, just within the range of the archers. Some of the men had brought wood with them or surrendered their wagons to what would obviously become a wall of fire. There had been a few volleys from the keep, but those working to establish the line of brush had been defended by others with shields. As soon as it was perceived that the arrows found no mark, the archers reserved their shots.

The Compagnie Rouge had assembled a variety of wood that had been in the wagon, and Antonio informed Ceara that the result was a trebuchet. Though she did not know the term, she could see that the device would launch a missile. Rafael tested it with a variety of rocks in the afternoon, adjusting it after each launch until he pronounced himself satisfied.

At dusk, he donned his hauberk and mail, a dark tabard and a dark cloak. He blacked his face and pulled up his hood, making himself a shadow against the night. The moon was hidden by clouds on this night, and even though it shone silver through their veil, it was dark on the ground. The line of scrub was lit as the drums sounded, orange flame licking against the night. Rafael and his men moved the trebuchet into place as the drumming gained in pace. Ceara's heart pounded in rhythm, her fascination ensuring that she was aware of the chill in the air. She gripped her crossbow, hoping there was some contribution she could make to her brother's success.

Antonio nudged her as Rafael bent over the trebuchet. The boy's anticipation was obvious and Ceara craned her neck to see. There was no need, for the Greek fire could not have been missed. Light flared as a flame was touched to the cloth that emerged from one of the missiles, then the trebuchet was loosed.

The missile soared through the sky, a magnificent banner of flame tailing it in glorious orange and gold. Ceara was not the sole one to gasp as the fire burned against the sky or to rise to her feet when the missile collided audibly with the roof of the keep. The fire spread in every direction, flowing down the walls like fiery water, sparking across the wooden roof with apparent glee.

Those within the keep shouted and struggled to douse the flames, even as Rafael lifted another missile in his hand. He assessed the distance, adjusted the trebuchet and released another blazing stream of fire across the sky. This one struck the gates, fire pouring down over the wooden portals, licking at the stone and dancing along the wooden walkways inside the walls. Meanwhile the roof of the keep burned like an enormous candle, sending torrents of smoke into the sky. The archers at the keep fired into the night but their shots found no mark. The fires were stoked on the protective wall of brush and Rafael stood in darkness, timing his next assault.

Ceara could only watch, enthralled by his effectiveness.

CEARA HAD NOT CONDEMNED HIM.

Rafael could make no sense of her reaction. He recalled her words and her reaction, over and over again, throughout that night as he did what he knew best.

And in a corner of his heart, he dared to hope.

The keep was damaged by the dawn but not destroyed, the plumes of dark smoke rising from what had been a wooden roof. All in all, it had withstood the assault well, to Rafael's thinking, a sign of good construction. He stood with Niall, watching the tide slide out. This day would be the reckoning. They nodded to each other, then Niall shouted to the men. Shields were raised, helmets donned and visors dropped as the men who had gathered outside the walls surged forth in pursuit of victory.

In that same moment, the remnants of the gates were opened and men poured out of the keep. The archers on the walls covered them, their arrows flying in fearsome quantity upon the attackers. Archers from the attacking side stepped up to what remained of the line of burning brush. They had buckets of pitch and worked in pairs. One dipped a bolt in pitch, then loaded his crossbow or bow. His companion lit the pitch, as time was of the essence, and the missile was loosed. Balls of fire rained down on the defenders and as they retreated, the attackers advanced. Soon the missiles were going over the wall, launching more fires within the keep.

Rafael was with Niall, both of them aiming for the slits used by the archers, any glimpse of an archer on the summit of the wall. Rafael spied movement behind a window in the tower and aimed for that, aware that Niall followed suit. Smoke unfurled in billows from the assaulted keep and he glanced back, seeking evidence that his men still fought.

When Rafael spotted Ceara, his mouth went dry. He should have guessed that she would not have remained behind as instructed. He should have anticipated her defiance of his command and in a way, he had. What astonished him was the vigor of her attack. She stood, behind what remained of the barrier of burning brush, Antonio fast at her side. Her hair was bound back, her face blackened, and he recognized one of his leather hoods upon her head. She wore her chausses and leather jerkin, and she lifted her crossbow again with confidence. The bolt had been dipped in pitch, for the end of it was rounded, and Antonio touched it with flame. She lifted the bow and fired, and though he lost the trajectory of her bolt in the frenzy, Rafael's heart glowed with pride.

How could he have imagined that she of all people would falter before the truth of war? He had done her a disservice with his doubts, with his assumptions that she was like other women and would desire a docile life of security and routine. Nay, she was a warrior maiden, through and through, and as Rafael watched her load her bow again, he realized that he would be seven kinds of fool to set her aside.

They were of a kind, just as she asserted, and Rafael finally ceded the truth of that. He surrendered to his own regard for her, and knew he had only to survive the day to act upon it.

The future was theirs to claim, whatever it might be.

Ceara had no notion of how many bolts she loosed that day. She knew only that others ran out long before she did. There were wounded men all around her as well as those who would not rise again, but she kept her gaze fixed upon Rafael and Niall. By midday, they were easing toward the road to the gates, and the gates themselves were utterly destroyed.

There was a bellow from within the walls, one sufficiently loud that Ceara was not the sole one to lower her bow. A heavily armored man appeared in the opening of the gate, an axe in one hand and a sword in the other. A whisper passed through the ranks of those around her and Ceara listened with surprise.

'Twas Angus, Aimil's sole surviving son, now chieftain.

He was a doughty warrior, a man nigh as broad as he was tall. He shouted at Niall. "Who is this son of a bastard who dares to assault my stronghold?"

Ceara realized that two bastards assaulted the stronghold in unison, but Angus could not realize as much.

"I am the tanist," Niall asserted. "Son of Aherne, son of Ruari, with the blood of Sommerled in my veins and honor in my heart. I have fought two decades with the galloglass and I am the most worthy to lead us all."

Angus stepped onto the road that joined the keep to land. "Prove it," he shouted. "I challenge you to mortal combat. May the best man win with the grace of God's favor."

Ceara stared in consternation. Angus weighed far more than her brother, it was clear, and she feared for his success. She wished he would continue their assault, but Niall raised a hand.

"I accept your challenge, cousin. Let us say axes."

Angus cast his sword aside, his retainer seizing it and retreating. He marched out to the middle of the causeway. Niall abandoned his crossbow and followed suit, his axe at the ready. The pair faced each other, then circled, each assessing the other.

Then Angus swung hard at Niall's knees. Niall jumped and landed with grace, swinging his own axe with vigor. Angus ducked out of the way, more agile than any could have expected, and Niall's axe struck the ground. He swung when Niall was at disadvantage but Niall evaded the blow. They circled again, both panting and wary.

When Angus swung his axe, Ceara could scarce bear to watch. She glanced over the men assembled on both sides, noting their avid attention, then found a man's gaze fixed upon her. Edward! She stood up in surprise, but he vanished into the company, making her wonder whether she had seen him in truth. The glimpse startled her, so that she nearly missed the end of the fight. She looked in time to see Niall swinging his axe at Angus, who stepped backward to avoid the blow. He stumbled then, his eyes widening in fear as Niall's axe moved closer.

There was the sound of a bolt being loosed from a crossbow on the ramparts. Ceara caught a glimpse of an archer there and was outraged that anyone would act so dishonorably. Niall ducked instinctively as the bolt shot over his head and buried itself in the dirt. He straightened and glared at the offender, even as a bolt flew toward the ramparts. There was a cry and the sound of a man falling behind the walls, even as Angus lunged toward Niall with his axe. Niall leapt to his feet and swung hard. His blade found purchase and Angus fell to his knees, his own weapon falling from his grip. He wavered there, his expression astonished as his blood flooded with vigor. There was not a sound from the company until he fell, face-first, into the mire on the road.

Niall bowed his head and turned to shake Rafael's hand. Belatedly, Ceara saw Rafael's grim expression and the crossbow that hung from his grasp. The men who followed Niall erupted in a cheer and surged toward the gates like a tide.

"Mercy!" a woman cried. She appeared on the ramparts like a vision of an angel. Her grey hair hung loose down her back and her kirtle wrought of undyed cloth. She raised her hands as if to bless them all and her voice rang over the assembly. "I pray that you show mercy, in the name of God and justice!"

"Name yourself!" Niall shouted.

"I am Aimil MacRuari, the heiress of Garmaron," she declared, her voice faltering even as glances were exchanged. Ceara strained for a better look at her aunt. "Abandoned by my lawful husband, I retired from the world and its woes here at my father's home." She raised her hands in appeal. "I entreat you for mercy!"

"Do you surrender the keep to us?" Niall cried.

"It is not mine to give," Aimil replied. "My son holds it, but he lies dead at my feet. I claim no holding." She dropped her face to her hands and her shoulders shook as she wept audibly. The men stirred, agitated by the sight of this elderly woman's grief. "My last son is dead. I am alone. My life is as naught. Mercy, I entreat you. Show mercy."

There was a moment of silence, then Niall called again. "Hold!" he cried, raising his hand, and the men lowered their bows. He stood in the midst of the road, hands on his hips and addressed her. "Fear not, Aunt. I accept your surrender. You will be left to your contemplation in peace. My cousin will be laid to rest as you see fit, as will all of his men who have fallen by his side. I will not compromise your grief."

She was aware that Rafael's brows rose and she wondered whether he understood the conversation. He could not doubt her aunt's sincerity, to be sure.

"She has suffered sufficiently," Ceara whispered, though Rafael could not hear her.

Niall's men roared approval again, though there was temperance in their manner. Niall strode into Eilean Tioram victorious and Ceara was smiling when Rafael turned. He scanned the company, obviously seeking her, and she watched him, waiting for his gaze to light upon her. When it did, he smiled slowly, then blew her a kiss from his fingertips.

Ceara's heart leapt that Rafael had made her brother's dream come true.

She could only hope he did the same for her own.

THE MOOD WAS merry as the sun set, turning all the sky to glorious shades of orange and pink as if the very heavens would celebrate Niall's victory. Niall entered the keep in triumph, the Compagnie Rouge behind him. His many followers trailed behind, hooting and cheering. While Niall and Rafael inspected the damage to the keep, the men dispersed throughout the stronghold.

The pantries were raided and a feast was prepared, the servants and squires of the many warriors aiding in the task. The gallowglass warriors themselves brought wood for the fire and assembled the trestle tables in the hall. They brought their own provisions to add to the meal as well as their ale. A keg of wine was discovered in the cellar and opened to much merriment, even as horses were brushed down and weapons cleaned. The damage to the structure by Rafael's Greek fire was surveyed and discussed, as was the merit of the weapon in general.

Soon the hall of the keep was packed with warriors who had come to celebrate. There were even some monks in their simple garb who had been granted permission to remain, the better to allow Aimil to continue her devotions. Niall granted his aunt a place at the high table where she could be both defended and watched. Rafael commandeered a table for his company and the boys served them all with enthusiasm. There was laughter and conversation, as well as music provided by some of the fighting men.

'Twas time.

Rafael went to Niall and bowed when that man glanced up.

Niall laughed. "You owe no homage to me, Rafael."

"But I would ask a boon of you."

"Indeed?" Niall's eyes were twinkling. "Would it involve my sister?"

"I would wed her in truth, but only with your permission. You are her closest kin and..."

"And I understood that you were wed already. Indeed, I attended the nuptials myself." Niall was teasing him but Rafael did not smile.

"Our match is made in name alone and you know it well," he charged softly. "I thought to defend her, but Ceara is no meek maiden in need of a protector. On this day, she impressed me mightily with her composure and her skills."

"Did she not warn you that we are warriors all?"

"She did indeed. I was fool enough to be skeptical."

"Tell me the sole detail of import," Niall said, a challenge in his manner that Rafael recognized well enough. "Tell me that and my approval is yours."

"I love her," Rafael said simply. "And she has confessed to loving me.

I know not how or why I have become so fortunate, but I would have her hand in mine for all my days and nights."

"Then I grant my agreement and willingly."

They shook hands in hearty agreement. Rafael turned then, seeking Ceara, but there was no sign of her.

Where had she gone?

THERE WAS one deed Ceara wished to do in Eilean Tioram.

She doubted they would linger long at the keep. Indeed, she expected to collect the mermaid's treasure in the next day or so. She might not have another opportunity for this errand.

She could have confided in Rafael, but recalled how he had said Maximilian was sentimental as if that was a trait to mock. Her quest was certainly sentimental, so she would pursue it alone.

It was easy to escape Rafael's attention. His concerns had eased since their triumph earlier in the day and she knew he was tired beyond all. She watched him approach Niall, doubtless to be congratulated on his contribution, and the weight of his gaze slipped away. She ducked into the crowd of warriors who waited to wish her brother well and crept toward the portal to the great hall. There was so much congestion and merriment that 'twas readily done.

Ceara surprised by how quiet the rest of the keep was in contrast to the great hall. The great hall filled the tower, save for the stairs, on the level above the ground. She already had seen the kitchens and storage rooms on the lower level and knew there were dungeons beneath them. The walls around the tower meant that there were no other structures to explore but she knew there had to be a chapel.

Her aunt had retreated here for a life of prayer and contemplation, after all. There were monks and there would be a chapel.

Ceara crept up the shadowed stairs alone. Her footfalls seemed uncommonly loud but she was alone, to be sure. There were chambers above the hall—Niall had secured the largest and best of them and her aunt had a modest one—and she suspected there was a treasury as well. There was no chapel. She took to the stairs again, but the tower opened onto the ramparts. She could see the damage wrought by the Greek fire and smell that thatch had burned, but no chapel.

If naught else, the height would give her a vantage point.

Ceara stepped onto the ramparts, noting that there were no sentries this night. She walked around the summit, taking care to avoid those places where the walls had been damaged. It was a clear night, the stars shining brightly overhead, and there was a crisp wind from the sea.

On the side of the keep that faced the loch, she found what she sought. There was a square structure built into the encircling wall, one with a cross on its roof. She would not have been able to see it from their camp the night before and from outside the walls, it would not have been discernible either.

What she sought would be there, if it could be found at this keep at all.

CHAPTER 16

*C*eara hastened down the stairs and past the great hall. The sentry on the door was inattentive, for he had savored his ale. She told him that she needed to pray and he nodded cheerful agreement, waving her onward.

Loch Moidart wrapped around the north side of the keep, an inlet that opened to the sea at the west. The wind was chilly from the water, but she ran along the empty walls. The door to the chapel was doughty. Ceara opened it with an effort and heard it shut audibly behind herself. There was a light burning upon the altar table, which was graced with a plain linen cloth, a cup and a plate. The cross hanging on the far wall was lit by the flickering golden light, and Ceara shivered at the dampness of the stone. Though it should have been warmer to step out of the wind, the chapel possessed a definite chill.

The floor was stone and swept clean. On either side, there were stone sarcophagi, four on the left and one on the right, a hint that she might find what she sought.

The first on the left was the oldest. *Ruari* was the name etched upon it. She had to fetch the lantern from the altar to read the inscription, and run her fingers across the carved letters to be sure. Her grandfather was entombed within this one. There was no embellishment save his name and the letters had not been carved deeply. She thought of her grandfather's love for his mermaid and wondered whether he would rather have been laid to rest in the sea.

The next was for her uncle, Raghnall, the chieftain assassinated by William, Earl of Ross. They must have carried him all the way from Elcho to bring him home to rest. His demise had seen the MacRuari lands pass to Aimil and thus to her husband, the Lord of the Isles. This stone was carved more deeply with entwined lines in the outline of a cross.

The third had Dugald's name upon it. He had been the eldest of Aimil's sons and Ceara had known little of him. He had passed less than ten years before, so he must have been in residence when her mother had come, seeking news of Aherne. Had he lied to Ceara's mother? Had he been the one who had injured her? The truth was lost forever, but Ceara was not impressed that his tomb was the most lavish of the four. Someone had doted upon him, to be sure, and paid for him to be so honored.

The fourth had Godfroy's name upon it. Ceara did not linger over it, for she did not mourn that man's demise. It bore a simple carving of a sword that might have been a cross if not for the detail upon the hilt.

There was space between this one and the altar, perhaps for Aimil's third son, Angus, who had died this very day.

Ceara pivoted to consider the single sarcophagus on the other side of the chapel. She held the lantern high and stepped closer. There was no inscription on this one. The stone was bare and unornamented, roughly hewn as if no one cared about the person within.

Ceara knew then who the occupant had to be. She had found her father's resting place. Not only was her father parted from his kin in death, a hint of the division in life, but it was clear that he had not been mourned in this keep.

She almost wished she had the strength to push back the lid and look inside. There would be naught but bones to see, though, and she knew it well. She ran her hands across the cold stone, hoping that Niall would have Aherne's name carved upon it.

She thought of her mother, so filled with despair upon returning from that short disappearance, and knew that her mother had stood in

THE DRAGON & THE DAMSEL

this very place. Ceara's tears flowed then, as she felt an ache for the mother she missed and the father she had never known. That they had been cheated of more time together only filled her with resolve to let no opportunity slip away.

She had to talk to Rafael. She had to convince him that they belonged together, stubborn protective man that he was, and persuade him that she would only be content by his side.

There was a sudden rush of air as the door was opened and Ceara spun so quickly that she dropped the lantern. Two figures were silhouetted briefly, then the door closed. Silence and darkness pressed against Ceara's ears and she considered that she should not have come to this place alone.

Then a tinder was struck and light flared, illuminating the lined features of her aunt, Aimil. A robed monk stood behind her, the hood drawn up on his dark garment and a wooden cross hanging from a lace around his neck. He must be a priest, come to pray with her aunt.

Ceara heaved a sigh of relief. "I am sorry if I interrupt your prayers, Aunt," she said. "I will leave you to your worship."

"I think not," Aimil said, her words steely.

Ceara hesitated at the older woman's unexpected manner.

Aimil moved closer, her gaze bright and her expression hard. She stopped before Ceara and lifted a finger to the younger woman's cheek. Her lip curled with disdain as she touched Ceara's tears. "You do not look like her, but you weep like her, silently and proudly." She said this as if it was an accusation. Ceara was affronted, then shocked as she realized Aimil had been present at her mother's visit to this very keep.

That cold gaze made Ceara wonder whether Aimil had witnessed her mother's humiliation.

She took a step back, finding the sarcophagus cold behind her.

"She was prettier than you," Aimil said, as if they discussed the weather. "And cursed loyal."

"She?" Ceara echoed, needing to know.

"Your mother. Your brother favors him more than you do." She tilted her head to study Ceara. "Nay, you take after our side of the family. Perhaps that is a good sign."

"A good sign of what?" Ceara asked.

"She denied you both," Aimil said as if she discussed the weather. Her words revealed that she had been present when Ceara's mother had been questioned. "She would not admit whether she had children by Aherne. She would not tell us any detail of import." She shook her head. "It did not matter how many fingers were broken, and what was done to her. She would not confess a single detail." She smiled at a horrified Ceara. "It does not matter, you know. People imagine that there is something noble in keeping secrets, but it only leads to pain and suffering, and that is generally their own. Of what merit is that?"

Ceara tried to move away but she could not retreat. She could only slide toward the altar, with that stone behind her back. "She was violated," she whispered.

"'Twas one way to verify that she had borne at least one child." Aimil shrugged. "I appealed to her, as kin, but she would not speak to me. It was not my fault that she had to be encouraged. Dugald did as I instructed him, as did Angus, but she was... *tenacious*, your mother."

Twice her mother had been abused. Ceara was appalled. "Yet you let her go."

Aimil laughed. "How else was I to discover the truth? We knew she would return to her child or children, wherever that might be, and she did." She shook her head. "Women can be so predictable."

"You sent the men who burned our home," Ceara guessed.

Aimil nodded. "Who would have guessed that she had the wit to anticipate me?"

"But why? What had we done to earn your ire?"

"You existed!" Aimil spat. "I was the eldest. I was the *first*. I was the one who wed well." She made a dismissive gesture. "My father had his mermaid mistress." She scoffed. "He would not tell me where to find the treasure, a legacy that should have been my own. He would not agree to a marriage for me. I had seen three and twenty summers, but he wished me to remain unwed and by his side. I was no better than a servant."

"He died of a broken heart," Ceara said.

Aimil laughed. "He died of a poison administered slowly and steadily by his devoted daughter." Her eyes lit. "I regret only that it took so long to work. He was more robust than I had expected." She backed Ceara toward the altar. "I learned of Aherne when he arrived that first time. Our father was dead so there was naught for him to gain here. I ensured he knew as much and he vanished for a decade. I knew he would be back and when he returned, my brother and I were prepared to make him disappear forever." She patted the stone sarcophagus. "Meanwhile, I wed Eòin, the most noble and influential man within these lands. I was a fine wife to him. I bore him three sons in rapid succession. I knew that he and I would rule the islands together and all would be mine, as it should have been."

"But your brother Raghnall became chieftain after your father's death."

She smiled coldly. "He did not remain so for long, did he? A mere thirteen years and he was a man who had not seen forty summers. 'Twas young for him to die, to be sure."

Something in her expression prompted Ceara's suspicions. "You could not have contrived Raghnall's demise," Ceara said. "He was killed by William, Earl of Ross."

Aimil smiled coldly. "And why was he so killed? Because my half-brother made poor choices. Doubtless it was due to his mother's inferior lineage. He provoked William, as only a fool would do. A man of passion, Raghnall was not keen of wit and never thought of repercussions. I encouraged that and he never guessed my true reasons. He seized Kintyre, a territory most precious to William, and I had Eòin convince the king to approve the transfer of the territory to Raghnall. The king also granted Skye to my husband." Her tone filled with satisfaction. "William was furious. I could not rely upon chance. I knew they were summoned to the king's parliament, so I sent a message to William, confiding that my brother intended to betray him and murder him. I assured him that William could be trusted and that it would be clever to strike first. The question of Raghnall was resolved with a satisfactory haste and I became the heiress of Garmaron."

She turned to walk toward the door of the chapel, her posture tense. Ceara noted that the monk kept his head bowed. Had he heard this confession before? She assumed he had and was bound to keep it secret. That Aimil was confiding in her was no good sign of her own future prospects.

Aimil continued. "And then, just as all was as I had planned, just when the legacy that should have been mine from the first was within my grasp, my husband discerned my hand in all of this. He was shocked and outraged. He called me unnatural. He put me aside, the fiend, dismissing me like a whore he no longer wanted in his bed." She shook her fist. "It was an outrageous injustice! And then, the wretch appealed to the king to claim my inheritance, on the argument that I was unfit to retain the lands. Wretch! I thought he could not succeed. I thought no one would believe him. I thought the law would keep him from stealing from me. Our match could not be dissolved for we had three sons. It was clearly consummated, we were not kin, and I had not been unfaithful."

"But the king agreed," Ceara said.

Aimil shook her head, rage filling her expression. "King David not only ensured a divorce between us, but he surrendered my lands to my former husband." Her voice rose. "And then he arranged a match between Eòin and the daughter of his successor, Robert Stewart, ensuring that my former husband would be advantageously allied for all time. As the final blow, he decreed that my sons by Eòin would inherit naught, that *her* sons would inherit *my* legacy." Her voice turned bitter. "She had five of them in rapid succession, the witch. And I, I was to have only this keep to sustain myself, along with my fury."

She spun to face Ceara. "And so I seethed. And so I schemed. And so I wrought a plan for vengeance. My hope was Godfroy, my youngest, who had never been afraid to do whatever was necessary to gain his will. He was my son in truth, blood of my blood, child of my heart. I sent Godfroy to seize his betrothed, Alys. She had some royal lineage. With proper management, he might have made a case to seize the crown for their son. I dispatched him to take what had been promised to him for I knew that if he did not act, he would be cheated as I have been."

Ceara considered that Aimil had sent her son to his death and thought it unwise to suggest as much. She eased toward the altar, unable to see how she might escape this woman. 'Twas clear she was not expected to do as much.

"But Alys wed another and my son lies dead." She caressed the tomb, shaking her head. "And now there is a new heir returned to Eilean Tioram, the son of the mermaid's bastard who lies behind you, the man who believes he will secure my dowry as well as this keep. He slaughtered my Angus this day, stealing the last of my hope, but I am not so weak as to surrender yet. Little does your brother know that there is a serpent in this garden, one that will see him dead with all haste."

It could not be a good sign that Aimil confessed this detail to Ceara. "And then?"

Aimil smiled. "And then I have another plan, of course." She walked closer, her eyes dark. "I see you thinking that you will warn him. You believe you can help him to escape and that you can save him." She raised a brow. "My scheme is better than yours."

But Aimil was an old woman. Even her fury could not give her the strength to fight Ceara and win. The monk had retreated to a corner, evidently sworn against violence, and Ceara dismissed him as a concern.

"We shall see!" she said, then lunged toward her aunt. She snatched the lantern that the older woman carried and flung it so that the oil spilled on Aimil's kirtle and the fabric caught fire. As Aimil tried to beat out the flames, Ceara tripped her, then leapt for the door. She did not reach it, for she was snatched from behind and held in an iron grip.

The man who held her captive wore the dark garment of the monk.

Ceara shouted and twisted, only to find herself flung to the ground and struck across the face. She saw stars, then opened her eyes to find a man leaning over her whose ear was notched.

"Edward," she whispered in terror.

A wicked smile curved his lips. "And so we meet again, my Ceara."

His expression convinced Ceara that he had no good intentions. She scrambled to her feet, her head pounding and charged toward him. He was not expecting her assault and she seized the cross around his neck. She tugged so hard that that the lace snapped and she clutched it tightly, as proof of his disguise. She kicked him hard, then raced for the door.

Her fingers had just brushed against it when he seized her from behind and flung her to the ground. She tasted her own blood and knew her knee was skinned. She stumbled to her feet, determined to escape but Edward seized her again. He punched her in the stomach so that she thought she might be sick, then shoved her to the ground and knelt atop her. She struggled against his weight but he struck her face again, then silenced her with a length of cloth.

"As troublesome as her mother," Aimil said with disdain. "I wish you luck with such a vexing bride."

"She will not be my wife for long," Edward said calmly. "Just long enough to inherit the family legacy then pass it to me." Ceara gasped in outrage, but he struck her temple with the hilt of his dagger.

She managed to do just one last thing before she knew no more.

RAFAEL COULD NOT FIND CEARA. He went through the keep from top to bottom, then he searched it again. She had vanished completely and he distrusted both her disappearance and its timing. Antonio and Matteo assisted him on the second search. If any of these warriors had touched her, he would ensure that man never was capable of making such an error again.

Finally, he stood at the gates, surveying the camp that filled the valley. It was only sparsely occupied, what with so many men in the hall. How could he find her if she had left the hall? The tide had come in and the water shone around the keep's exterior walls, ensuring that no one could have left by any way other than the gate.

The gatekeeper was dozing, but Rafael shook him to wakefulness. "Have you seen the laird's sister?" he demanded using every language he spoke in succession to no avail. Finally, he gestured to indicate a woman's shape and the gatekeeper grinned.

He pointed to the far side of the keep, then lifted his hands together as if in prayer.

'Twas not a choice Rafael would have expected Ceara to make, but they followed the sole indication. Sure enough, there was a chapel on the loch side of the keep, built directly into the protective walls.

Rafael strode toward it, passing through the men working in the small bailey. They were gathering the fallen warriors and loading their corpses onto wagons. Several of the monks who had been in residence were assisting in this grim task. A monk carrying a body wrapped in rough cloth collided with Rafael, his hood pulled so far over his face that it was no wonder he could not see where he was going. Rafael shook his head and continued, only barely noting that the monk called out for a wagon to halt.

When he looked back from the door of the chapel, that monk had deposited his burden on that wagon then climbed atop it. He had taken the pony's reins and was urging them toward the gates with a haste that seemed unnecessary. The men, Rafael knew, would not be buried until the morrow.

But the matter was scarcely of his concern.

Rafael opened the door of the chapel to complete darkness, then Matteo struck a tinder. He had time to see that there was an oil lamp shattered on the floor before the light went out.

There was no one within the chapel, but he smelled burning cloth.

At his command, Antonio raced back to the keep to fetch a torch. The boy returned quickly as Rafael paced with impatience.

"She will be well," Matteo said in an attempt to reassure him.

"I will believe as much when I see her," Rafael replied tersely.

The torch revealed little at first glimpse, save a small ornament on the floor. Ceara was not within the chapel. Rafael bent to study it and realized it was a wooden crucifix on a cord, of the style worn by the monks who had been resident in the keep to serve Aimil's needs. When he picked it up, mystified as to its presence, he saw the blood that stained the stone.

The blood was still wet.

And the light glinted on an item cast against the far wall. Rafael felt an echo of dread when he retrieved the familiar dagger, then displayed it to Matteo and Antonio.

"Her dagger!" Antonio said with dismay.

"Did she not leave it before?" Matteo said.

Rafael nodded. "She has been abducted," he said with surety, knowing that Ceara had left the dagger by choice. "And likely by Edward again."

"What is amiss?" Niall said from behind them, his tone light. "I heard you sought a woman and knew it had to be Ceara."

Rafael was yet crouched on the floor and he pivoted to show the dagger to Niall.

"Again?" that man said, sobering immediately. "How can Edward be here?"

"He must be," Rafael said. "He must have hidden in the crowd. Or perhaps he donned a disguise." He held up the wooden cross. "What do you know of the brethren who serve your aunt?"

"Little enough. I assumed them above reproach."

"At least one of them is not. There is blood on the floor." He stood, battling his sense that he had failed Ceara even as he realized a key detail. "The monk who passed us," he said to Matteo with urgency. "Am I wrong that he wore no crucifix?"

His friend shook his head. "He had none."

"They all wear crucifixes," Niall insisted.

"They may not all be monks." Rafael said, standing as he surveyed the chapel one last time. "Ask your gatekeeper about your aunt's activities this night."

Niall paused. "You suspect her?"

"I think the easiest way for anyone to enter this keep disguised as a monk would be with her assistance."

"And you?"

"I intend to follow a corpse. If I am right, someone intends to steal the mermaid's treasure."

Niall's lips thinned to a taut line and he strode away with purpose. Rafael noted Antonio's concern and ruffled the boy's hair. "She will be well," Matteo insisted, but the boy watched Rafael and he could give no such assurance.

"I will do my best," he said instead and Antonio nodded agreement. "I will leave my hauberk and my armor, for the weight is too much," he decided. "But will take my cloak and crossbow. I will meet you at the gate." The boy hurried away, relieved to have a task.

Matteo opened his purse and gave Rafael the last of his bolts. There were only three but Rafael had none. "Do not miss," Matteo said softly and Rafael nodded grim agreement.

This time, Edward de Leslie would not escape.

NIALL FOUND his aunt in her chamber above the celebration in the great hall. She looked up at him and smiled, her expression docile. She appeared to be both fragile and weak, and he felt sympathy for her that she had lost her son this day.

She knelt at a small altar in one corner, a plate before her with a piece of bread upon it.

"I pray for his soul," she confessed, her voice breaking. "I would order a thousand masses, if I could."

"I will see what can be done, Aunt," Niall said. In this moment, he doubted Rafael's suspicions, but he had to ask.

"Take the body of Christ with me," Aimil said, urging the small plate toward him. "Pray with me."

In that moment, he saw a glitter in her eyes, one that he did not trust.

"I have not confessed my sins of this day, Aunt, and am unprepared for the Lord's blessing," he said smoothly.

"Perhaps on the morrow."

"Perhaps. What can you tell me of the monks who reside here?"

"They are good simple men, chosen by Angus for their piety. Seven in all, two of whom have taken holy orders and are priests." She smiled. "I rely upon them utterly." She clutched his hand as if in sudden fear. "I beg of you, do not send them away. I must pray for my son! I must have masses sung for his soul!" She became incoherent in her entreaties and Niall gripped her hands tightly.

"I asked only who they were, Aunt, no more than that."

"Men of these lands. Loyal men." She lifted her chin, and he saw a cold glint in her eyes. "Good men."

Niall thanked her, considering his impressions as he left her to her prayers. Was he wrong to distrust her invitation to partake of the bread? Had he been at war so long that he could suspect an elderly woman, bereft of her last son?

He might as well be Rafael, whose suspicions of all were boundless.

Seven men. He was certain he had counted eight monks this night. Niall would count again.

RAFAEL HEARD the wagon before he saw it. To his relief, its creaking disguised any sound that he made. The axle had not been greased of late, 'twas clear, for the conveyance was noisy beyond all. He spent some time fearing that he had chosen the wrong wagon, but this one had turned for the west almost immediately after leaving the road to the keep. It made its way along the coastline, far beyond the place where the other corpses had been taken. When the driver paused and removed one burden from the wagon, Rafael knew.

The size of that bundle was right for Ceara, and the monk lifted its weight readily. When he turned, the moon slipped from behind the clouds and Rafael saw that he wore no crucifix. The supposed monk set down his burden and Rafael flattened himself on the ground to watch. He had no doubt that this was Edward and that the other man took Ceara to fetch the mermaid's treasure.

What he did not know was what he could do to stop him. The line of sight was obstructed from his current location. There was no merit in injuring Edward again, for he might kill Ceara. Rafael had no doubt the other man was armed. He also wondered at Edward's allies within Eilean Tioram. Niall's victory would be an empty—or a short-lived—one unless they were all named and ousted.

As much as Rafael would have preferred to attack Edward and secure Ceara's release, he knew it was better to wait.

CEARA AWAKENED IN COLD SUNLIGHT. She was bound with ropes and lying on the rocky ground. There was a rag in her mouth and she could see only rocky hills before herself. She wriggled but a hand landed upon her. "Save your strength, Ceara," Edward advised her. "You have much swimming to do this day if you mean to see night fall."

She twisted around to discover that the loch was behind her, the water shimmering in the morning light. There was mist upon the water and a wagon piled with sacks was behind her. The smell and the blood told her what was inside those bundles and she shuddered as she averted her gaze.

"You could join them, if you choose to call out," Edward said. He was wearing the dark robes of a monk, though he wore boots instead of sandals. As she watched, he tugged off the garment and cast it aside, revealing that he wore his customary garb beneath it. There was a great notch out of his ear and that sight gave Ceara tremendous satisfaction.

"Silence?" he asked, brandishing his knife. "I could cut out your tongue if you prefer."

Ceara had no doubt he would do as much. She nodded agreement and he removed the gag. He unbound her legs but left the rope tied to one ankle. Her hands were bound together before herself and he passed her a vessel. It smelled of thin ale and she took a sip, realizing only then how parched she was.

"I assume there is something you desire," she said quietly.

He smiled. "The mermaid's treasure, of course. You will fetch it for me."

"And then?"

"And then we will wed, the treasure as your dowry."

"But Niall…"

"Will have little need of it by then. You will be the sole surviving descendant of Ruari MacRuari, the obvious claimant to all of his legacies. We will wed and your inheritance will become mine."

"And then you will have no need of me," she guessed.

He smiled and tickled under her chin with the tip of his dagger. "You might be able to change my thinking upon that matter, Ceara."

The very prospect made her innards churn.

She averted her gaze as if to study their surroundings and recognized where they were. Eilean Tioram was to the east, out of sight and too far for any to hear her call out. They were even well beyond the outer perimeter of the camps of the men who had come to fight, so far past them that she could not see them. Mingary would be at least a day's ride to the south. She was alone on this remote coast with a man who would kill her if he took the whim to do as much.

On the other hand, she knew where the treasure was. She would live at least until she had retrieved it for him.

She could only hope that Rafael had found the clue she had left and understood it. She wished she still had her dagger but Edward would have taken it from her by now if she had not left it behind. Her head ached and she was hungry, but she was alive.

She surveyed the coast, then pointed. "That is the mermaid's favored rock," she said, pointing to the one in question.

"Do you think she will come to your aid?" he asked with a smirk.

"I know that it marks the entrance to the cavern where her treasure is secured," Ceara said and rose to her feet. She did not bother to wait for him, but began to walk along the coast toward the hidden sanctuary.

She prayed that Rafael found her in time.

CEARA LED Edward along the rocky shore, descending toward the mermaid's favored rock. The tide slid out, revealing a cavern, one with an entrance so well hidden that few would have noted it even when the tide was at its lowest point.

She halted beside it and held out her bound hands. "The way is not easy," she informed her suspicious captor. "We both will need our hands."

He left the rope around her ankle and bound the other end of it to his waist. "No tricks," he muttered as he unbound her hands and Ceara smiled at him.

"Of course not," she said with such sincerity that any soul who knew her would have been warned.

Edward smiled, reassured.

They crept through the opening together, only to find themselves in a larger cavern, one with a still pool in its center. It was dark and cold, the cavern completely sealed from the outside. There were loose pebbles underfoot and they slid on the slope, dozens of small stones dancing downward to splash into the still water. Edward struck a tinder and lit a torch, which cast shadows over the high walls.

Ceara pointed. "This entire coast is riddled with holes and caverns. Down there is an opening that is never revealed to view. It is a tunnel, which leads to another small chamber. Within that chamber lies the mermaid's secret."

"Do not imagine that I will let you escape!"

"Then swim there with me."

He looked uneasy. "I cannot swim."

"I have been there before," she said, even as she cast aside her cloak. She unfastened her leather jerkin with quick gestures. "It has been years, but I have touched the mermaid's treasure with my own hands. If you desire it, I must retrieve it."

Edward eyed the water, which looked dark in the cavern and filled with ominous secrets. "How do I know there is not another passage for you to escape?"

"I will have no garments," Ceara said with impatience. "I will not be able to journey far thus."

He lifted the end of the rope and she knew he would bind her to him again. 'Twould be folly to do thus, for she might be snared on the rocks and drown.

She retreated into the water, then glanced down at her boots. "I cannot swim with these. I will drown and you will be left with naught."

"You will cheat me."

"'Twill take me three trips if not four, while you guard the passage," Ceara said speaking with impatience in the hope that he might be provoked. "Make haste! I must go quickly because the water is cold." She turned her back upon him then bent over from the waist, hoping to distract him with the view.

He swore softly, vowing all manner of vengeance upon her if she tricked him, but Ceara had already untied the rope. She quickly shed her boots and her chausses, keeping only her chemise as she waded into the icy water.

She extended her hand. "Cast me your satchel."

He warned her again, then cast her the bag.

Ceara did not linger but dove beneath the surface. She could only hope that all was precisely as she recalled. She had to find the tunnel by feel, coming up for air at intervals. When she found the opening, she took a deep breath, then ducked through it.

It was longer than she recalled and farther to the hidden cavern. She emerged with her chest tight and smiled at the familiar sight. There was a crack in the rock high overhead, one that was not noticeable from above but which allowed a slender finger of light into the cavern. She swam across the water and hauled herself onto a rocky shelf. Behind it was a hidden space and she reached into the darkness, praying that naught had changed.

When her hand closed around cold metal, she nearly wept with relief.

Ceara pulled bracelets and coins out of the space, recalling the day that she and Niall had spread them out on this very shelf to admire them all. They had counted them, as well, and she did as much now, arranging the entire hoard upon that rock. There was one piece that was particularly magnificent and she left it for last, filling the satchel with loose coins and armbands.

Then she slid back into the water and retraced her path, breaking the surface on the far side with relief.

She swam hard across the pool and emerged to silence.

Rafael stood on the shore, held captive by Edward. Though Rafael was larger, Edward held a dagger against his throat, the blade pressed so deeply into the skin that she could see a line of blood. Rafael watched her, his gaze dark and his expression inscrutable. Ceara watched as Edward claimed Rafael's dagger and tucked it into his own belt.

What could she do?

"It looks as if I will triumph this time," Edward said. "Tell me, how fond are you of your ears?"

Rafael granted him a dark glance but did not respond.

"This is half of it," Ceara said, emptying the contents of the satchel onto the stony shore. The gold and silver shone in the light cast by the torch and both men surveyed the spoils eagerly.

Ceara's heart sank. Had Rafael pursued her or the treasure? By his expression, she feared she knew, though she did not like that truth. The dark suspicion could not be shaken once it had occurred to her.

"You said three trips," Edward charged. "If not four. Cheat me, Ceara, and he dies." He pushed the knife a little deeper and a trail of blood began to run down Rafael's flesh. "Perhaps he should die anyway. He is of no import to this task and we must be rid of him to celebrate our own nuptials." Rafael's gaze simmered as Edward moved the blade.

Ceara had to distract Edward to give Rafael an opportunity, and she knew one way to do as much.

CHAPTER 17

$\mathcal{R}$afael had not expected the loose pebbles in the cave, much less that they would reveal his presence. 'Twas Edward who had surprised him, not the other way around, much to his dismay. He had erred in his haste to save Ceara and he feared she would pay the price. As he had suspected earlier, he and Edward were evenly matched, save that there was a viciousness about Edward.

He chose to let the other man triumph over him in the short term, wanting to be sure he guaranteed Ceara's welfare.

The disappointment in her expression when she reappeared in the water had torn his heart in two. He had the opportunity to admire how she considered the situation, and he knew she was seeking some advantage.

He did not anticipate the one she chose.

Beyond doubt, Ceara was a marvel.

She stood up abruptly in the water, then walked into the shallows. The wet chemise clung to her curves, much as a chemise had done that long-ago day she had lured him into the fen. The sight of her was just as enticing. She raised one hand to her own breast and fondled it, drawing Edward's attention to the way the nipple had beaded in the cold. Her braid hung wet down her back and her beauty was only surpassed by the bold confidence in her expression.

He loved her with all his heart and soul.

Edward stared for a moment, then shook his head and retreated, his blade still at Rafael's throat. "You will not distract me, Ceara," he snarled, proving his desire was not for Ceara. "I will have time aplenty to savor your charms."

He would not, if Rafael had much to say upon the matter.

Ceara's eyes flashed in the barest of warnings. She cast the satchel at Edward then, aiming for his head. Edward anticipated her and ducked in time, though Rafael stumbled, ensuring that the coins scattered across the pebbles. Edward was distracted by the sound of the coins and twisted to watch as several of them vanished into the dark water. "Nay!" he cried, forgetting his captive for a precious moment.

Rafael moved like lightning. He spun out of harm's way, seizing the hilt of the knife and twisting it from Edward's grasp. The dagger fell and landed in the water with a splash, both men looking after it.

In the meantime, Ceara dove back into the water and seized the loose end of the rope, giving it a hard tug. Edward cried out and fell to his knees in the shallows.

This was the fight Rafael desired.

Edward fought by no rules and no conventions, but Rafael had learned to fight in the streets of Venice where it was not possible to cheat. He fought with his hands and his wits, tripping Edward abruptly so that man fell into the water. When Edward emerged with the dagger, Rafael ducked the wickedly sharp blade that he had honed himself and finally kicked it out of Edward's hand. It fell on the dry floor of the cavern, and Rafael made the mistake of reaching for it.

Edward leapt on Rafael's back, his weight fairly taking him to his knees. Rafael ducked low, letting his opponent think he was more surprised than he was, then reared up and flung himself onto his back. Edward fell beneath him, that man gasping as he was plunged into the cold water. He gasped again when Rafael's weight fell atop him, then once more when Rafael drove his elbows into Edward's sides.

The man was like an eel. Each time Rafael thought he was defeating Edward, that man twisted out of his grasp. That his opponent had claimed his own dagger and meant to use it against him was an insult

Rafael could not bear. The sole consolation was that Ceara was beyond Edward's reach.

Edward stuck Rafael hard in the back of the head and Rafael saw stars. He rolled to his feet, still grappling with the other man, then heard Ceara inhale sharply. He glanced up, saw that she aimed his crossbow, and drove his elbow into Edward's jaw. That man choked and fell back, his hands still locked around Rafael's neck, but Rafael ducked.

He heard the whistle of the bolt and felt his opponent's weight drop. Edward was gasping for breath, the bolt being buried in his throat, and still trying to fell Rafael. Rafael stepped away, evading Edward's kicking feet and snatching hands, and retrieved his dagger. He returned to look down on Edward, who struggled for breath.

"Let me aid you," he said softly, then bent over the other man and slit his throat. He cast Edward's carcass aside and spat upon it, then turned to confront Ceara. "Are you hale, *bella?*"

She nodded and averted her gaze. "But I must fetch the rest."

She waded into the water, without waiting for his reply. Rafael wondered what was amiss, then saw her shiver. They had to retrieve the rest with haste, lest she fall ill. He could not imagine that there were apothecaries of merit in these remote lands.

"Nay," Rafael said, then began to disrobe himself. "You are not the sole one who can swim, *bella*. We go together or not at all."

Ceara eyed him warily and he wondered at her expression, until she spoke. "You can swim?"

"I grew up in Venice."

"I know but I do not understand."

"It is a city built upon the very lip of the Adriatic, a city of canals and waterways. One travels by boat within the city or on foot, but the distance is usually shorter by water."

"Someone should guard the treasure," she said, glancing at what she had already brought.

"We are alone, *bella*. Edward will threaten you no more." He spoke with impatience, thinking only of her comfort. He would not lose her to an ague now. "Make haste!" He walked into the water, flinching at the chill.

Still she lingered, until he turned to look at her. There was something in her expression that troubled him, an uncertainty that was utterly unlike her, but then her lips set with familiar resolve. She marched into the water, undeterred by its temperature and cast him a glance that could have been furious.

Though that made no sense.

"The treasure then," she said, her words hard. "With all haste." Rafael strode into the water after her, stunned that it should be so cold. His very blood was turning to ice, but Ceara did not falter. She ducked beneath the surface without a backward glance, swimming with the agility of a fish.

Or a mermaid.

~

THE TREASURE.

After all they had endured together, after all the battles they had fought and obstacles they had overcome, the truth was clear. Rafael cared only about the treasure. Doubtless he would sit, chilled to his marrow, and divide the spoils, counting each coin to ensure that neither of them cheated the other. Ceara swam with furious strokes, livid with him for being precisely the man he had claimed to be—and hating that she had been fool enough to expect otherwise.

If naught else, though, he could swim.

If Ceara had feared Rafael's skills, she had no reason to do as much. He moved through the water with powerful strokes as he matched her pace. Perhaps the goal gave him strength, though she had thought the cold water might make him falter. She bade him take a breath when they reached the far side of the pool and he nodded. They dove together, his fingertips brushing her ankle as he followed her through the dark tunnel. They surged through the icy water with purpose, then broke the surface together, gasping for air.

"A marvel," he murmured and she saw the cavern with new eyes. That meagre finger of light illuminated the water so that it glowed azure, and touched the shelf where the treasure was concealed. Though naturally formed, it was smooth and regular, as if a mason had created this place for an offering.

"*Dìomhair na maighdeann-mhara*," Ceara said, feeling her awe again, then swam toward it. She thought of the mermaid who had claimed Ruari's heart and how she had come to love Ruari against her will. She thought of the price the mermaid had paid for that affection but could not be glad that she and Rafael had never coupled.

She would have liked to have known what it was like.

She did not like her conviction that she would never know, much less that he would soon depart. Would he escort her back to Kilderrick? She expected not. He would simply leave, perhaps in the night, returning to his trade and leaving her in Niall's protection.

Ceara would not beg him to take her with him.

She pulled herself onto the shelf and looked back as Rafael emerged behind her. He looked like a pirate or a ruffian and her heart skipped at the sight of his wet hair and the growth of beard on his chin. He gripped the lip of stone and pulled himself from the water, and she could not keep herself from looking upon the splendor of his body.

He picked up a brooch with an admiration she shared, angling it toward the light. She would not think that he had selected the best piece first, that he had an eye for value. 'Twas wrought of gold and circular in design, with fine braids around its perimeter. In the middle was a crystal orb, set deeply into the brooch, surrounded by eight polished garnets of goodly size, stones that fairly glowed red.

"Such fine spirals of gold," he mused. "I had no notion that mermaids were such skilled goldsmiths."

"I think it is of Viking craftsmanship." Ceara gathered up the rest of the plaited silver bracelets, but Rafael halted her with a fingertip to study them.

"Fit for a mermaid queen," he murmured, then added them to the satchel.

They worked together, placing the treasure in the satchel so that it bulged with the volume of it. Rafael laid out his chemise, piling more into the middle of it, and she guessed that he would knot the cloth around the precious burden.

He paused regularly to admire the hoard, holding up many pieces to

THE DRAGON & THE DAMSEL

the light, his expression awed. Ceara's heart twisted, for she could see his true interest, as much as she wished it might have been otherwise.

There were pins of gold, as a lady might place in her hair, and many golden beads that the light shone through. Some of them were large enough to fill her palm and others were smaller than a fingernail. Some beads were carved and others faceted, but most were smooth. Ceara had admired them before, and despite herself, she realized that Rafael might know more of them than she did.

"Are they glass?" she asked.

"Amber," Rafael said, turning one in his hand, then placing it in her hand. "Feel the warmth of the stone. It is this dark gold hue in the northern seas."

"And in the southern?"

"In the Magreb, it is pale yellow and cloudy. Women wear it threaded in necklaces with silver beads as their dowries."

How Ceara yearned to see such faraway places, though she knew she never would.

In fact, she hoped there was yet a place for her at Kilderrick.

With impatience, she piled the rest upon his chemise, frowning at her own mood.

Rafael flicked a glance at her. "Is aught amiss, *bella?*" he asked softly, his tone making her want to weep.

"I am cold," she said curtly.

"Then we must hasten," he said, knotting his chemise into a bundle. Rafael jumped into the water again then broke the surface gasping. "God in heaven, *bella*, 'tis an intrepid soul who can swim in these waters."

She jumped into the water and broke the surface beside him, feeling the weight of a hundred things she wished to say to him. Their paths would part now and soon he would leave her side forever. She would not weep or beg, but she would miss him with all her heart.

Should she tell him again that she loved him?

Would it matter?

It had not mattered before.

Perhaps he had not believed her? How could she convince him?

Ceara hesitated, indecisive for once in all her days, and the moment was gone. Rafael swam toward the tunnel, not even hampered by the burden he carried against his side with one arm. Ceara slung the satchel over her shoulders as she had done before and followed him.

They nodded at each other, then took deep breaths, diving under the surface as one. 'Twas easier to swim through the tunnel from this direction, for the light was blindingly bright ahead of them. When they broke the surface in the outer cavern, Rafael swam on ahead of her with speed. She wondered at that, then saw that someone crouched beside the treasure on the shore.

'Twas Niall.

Her brother stood, grinning as they hauled their prize ashore. He had brought heavy cloths and dry chemises. Rafael seized one of the rough clothes, turning immediately to Ceara and wrapping her within it. Had she not seen his interest in the treasure, she might have thought he had a concern for her.

Perhaps his actions were for Niall's benefit. She turned away from him, shedding her wet chemise from beneath the shelter of the cloth. His eyes narrowed but she turned her back upon him lest he see how her heart was breaking.

"You will be chilled," she said curtly. "Garb yourself with haste."

Something was amiss.

The change in Ceara's manner was not because she was cold. 'Twas more than that at root. Rafael realized she was disappointed, though he could not fathom why. The treasure was splendid, far beyond his expectations, and he had anticipated that she would be triumphant in her success. Edward was dead, unlamented, and all seemed to Rafael to be resolved most satisfactorily.

But there were tears in the eyes of his bold huntress, as if she might weep. He could make no sense of it.

Niall exclaimed over various items as he packed the treasure into several trunks he had brought. Ceara seemed to have no interest in it any longer, but Rafael felt obliged to be polite.

Niall shook his head as he studied each piece in turn. "I will never forget the day we found it," he said quietly, then smiled at Rafael. "'Twas Ceara, of course, who was sufficiently bold to swim further into the cave."

Rafael was not surprised.

"And Ceara, of course, who reclaimed it." Niall smiled at her. "What share will be yours, sister mine?"

"None of it," she said, her expression set. "My share is yours." She flung her cloak over her shoulder and strode for the opening to the coast.

"But it is our shared legacy," Niall protested.

"And you have more need of it, as chieftain," she replied.

Niall looked between her and Rafael, clearly sharing Rafael's suspicions. "But what is the Dragon's share?" he asked lightly, as if he would provoke her smile.

She turned and glared at the pair of them and this time, Rafael did think she might weep. "I do not care. Settle the matter between yourselves." She pivoted then to depart.

"Ceara!" Niall cried. "Do you not owe some loyalty to your husband's side?"

"We are not wed in truth," she said softly without turning. Her head bowed and Rafael saw her shoulders shake. "'Twas only words, Niall. Only words. Doubtless he can seek his annulment from the priests at Eilean Tioram."

Niall raised his gaze to Rafael, confusion in his gaze.

Rafael's heart fairly stopped. She thought he desired only the treasure and he was astounded that she could have concluded as much. He shook his head minutely and Niall turned back to Ceara.

"But you must take a share," that man protested, holding out the brooch that was the finest token in the hoard. "I insist upon it."

Ceara returned with heavy steps to look down at the brooch. She did not even glance at Rafael, proof that his conclusion was correct, and he saw her throat work with rare vulnerability. She looked both brave and defeated at the same time and he knew her manner was entirely his fault. "'Twas always your legacy," she said to her brother. "Intended to help you gain the leadership of the clan. I fetched it only for you." She shook her head and made to turn away again. "Take it, Niall."

"Take it all," Rafael added with resolve.

The pair looked at him in surprise and wonder.

Rafael did not care for Niall's reaction. He held Ceara's gaze, hating that he had caused her any doubt. "I have never been in the habit of stealing the birthright of others, no matter what has been said of me. I accept only what I am owed, or what is surrendered by choice." He nodded at the treasure and let his voice deepen to a command. "Take it, Niall. It is yours. The mermaid was your forebear, after all."

"You do not have to surrender your share," Ceara began to protest, but Rafael dropped to one knee beside her.

She fell silent when he removed the ring from his right hand, her eyes wide. "Our bond was more than words, *bella*," he declared, offering the ring to her. "I would defend you with my life, for that is all I possess."

"You had treasure but a moment past," she noted, her eyes beginning to sparkle with mischief. "You might wish to reconsider your choice."

"I never desired the treasure," he asserted, hoping he could convince her of that. "'Twas always you alone who fed my desire. We embarked on this journey because I could not leave you undefended, and now, I would not leave you at all." He lifted the ring beside her hand and her gaze flicked between it and his eyes. "I have only myself to offer, but I am yours to my dying breath if you will have me, *bella*."

"What of the Compagnie Rouge?"

"Another will lead them in my stead. There is always trade for mercenaries, whoever they follow. Maximilian once offered me the post of sheriff in Rowan Fell, or perhaps I might become his captain-at-arms. We will find a way together, Ceara, if you put your hand in mine."

"Together," she echoed with glowing eyes. She tilted her head to survey him, a smile upon her lips. "But I am yet a maiden, sir."

Rafael chuckled. "I believe we can resolve that matter this very night." He lifted the ring again and she laughed, pushing her finger through it once again. It suited her hand better than his own and he was relieved to see it in its rightful place.

She then flung herself at him and Rafael caught her close, standing up to swing her in his arms with joy. "You are the only prize I desire, *bella*," he murmured to her, watching her eyes light with pleasure. "Never doubt as much."

"I never will again," she vowed and they smiled at each other for a potent moment. He could feel her heart beating against his own and welcomed the weight of her in his embrace. He smiled at her, letting his expression turn wicked.

"You are cold, *bella*. Let us see you warmed." With that, he slid his hand into the fire of her hair and cupped her nape, drawing her closer for a triumphant kiss.

~

IT WAS a merry trio who returned to the keep with the mermaid's treasure. Niall had brought a pair of palfreys when he pursued them and Ceara rode before Rafael, content to be nestled against his chest. Her brother sent a party to retrieve the corpses and wagon, to ensure the men were buried as they should be. As they rode, she told them both what Aimil had confessed to her and watched both men's expressions become stern.

They entered the keep, which already bustled with activity, and dismounted.

"This injustice must be resolved," Rafael said and her brother nodded.

"I would ask you to come with me," Niall replied, his manner mysterious. "I have a notion."

Rafael took Ceara's hand as Niall led them up the stairs to the chambers above the hall. She exchanged a glance with Rafael, who looked grim, for she did not understand what would transpire.

"Aunt?" Niall called and Ceara caught her breath. "I have come to pray with you, as promised," he said, continuing into one of the chambers.

"Have you confessed?" the older woman asked, as yet unaware that Niall was not alone.

"I have, and indeed, I have heard confessions myself."

279

"But you are no priest," she countered with a laugh. "What is this jest you make?"

"I make no jest, Aunt," Niall said, steel in his tone. He stepped aside so that Ceara and Rafael were revealed. "Your treachery has been uncovered. Your ally lies dead."

"Edward?"

"You should never have attacked my sister, Aunt, for now you have earned the ire of her husband."

Rafael took a step forward and the older woman stumbled backwards. She looked between them, her manner wild, as she strove to concoct an explanation. She managed to smile. "She lies," she said, pointing to Ceara. "Edward told me their marriage was a ruse. She is as untrustworthy as the mercenary she has taken to her bed."

"My sister does not lie, Aunt."

"But Edward…"

"I slit his throat," Rafael admitted, his voice low. "For the bolt from the crossbow did not kill him outright. 'Twas only merciful to ensure that he was dead."

"He will be brought to the bailey, if you wish to look upon him," Niall offered.

Aimil looked between them with dismay. "But, but, he was my last hope. He was the sole one who could reclaim my legacy for me."

"You would have killed Niall, then me, after Edward had forced me to wed him," Ceara said, her voice as hard as Niall's. "You contrived Raghnall's death and you killed my father, Aherne."

Niall shook his head. "The king's justice will be harsh, Aunt, but perhaps by the time the court is heard, you will be glad of release. Your time in the dungeon is as unlikely to be pleasant as it is to be of short duration."

"You cannot do this to me!" Aimil cried, launching herself at Niall. "You are merely the son of a bastard. *I am the heiress of Garmaron.* I am the one who should claim it all!" He rebuffed her easily, casting her back into her chamber.

"I will send guards to take you to the dungeon," he said softly. "I grant you one last chance to pray in this place."

Her eyes flashed and she turned to the altar, falling upon the bread on the plate as if she was starving. 'Twas then that Ceara guessed the truth, understanding the reason why Niall had been invited to pray with Aimil. She took a step forward in the same moment as Rafael. "Poison!" she said. "She said she had poisoned her father!"

But it was too late. Aimil had swallowed the bread and braced herself in the corner of the chamber, a dagger in her grasp. They could only watch as her expression changed to one of dismay, as her features contorted and she crumpled to the floor in pain. She moaned once, a pitiful sound, then groaned as she fell silent.

Rafael crouched beside her, listening for her breath, then stood again, shaking his head. He came to Ceara and took her hand. "'Tis done, *bella*."

"And for the best," Niall agreed.

Ceara nodded, her heart heavy. Despite all her aunt's misdeeds, Ceara would not have liked to see her consigned to the dungeon or compelled to face the king's justice. 'Twas better thus, though she would always regret it could not have been otherwise.

"So much anger," she whispered when she and Rafael were alone in the corridor. Niall was calling for aid and Rafael pulled her into his embrace.

"The fury of a woman scorned," he agreed.

They simply stood entwined for long moments and Ceara closed her eyes to listen to the steady pounding of his heart. She felt more chilled than she had in the water earlier in the day, sensing that both wickedness and death were overly close. She held Rafael tightly, glad beyond words that he had set his former trade aside.

He cleared his throat finally, then whispered into her hair. "Niall would likely invite us to linger here this night in the comfort of the hall, but I yearn for simple pleasures. What say you, *bella*?"

'Twas the perfect suggestion and she could not have agreed more.

"Your tent is the sole place I wish to be this night," she said, tipping back her head to smile at him. "Provided, sir, that you accompany me there."

Rafael grinned then his triumphant kiss left her in no doubt of his reply.

∽

RAFAEL AND CEARA walked hand-in-hand from Eilean Tioram as the sun set once more in splendor. Rafael surveyed the sky, certain he had never witnessed such a glorious display of color. There was still debris from the battle, but his trebuchet had been removed from the field. He had no doubt that it was disassembled and in the wagon once more, his men prepared to depart. He and Ceara climbed the hill to the site where the Compagnie Rouge had made their camp and found Helmut and Lambret drinking ale by the fire. The pair saluted them with good cheer, but had the sense not to expect their company. Antonio appeared out of the shadows, his eyes alight, and swept open the flap of Rafael's tent.

All was precisely as it should be, save that there were no vessels for Greek fire and no ingredients to make more. For once, Rafael did not care. He asked only for some hot water and the boy darted away on his quest. He removed his boots as Ceara did the same, then laced his fingers with hers and led her toward the bed.

"I was certain you desired only the treasure," she said for the second time and Rafael smiled.

"I knew you were vexed with me but could not fathom why," he explained again, waiting for her to laugh as she had before.

She did. "I suspect you are not so fearsome as your repute," she teased and he chuckled.

"Perhaps I shall cultivate a new reputation," he said, glancing back as Antonio appeared. The boy put down the steaming bucket and would have done more, but Rafael halted him with a touch. "Go and sleep, Antonio," he said quietly. "We will be fine."

The boy hesitated, glancing between them for a moment, then bowed and stepped away. Rafael saw his silhouette as he stood guard outside the tent, but knew the boy was too exhausted to persist for long.

"He would do any deed for you," Ceara noted.

"He has no kin."

Ceara shook her head as she set aside her belt. "He has you," she said with soft heat. "And no one could have need of more." Her words filled his heart with a joy beyond any he had felt before, and he was humbled anew that she was his bride.

Then she set aside her jerkin and unlaced her chemise, and Rafael could only stare like a man enchanted. She smiled and untied the lace that held her braid, shaking out her hair like a burnished cloud. He was reminded of the sunset and smiled as she unlaced her chausses and cast them aside. She wore only the chemise her brother had brought, but even that soon landed on the carpet.

She was nude and as beautiful as the first time he had seen her, perhaps more so for she held his heart fully in thrall.

She came to him and he waited, his throat tight, wanting her to set their pace. She unfastened his belt and set it aside, showing as much care for his weapons as he would have done—nay, more, for on this night, he would have been impatient in setting them aside. She unlaced his jerkin and let it fall to the ground, then loosed the tie of his chemise. It, too, went over his head and fluttered to the carpet as she ran her hands across his chest. She pinched one nipple and gave him that impish smile before her hands lowered to the lace of his chausses. She caressed him through the cloth as she unfastened them, tormenting him sweetly so that he clenched his fists to await her desire.

When he stood before her nude, she walked around him, letting a fingertip trail around his hip. Her eyes were dancing, as green and filled with mischief as ever he had seen them, when she stood before him again, and he inhaled sharply when those fingertips caressed him.

"*Bella*," he whispered and she laughed lightly, savoring her effect upon him. Then her hands slid up his chest and over his shoulders, her fingers spearing into his hair. She stretched to her toes to kiss him, but Rafael swept her off her feet, catching her close as he claimed her mouth with a sultry kiss. She fairly wrapped herself around him, surrendering to his kiss and inviting him to demand yet more. As ever, he was filled with a fire that he knew would never be quenched so long as this woman desired him.

He crouched down with her cradled in his lap and plunged the cloth into the warm water. He washed her face and her throat, laved her breasts, then followed the path of the cloth with his mouth. He trailed his tongue over her warm flesh, capturing first one nipple and then the other in a slow sweet kiss. She squirmed against him, her every movement a delicious torment, but Rafael was determined to make this moment last. He teased each nipple to a taut peak, moving from one to the other so that both were hard and ruddy. He dipped the cloth in the water again, stroking it over her skin and between her thighs. She gasped and he dropped the cloth, caressing her with finger and thumb as his mouth locked over hers. He kissed her deeply and possessively, even as he conjured her slick heat. She moaned into his kiss and arched against him, her fingers digging into his shoulders in demand as he tormented her with pleasure. He felt the tide rising within her and retreated, leaving her eyes flashing and her cheeks flushed.

She seized the cloth then and he smiled, knowing that she would retaliate in kind. She did, washing him slowly and seductively, trailing her hands across him, then following with her lips and teeth and tongue. He claimed her mouth and kissed her again, wanting all she had to grant and more. When his fingers slid through her slick heat again, she nipped at his lip and dropped her voice to a growl of demand that thrilled him to his toes.

"More," she commanded and he was only too glad to comply.

He set her on the bed, on the pile of fur pelts that were there and eyed the contrast between their silvery darkness and her fair skin. She beckoned to him and once again, he could not resist her siren's call. He lowered himself over her, loving how warmly she welcomed him. There was no trepidation in her expression, no doubt, and he was honored by her trust. Her eyes were glittering with desire and her lips were swollen from his kisses. He braced his weight over her as he kissed her languidly, his one hand gripping her nape and his fingers in her hair. They had all their lives to explore the passion that rose between them and Rafael knew he would never tire of it. He eased between her thighs and Ceara wound her legs around his waist, welcoming him with such enthusiasm that Rafael had to halt for a moment lest he injure her.

"What is amiss?" she whispered, her fingers stroking his neck.

"I nigh forget that you are a maiden," he said with a smile then nudged against her. She was hot and wet, so tight that desire roared hot within him. He watched her intently as he moved deeper, swallowing her gasp with a kiss, stroking her as he moved ever deeper. He paused and she smiled, his bold huntress. She slid her hands over his shoulders, drawing him onward, then dug her nails into his flesh in silent demand. Despite her ardor, Rafael moved with excruciating slowness, gradually easing inside her. It took forever to bury himself within her but when he felt her tight sheath surrounding him, he closed his eyes and shuddered.

Ceara kissed his throat. "There must be more," she whispered and Rafael smiled against her skin.

Then he moved and she gasped aloud. He arched back and moved steadily, taut with control as he watched her, determined to make this union a satisfying one for her. In but three strokes, Ceara matched his rhythm, arching against him when he moved inside her. When he growled with satisfaction, she rubbed her breasts against him, pulling him closer for a kiss. Rafael could resist her no longer then. He moved with vigor, ensuring that he rubbed against her to conjure her own pleasure, and watched her eyes light.

She flushed with the rising tide and he rolled to his back, letting her straddle him. She knelt above him, eyes shining. She was a vision of beauty, her hair flowing wild and red, her expression filled with joy. She moved slowly until she learned how best to do so, then moved more quickly. She drove him wild with every roll of her hips, making him dizzy when she caressed her own nipples before his eyes. She conjuring the tempest so expertly that they might have loved a hundred times.

Her eyes sparkled that she had him at her mercy, then Rafael slid his finger beneath her and rubbed that most sensitive spot. Her eyes widened and she gasped in astonishment, then he laughed. Their gazes locked—indeed, the air fairly crackled between them and Rafael knew that he would gladly pay any price for decades with this woman by his side. Higher and higher they climbed, and it seemed to him that their union was of more than their bodies, more profound than the pursuit of pleasure. Rafael felt they were joined as one heart, one soul, and united in a single purpose, one that could not be denied and might never be fully sated.

She whispered his name, an entreaty he could not deny, and Rafael pinched her. He had the gift of seeing the flush suffuse her skin as she cried out in her release. There could have been no finer view and Rafael felt the tumult rise within himself. Ceara was yet gasping when he rolled her beneath himself and drove deeply, seeking his own release.

She nipped at his ear, the temptress, then slid her tongue across his skin, loosing the tide with that sultry caress.

"Ceara," he whispered, hearing the strain in his own voice. He drove hard into her once, twice, three times, then roared as his own release claimed him completely. He sank down atop her, his heart thundering at the power of their union, and Ceara wrapped her arms around him to hold him close.

Once again, there were cheers in the distance and he felt Ceara smile against his skin.

He braced himself on his elbows to look down at her, smiling at her evident satisfaction. "Now, we are wed in truth," he said with amusement. His other hand tangled in her hair, winding a tendril around his finger as he surveyed her. "There can be no annulment, *bella*."

Her expression turned wicked in a way that suited her well. "Perhaps we should be sure," she whispered, eyes dancing with merriment, and Rafael laughed.

"A moment, *bella*, if not more."

He retrieved the cloth and washed her with reverence, admiring how she lounged before him. Rafael found himself smiling at her, the temptress he had been determined to possess.

And now he would never relinquish her.

Niall was right in that: such opportunities seldom presented themselves. They had to be seized and cherished, lest they be lost forever. This night would affect his choices for the rest of his life and Rafael knew it would be folly to regret any of it.

The sole error would be letting such a chance slip away.

"What are you thinking?" Ceara asked and Rafael realized she had been watching him.

"That trust must be earned, but that it is also a matter of choice," he admitted. He turned his wrist so she could see the scar there from the wound that had healed. "This is the evidence of an oath sworn with my blood brothers, Maximilian and Amaury, at our father's funeral. We pledged to each support each other and to find our way together. Each of us inflicted our own wound and we mingled our blood together as evidence of our vow."

"There must have been other witnesses, too."

"Does it matter? The vow hangs upon my heart, a pledge that will ensure I never betray either of them, even if it cost my life."

"They are fortunate to have your loyalty."

On impulse, he leaned across the bed and picked up his dagger, the one she had taken from him, and the crystal pommel caught the light. She watched him, her eyes dark. "That day at Château de Vries, I trusted Maximilian for he had earned as much, but I knew little—and less good—of Amaury. I chose to trust him, on our shared lineage, on Maximilian's assurance, on faith." He cut the inside of his right wrist and the red blood beaded along the wound. He spun the knife, handing the grip to Ceara. "Let us pledge to our mutual protection."

"We are already wedded," she said, even as her fingertips brushed the hilt. "Surely that binds our paths together."

"This is the kind of vow I understand best," was the sole explanation he could give.

She smiled. "It is the one you trust," she said softly, then took his knife and cut her own wrist, echoing his gesture perfectly. "I pledge myself to you again, Rafael di Giovanni. I would be your wife, your lover, your companion, the mother of your children and the warrior who defends your back."

Rafael smiled even as he took her hand and pressed their wrists together. Her choice of words was more persuasive than aught else could have been. They were two of a kind—or two halves of a whole. He could have sworn that he felt the moment her blood mingled with his, that it surged through his veins and made him a better man than he would have been without her. "And I pledge myself to you, Ceara MacRuari," he said. "I will be your husband, your lover, your companion, the father of your children and the warrior who defends your back."

"Forever and ever," Ceara added.

"Indeed," Rafael agreed, then sealed their vows with another potent kiss.

Of course, the lady who was his equal if not more, his partner and his companion forever, wound her arms around his neck and kissed him back.

Their paths were bound together for all time, for better and for worse, and Rafael could not have imagined a better fate.

EPILOGUE

$\mathcal{I}$t took the Compagnie Rouge a fortnight to return to Kilderrick but Rafael did not care. So long as they did not reach that keep, he could consider their shared future.

He could regret that he had no good destination for his bride.

They were greeted with great joy and welcomed to the hall like old friends. Everyone wished to hear the tale of their adventures and the board fairly groaned with Maximilian's generosity. Alys was so ripe that she was unsteady on her feet but between Maximilian and Nyssa, there was little chance of her stumbling. The hall was merry again that night, the company fascinated as Rafael recounted their adventures. The completion of his tale was greeted with a cheer and more ale.

"But did you learn your mother's name?" Yves asked as he filled Rafael's cup.

"Francesca. That was all Jean le Beau confided in me."

"Francesca? Your mother was Francesca?" 'Twas clear that Yves was startled by Rafael's response for his words were sharp. Indeed, he nigh dropped the pitcher of ale.

"Aye," Rafael agreed, wondering at this reaction.

"Do you know her family name?" Yves demanded.

Rafael shook his head.

Yves frowned and sat down on the bench, obviously recalling

details. "Francesca Dandolo was expected to arrive as a guest at Château de Vries." The older man spoke with excitement. "I did not know what happened to her. I forgot that her anticipated arrival was so near the day that Jean le Beau attacked. Matters were most unsettled, what with the mercenary's invasion with his company and I fear I was not at my best."

"He killed the lord," Alys reminded everyone softly.

"Frederick de Vries, my lady. Aye, he did." Yves shuddered. "And then he took Mathilde forcibly as his bride, leaving no doubt of his claim."

"He possessed her before the company," Henri whispered and those who had not known as much exchanged glances of horror.

Yves continued. "Aye, 'twas a wretched day, one of foul deeds and suffering beyond any day before." The older man cast a quick smile at a watchful Maximilian. "Though there was one matter of merit to result from events of that day," he added quickly.

"I thank you for the qualification," Maximilian murmured into his cup of ale.

The châtelain shook a finger at Rafael. "But Francesca was the niece of Giulia Dandolo, Frederick's first wife. Giulia died in the delivery of Gaston de Vries and Frederick had not wed again. There was a negotiation at the time, a scheme that he should wed again and have another son. She was offered as a choice in correspondence between the families. There is a likeness of her in the treasury of de Vries."

Rafael straightened, finding new reason to return to Château de Vries. "Then you met her?" he asked.

Yves shook his head. "She never arrived. I assumed she had been delayed upon the road, or that she had departed late." The older man colored. "I confess that I forgot about her."

"We could not keep him from her," Eudaline muttered, drawing every eye.

Yves straightened with purpose. He exchanged a glance with Maximilian who raised his voice. "Eudaline, do you know what happened to Francesca Dandolo?"

The old woman shook her head, rocking in agitation on the bench.

"She was a maiden, black of hair and dark of eye, a beauty. Dragged from her carriage when he arrived. 'Twas horrible. Horrible!"

Those in the company exchanged shocked glances and Rafael felt Ceara's hand close over his own.

"We could not save her," Eudaline whispered.

"But what happened to her?" Nathalie asked when the older woman fell silent.

"They said she was locked away for his pleasure, from the day of his arrival and hers." She sighed. "He took her with him when he departed. Who can say what befell her?"

"God in Heaven," Alys whispered into the silence that followed the old woman's words.

"Francesca Dandolo," Yves said with reverence. He bowed to Rafael. "Sir, your lineage is a mighty one, indeed."

"Dandalo," Rafael murmured and met Ceara's gaze.

"They were her family," she said, gripping his hand. "They should not have cast her out."

Rafael could scarce take a breath.

Maximilian raised a finger. "We are brothers, both sons of Jean le Beau. How curious that if your mother had wed my grandfather, we would have been related on our mother's side as well."

"But they *would* have wed," Yves said. "There was no question about it. The agreement was signed. Francesca was sent a betrothal ring to seal the contract."

Rafael looked at Ceara who looked back at him. She raised her left hand, showing Yves the ring Rafael had placed upon her finger. "This one?" she asked softly and Yves' eyes lit, his reply clear even before he spoke.

"The very one! It appears modest but it has a cross engraved inside, along with Frederick's initials."

Ceara removed the ring and they each peered at it in turn.

"It was said to have been brought back to de Vries by a crusading knight."

Rafael looked at the ring with more admiration than he had before. Francesca Dandolo. There was a name. And Frederick de Vries might have been his father, if not for Jean le Beau.

Maximilian grinned at him. "I cannot appoint a Dandolo as a mere sheriff," he said with amusement and Rafael could only smile.

"Of course not," Yves said sternly, then bowed before Rafael. "But if I may be so bold, sir, it seems that you would be the best candidate to become the Lord de Vries. You already hold the seal, after all."

"I expect the claim would be contested," Rafael had to note.

"You could reclaim it from Philip, if that were so," Matteo said, but Ceara shook her head.

Her grip was tight upon Rafael's hand. "I think my lord husband does not wish that prize," she said when he could not. "It is where his mother was seized and abused, and that is not an event he could ever forget."

Rafael kissed her fingers. "We will find another home, *bella*." He promised her, his heart warmed by her smile.

"I do have another suggestion," Maximilian said in the tone he used when he was proud of himself. Rafael looked up to find his brother's eyes sparkling. "Though, of course, it may be too close to family for your satisfaction."

"What have you schemed?" Rafael demanded, wondering how his brother had contrived any alliance in the Veneto.

Maximilian laughed. He reached into his purse and set a seal upon the board between them, his manner expectant.

"I do not recognize it," Rafael said.

"Nor will any other," Maximilian said. "For the Barony of Gisroy has been unassigned these past twenty years." He winced. "That explains the matter of Bewcastle remaining unoccupied and the reivers taking their trade through those lands, laying them waste. 'Twill take a certain manner of warrior to return that territory to a lawful state." He eyed Rafael.

"How did this seal fall to your hand?"

"It has not. It fell to Amaury, for Gisroy was granted decades ago to a cousin of Elizabeth, one who died without issue. The seal was sent to Amaury, because of his obligation as Warden of the March to see the position filled."

"But surely someone else desires this barony?"

"It must be bestowed upon a candidate with suitable credentials. It should be noted that Amaury thought immediately of you. He appealed to the other Wardens of the March, who suggested that I present the possibility to the king." Maximilian smiled. "Robert very much likes the notion of another former leader of the Compagnie Rouge pledging fealty to him."

The company erupted in laughter and Ceara gripped Rafael's hand, her anticipation most clear. Still he had to ask her. "Does this solution suit you, *bella*?"

"Of course. I think the post will suit you well, if it can be arranged."

"Will the holding suit you?"

Her smile was radiant. "Aye, for I will be with you."

Rafael's heart pounded with vigor at that.

"We should go to de Vries to retrieve the likeness of your mother and ensure that Philip compensates you for the seal, though," she said.

"And then we will return, to breed horses at Bewcastle and rout reivers?"

"I can think of little better." She settled against him with a smile.

"What of sons?" Rafael asked in a wicked whisper and Ceara laughed aloud.

"I would have a dozen of them," she replied with surety.

Rafael could have no argument with that.

Maximilian called for a cask of wine, but Alys stood up abruptly, her expression stricken. She gasped aloud and Maximilian was immediately on his feet.

"'Tis time," Nyssa said with authority and caught Alys' elbow.

Maximilian swept his wife into his arms and carried her to the solar, Nyssa fast behind him.

"A son," Eudaline murmured, nodding to herself, but Rafael could not tell whether that was a hope or a prediction.

By dawn, when the boy's cry filled the hall, 'twas clear that Eudaline, for all her blindness, had seen the truth.

CEARA AND RAFAEL left Kilderrick in late June to return to Château de Vries.

Ceara was fascinated that each day they rode or sailed south, the view changed. The people's languages and appearances changed. They passed fearsome keeps and tidy villages, and she scarce wanted to close her eyes to sleep lest she miss some wondrous detail. She had never anticipated that there was so much diversity in the world. Rafael was always at her back, pointing out what she might have missed, explaining what was different in these parts, and she could not have been more content.

Once in France, Rafael gathered the Compagnie Rouge again, arriving at the gates with a veritable army at his heels. He did not cross the threshold, much to Ceara's relief. As Rafael had anticipated, Philip desired the seal to that holding above all else. His astonishment when Rafael offered it to him for a price was evidence enough of that. The way Philip's gaze flicked over the warriors arrayed behind Rafael revealed that he might have battled for it, if his forces had been sufficient. He invited Rafael into the keep, but Rafael declined, recalling Gaston's trickery.

The pair made their agreement outside the walls, in the middle of the veritable road, encircled by the Compagnie Rouge. Philip's agitation was palpable, but so was his desire for the seal. He readily surrendered the portrait of Rafael's mother—Ceara doubted he had realized who the lady was—as well as the coin in exchange. Once the agreement was made and the fee paid, the Compagnie Rouge departed the lands, riding south and east.

Ceara could have sworn she heard Philip breathe a sigh of relief.

Rafael ceded the command of the Compagnie Rouge to Bernard, who had no desire to leave that life. With Rafael's endorsement, there was no argument from the warriors who had followed him. They had word of a baron in the Low Countries who sought their aid in his feud with his neighbor, and Bernard led the men to the north.

Matteo, Antonio and Louis remained with Ceara and Rafael. By unspoken agreement, they rode to Venice, with the plan of presenting themselves as merchants at the city gates. En route, Ceara taught the four men Gaelic as they rode, while Rafael tutored her in Venetian at night. She marveled at the towns with their tiled roofs, the abundance of flowers and fruit, the warmth of the sun. She had never imagined a city like Venice could exist, sparkling like a gem on the shores of a turquoise sea, its twisted streets lined with canals and hidden courtyards. She saw its splendors, as well as one of its poorer neighborhoods when Matteo led them to the house where he and Rafael had grown up.

The area had changed, Matteo's mother gone, as well as many of their former neighbors, but he and Rafael found one couple who recalled them as mischievous boys. They shared a merry afternoon together on a sunny patio, reminiscing over cups of red wine. 'Twas they who confirmed that Matteo's mother had been Francesca's maid but had left the family's service when she rounded with child. One of Francesca's cousins had apparently been the seducer, but the timing of her pregnancy meant that Matteo's mother had not gone to Château de Vries with Francesca. Upon her return to Venice, Francesca had sought out her former maid and friend.

Matteo and Rafael saluted the fact that they were cousins at least.

Later, before the new palazzo that rose from the ashes of his family's former home, Rafael pointed across the seas to Byzantium and told Ceara of its wonders. She knew the crucifix he wore had come from there and looked east, only to find that her curiosity dimmed.

"We can find passage and go," Rafael murmured into her ear, his arms wrapped around her as they stood looking. "We need not return to Scotland if you do not desire as much."

She turned to look at him. "Do you desire the barony?"

"I would live wherever you are happy," he said, then his eyes began to twinkle. "But I would not decline such a new challenge as that." He met her gaze, awaiting her choice.

"I think journeying abroad is all well and good," she said, nestling against him. "But there comes a time when one would be home again. Let us go home to Gisroy, Rafael."

And he kissed her so soundly that she knew their hearts were as one.

Before their departure from the city, Rafael bought provisions. Ceara accompanied him to obscure corners, to the shops of men who sold powders and weaponry. Only when he had acquired all he desired, including more of the ceramic vessels he favored, did they depart.

They rode north this time from Venice, taking a different path. This route led through the Alps and St. Bernard's pass, a wondrous climb of dizzying heights. Ceara could not believe such mountains existed, much less that their peaks would still be capped with snow in summer. Paris was their next destination and she knew that Rafael intended to show her as many wonders as possible. Louis led them in that city, guiding them to cathedrals and markets, to inns where he had labored as a stableboy, to bridges where he had huddled in the night before Maximilian had found him. They lingered a few days while a seamstress completed two new kirtles for Ceara at Rafael's insistence, one of sapphire blue embroidered with gold and one of a deep red wool, as richly hued as fine wine.

By then, Ceara was anticipating the quiet of the forests, the comparative solitude of the lands she knew best, and even the task of routing the reivers.

They crossed the channel from Calais, passing through London swiftly for all of them tired of cities and their filth. They rode north with all speed, the increasing familiarity of the land with its smaller trees and rocky outcroppings making Ceara's heart sing. Finally, they passed through the milecastle on the old Roman wall, saddle-sore and tired, but unable to halt so close to their destination.

'Twas early October and the leaves were changing hue, yellow taking precedence from green. The skies were stormy and the wind had a new bite. They followed the path through the forest, dappled with sunlight in the late afternoon, and came finally to Bewcastle.

The ruined keep had utterly changed. Not only had its walls been rebuilt to rise tall and square, but the clearing around it was crowded with tents, wagons, horses and men. Fires burned and horses nickered. Men labored and boys darted between them, bringing supplies and running errands. The arriving party remained in the shadows, simply looking in their astonishment, and Ceara doubted she was the sole one filled with relief and joy.

They were home. She saw Nyssa, assisting Denis by the fire, while Denis' wife, Marie, hastened around him. Royce was there, directing the installment of the heavy wooden gates and Alys sat beneath a canopy nearby, nursing her son. Maximilian stood on the newly-built curtain wall, directing the efforts of his masons, and the smell of venison stew made Ceara's stomach grumble. There were two tents larger and more ornamented than the rest, but Ceara did not recognize them. Her heart was full at just the sight of so many familiar faces.

Rafael reached out and took her hand, his own strong fingers closing over hers. She saw his throat work, then they were spotted and a shout rose through the company. Maximilian leapt down from the walls and came to shake Rafael's hand, his satisfaction more than clear. The two men conferred for a mere moment, Maximilian confiding that Elizabeth had borne a daughter to Amaury just weeks before. The new arrival was named Florine.

Then Maximilian glanced over his shoulder. "'Tis done," he said simply and gestured to the largest tent.

Robert, King of Scotland stood before it, watching intently. When Rafael inclined his head, the king extended his hand, offering his ring to be kissed.

Rafael reached back to take Ceara's hand, leading her to the king at his side. She wished, in truth, that she had worn one of her new kirtles, but they had expected Bewcastle to be empty. Rafael dropped to one knee and she stood behind him, head bowed.

"You have challenged me, Rafael Dandalo," the king said once Rafael had kissed his ring. "You have deceived me and you have aided a rebellion in my lands without my authorization. You have fostered discontent in one of my allies as a result of that rebellion and you have even killed my godson."

Ceara's heart fluttered. Rafael did not so much as breathe.

"But in all these matters, you have pursued a rough justice. You defended the woman who has become your lady wife in truth, you ensured that his legacy was restored to her brother, the rightful heir and tanist, and truly, the toll you took from my godson was in retribution for his own crimes." He waved a hand. "The Lord of the Isles has territory aplenty and can be made content in the interest of peace in the highlands." The king drew his sword and Ceara felt her eyes widen before he rested it upon Rafael's shoulder. "I believe, Rafael Dandalo, that you are a better ally than opponent."

"Hear, hear," Maximilian said softly.

The king spared him a glance before continuing. Ceara saw that his eyes were sparkling. "If this is the sum of the insolence you maintain from your father's tutelage, I suppose I can endure it."

Maximilian grinned.

The king returned his attention to Rafael, seemingly fighting his smile. "Though you have been a warrior for many years, Rafael Dandalo, I dub thee a knight and one pledged to my service and that of Scotland."

Rafael bowed his head in agreement as the blade touched his other shoulder.

The king put out his hand to an attendant and two items were given to him. "And I grant to you the Barony of Gisroy, with the trust that you will continue to serve justice, as well as me." He held out the signet ring and Rafael lifted his hand. Ceara watched as the golden ring was placed on Rafael's finger, then the king surrendered the seal to Rafael. He bent and kissed Rafael's cheeks, one after the other, then bade him to rise.

"All hail Sir Rafael Dandalo, now Baron of Gisroy!" the king cried and a cheer rose from the ranks of all assembled at Bewcastle. Maximilian was the first to shake Rafael's hand and the king was the first to kiss Ceara's hand. They were surrounded by a crowd of well-wishers, though Ceara found her hand securely in Rafael's grasp. There was laughter and merriment on all sides, and she was surprised when a familiar woman halted before her.

"Euphemia!" Ceara whispered, for she would have known the earl's daughter anywhere. Little had changed in Euphemia's appearance. She had gained a little weight and there were a few lines around her eyes, but she still exuded a serenity that Ceara would never forget.

"Ceara," Euphemia said with unexpected pleasure, grasping her hands and kissing her cheeks in turn. "I had to come. I had to see you and meet your husband." A man appeared behind Euphemia then, a tall and broad warrior with a steely gaze and silver in his hair, and Ceara feared the day would not proceed well after all.

"Walter de Leslie," she whispered, just as she felt the weight of Rafael's hand land upon the small of her back.

Euphemia glanced back at her husband, as if for encouragement, then spoke haltingly. "I could not bear for there to be any dissent between us," she said, gripping Ceara's hands more tightly. "I was prepared to welcome Walter's son but I could never like him. There was an avarice in him that left me uncertain of his intentions, and when our son was born, Edward could no longer disguise his resentment."

Walter placed a hand upon her shoulder, his expression turning somber. "He assaulted our son," that man said. "And clearly intended to see the infant killed. He attacked Euphemia and her nurse when they defended the boy, and I am only glad that I returned early that day from the hunt." He looked down at his wife, his adoration of her clear. "He was cast out from Delny and I knew not where he went." He bowed. "I beg your forgiveness, Ceara MacRuari, that my first son acted so grievously toward you."

Ceara exhaled in her relief.

"Praise be to God that your husband was able to come to your aid," Euphemia said with unexpected heat.

'Twas on the tip of Ceara's tongue to confess that she had been the one to execute Edward, but the weight of Rafael's hand increased slightly and she knew that he was right. He reached out and introduced himself to Walter, the pair of them shaking hands even as they assessed each other, then Euphemia reached for a small chest offered by a maid.

"Your brother sends you a wedding gift," she said. "We halted at Eilean Tioram on our journey south and he sends you good will as well."

"Niall had no need to send me a gift," Ceara said, even as she accepted the small chest.

"I vowed I would place it in your hands alone."

Ceara opened the lid and gasped at the sparkling trinket within. It was the brooch from the mermaid's hoard, the engraved gold circle studded with garnets, with that crystal sphere in its middle. She could see now that within the crystal was a shard, much like the piece of the True Cross in the pommel of Rafael's dagger.

"He said the mermaid would have desired you to have it," Euphemia said. "Though I can make no sense of that."

Ceara smiled and closed the chest, holding it close. "I can," she said. "I must send him my thanks."

Rafael slid his arm around her waist, then raised his voice to the company.

"I welcome you all," he cried. "And I thank you all for your efforts in welcoming us to Bewcastle and the Barony of Gisroy. I would wager that a feast is being prepared, thanks to the efforts of Denis—" He gestured to that man who beamed and nodded. "And I invite you all to the hall at sunset, that we might celebrate the events of this day." He had spoken in Norman French, but he then repeated himself in perfect Gaelic. Ceara smiled at Maximilian's obvious astonishment, then the company cheered approval. They called for a kiss and Rafael turned to Ceara, gathering her in his arms.

"We are home, *bella*," he murmured and she smiled up at him.

"Home, husband," she replied in Venetian, watching his smile dawn. "We shall have a child in the spring, and, God willing, 'twill be our first son." Rafael's eyes lit and he gave a hoot of delight. He swept Ceara off her feet and swung her around, then caught her close and kissed her soundly.

Ceara kissed him back, scarce able to contain her joy.

THERE WAS INDEED a feast that night, along with much merriment and dancing. The king had brought his minstrels and they sang long into the night. Every squire and warrior came to the hall to dance for an interval, and ale from Rowan Fell flowed in abundance. Ceara wore one of her new kirtles to the approval of all, and the mermaid's brooch upon her shoulder. Rafael was so elegant, his jewelled crucifix gleaming against the dark cloth of his tabard, that even the king was impressed.

Only Nyssa heard the howl of the wolf in the forest over the din of the celebration in the hall that night. Only Nyssa shivered at the sound. 'Twas the wolf of her dreams and she knew it well.

She also knew it awaited her.

Once she had thought the hungry wolf in her dreams was Maximilian de Vries, the notorious *Loup Argent*, but this summer, her dreams had revealed otherwise. The wolf she feared was still unsated, still seeking his vengeance.

She raised her cup and forced a smile, reminding herself that she was happy for her three former companions and glad to know that they were content. As for herself, she would go to the Ninestang Ring, as always, on the full moon after the high quarter day.

And this time, Nyssa knew, the ravenous wolf would await her there. He was her destiny, just as she was his, and though she knew their encounter could not be evaded, still she shivered in dread of what would be.

~

AUTHOR'S NOTE

As is so often the case in my books, I've started with historical fact and built fiction in and around what is known to be true. In the case of the 14th century MacRuaris, there is a lot of opportunity to play. Ruari MacRuari, presented here as Niall and Ceara's grandfather, did have a daughter, by his wife, as well as a son, probably by his mistress. The daughter was named Áine (sometimes written as Amy) and married John of Islay (Eòin Macdonald), Lord of the Isles, around 1337. Ruari's son by his mistress was Raghnall. When Ruari died, the chieftainship passed to his oldest son, Raghnall, and when Raghnall subsequently died (assassinated by William III, Earl of Ross) the family holdings passed to Áine and through her to her husband. There also is a suggestion that Ruari may have had a second son (and third child) who vanished around the time that his father died.

Áine and Eòin had three sons by 1350 when he divorced her. It does not appear that this because Áine had been unfaithful, the usual reason for a medieval divorce. The connection may simply have become inconvenient, as Eòin then married Margaret, the daughter of Robert Stewart (who would later become King Robert II). King David not only granted the divorce but decreed that Áine's inheritance would be retained by Eòin and her sons by Eòin would be disinherited. What little record there is of Áine suggests that she retreated to those

MacRuari family lands. She may have built Borve Castle on Benbecula and also reinforced the structure of Eilean Tioram in Moidart. She is said to have retired to Eilean Tioram to a life of contemplation.

The MacRuaris were fierce, and numbered among the galloglasses who fought in Ireland. The MacRuari women were equally fierce, particularly Christina (Cairistíona Nic Ruaidhrí) from the early 13th century and from this, I derived Ceara's nature. I thought it would be interesting to give Eòin a more interesting reason for ending his marriage and for Áine to be bitter as a result of his choices. The character Aimil in **The Dragon & the Damsel** was inspired by Áine, albeit with more than a few fictitious additions—including the names of her sons. There are other fabrications, as well. Ruari's lover was not a mermaid, as far as I know—let alone one who surrendered a treasure to him. I like the idea of Ceara's grandmother being a mermaid and I hope you liked this story, as well.

THE SCOT & THE SORCERESS

BLOOD BROTHERS #3

Embittered by his losses and thwarted in his pursuit of vengeance, Murdoch is sworn to avenge his father. The sole means of striking a blow against his enemy, the Silver Wolf, is to seize that man's beloved wife, Alys—but Murdoch cannot bring himself to injure a woman he has known all his life. When the wise woman of the woods offers herself in exchange for Alys' freedom, Murdoch cannot resist temptation. The mysterious beauty lights a fire in his blood, a need for more than vengeance, and Murdoch finds himself enchanted. He never expects Nyssa, his apparent opposite, to burn with a similar desire for vengeance—but once she asks for his assistance, Murdoch swears gladly to do her will.

Nyssa is a healer and a wise woman, blessed with visions of the future to come. When her dreams fill with horrors for her kin in the distant north, she knows she must return to aid in their defense, no matter how long the odds against her. She strikes a bargain with Murdoch, a man with fearsome fighting skills, to aid in her quest, never guessing that her need to heal his hidden wounds will be so overwhelmingly powerful. Her visions warn that she has made an unholy alliance and that Murdoch's anger will destroy her utterly—yet Nyssa cannot resist his fiery touch or the gift of watching him heal.

Bound together by passion and fury, Murdoch and Nyssa journey north, where they find her family snared in a battle that pits brother against brother. When Nyssa's father surrenders her to his enemies for the sake of peace, Murdoch realizes that he must defend justice everywhere, beginning with the rescue of his beloved—no matter the cost to himself

The Scot & the Sorceress
Coming spring 2023!
Pre-order available at some portals.

ABOUT THE AUTHOR

Deborah Cooke sold her first book in 1992, a medieval romance called **Romance of the Rose** published under her pseudonym Claire Delacroix. Since then, she has published over fifty novels in a wide variety of sub-genres, including historical romance, contemporary romance, paranormal romance, fantasy romance, time-travel romance, women's fiction, paranormal young adult and fantasy with romantic elements. She has published under the names Claire Delacroix, Claire Cross and Deborah Cooke. **The Beauty**, part of her successful Bride Quest series of historical romances, was her first title to land on the *New York Times* List of Bestselling Books. Her books routinely appear on other bestseller lists and have won numerous awards. In 2009, she was the writer-in-residence at the Toronto Public Library, the first time the library has hosted a residency focused on the romance genre. In 2012, she was honored to receive the Romance Writers of America's Mentor of the Year Award.

Currently, she writes contemporary romances and paranormal romances under the name Deborah Cooke. She also writes medieval romances as Claire Delacroix. Deborah lives in Canada with her husband and family, as well as far too many unfinished knitting projects.

Visit her websites to learn more:

http://DeborahCooke.com
http://Delacroix.net